Advance praise for
AMARYLLIS IN BLUEBERRY

"Christina Meldrum is a fresh, invigorating new voice in women's fiction. *Amaryllis in Blueberry* is a beautifully written, completely compelling novel that grabbed me from the very first page and wouldn't let me go. I especially loved the African setting."

—*New York Times* bestselling author Kristin Hannah

"*Amaryllis in Blueberry* is a rich, evocative story about an unusual family that will sweep readers away to another place and time. Amaryllis's voice is a spellbinding and unique blend of naiveté and wisdom. A perfect melding of family saga, mystery and a meditation on faith, loyalty and love, thi will both haunt and entertain you."

—*New York Times* bestselling author Susar

"Told in prose that is rich and evocative, *Amaryllis in Blueberry* will stay with readers long after its surprising and satisfying ending, and leave book clubs talking late into the night. This lovely novel spans continents and cultures in a love story, a family saga, and an exploration of faith that is colored by Africa and flavored by the impurity that is love."

—National bestselling author Meg Waite Clayton

Amaryllis in Blueberry is also available as an eBook

Awards and accolades for Christina Meldrum's debut novel, *MADAPPLE*

William C. Morris YA Debut Award Finalist • PEN USA Literary Award Finalist

ALA Best Book for Young Readers • *Vanity Fair* "Hot Type" Pick

Chicago Tribune "Hot Summer Read" • *Booklist* Editors' Choice Pick

Kirkus Reviews, First Fiction: 35 Promising Debuts

Amazon, Best Book of the Year . . . So Far

Booklist, Top Ten First Novels of the Year for Youth

Kirkus Reviews, Best Young Adult Book

New York Public Library Book for the Teen Age

"[A] mesmerizing literary mystery."

—Vanity Fair

"Exquisite myth of a girl who grows up in isolation and, when her mother dies, must contend with the odd convictions of a strange world."

—Chicago Tribune

"An ambitious, often haunting debut, a unique meditation on language, rationality, and faith."

—San Francisco Chronicle

"With this spellbinding debut, Meldrum marks herself as an author to watch."

—Kirkus Reviews (starred review)

ALSO BY CHRISTINA MELDRUM

Madapple

AMARYLLIS

in

BLUEBERRY

————

Christina Meldrum

Gallery Books

New York   London   Toronto   Sydney

Gallery Books
A Division of Simon & Schuster, Inc.
1230 Avenue of the Americas
New York, NY 10020

First Gallery Books trade paperback edition March 2011

GALLERY BOOKS and colophon are trademarks of Simon & Schuster, Inc.

For information about special discounts for bulk purchases, please contact Simon & Schuster Special Sales at 1-866-506-1949 or business@simonandschuster.com

The Simon & Schuster Speakers Bureau can bring authors to your live event. For more information or to book an event contact the Simon & Schuster Speakers Bureau at 1-866-248-3049 or visit our website at www.simonspeakers.com.

Designed by Jaime Putorti
Photograph from istockphoto.com

Manufactured in the United States of America

10   9   8   7   6   5   4

Library of Congress Cataloging-in-Publication Data is available.

ISBN 978-1-4391-5689-6
ISBN 978-1-4391-9536-9 (ebook)

BOOK ONE

West Africa

Dick is dead. Seena knows this, of course: her husband is dead. Yet she keeps expecting him to barrel in, his enormous, gangling self plodding along, a spectacle unaware that he is one. *Was one,* she thinks. *Was one.* Still, she finds herself waiting for him to call out, make some pointless point, make it clear to everyone that he just doesn't get it. She anticipates the annoyance she so often would feel around him. She almost longs for it—this longing he'd disappear, shut up, let her be. Because he has disappeared, shut up, let her be. He is dust from dust. Ashes from ashes. As dead as a doornail.

And she has the devil to pay.

Like Dick would say, "The devil take the hindmost."

Dick's moved on, and she's left to pay. Alone.

Because he did get it, more than she did—she knows this. But the recognition came only after the trigger was pulled, so to speak, after the poison went flying, when it pierced his pale chest, when it was long past too late. Now she understands she was the spectacle unaware: she was the fool.

And she wonders, How can you live with someone for years—know the softening ring around his still-thin waist, the changed texture of his graying stubble, the scent in the hollow beneath his Adam's apple—and see only your imagination reflected?

Seena is on trial in a village in West Africa, in a "customary court." The courthouse is the schoolhouse, transformed. The village elders—one a witch doctor, one a queen—are her accusers, judge and jury. She was indignant when she learned this, sure it couldn't be. She's an American, she'd said. She's entitled to due process. "These customary courts, they must be illegal. There are laws—aren't there?—even here, even in this hell?"

But she's a murderer, the elders said: she's entitled to nothing. "Our courts are based on our traditions, which are different from yours. Americans think they alone make laws, but we have our own rule."

They have their own rule.

"Christina Slepy?" the witch doctor, this so called "wise man," says. He speaks to Seena, and watches her. Every person in the crowded room watches her; she feels this. And she knows if she were to look up at them, she would see only the whites of their eyes, and perhaps a shock of color from clothes that now seem mocking. They've told her the reasons women kill, and they've told her no matter her reason, she had no right. Still, they demand to know her reason, and she wonders which to choose. Which would they believe, or not? Which would solicit less loathing?

Even as she ponders these questions, she is aware she has no idea what they would believe, or not—no idea of the seed of their loathing, the fruit of their pity, whether they ever would feel pity for her. This is a world of rules turned inside out, a world where all she took for granted has been stripped away.

She is a carcass, ripped clean of flesh. A skeleton of holes. No longer can her mind set her apart, give her that private space where the real world could seem a dream. No longer can she fill her holes with assumptions: that rationality wins in the end, that humans have rights, that *white* humans have rights. She never appreciated this distinction before—appreciated that she made this distinction. She never thought of herself as racist. Dick was a racist, she knew. Not a malicious racist. A do-good kind of racist. A feel-sorry-for kind of racist. A thank-God-I'm-white kind of racist: there but for the grace of God go I. But not her. Not her. How could she be racist, given the only man she'd ever loved?

Yet she set foot in this dusty African world never believing its dust and rules would apply to her, her children, her mind. But why wouldn't they apply? Because she's white, she thought, that's why. Only, she didn't really think this, she *knew* this. It was in her flesh—what made her feel whole. She never had to think it; it just was. She never had to come to terms with being racist; she just was. As she sits here condemned, she knows this. And she knows she should be condemned, if for this reason alone—especially given her child of light.

"Do you have anything to say?" asks the elder, who is not even old. He is forty perhaps. At max. And Seena thinks, He is neither wise nor old, yet he has the power of Zeus, here. He and the queen of this village—Avone—are the gods of this universe, painting this African sky. Painting me, the African version of Clytemnestra.

"What don't I have to say?" she would like to say. "You want me to admit guilt? I'll admit it. I came here having little respect for your beliefs and laws and I flouted them willingly. You want me to say I hated my husband—that I wanted him dead so I could be free to love my lover? I'll say it. You want me to tell you I committed adultery and squandered the welfare of my children for the sake of lust while I spit in God's face. It's all true."

"No," she says. "I have nothing to say."

Yllis

Danish Landing, Michigan

Mama said I was born in a blueberry field—that she was squatting, not to birth me, just to pick. Her hands were stained that purple-blue, and her lips were ringed black-blue, and a once-plump blueberry teetered on her tongue, staining her teeth as gray as a November sky. But it wasn't November, it was steamy July, Independence Day. And in the distance Mama could hear the sizzle on the Landing, where long-legged Mary Grace, always-obedient Mary Catherine, and troublemaker-in-training Mary Tessa swirled their sparklers, their sun-streaked hair dancing so close to the ephemeral glow that three-year-old Tessa singed her golden tips a crispy black.

"What in God's name?" Mama asked, as if she didn't know. She'd birthed the Marys in a steady succession like they were part of a fugue. Every two years a new one appeared, almost to the day: their bald heads glistened like the harvest moon and their dark lashes crept down their faces, giving them that startled look they have to this day. Even so, when Mama felt that wrenching tug, what she later described as her "rearrange-ment" (for she swears her internal makeup was never the same), and when she realized she was pushing whether she wanted to or not, she asked that very question, "What in God's name?"

I expect the question was a bit of an omen, as Mama seemed certain from the start I was going to be far more different from my sisters than they were from each other. While the Marys all came "as civilized children should" (Papa said) in the sterile world of white walls and white floors and white-clad, rubber-gloved professionals, I splattered down into a blueberry bush, wasting a full morning of Mama's toil. (No one would eat the berries she'd picked, convinced I'd splattered myself into her bucket as well.)

My mop of black hair was so tangled in the scrawny bush, and Mama's hands so slippery with blueberry juice and the mess of me, she couldn't free me, so she pulled a pair of pruning shears from her skirt and gave me my first haircut right then and there, while I wailed like a robbed jay. When she'd finished I appeared a shrunken old man, a bald sun on the tiptop of my head with a halo of greasy hair matted about it, and a forehead so furrowed in fury, the lines didn't soften for days. "With the way you carried on," Mama said, "there was no need to phone the doctor. Anyone within earshot knew you were in this world for the long haul."

Before traipsing back to the Landing, Mama clipped the cord with those same shears then swabbed me with her skirt in attempt to make me presentable to Papa and the Marys. Papa was fuming at the eldest Mary, leggy Grace, over tiny Mary Tessa's singed hair, and all the Marys were weeping. Mama had to tap Papa thrice and knee him once just to get his attention. When he did turn toward her and saw my sticky skin and haloed hair and the partial blueberry that dangled from my left ear, he screeched as if a Mary, then bellowed, "Mary, Mother of God!" And the Marys cried louder, and I wailed again.

"Your daughter," Mama shouted, to be heard over the racket.

"But what about her hair?" Papa said.

"She came when I was picking," Mama said. As if that explained it.

My hair has always had a touch of blue when struck by morning light, and my skin is nearly as dark as my sisters' is light. And my eyes are that pale, just-ripe-blueberry blue. When I asked Papa as I grew why I look the way I do, all swarthy skinned and swarthy haired and icy eyed, so different from he and Mama and the Marys, he asked me what exactly did I expect given the way I came crashing into the world?

Mama named me Amaryllis, right out there in the blueberry field, and when Papa's mustache quivered after she told him the name, and his eyes took on the glassy, stunned gaze, Mama straightened her long back and stretched her giraffe's neck and flounced that Mary-hued hair as she pointedly turned away, and Papa knew the name was not negotiable.

Mama told me this story at least a hundred times as I grew up—claimed she'd named me Amaryllis after a shepherdess in her favorite Virgil poem. "You seemed partial to fields," she said, and she didn't even crack a smile. The name Amaryllis comes from the Greek *amarysso*, meaning "to sparkle," Mama said, "to shed light." She was wont to remind Papa there is in fact a "Mary" in the name. Mama insists she'd intended to call me Marylla for short, or maybe even just plain Mary, but these nicknames never stuck. I was Yllis from the start. "I'm Yllis,"

I'd say, when I'd meet new people. "Phyllis?" they'd say. Some-times, "Willis?"—as if even my sex was a mystery.

Papa's deceased mother had been christened Mary Ann, and until that moment of truth in the blueberry field, Mary Ann was to be my "blessing," as Papa would say. But I've no doubt Mama knew it would have been a sort of sacrilege to name me after dead Grandma Slepy, let alone the Mother of God.

Mama herself was named Christina, after God himself according to Pa. Perhaps that's why the name made her itch. Whenever Papa introduced her as such, she'd claw behind her ear and up her right side and correct him. "Seena," she'd say. "Call me Seena."

"What kind of name is Seena Slepy?" Papa would mutter to himself. Then he'd go on to introduce himself, Dick, and the Marys. And me, Yllis.

I myself have an affinity for the name Seena, perhaps because it contains the word "see." Long before I had any understand-ing of who I am—what I am—I could see Mama's instincts were right: I was different, and not just on the surface. I didn't fit in my family, I didn't fit in at school. Classmates and teachers (and Mary Tessa) so ridiculed me for my "wild imagination," I wasn't sure I belonged on earth. Yet I knew things about earth—about people on earth. I often knew what people would say before they spoke. I knew whom people loved, whom they despised. I knew what gave others joy and fury and envy, even when they didn't seem to know themselves.

Just to set the record straight, envy is not green. And rage isn't red hot, and the blues have nothing to do with blue. Envy is more dust colored, a transparent sort of gray. It quivers, like heat rising. Rage itself is not any shade of red—it's not any color at all. It's a smell, like fried-up fish. Melancholy? The blues? Melancholy's more of a shimmer than any color. And it creeps: blues on the move.

People say joy is infectious, but that's a myth. It's melancholy that's infectious. And sneaky. It skulks about, climbing legs, mounting skirts. It's particularly active when joy is in the room. Joy shows up, a sort of humming, and melancholy gets the jitters. I've seen it time and again. While joy bathes one person—who purrs almost, like she's been plugged in—melancholy makes the rounds. And those closest in proximity to joy are melancholy's most likely targets. That's not to say joy's humming doesn't sometimes spread—it does—but melancholy is crafty and determined, while joy spreads mostly when it tries not to. At least when it doesn't try too hard.

Guilt, in contrast, is tricky to see, smell, hear, because guilt is a mush—a combination of envy and anger, joy and melancholy. And love. But I know guilt. I know the taste of its quivering, shimmering, cloudy, smelly, buzzing self.

I met guilt first in the time BEFORE—before Africa, before Papa's death, before my love for Mama took on a taste I couldn't recognize—when envy may as well have been green, and anger could have been Papa's flush, and joy might have been quiet, not a hummer. And sadness? As far as I was concerned then, it was my mother. Snug in the world of her mind, Seena was the goddess of deception, Apate herself, ensnared in Pandora's storage jar. But at the time, I mistook her cunning for sadness.

It was the day of my eleventh birthday and the bicentennial and we were summering on the Danish Landing, a hodge-

podge of cottages owned by Rasmussons and Sorensons and
Jorgensons and Eihlersons. And Slepys. When Mama convinced
Papa to buy the cottage we'd been renting in a probate sale, he
said, "At least we all look Danish." Then his eyes dashed to me,
and the skin beneath his pale mustache went pink, and his ears
looked hot to the touch.

The cottage is on a lake named Margrethe, in a mite of a
town named Grayling. The prior owners named the cottage
"Deezeezdaplas." Papa left the name hanging near the front
door as a "welcome" sign. (Mama said it was more of an unwel-
come sign.) And he painted the cottage the Danish-flag red and
white "to fit in." But Grayling sits nearly two hours' drive north
of our hometown of Midland, so there was no fitting in for Papa.
While Mama and the Marys and I spent the whole summer at
the Danish Landing, and some long weekends in the spring and
fall, Papa was purely a weekender, and what the locals called
a half blood—making ill-reference, Mama said, to the Ottawa
and Chippewa Indians who'd inhabited the area long before the
Danes arrived. And making Papa's pure Polish blood boil.

But it was a weekend, and fourteen-year-old Tessa—by then
a seasoned troublemaker—and I had headed down the Old
Trail to gather kindling for the campfire Papa was determined
to build, even though the wind had blown the lake to foam and
was spitting acorns from the trees, and the moss beneath our
feet felt more like moist flesh, and the kindling we'd gathered
was as wet as the towels dripping on the line and as likely to start
a fire as a mound of tomatoes.

"Snake!" Mary Tessa said. Her braided hair jerked as if
lopped as she sprang back. The kindling rolled down her legs.

Tessa—the closest Mary to my age, but still three years my senior—was no rookie when it came to snakes. She and I had kept a box of garters on more than one occasion. But her voice was high pitched, her body stiff.

"Where?" I said. "What? Is it a rattler?"

I knew there were rattlers in these woods. Papa had told us of them. "The eastern massasauga rattlesnake lives in these woods, girls."

"What kind of name is massasauga?" I'd asked. But Papa ignored me.

"It's the only venomous snake in Michigan," he'd said. "And it's rare. But it's out there. Make noise when you head onto the Old Trail. Scare those snakes away. Clap your hands. Bang sticks together." Then he'd sent us off to carry back loads of kindling, reminding us to never talk to strangers, "especially those red-skinned natives." I assumed at the time he was referring to the Rasmusson boys, whose sun-fried Danish skin was a peeling hot pink. I'd seen Papa watching them watch bikini-wearing Grace—who was eighteen going on eight, as far as Papa was concerned.

I tried to push past Tessa to see the snake, but she spread her own sunburnt arms wide. "No, Yllis," she said. "No. Go back."

"I'm not going back," I said. "I want to eye that snake." I slipped under her outstretched arm, but she caught me by the hair.

"Hey," I said. I dropped my kindling, swatted at her, but my efforts were fruitless. At just three years older, Tessa was twice my size. "You can't do that. You let me go."

"I said go back." And she dragged me by my hair, but she couldn't stop my looking, she couldn't stop my *seeing*. The snake was a rattlesnake. But it was dead. Not just dead. Someone had sliced off its flat triangle head and carefully slit its body wide, pinned it flat. Its entrails lay exposed there, in all their completeness—and the rattle, too. And I saw there was an amazing beauty about those entrails, that hollowed-out rattle and that decapitated head with its cat-pupil eyes. Yes, there was a beautiful, remarkable mystery in how perfect it all was. How smart. As if someone had sketched out those innards again and again before getting it just right. The plump blob of heart beneath the elongated left lung, and the right lung snaking thin between the stretched stomach and liver, ending alongside the coil of small intestine. The greenish gallbladder ball hugged by the darker pancreas ball. The kidneys like worms, one chasing the other. I knew these body parts—I'd found Mary Catherine's *Sophomore Anatomy* discarded in the trash, and I'd hidden the book beneath my bed. But there lay what I thought were human parts, all thinned out as snake parts.

It wasn't the similarities between humans and snakes that surprised me, though, it was the crispness—the clean, clear crispness. With the snake dead, it wasn't smelling sweet with fear, it wasn't colored with emotion. It wasn't hazy or shimmering or buzzing.

It just was.

"You didn't touch that snake, did you, girls?"

I rotated my seeing from the snake to one of those ill-referenced Indians. He stood on the Old Trail with midnightlike hair streaking down his sides. But he had these blueberry eyes.

"You an Indian?" I asked.

"That's one way to put it."

"What do you mean?" I thought of his eyes. "You a half blood?"

"Hush, Yllis." Mary Tessa tightened her grip on my hair.

"Even dead rattlesnakes can bite," the Indian-man said. "Even when they've been decapitated. Pick up that chopped-off head, and it just might bite you."

"That was sick," Tessa said, after we'd left the Indian and the rattler.

"No," I said. "It wasn't. It was beautiful."

Tessa was moving along at such speed, she nearly yanked the hair from my head when she skidded to a stop. "What did you say, Yllis?" Her startled expression contorted some, and I saw she truly was startled. "You thought that snake was beautiful? Someone killed it. You know that, right? Cut it open. Pinned it there. I mean, that's really sick. It was a rattler, but still . . ."

Coming from Tessa, that meant something. Tessa was good at sick. And cruel. And killing that snake—pinning it and such—was cruel. I'd give her that. I wouldn't have had the stomach for it. Yet it seemed to me in that moment there is a painful sort of beauty in seeing things for what they really are.

———

When we arrived at the cottage, Mama sat coiled on the couch, her white peasant blouse a pillow about her and her ever-present pearl necklace snug as a noose. Even standing at the door, I could smell her Primitif tainted by Noxzema. Hesiod's *Theogony* lay on her lap and her face hovered above the Greek dictionary she held in one hand. Mama had wanted to be a classics scholar. "But I dropped out of college in fifty-seven to get married," she'd recently told us girls. "That means Grace is a bastard," Tessa had whispered to me, which had confused me. Based on previous comments Grace had made, I'd thought Papa was the bastard. (Tessa later set me straight.)

My birthday cupcakes sat uneaten on the table. Their fingered-over frosting had grown rock hard—as hard as the cupcakes themselves. Mama had used blueberries when making the batter—in honor of my birth—and they had turned the batter into blue soup, the burnt cupcakes into blue-gray rocks. Mama had frosted them red and white, in honor of Independence Day. We'd all tried to eat the cupcakes: a futile effort to protect Mama's feelings. But even during the singing of "Happy Birthday"—before any of us had tried to take a bite—I'd smelled that faint sweet scent of trepidation: the Marys' and Papa's and mine. And I'd smelled Mama's fear, too—only hers was not faint but powerful, longing as she did to celebrate my life yet suspecting she'd failed. Again. Surprisingly, Tessa had made the best effort to look after Mama's feelings: she'd managed to dent the rock by chiseling it with her incisors.

But after meeting that snake, Tessa was in no such generous mood. "Apparently your cupcakes are better than dog food," she whispered. She motioned toward Lint, our colorless mutt, who crouched beneath the table, lopping up the shards of red, white and blue that speckled the floor. "Well, I guess that's something."

HAPPY BIRTHDAY YLISS!!! hung lopsided on the wall behind Mama, the banner speckled with poster-painted *x*'s and *o*'s and blobbed with what sixteen-year-old Mary Catherine insisted were fireworks—although similar "fireworks" decorated the seat of her well-pleated shorts. Captain and Tennille spun on Mama's old phonograph, insisting love would keep us together. Grace and Mary Catherine lay stomachs flat on the floor, their knees bent, their bare feet dangling over their rears. A game of Scrabble sprawled before them like a sadistic maze: no way out.

Papa circled the game like a parched horsefly, but his eyes were on Mama. He and Mama often joked about Mama's "interests," as Papa called them. (Always the same joke.) She would spout off some poem, and Papa would say, "What is that, Greek?" Mama would confirm that it was in fact Greek, and they'd both guffaw; they'd squeeze their sides and swab their eyes. But behind their swabbing, their eyes weren't laughing. That was obvious enough to me.

"Some say Pandora is the story of the first woman," Mama said, in response to a question from Papa, I guessed—even though she wasn't looking at him—because Papa squinted at Mama, like she was blurry or too bright. "Some say it's the story of the birth of all evil."

"Arguably the same," Papa said, but barely. Unlike Mama, I saw—and read—Papa's lips.

"Hmmm?" Mama said.

Papa added, "I thought it was about a box—about a woman opening a box."

"It was a jar, actually," Mama said, although still she didn't look up. "There are various versions of the story, but it essentially goes something like this. Zeus went to Hephaestus, the god of artisans and fire, and asked him to create a woman." She flipped a page in the Greek dictionary, scanned the words on the page with her index finger. "Zeus wanted to use the woman as a means of revenge against mortals. So, Hephaestus molded the woman, gave her form. Athena taught the woman how to weave. Aphrodite gave the woman beauty. Apollo gave her a gift for healing. Poseidon gave the woman the security she'd never drown. Hermes gave boldness. Hera, curiosity."

Mama shifted her gaze from the dictionary back to Hesiod, then. She didn't notice no one was listening to her—no one, that is, but me. Papa had opened the newspaper, and he read while he paced. Tessa had nabbed Papa's camera off the kitchen counter and zoomed in to spy on Old Lady Clara, who lived in the cottage across the way. Mary Catherine alternated between studying her Scrabble letters and examining her rosary beads, all while chewing her nails. Grace yawned audibly, rolled onto her back, stretched her long legs skyward and closed her eyes— clearly intending to make the point Mary Catherine's turn was taking far too long.

"Zeus named the woman Pandora," Mama continued. "He sent her as a gift to Epimetheus, who married her. At the wedding, Zeus gave Pandora a storage jar as a gift. Epimetheus, wary of Zeus, told Pandora to never open the jar. Because Hera had given Pandora curiosity, however, one day Pandora slightly lifted the jar's lid. Before she realized what was happening, she'd released Apate, the spirit of deceit; Geras, the spirit of old age; Moros, the spirit of doom; Eris, the spirit of strife; Momos, the spirit of blame; Oizys, the spirit of suffering; Nemesis, the spirit of hatred; and Ker, the spirit of carnage and death. When Pandora again sealed the jar, only hope remained."

"Would you look at this, Seena?" Papa said, apropos of nothing. He held the newspaper in one fisted hand as he circled and he waved it about as if swiping his way through a horde. "The Supreme Court agrees with me, even if Pope Paul doesn't. Says here the court decided Friday. There's nothing cruel or unusual about killing a killer."

"Mmm-hmm," Mama said. She turned another page. She was no more listening to Papa than Papa had been listening to her.

"Is it like dominoes, Papa?" I said, trying to dodge his noticing Mama's obvious lack of interest.

Papa was fairly adept at failing to see the obvious, actually. Neither he nor Mama had noticed Tessa and I had arrived. He jerked toward us, startled. "Dominoes?"

"You said there's nothing cruel about killing a killer." I was thinking about that snake. "You have to be a killer to kill a killer, right? Doesn't it just keep going?"

"What are you talking about, Yllis? Human beings are not like dominoes. Killing is not fun and games." And then: "Tessa. Hey. What are you doing? You put my camera down. Now."

Tessa turned from the window, slid the camera down the counter just as the wind threw a branch against the window to Papa's left.

"Where's the kindling?" Papa said.

"We found a snake," I said.

"Where's the kindling?" Papa said again, and louder, as if somehow we'd failed to hear, although the entire cottage is the size of a two-car garage. You might be able to choose to not listen while in the cottage, but you pretty much couldn't choose to not hear—the Marys and I had learned that well enough when Papa had rushed us to bed so he and Mama could "sleep."

A storm was brewing. I could see through the front windows on to the lake, where the waves had been stirred into such commotion, it was hard to be certain the lake was water at all. I imagined it rising up, some humongous animal with mounds of white fur and dark, wet eyes.

Another branch smashed the side window. And then another. "That'll do for you," Tessa said. She pointed to the window just as a large something hit the roof. "There's your kindling."

"Did you hear that, Seena?" Papa said. He looked first at Tessa then at me. Then he looked at Mama. But Mama (true to form) wasn't listening. The Greek dictionary sprawled her lap; she pressed her face into Hesiod. "Seena!" Papa said. He raised his voice louder than I expect he intended. Lint whimpered. Still Mama didn't budge. Papa ripped *Theogony* from Mama's hands and shook it to the floor, like one might shake off a leech. In so doing, he slid across Scrabble, scattering the maze.

"I was winning!" Mary Catherine said as she snatched up letters. Her rosary beads, made of olive seeds from the Garden of Gethsemane, swung like clinging seaweed from her wrist. She was quivering gray with envy, as was usual, but her mood ring was dark blue. According to the mood chart, which I'd studied that morning, she was "very happy, full of love, passion and romance," which served to confirm Tessa's claim the ring was nothing but liquid crystal, a temperature gauge.

"You weren't winning," Grace said. "I thought saints didn't lie." Then she turned her attention to adjusting her chain belt, as if to say, "I really couldn't care less."

"What's happened?" Mama said. She grabbed *Theogony* and

dusted it, then she looked at Papa like she'd just watched him murder a babe. "Who's hurt?"

"Mary Tessa and Yllis are being disrespectful," Papa said.

"And Papa ruined our fun," Mary Catherine said.

"What's new?" Grace said.

Papa zipped around to face Mary Grace and the newspaper grazed her golden head.

"I was talking about Tessa. And Yllis," Grace said.

"Pants on fire," I said.

"We saw a rattler," Tessa said.

"A dead one," I added, "with its insides all laid out and its head chopped off."

"And Yllis said it was beautiful."

"Gross," Mary Catherine said.

"We met an Indian, too," I said. "A real one. Well, he probably was a half blood."

"We didn't talk to him, though," Tessa said.

"Yeah we did . . . ," I started, but I stopped myself, remembering Papa's instructions about strangers.

I knew I should change the subject when I realized everyone but Mama was looking at me. It seemed Mama's Pandora story was a sure way to lose their attention. "Where was truth in that story you told about Pandora, Mama?" After that experience with the snake, truth was on my mind. "You told me before there's a goddess of truth. What did you say her name is? Aletheia? Why didn't Aletheia give Pandora truthfulness? Why wasn't truth still in the jar, along with hope?"

Up until that point, Mama still had been thinking in Greek—I'd seen the distance in her eyes. But my words yanked her back in a way Papa's hands hadn't. She looked at me, then—only me. Not at sassy Tessa. Not at dusty Mary Catherine. Not at hot-pants Grace. Not even at Papa. Still, she didn't say a word.

"Maybe Aletheia couldn't be found to give Pandora truthfulness." I answered my own question, as it seemed Mama had no intention of answering. "Maybe, unlike hope, truth couldn't be contained in the jar."

It was at that very moment that BEFORE passed away. For a second or so I thought I was seeing Mama like Papa had minutes before: she seemed both blurry and bright. She looked dusty, yet the dust had a white-yellow shimmer. And she waved, not with her hands. Her body waved, undulated, but barely. Just barely. And the smell. It was stronger than Papa's, as if Papa had dragged in his bucket of fish guts, and fish heads with their bulging fish eyes, and cooked them up. I looked toward Papa, away from Mama, and the smell faded, as if it blew away. Then I looked at her again. Wham. It blew back. Like someone had cut the cheese. The phonograph needle lifted, the room fell silent. Then the hum began: the monotonous chorus. It started out softly then picked up volume. I looked toward Tessa, wondering whether the joy I heard was hers, but while looking at Tessa, I heard only silence. So I looked again at Mama. The hum began softly then picked up volume.

The taste came then. Sort of an aftertaste. It was the first time I'd ever experienced this taste. It wasn't sour or salty, yet it made me pucker. Even though I didn't like the taste, I felt myself relishing it. So later, when the taste became an afterthought, I longed for it.

"You thought that dead snake was beautiful, Yllis?" Mama said.

I nodded my head. I wasn't sure what I was sensing—I didn't know it was guilt. But I knew the experience was real. I wondered why I hadn't sensed it before. And I thought about the painful, beautiful truths that hover about like gnats—about how so often we just swat them away: Papa wasn't my papa, that blue-eyed half blood was. It wasn't Papa who was the bastard. It wasn't Grace.

It was me.

All the emotion swirling around this fact had distorted it for me before. But there it was, spread out before me on my birthday, just like that snake.

"Did you kill that snake, Yllis?" Mama said, although she knew I wouldn't do such a thing: I'm no killer.

"Nuh-uh."

Our dog Lint moseyed over and lay on my feet, as if trying to back me, as if to say, "How could you ask her that?" Given all I'd seen and heard and smelled, I thought I might look down and find that colorless Lint had a color after all. But Lint was hued as always, that color that was no color and every color, like lint.

"Well, at least it can't bite anybody now," Papa said.

"Even dead rattlers can bite," I said. "Even a rattler with its head chopped off can bite."

"Stop being contradictory, Yllis," Papa said. "Show your father some respect."

"You're not my father. That Indian we saw? He's my father. I know for sure he is."

"Your father?" Tessa said. "Hah. I knew it. I always figured you were adopted."

"What?" Mama said. "Why would you say that, Yllis?"

"Stop that, Yllis," Papa said. "You stop that right now."

"That's ridiculous, Yllis," Mary Catherine said, but she strangled her wrist with her rosary beads.

"Now whose pants are burning?" Grace said.

Somebody needs to tell Aletheia's story, I thought: truth should have her day. As far as I could tell, I was the only one whose pants weren't burning—that is, until Papa gave me the paddling.

But now? Now I know Aletheia didn't need my help. She was perfectly capable of telling her own story.

Dick

Ann Arbor, Michigan
1956

◆ There are fifty ways to leave your lover. You just slip out the back. Make a new plan. Hop on the bus. Drop off the key.

Seems obvious to Dick Paul's never been in love.

Seena. Dick loved her before he knew her. Sat behind her in Latin, September of '56, first semester of his senior year. He barely knew her face; it may as well have been the wind. Whenever he glimpsed her, she moved. He'd try to imagine her at night as he lay sandwiched between his roommates in the triple bunk, while asthmatic Frank wheezed above him and Sam reeked below him. But Dick could conjure up only Seena's neck—that he knew. She'd twist her hair up in a high chignon, expose the silk of her skin. Day after day, she wore the same pearl choker. Wisps of fine hair hovered along her hairline, and when the air was humid, the hair wisps curled into a sort of tiara, just like Dick's mother's had when Dick was a boy.

Their professor was a loudmouth Englishman named Welton who was far too fond of his own voice. Fortunately, Welton's voice rarely distracted Dick from Seena's.

Her voice seemed tangible to Dick, as if it seeped from the linoleum, dripped from the ceiling. He'd catch himself looking around when she'd speak to see if the other students noticed her voice, how it seemed to be everywhere at once. But George to his left would be chewing his eraser, and Jackie to his right would be recording Seena's every word, same as she recorded everyone's every word.

Dick learned more Latin listening to Seena than he did listening to Loudmouth. That's not to say he learned much. He was headed to medical school, like his father and his father before him. Dick's grandfather had been a medical missionary who traveled through Africa, healing the sick, doing something practical. Impractical Latin (a dead language?) fulfilled a requirement, nothing more. It was one of the classes Dick nearly didn't take. Dear God, how his life would have been different.

Dick slipped Seena a note one day, just like he did when he was in grade school and had a crush on Lizzie Schrater. Lizzie turned fidgety pink when she read the note, and part of Dick expected the same from Seena. Dick was handsome, he knew. He looked more Scandinavian than Polish with his height and the height of his cheekbones. His hair was blond sans dishwater and his eyes were a pale aqua green, "like the water of Lake Huron when it laps the shores of Mackinac Island," his mother used to say—before she stopped noticing. Girls never seemed to mind when Dick paid them attention. He even wondered whether Seena might have a secret crush on him herself, thought maybe her refusal to look at him directly was a byproduct of that crush.

He tapped her on the shoulder before he handed her the

note, just as Loudmouth conjugated *amare,* "to love"—Dick hadn't planned that. Seena turned, and it was the first time Dick saw her straight on. He felt like pulling the note back, ripping it to shreds. Because Seena looked at him with the eyes of the devil. Dick had never seen eyes like hers. Never knew people had yellow eyes. Thought only cats had those eyes. Cats and the devil. As Dick looked at Seena's flushed face and piled-up hair, an image from childhood—from catechism—set fire in his mind: the devil with red skin, a gold crown and pastel eyes.

Seena took the note and unfolded it. Dick watched as she mouthed his words, MARRY ME. It was meant as a joke, the note. He'd just wanted to get her attention, start a conversation, maybe make her laugh.

She didn't laugh.

She folded the note, seam by seam, then slouched to tuck the note inside her bag.

"Ms. Michels," Loudmouth said, referring to Seena. "Perhaps you'd like to read Mr. Slepy's note out loud."

And once again Dick was transported to grade school, to Lizzie Schrater and his teacher, Ms. Zimmerman. "Lizzie?" Ms. Zimmerman had said. "Why don't you read Dick's note to the class?" Lizzie wept while Ms. Zimmerman scooped up the note, read it, then deposited it with fanfare into the trash.

"Sure," Seena said, with that voice that was everywhere, "if you insist." But it seemed clear she would have read the note aloud without any insisting at all. She lengthened that coveted neck, as if preparing to relay a long-awaited answer. Her shoulder blades sharpened against her straight sweater dress. She unfolded the note the same as she'd folded it, seam by seam, and with every unfolding the noise around her shriveled. By the time the note was spread wide before her, anyone in the class of voyeurs could have heard the proverbial pin drop. Seena wiggled a bit to the left, then the right, as if repositioning the dress's belt, then she cleared her throat and "read," "Professor Welton is a pompous ass."

Welton expelled Dick from class. But Dick couldn't expel Seena from his mind, hard as he tried. You'd think her stunt would have made him hate her. You'd think those eyes would have sent him running. But, in all honesty, it was a relief for Dick never to have to conjugate again; there were other classes that could fulfill the requirement. And not having to see Loud-mouth was no heartache. Not seeing Seena, however, was another matter altogether. Funny thing was, once Dick had seen Seena's face, he couldn't think of anything else. Not even her neck. Those eyes that at first seemed demonic came to seem like burning-hot suns, exposing parts of him he barely knew. She'd become the perfect woman to him. An angel. The Virgin Mary. Despite the "pompous ass."

Growing up, Dick had fallen in love with the Virgin Mary. He was eleven when he fell in love. It was the year his surgeon father lost his license and took his own life. It was the year his mother lost her soul, when depression became her offspring and Dick became her burden. Dick longed to go to mass, then, just to see Mary's image, standing erect in her celestial blue mantle, her hands reaching out to him. For him. Not for his friend John Mark. Not for John Mark's sister, Martha. No, the Blessed Virgin reached for Dick alone—she desired to care for Dick alone. And she did. She was Dick's solace when he had no father to turn to for guidance, when his mother was needier than Dick was himself. Dick carried his burdens to God through Mary, and Mary lifted those burdens away. By the time Dick was a teenager, every time he said the rosary, it felt like a love poem. Hail Mary, full of grace, the Lord is with you. Blessed are you among women and blessed is the fruit of your womb.

But after the incident with Seena, whenever he said the Hail Mary, it felt like a love poem to Seena. He'd do his five Our Fathers and five Hail Marys as penitence for the way he felt, but it only made the problem worse. To say it was a vicious cycle is an understatement: it was a vicious Holy Labyrinth.

Dick sought counsel with Father Quinn, the senior priest at St. Francis of Assisi, and Quinn led Dick from the labyrinth. Father Quinn reminded Dick that marriage is one of the seven holy sacraments. "The apostle Paul compared the union between a man and a woman to the union of Christ with His church," he told Dick. "Your conflation of the Virgin Mary and this girl is biblical in a sense. Holy matrimony is, in a manner of speaking, a union with Mary, Mary being a symbol of the church. The apostle Paul said husbands should love their wives as Christ loved the church and delivered Himself up for it." But Father Quinn cautioned that Seena seemed to need some reining in. Quoting Ephesians, he said women should be "subject to their husbands, as to the Lord, because the husband is the head of the wife, as Christ is the head of the Church . . ."

Dick knew then: he had to marry Seena—he would marry her. The note he'd given Seena asking her to marry him wasn't a joke after all: it was the Word of God. God wanted Dick to marry Seena. God had written that note through Dick. And Dick was determined to abide by God's wishes, rein Seena in.

Since Dick no longer saw Seena in class, he spied. He knew she was a classics major and her full name was Christina Michels. He'd learned she lived in Betsy Barbour. And he'd deduced she was a skater, having seen her haul a pair of flesh-colored skates, laces over shoulder, clearly comfortable wielding those blades as she stomped through the snow to catch a bus to the rink.

Wearing his tweed overcoat with its raglan sleeves and a narrow-brimmed hat, brim down, Dick was Jimmy Stewart or Cary Grant in a Hitchcock movie. He carried his camera with him always, hoping to get a slice of her. Sometimes he'd get a small slice—a small, blurry slice.

It was a game, in a way, yet it wasn't. His grades suffered. He couldn't eat. As he sat on the steps of Angell Hall, waiting to catch sight of Seena when she slipped out the grand doors after Loudmouth's class, or as he stood with his feet frozen in a snowdrift near the bus stop, or as he circled Betsy Barbour, Dick was a predator. When he'd eye her, he'd swallow her whole. Her nylons. Her emerald green coat with the enormous collar. Or her bright red coat with no collar at all. Her hair, caught inside her deep-crowned swagger hat, those feather hairs teasing him. Sometimes, when the weather warmed a bit and spring seemed a possibility, she'd step outside holding her coat, and he'd imagine her thin arms beneath those wide sleeves she'd wear, and the waist-deep armholes and tight corselet belt of her dress would taunt him with her silhouette. He felt mad. Crazy. A beast. He was frightened of himself—of what he'd do if he ever found himself alone with her. She was his, his Christina. Even her name implied God wanted her to be his, holding Christ within it as it did.

And yet—like Dick's father and his mother, who should have been his, too—Seena wasn't Dick's at all.

Dick was outside Angell Hall the day it happened, his body wrapped around his biochemistry book, his mind wrapped around the anticipation of Seena. It was one of those days when he knew she would emerge from Angell Hall, coat in hand. He knew he'd see that neck, and the array of collarbone. He knew he'd see her legs from the knee down, swathed in those stockings that seemed a mystery in and of themselves. He knew he'd see her waist, hugged by a wide belt or a sash, or by a sweater dress that hugged more than her waist. But he didn't know he'd see her eyes, because he rarely did. Those devil-cat eyes were the hidden treasure—the jewels—veiled from Dick by distance, angle.

And will. Seena's will, although Dick didn't realize this—not at the time. He didn't know she'd spotted him preying on her. He didn't know she was afraid of him; it might have given him courage had he known. He didn't know she feared his fury, that she assumed he had fury and that it was aimed at her.

She touched him from behind. He thought she was an insect, or the breeze. She cleared her throat. He believed she was the entrance door to Angell Hall opening, scraping across the stone. She spoke: "Hi." He presumed she was not she, and that whoever this non-Seena was, she was speaking to someone else, someone who cared about something and someone other than Christina Michels. "Seena is a pompous ass," she then said.

And time stopped.

Truly. Dick remembers this moment as clearly as he remembers any moment of his life. It seemed he'd plunged into a hammock and was caught, deep in its confines. The hammock swayed and swayed, but he was still. Time was still. And Dick felt he would stay there, in that place that was at once soothing and suffocating, forever.

"Dick?" Seena said. "Dick Slepy?" She walked around him. Faced him. And her devil-cat eyes studied his Lake Hurons.

"I can't move," he wanted to tell her. "I can't breathe."

"I'm sorry," she said. "I am. I didn't mean for you to get in trouble, to get kicked out of class. You must hate me. I'd hate me. I was a coward. *Am* a coward. I should have told Welton I was lying—that I'd made it up, the note, what it said . . . But I loved that class—*love* it . . ."

Somehow Dick managed to stand and touch his fingertips to her lips. Her lips were dry, not at all how he'd imagined they would feel. Seena fell quiet. And for a second Seena and Dick stood on the steps of Angell Hall, his fingers kissing her lips.

"Can I call you Christina?" he said then.

She stripped his fingers aside. "No, you can't." Then she truly kissed him. Just like that. This thing he'd fantasized about for months happened as if it were the most normal thing in the world. She'd lowered his hand from her mouth, and her mouth was on his.

They made love that afternoon, with a chair jammed under the handle of Dick's dorm room door to seal out Frank and Sam.

"I feel like the goddess Cydippe," Seena said afterward, as they lay disheveled, the chair still propped against the door despite Frank's efforts. "And you are Acontius. You've tossed me the quince."

He had tossed her the quince.

Seena became pregnant that very day.

God moves in mysterious ways. He may have taken Dick's father, He may have taken Dick's mother's spirit. But He had given Dick Seena. And He gave Dick lovely Mary Grace, then sweet, God-loving Mary Catherine, then smart-as-a-whip Mary Tessa.

Then there was Yllis.

Yllis.

———————

Danish Landing, Michigan
1976

Now Dick stands on the Old Trail, in the sweet smell of decay from leaves and logs. The pine trees and maples and birches rise up in the moonlight like ghosts of forgotten soldiers, urging Dick toward death. It's four in the morning, two days after Dick discovered the rattler and Yllis discovered the Indian. If Dick finds Yllis's Indian now, he'll kill him, butcher him, like he butchered that rattler to protect his girls, his wife. *His* wife. God gave Seena to him. Dick tossed the quince.

Dick turns to the side of the trail and empties his insides. He heaves until his throat burns raw. And then he heaves more, until the raw fire inflames his esophagus. He feels the burning deep in his chest. He feels it reaching for his gut, as if he might lose the lining of his stomach as well.

Didn't I always know? he thinks. He swipes his mustache with the back of his hand as he draws back the curtain of lies and excuses and explanations that have defined the past eleven years. Of course I knew, he thinks: of course I did. How could I look at Yllis and not know? How could I speak her name and not suspect? How could I listen to her blabber about the color of feelings and the taste of feelings and believe her makeup had anything to do with mine? I even imagined it was a native—an Indian who'd fathered her. Someone with a name like Spirit Warrior or Painted Arrow, who himself espouses Yllis-type non-sense. Somewhere deep inside me, even this I suspected—didn't I?—given Yllis's coloring, given Seena's absurd account of Yllis's birth. Given Yllis's contorted mind.

At times Dick made intimations of his suspicions to Seena, and to the girls. He warned the girls to steer clear of the Indians. He prodded Seena to attend confession, needled her. She was a sinner, he told her. They were all sinners, of course. But Seena: perhaps she was more of a sinner than most.

Yet he hadn't allowed himself to comprehend his own intimations. Instead, he'd made excuses to himself and to the many others who raised eyebrows. There must be mixed blood buried somewhere in his past, or in Seena's past: Yllis was an expression of that buried blood.

But why had he lied to himself all these years? Why?

Because the thought of Seena's betrayal was more than he could bear.

More than he can bear.

After Dick's father's betrayal, and his mother's betrayal, Seena's betrayal is more than Dick can bear. Yet he must bear it now. Yllis spoke the truth aloud, and her speaking it gave it life. And, now, like the rattler, Dick must take its life.

I'll kill him, he thinks again. I'll find Seena's lover, and I'll kill him. I'll wait here. And when I see him, I'll do it with my own hands. With my hands.

Yet he wonders how he'll manage given his hands won't stop shaking, given his body can't stop heaving.

Given there is no reason the damn Indian would be on the Old Trail in the middle of the night.

Help me, God, he thinks. Oh, God, please help me.

But Dick feels further and further from his God.

He returns to the cottage, to the sound of breathing. He steps into his and Seena's bedroom, finds Seena dreaming on her back, her mouth slightly open. He picks up his pillow—the down prickles his fingertips. He holds the pillow inches from Seena's breath. The pillow blocks her face from his view, he knows it could block her breath, that she could never hurt him again. He feels the wet tears on his face evolve from warm to cold. He lifts the pillow to his chest, sees Seena's sleeping face again. Then he sets the pillow down near the edge of the bed, gently, so as not to wake her.

Dick drops to the ground, pulls the stack of magazines from beneath the bed and carries them with him to his Cadillac, which is parked in the sandy yard of the cottage, just behind Seena's station wagon. Dick climbs into the front seat, turns on the overhead light. He thumbs through the magazines, through page after page of breasts and spread thighs and come-hither looks, until he chooses one set of breasts and spread thighs, one come-hither look. And for the few minutes while he is with this paper girl who is not his wife, he forgets he loves his wife.

But it is not enough, this forgetting.

It is far from enough.

The newspaper deliveryman rounds the corner, pulls onto the Danish Landing. The lights from the car expose Dick. Dick ducks. He hears the newspaper thump onto the porch, hears the delivery car move on.

Dick collects the newspaper and returns to sit in the car. He tries to read, but his eyes keep finding the same advertisement. He has seen it before, this advertisement. "Rent-a-Girl. Our Companions *Want* to Serve Your Needs." It is an escort service, he knows, supposedly intended to provide company for executives while away from home. The girls will be dinner companions for the executives, or theater companions. But Dick is no fool: he can guess what really goes on.

Dick climbs from the car, reenters the cottage, replaces the magazines beneath the bed. He enters the kitchen, lifts the phone, untangles the curled cord. He glances out the window at Old Lady Clara's cottage and sees the lights are all out, his only assurance Clara isn't listening in on the party line.

He dials.

"Rent-a-Girl," he hears a woman's voice say. "We want to serve your needs."

"I'd like a companion," Dick says.

Dick meets the girl in a hotel in Traverse City. It takes forty-five minutes for him to drive there, but he never wavers. He has needs. So many needs.

She has red hair and wears lipstick that clashes with her hair. But her hair is not really red. Dick thinks this after she undresses and he sees her hidden hair. She parades around the room as if she's obliged to display the goods. Then she asks Dick what he wants, as if he is ordering from a menu.

What do I want? Dick thinks.

What don't I want? What don't I need?

———

At ten in the morning, the local Grayling priest, Father Amadi, finds Dick asleep in the Cadillac, in the parking lot of the rectory. Dick's head rests on the steering wheel. Father Amadi wakes him with a tap on the window.

"Get in," Dick says when he remembers what he's done and where he is and who Father Amadi is.

Father Amadi hesitates before he rounds the car and slips into the passenger's seat.

"I'm going to kill the son of a bitch if I ever find him," Dick says, and he sees the fear in Amadi's eyes.

But Amadi's voice is calm. "What is it, Dick? What are you talking about?"

Dick tells him; he tells him everything. Of Seena's betrayal, of the Indian, of Yllis, of the Rent-a-Girl. "I'm a monster," Dick says. "I've become a monster. I could kill a person. I could."

And Father Amadi tells Dick to run from death. "You need to flee from wanting to kill," he says. "It's destroying you inside. You need to run toward preventing death, preserving life. There's so much need in this world, Dick. Find a way to give of yourself. Giving is healing. It will help heal you inside. We can't control what others do. You can't know whether Seena's been unfaithful to you. You can't control Seena."

But I can, Dick thinks: I have to.

"But we can control our own behavior, Dick. You can control where you go from here. Choose life, Dick. Choose *life*. You're a doctor. You have much to give. You could do great good in this world. You told me once about your grandfather. The one who was a doctor. You told me how giving he was, how much you admired him."

"He was a medical missionary," Dick says. "In Africa. I never knew him. But my father told me of him when I was young. My father was a doctor, too, but he chose a different path. Cared more about personal comfort . . ." Until he botched a surgery and was stripped of his license. Then he lost that personal comfort, so he took his own life and left Dick and his mother to fend for themselves.

"You could be like your grandfather, Dick," Father Amadi says. "We have choices in life. *You* have choices. You don't have to live your life trapped in a box. You don't have to be the person you've been. Be the person you want to be—the kind of person you admire. Control what you can control."

"You don't understand," Dick says. He presses his palms into his eyes. "I can't control my feelings. I can't control my rage. You should have seen me last night—you should have seen me . . . I can't let her be with him."

Father Amadi says nothing at first—nothing until Dick lowers his hands and turns Amadi's way. And even then Amadi hesitates before he speaks. "Go away, Dick," he finally says. "Take your family and go away. You could go to Africa, you know? You could go there. Like your grandfather did. You could take your family and find peace through giving of yourself." Amadi describes his homeland in West Africa and the great needs there.

He tells Dick of his nephew, Mawuli, who runs a West African aid organization. "Mawuli could work with you to set up a clinic in a village, someplace where there's no access to formal health care."

And Dick knows in his spirit Father Amadi is right. Dick should take his family to Africa, like his grandfather did. It's his heritage; it feels like his destiny. Just like Seena was his destiny. God spoke to Dick through Father Quinn those many years ago—guided Dick to understand Dick's marrying Seena was God's will. Now God has spoken to Dick through Father Amadi, and once again Dick knows God's will. Dick should take Seena away—far away—to a place no lover will ever find her. And he should atone for his sins through good works. Perhaps in this way he will pass, if not from hell to heaven, at least from hell to purgatory.

Mary Tessa

Danish Landing, Michigan
Summer 1976

Life is a feast. Like the concoction Yllis and Tessa brewed up this morning after Pa left for Midland, while Ma was in Never Never Land. Ma was burrowed in the beanbag chair at the time, mouthing Sappho purportedly to them, although neither was listening. Instead the girls were doing their own mouthing, but of the marshmallows they'd roasted on the gas stove, smeared with Jiff, rolled in mashed graham crackers and decked with the barely ripe blueberries they'd picked that morning along the Old Trail. The taste of those gooey marshmallows was at once gritty, sweet and tangy. Every one Tessa ate, she just wanted more.

That's what Tessa wants in general: more. You get one life, she figures. You may as well live it up. Pa can lecture all he wants about this life being a precursor for the next, and Tessa's (holy) sister Mary Catherine can believe him for all Tessa cares, depriving herself of every sweet, tangy, gritty joy on this earth. But it seems to Tessa you'd best hedge your bets. You know you've got one life. The next life? That's a crapshoot at best, as far as Tessa can tell. And, frankly, Mary Catherine describes heaven as a place of eternal happiness where the blessed want for nothing. Sounds like divine dullness to Tessa, even in the off chance it exists.

Chances are when we die, we die. It's pretty hard to have a ma like Ma and think otherwise. The woman crosses her fingers when she takes communion (not literally, but she may as well). Each time Father Amadi gives Ma the host, she looks at her feet, not him. Tessa half-expects her to burst out laughing. And when Father Amadi speaks about God, seems Ma has to bite her tongue to stop from asking which one. Why on earth Ma married a Catholic like Pa, who truly believes he's chomping down Christ when he eats that communion wafer, is a question only God himself could answer—assuming there were such a God.

Tessa thinks these things while hidden behind the rowboat, which is propped upright to drain yesterday's rain, as she spies on her eldest sister Grace—and while her youngest sister Yllis spies on her. The rowboat's underside crawls with all manner of life, from spiders to salamanders to red ants to beetles to termites. A few spiders and ants have made their way to Tessa, but she only gets the willies when leeches are involved. Yllis continues to tiptoe around the acorns and slither along the walls of the cottage like she's some Charlie's Angel.

Yllis is a brat; there's no question about that. Ma and Grace and Mary Catherine like to think Tessa is the Chief Trouble Maker, but Tessa sees Pa knows: Yllis is a pot stirrer. She's Ma's Eris, the goddess of discord. The apple stealer. She makes people squirm with those eyes of hers. They're sort of see-through, her eyes, all pale and glassylike. And they seem to *see through*. Even Tessa can't lie to her.

Still, Tessa likes Yllis all right. Partly because Yllis's stirring detracts from Tessa's own, meaning Tessa can get away with plenty more. Partly because Yllis gives the skinny, which can be hilarious, depending. But mostly because Yllis has an imagination as plentiful as June bugs in June. Makes Yllis seem a bit off at times but, given Tessa is deprived for the entire summer while at the cottage of both an Atari and a TV, Yllis is the next best thing. Grace spends most of her time changing her clothes, or gazing at her ears, which she's convinced are too big. And Mary Catherine is what that old biddy, Clara of the Bowed Legs and Beehive (her hair), who lives in the cottage across the path, calls a navel gazer. (Mary Catherine, otherwise known as Saint Catherine of Siena—in her dreams—claims she is in fact gazing at God, meditating on the Holy Mysteries: the Joyful on Mondays and Saturdays, the Luminous on Thursdays, the Sorrowful on Tuesdays and Fridays, blah, blah, blah, blah, blah. Why a sixteen-year-old girl would prefer to be a fourteenth-century saint is the ultimate Holy Mystery as far as Tessa is concerned.) Needless to say, Tessa will take bratty Yllis any day. Even with her pot stirring and apple stealing.

The most recent pot Yllis has been stirring has to do with what Pa calls "procreation" and the old biddy Clara calls "the birds and the bees" (apropos of her hair) and Ma doesn't call at all. Yllis is convinced she was fathered by an Indian warrior named Running Buffalo (Yllis looks more like a scampering rodent) or Stand Tall (that, she does not) or Night Sky (well, she does have that hair). But Tessa just gives it to her straight. "Yllis," she says, "Ma found you along the Old Trail and mistook you for a rodent, so she brought you home so Lint would have something to bat around."

Truth be told, Tessa feels a bit guilty about Yllis's most recent pot stirring. Figures she may well have provided the soup for this pot, given the number of times she's intimated the very same thing. "You half blood," Tessa's said to Yllis, no less than a hundred times. "You know you're adopted, don't you?" But she never thought Yllis would take her seriously. How many times have Mary Catherine and Grace said the very same thing to Tessa? Well, not the very same. Everything but the half blood part.

Tessa picks up an acorn and hurls it at Grace, who circles a stump while conversing (that is, giggling) with Rocky Rasmusson. The acorn nearly hits Rocky in the rear, and Yllis sputters, trying not to laugh. Tessa picks up another acorn and whips it toward Yllis, just as Yllis ducks behind a narrow birch tree, her black hair flanking the tree, giving it zebra stripes. Yllis clearly is more Kate Jackson than Farrah Fawcett. Even without the hair.

"Shut up, Yllis," Tessa says. "I'm spying."

"Spying what?" Yllis says, and those see-through eyes inch out from behind the birch.

"The birds and the bees. Now, shut up."

"You're spying on Grace and Rocky," Yllis says matter-of-factly. "If you don't want them to see you, why d'ya try to peg Rocky's bum?"

Will there ever be a day when Yllis fails to point out others' failings? That was an asinine thing to do, now that Tessa thinks of it. But she doesn't intend to give Yllis the satisfaction. "I know what I'm doing," she says.

Yllis slinks across the moss on her tippy toes. "She's got it," she whispers into Tessa's back, and Tessa feels Yllis's hot breath wetting her bikini strap. "What's she done?"

"Quit slobbering on my back." Tessa nudges Yllis, but not too hard. She doesn't want her to trip and blow their cover.

"What's she done?" Yllis says again.

Tessa strains her neck to look at Yllis, and she sees Yllis has that look she gets sometimes: her mouth is all soft and her eyes are squinty. Those see-through eyes are seeing something. "What?" Tessa says. "Who?"

"Gracie. Mary Grace. Look at her."

Grace leans on the stump then rubs her bare left toe up and down her bare right calf. "What are you talking about, Yllis?" Tessa says. "Shut your trap before they spot us."

"I don't have to listen to you," Yllis says, but she does shut her trap.

Grace pets her own hair now, like she used to pet Lint in the long-ago days when she actually paid attention to Lint. Grace has hair like Tessa's. Sexy hair. Far more Farrah than Kate. Pa would no doubt be surprised Tessa understands "sexy," even though she's fourteen and well aware there's been a sexual revolution. Tessa knows about women's lib and free love and the pill. She's seen *Maude*. Still, Pa, the good Catholic, insists sex is for making babies. And he fools himself into thinking his girls don't see the way he looks at Ma, as if they haven't heard him call her that very word, "sexy," when he thought they were asleep. Tessa has to admit, hearing Pa use the word in the context of Ma seemed a bit shocking at first given how annoyed Pa is with Ma 100 percent of the time. But she's come to see Ma's sexier to Pa the angrier he is. Go figure.

Yllis has pressed herself against Tessa's back again. She's sweating and Tessa is sweating, and Tessa can feel Yllis slipping up and down with each inhale. Tessa is tempted to butt Yllis away, but when Yllis gets that look, Tessa knows she's fragile. Like a disoriented butterfly. Nab her and you'll rip her to shreds. Tessa has made that mistake more times than she'd like to remember. So she pretends to not notice Yllis there, slip sliding away.

Rocky makes his move. He lifts Grace from the stump and turns her to face the lake. He stands behind her now, pointing over her shoulder toward the sand hill, as if directing her gaze. His hand circles her waist, and Grace is as still as the stump, like she's not breathing at all. If Pa were to see this, Tessa thinks, it would be Rocky who'd cease to breathe.

"Ma's done it again," Yllis whispers, after a minute of silent steaming.

"I thought it was Grace who's done whatever it is you're yapping about."

"Different," Yllis says.

"Just tell me, okay, Yllis?" Tessa says, although she doesn't really care. But she knows Yllis. She got Yllis to shut her trap once. The chance of Yllis shutting it twice in a row is a statistical impossibility.

"Fish. It's Friday. We ate meat."

Big whoopy, Tessa thinks. Has anyone in this family heard of Vatican II?

Grace bends her head upward, then, as if to look at the sky. Her hair falls against Rocky's shoulder. Grace reaches up, lifts her hair free, then drops it over his shoulder, down his back. Tessa can't help but wonder where Grace learned *that*.

Rocky's definitely breathing now. And so is Grace. Seems

they might hyperventilate in unison. Tessa wonders whether Yllis should be watching this. She's just a kid. You'd think Ma might watch out for her, but no: ends up being Tessa's responsibility.

"Mary Catherine says it's a mortal sin," Yllis says.

"What?" Tessa looks back at Yllis. Once again the little twerp has read her mind. "It's not a mortal sin. Not that you should be watching it."

"Watching it?" Yllis says, and Tessa realizes she wasn't watching it. What on earth was she blabbing about, then? Yllis tucks her head beneath Tessa's left arm to improve her view, apparently realizing she's been missing some action.

"I saw that one on Papa," Yllis says, after a minute more of extraordinary silence. "That color."

With Yllis's head where it is, it would be so easy to give her a noogie. "What color?"

"And the smell. You smell that? That's sweeter than Papa."

"I smell your stench, if that's what you mean"—although Yllis actually smells pretty good. Must be that Breck shampoo. Or Tessa's Love's Baby Soft, the little thief.

"It's all kinda jumbled though. And it keeps changing."

"Yllis, there are times when I think you're a complete and utter freak," Tessa says, which is true. But as soon as she says it, she regrets it. She'd forgotten about the disoriented butterfly thing.

Yllis backs away. She's out in the open now. She may as well be neon. The only saving grace is that Rocky and Grace's attention most certainly is elsewhere. Even so, Tessa figures she's damned. Yllis eyes Tessa as if Tessa just said something Yllis has been wondering herself for a while now. And Tessa's saying it confirmed it: Yllis is a freak.

The screen door slams and Mary Catherine streams into the yard. She's got the sexy hair, too. Wings and all. It's even blonder than Tessa's. Clearly Mary Catherine has been sneaking Grace's Sun-In. Mary Catherine had insisted on going to confession this morning with Father Amadi, probably seeking penance for her Sun-In stealing.

"Catie," Yllis says to herself, and Tessa sees Yllis has sunk further down into that strange place. She looks about, sort of stunned like, as if the world is passing by her fast.

In reality, it's Mary Catherine who's passed by fast, along with Tessa's opportunity to spy on Grace. When the screen door slammed, Grace and Rocky parted ways, wide enough for the setting sun to pass between them as it streaked the lake an inky red. The Red Sea, Tessa thinks: my parting sea of opportunity.

Grace gawks from Yllis to Mary Catherine and back, looking like she's trying to figure out whether she's been caught with her hand in the cookie jar or whether she's p-oed because she's been deprived of her cookie. She's yet to see Tessa, as Tessa had the smarts to stay put here, behind Noah's ark. Grace's bikini top is just a tad off center, showing off her tan lines and making those breasts she's so proud of look lopsided. Rocky's got his hands dug down deep into the pockets of his shorts, as if the rules of gravity were inapplicable when it comes to shorts, necessitating his pinning them to his thighs to keep them from floating away. He mumbles something to Grace, his pale hair taking on a peachy halo in the sunlight. Even Grace looks a bit off-color, like she's used too much of that tanning lotion, turned herself orange. Tessa wonders whether what she sees now is what Yllis commented on before when she ran at the mouth about the color she was seeing and how it was changing, et cetera. Ma says Yllis is just sensitive, that she sees things others miss, that when she goes off talking nonsense, she's really talking sense. Well, maybe. More likely Ma's just making excuses so she can return to the likes of Adonis. Leaving Yllis to go off the deep end.

At the moment, it's Mary Catherine who's gone off the deep end. Passing directly between Grace and Rocky, wielding scissors (to make a point?), she headed down to the dock and jumped—fully clothed—into the still-Red Sea. Apparently the parted sea of possibility no longer is parted, because Mary Catherine emerged with her yellow halter and shorts pasted to her white skin and her pale hair slick down her back, making her resemble the dreaded leech. Even so, Tessa feels a tinge of envy, imagining the feel of that cool water licking her skin. Standing where she is, crawling with bugs, she's hot as Mary Catherine's Hell: that pool burning with fire and brimstone.

Mary Catherine stands on the dock, now, still wielding the scissors, and she has the full attention of Grace, Rocky, Tessa and Yllis. Tessa expects getting their attention was the point of this full-attire dip. Knowing Mary Catherine's tendency to secure an audience for her various ablutions, Tessa expects Mary Catherine would love to turn back now, make sure they're all riveted (which they are), but she controls the urge. With the scissors hooked to one pinky, Mary Catherine pulls her hair into a ponytail on the crown of her head. She adjusts the scissors from her pinky to her thumb and forefinger. She spreads the scissors wide. And she slices, smack through the base of the ponytail, where a rubber band would have been if she'd used one. It's not easy, this slicing. It happens in slow motion, and her whole body gyrates with each squeeze. Eventually she holds the scissors in one hand, the hair rope in the other. And her hair is no longer sexy. No siree.

Yllis weeps, but her face is dirty and it looks more like she's seeping tar. "Why?" she says. "Why would she?"

Grace backs away, as if Mary Catherine were in fact a leech. Rocky has disappeared, although when and how Tessa couldn't say. Apparently a histrionic younger sister is more than he'd bargained for (and that on top of the histrionic father he regularly has to deal with). Tessa figures she'd best head down to Mary Catherine: Grace and Yllis are useless (big surprise, there). But just as she surfaces from behind the boat, Ma bangs open the door and trips down the porch steps. She sprints across the acorns in her bare feet, and Tessa knows she's getting stabbed by the way she jerks now and then. When she reaches the dock, she halts. Apparently she's spotted the hair on the head, the hair in the hand. What to do?

Mary Catherine turns. She part spits, part shrieks, part laughs. Tessa finally thinks she understands the term "screaming meemies."

The screen door slams again. Tessa turns and sees Lint, who stands on the porch looking confused. Apparently he pushed the door open when he heard the meemies, momentarily forgetting he's a scaredy-cat who most certainly is not coming to anyone's rescue.

Tessa turns back to the goings-on, knowing full well Lint has little going on. Ma stands like Mary Grace did when Grace was the stump. "What are you doing?" Ma says. She doesn't yell, per se, but Tessa sure has no trouble hearing her. "What have you done?"

Mary Catherine loops her tail of hair above her head, like a lasso. Watching that hair-tail circle reminds Tessa of the decapitated rattler she and Yllis found—that headless rope of death. Mary Catherine is freaking Tessa out.

"I was praying, Mama. Because it's Friday, Mama. It's Friday. And we ate those frankfurters, Mama. But I didn't know. I didn't remember. And then I did remember. I realized after we'd sinned that we'd sinned. And I was telling Jesus I'd sinned without knowing and asking that the sin not destroy the grace of God in my heart, 'cause it was an accident. I told Jesus I'd do penance. That I'd stay in the cottage, praying. That I wouldn't go swimming, I wouldn't go to the bonfire later."

"Sweet Jesus," Mama says. And she tries to embrace Mary Catherine, but Catie backs away. "Jesus doesn't blame you, Mary Catherine. It was my fault . . . Jesus holds me accountable. Not you. Jesus loves you, honey. He loves you."

But Tessa knows Ma is just saying this, not believing it. Ma doesn't believe in Jesus. Certainly not a sweet Jesus.

"Listen to me!" Mary Catherine spits-laughs-shrieks. "Jesus came to me, Mama. When I was praying. I saw Him. I really saw Him. Like Saint Catherine did. He stood in the doorway and He said to me, 'Mary Catherine, you must come out.' Just like He said to her, to Saint Catherine. But I didn't know what He meant. Then I overheard you arguing with Papa on the phone. I heard about Africa. That we're going. And I realized what Jesus was saying—why He was saying it. Jesus was calling me like He did her, telling me it's time, that I'm being called."

Not this again, Tessa thinks. This Saint Catherine of Siena crap. It's all starting to make sense—as much sense as it could make. Tessa remembers Mary Catherine droning on about Saint Catherine cutting off her hair. Something about perpetual virginity, about preserving herself for God, about being called to action. Even so, Tessa thinks, if I were God watching this, I'd be scratching my Holy Head.

Ma faces sideways now and Tessa sees she is widemouthed, as if she intends to say something but the words just won't come out. Mary Catherine tosses her hair rope high, in some form of exultation, it seems. Tessa expects the hair to scatter, but it plops on the dock in a lump, with a thud. Ma looks at the lump, then turns to face Grace, Yllis and Tessa, knowing she has some explaining to do.

"Africa?" Grace yells. Her ears do look huge all of a sudden, and red, as if all the blood in her body rushed there, ballooning them. "What the hell? Africa?"

"Watch your mouth," Ma says. But it seems to Tessa that Ma herself is thinking: What the hell? And then Tessa thinks, Yeah, what the hell? Africa? What's Africa got to do with anything?

"Sure," Grace says. "No problem. I'll watch my mouth, and you watch my ass as I run away." She swings her bikinied rear, gives it a swat, as if she needs to clarify she's not talking about a donkey. "'Cause I'm not going to Africa."

"You talk that way again in front of Yllis, and I'll wash out your mouth," Ma says.

"Yllis this, Yllis that, Yllis this, Yllis that," Grace says, gesticulating like the skinny birch in a storm.

"This is about your father," Ma says. "This is something he wants. This has nothing to do with Yllis. Or Mary Catherine, for that matter."

Mary Catherine has this confusedlike expression, as if she's just woken up. And with serious bed head. She studies Ma like she's trying to figure out whether it's a real Ma or a dream Ma standing before her. She reaches up with one hand and feels her hair—that bit that remains. And she wakes up. Totally wakes up. Realizes she's Dorothy Hamill on a very bad hair day. Even from this distance Tessa sees Mary Catherine's mouth hang and her neck flush, and she knows Mary Catherine is crying, although she can't see the tears.

"Liar," Yllis says.

Tessa had nearly forgotten about Yllis standing there, despite Yllis being the current topic of conversation. "What? You know about this? This Africa thing? What d'ya know? Who's lying?"

"I don't know anything about Africa," Yllis says. "But Mama's lying."

Mary Catherine

The beauty. The symmetry. God's perfection. Mary Catherine sees it without trying. And she feels for those who don't see it, who can't. Like Mama, who's stuck in her brain; and Gracie, who's stuck on herself; and Tessa, who's too bullheaded to appreciate she's not God herself; and Yllis, whose imagination borders on psychosis, who insists on seeing what God never intended.

Unlike them, seeing God, believing in Jesus, is like believing in air for Mary Catherine. She can't imagine not believing—although she's tried. When she's wanted something she knew Jesus wouldn't want her to have, she's tried testing God—His omnipresence—just like Tessa has tried testing air, plunging her head into that icy water of Lake Margrethe and staying there, thinking she'd outwit oxygen, prove she didn't need it. That didn't last long, obviously. Tessa's alive, breathing air. And that mere act—the act of breathing air—proved sufficient for God to pass Mary Catherine's test. Because, unlike Papa, Mary Catherine believes in her heart, her soul, her *lungs*—she believes with every breath—not because Father Amadi says so.

Father Amadi: he's a man, he's not God. Mary Catherine reminds herself of this. She reminds herself Father Amadi is just God's vessel. An embodiment of what she loves, not the very thing. Not the very thing. It's God that's the thing. It's Jesus. Because the reason Mary Catherine believes has a lot less to do with what Father Amadi does or says, and a lot more to do with the painting of the sun setting over the lake—that swell of shimmering pink or splashed red or purplish haze. It has a lot more to do with the lake itself as evening melts over her and the lake shows like glass—a smooth expanse of the flawless. Yes, unlike Papa, her belief is driven not by need or the need to please. Life is too beautiful, too perfect, too abundant, too gloriously designed to be an accident, a fluke, some chance confluence of events.

And she feels so much love for the great designer of this masterpiece. So much love. Sometimes the love feels big, out of bounds. Sometimes she thinks it's a person she loves. But then she takes a good look and she sees people are flawed, too often incapable of sensing beauty—let alone producing it. And she knows she could never love a human the way she loves God, Jesus. Because it's the perfection she loves, the refusal to settle for the mundane. When God does something, He does it with splendor. Human beings? They undo a lot of God's doing. God rolls out an evergreen forest. Humans hack down the trees, slap down a road. God rains in a lake, blue as huckleberries. Humans zoom around on it, poisoning it and the silence. God designs deer—animals with such elegance, such grace—and humans gun them down, strip them of their antlers, hang them from their hoofs at the edge of the road, displayed there for all to see, measure. Treasure? "Did ya see the size of *that* beauty?" Tessa will say when they visit Grayling during deer season, see the bucks hung like laundry along the road's edge.

But the God Mary Catherine knows and loves weeps at that buck, at the denigration. He doesn't just talk about beauty and love and pain. And passion. He *feels* it. And the God she loves, loves her more because He knows she feels it, too. He caresses her skin with cool water and warm breeze to comfort her. When she kneels on her knees in prayer, the smoothness of the rosary beads like petals dusting her fingertips, she loves God, Jesus, with passion. She imagines Jesus holding her. She imagines looking into his blue eyes, seeing the love in His eyes. And she knows Grace, with her tube tops and short shorts, wouldn't know passion if it licked her in the face. I mean, Rocky? Please.

And yet. Mary Catherine feels caught. As she sits looking at her thicket of hair, she struggles with what she loved more: her hair or Jesus. Because losing it—her hair—makes her feel like Samson, it's drained her strength. She wanted to show Jesus she loved Him so, she'd give up her beauty to be His bride. When she overheard Mama talking on the phone, arguing with Papa about Africa, she wasn't praying like she told Mama she was. (Forgive her, Jesus, for that lie.) She'd gone to pray, remembering about the meat. But she got distracted by her hair. She was admiring it, and imagining it being admired, running her fingers not along her rosary but through her golden streaks, thinking her hair was prettier than Grace's, Tessa's. Prettier even than Mama's. Then she heard Mama talking like Mama does when she talks to Papa on the phone. A lot of "Uh-huhs" and "Mmm-hmms" peppered with a "Really?" or an "I see" or an "Interesting" (not). Mary Catherine figured Mama was three-quarters reading, one-quarter listening. At first she didn't pay much attention. As Tessa has pointed out, eavesdropping on Mama and Papa's conversations is rarely worth the effort.

But then Mama's voice changed; she was no longer reading—Mary Catherine was sure of that. "What?" she said. "Where?" And then: "Oh, for the love of God." (This one, in particular, got Mary Catherine's attention, coming from Mama.) "West Africa? But, Dick, honey, you're a pathologist . . . How can a pathologist really help? They need practitioners . . ." (Honey? She called him "honey"?) "This is something we would need to decide to do as a family. You can't just decide to do this on your own. What do you mean, it's already decided? How am I going to stop our going? Seriously, Dick. You don't need to yell at me. I know perfectly well I don't have a job—I know I can't support myself and the girls. But we can't just up and leave. You're hurting my ears, Dick—please stop yelling. I'm just being practical. What about Gracie? She's starting college. What? We're going to drop her off at college and disappear halfway around the globe? She's young, Dick. Immature. More immature inside than outside. She's lucky she got in . . . Well, what about the other girls, then? What about their schooling? It's Yllis's first year in middle school . . . What do you mean, "Not Yllis *again*"? Someone needs to care about Yllis, Dick. All you ever do is criticize the child. Unlike saintly Mary Catherine, whom you never criticize. Maybe the two of you should go save the world by yourselves, save the rest of us the headache. No, of course I don't mean it. I was just making a point. Well, *that's* not the point. Okay, what about Lint, then? Who's going to take care of him? Have you thought of that? These aren't minor details, Dick. They're not. What do you mean it's your duty? To whom? The heathens? What, are you trying to save me? Father Amadi? Why would he suggest we do this? Well, of course I know there are people who are far less fortunate than we are in the world. I know that . . ."

Mary Catherine looked at herself looking at herself in the mirror. Papa was talking about saving the heathens while she flattered herself. She'd disparaged Papa's simple faith, thought Jesus loved her far more. But, here, Papa was talking Mama into going to Africa—it was Papa who was dedicating himself to good works, like Saint Catherine did—and Mary Catherine was as much a heathen as anyone. "I'll do anything for you, Jesus," she said out loud then. "It's you I want. I was confused before. But I understand now. It's you I love. I'll give you my hair—cut it off—like Saint Catherine. I'll forego my beauty to be your bride, just like she did."

That was so much easier to say—to think—when Mary Catherine actually had beauty to give. Now she looks like some horrific version of a female Rocky Rasmusson, electrified. She's having a hard time seeing any symmetry, beauty, perfection in that.

She slips open the bureau drawer—tries to, but it sticks as usual, and she has to jerk it out, which makes far too much noise. She pushes the panties aside, Grace's frilly ones and her sensible ones. She sees Grace's bra, the one she'd sneaked, along with the matching black panties. She picks the bra up, stretches it across her breasts. She wants to burn them: the bra and her breasts. The bra was too big on her, but she'd worn it anyway. She chucks it back in the drawer, buries it. And she finds the razor blade.

She's cut herself three times so far—this will be the fourth. She did it on her inner arm, beneath her armpit, near her breast, so she could run her fingers across the cuts whenever she needed to remember the feeling, the pain. Her tank top is yellow. A sort of mustard color now that it's wet. The blood might stain it, she knows. But she doesn't care.

She hovers the blade above the first three cuts. Each is an inch long and perfectly straight, perfectly aligned, one over the other. There's something beautiful about their symmetry, about this intersection of perfection and pain.

Mary Catherine slices, the skin pops—a flesh-filled balloon. The pain stabs and builds. The blood runs. She feels a release, almost like joy.

But nothing like joy.

She removes a sanitary napkin from the box stashed in the opened panty drawer and she presses it hard against the blood until the bleeding stops. She rolls the napkin into itself before she tosses it in the trash. As she pulls on a T-shirt to hide the fresh cut, she hears Mama.

"Mary Catherine?"

Mama hangs her head through the part in the curtains, this makeshift doorway to the bedroom. Mary Catherine sits down on the bed. Its springs are knuckles jabbing her rear. She pretends she doesn't see Mama's curtain-decapitated head, that she doesn't hear Mama's voice trying to massage her. Mama will say something she'd never herself believe, like, "Jesus loves you just the way you are," or "You are precious in Jesus' eyes."

"Catie. Honey?"

Honey, Mary Catherine thinks: I've heard *that* one before.

Mama parts the curtains, enters the room. She holds the scissors, and Mary Catherine wishes she were Yllis, that she could make up a world rather than live in this one. The rush from the cutting has withered to a weak pulse. All the beauty and perfection in this world suddenly doesn't seem all that beautiful or perfect, and Mary Catherine wonders whether she's like Samson after all, whether her power was in her hair.

"I'm gonna fix it, honey," Mama says. And she scalps Mary Catherine.

Hot tears boil down Mary Catherine's cheeks as Mama cuts, as she tries to even out what can't be evened out. Mama pretends not to notice the tears and the snot puddled above Mary Catherine's lip. When Mama finishes, Mary Catherine's arms and chest are furry.

Mary Catherine wants Mama to say something now. She wants Mama to tell her she's beautiful, no matter what, that Jesus loves her, no matter what.

Instead Mama dusts Mary Catherine's nearly hairless head, her fuzzy shoulders, her neck. Then she swipes the bed. Hair dives from the bed to the floor. Mama piles it, scoops it into a paper cup. Mary Catherine wants to grab it from her, drink it down.

Because the bulk of Mary Catherine's hair ended up in the lake. If only she'd thought to keep it, her relic. It had been lying like a lopped tail on the dock, but after it dried, it departed, piece by piece, slithering off with the wind. She watched it go, every last strand of it. Mama and Grace had spun themselves into a whirlwind, Tessa watched it all with a smirk, Yllis sealed herself off in fantasyland. And Mary Catherine watched her hair fly, fall, float.

"At least you won't be hot in Africa," Mama says. Then she wishes she hadn't said this, it seems, because she's reminded herself: Africa. Mama doesn't want to go—that's clear. And Mary Catherine wonders why. Mama can take her books anywhere.

"Yeah," Mary Catherine says. "I don't care what I look like, Mama. Saint Catherine—"

"Don't," Mama says. "Not now . . ."

And Mary Catherine realizes Mama knows she's lying. Yllis is her daughter, without a doubt. Yllis may live make-believe, but she can hone things down when she wants to, make them all see what they'd rather not. She didn't inherit that sixth sense from Papa. But Mama rarely uses her sixth sense, seems she's usually flicked the switch, turned it off. But it's on now.

And Mary Catherine feels switched off. Cleaned out. Wiped away. Who has she been fooling? Who, but herself? Life seemed beautiful when she was an angel, but now she looks like a devil child, and she feels like the devil.

It all seemed so clear before: life was a pure glass of water, just drink it down. But Mary Catherine chokes on that water now. Mama's beauty—her sun-kissed hair matching her golden eyes—chokes her, like the smoky scent of the bonfire that's made its way from the fire pit, through the screened window, into Mary Catherine's throat. The sight of Old Biddy Clara chokes her. Mary Catherine sees Clara through the screened window, hobbling down toward the bonfire, seemingly intent on complaining about something, the smoke or the noise. But it's not Clara's complaining Mary Catherine fears, not this time. It's Clara's mound of hair. The hair twists around Mary Catherine's neck, strips her of her breath. And Grace. Grace's voice chokes

Mary Catherine, too. The voice rides on the smoke from the campfire, where Grace sings Peter, Paul and Mary. Her voice is melodious and light, reminding Mary Catherine of Grace's waves of hair, the waves of her body, the way Rocky looks at her.

Reminding Mary Catherine of what she's not. Now. She looks so different without her hair, as if chopping off her hair somehow infected her features, diseased them. Her nose is super shiny and red. Rudolph. Her eyes are sunken and bulging at once—sunken around them, bulging inside them. Her skin is peeling dry. Scaly. Like a lizard. Rudolph the Red-nosed Lizard. And the hair she thought was golden blond is dishwater at the roots. A head of scummy water. Porcupine quills of scum.

And she thinks, How does Yllis live looking like she does? All scrawny and mousy and dark? Like an ink blot.

Mary Catherine knew Papa loved her more than he loved Yllis. Whenever Papa would explode, his rage reaching even Mary Catherine, he'd come to Catie later, apologize. He'd tell Mary Catherine what she already knew: he's an imperfect man, he needs God's help, he wants to be a good man, he loves her. Mary Catherine took this love for granted, just like she took Father Amadi's love for granted. And Jesus' love, and God's.

But now Mary Catherine wonders, What did Papa love? Was his love for me wrapped up in my hair, and now it's floated away?

Papa often told Mary Catherine how much she looks like Mama. Even Father Amadi told her this. "You're her spitting image," he said. Mary Catherine hated this—hated she looked like Mama. Because people would impute Mama's character to Mary Catherine, as if Mary Catherine herself were unbelieving, unfeeling, barely loving. At times Mary Catherine would find herself hating herself for being this self-centered woman whom she wasn't. But now Mary Catherine looks like Mama's spit, not her image, and she longs for that which she hated, because she can't help but question, Is that what Papa loved? Mama's image? And what of God? Jesus? Somehow Mary Catherine's ugly outside has made her insides ugly, too. She's angry. Jealous. Even of Yllis. At least Yllis has that sixth sense. And those eyes.

Yllis this, Yllis that, Yllis this, Yllis that, Mary Catherine thinks. "You love Yllis more," she says now to Mama, not sure why she's saying it. Not even sure she believes it.

"What?" Mama says. Her fingers work in vain to style the quills.

"Yllis," Mary Catherine says. "You love her more. Always have."

It's at that moment Mary Catherine sees it, the truth. It's in Mama's swallow, the choppy wave down her neck. It's in her teeth, which grip the interior of her cheek and chew. It's in her eyes that skirt. It's in her breath—in her forgetting of it, then grasping for it, gulping it down.

Mama does love Yllis more. Always has.

"No," Mama says. "I love all my girls. Each one of you the same."

But she's lying. Like Yllis would say, "Liar, liar, pants on fire." Mama may be a barely loving woman, but Yllis made the cut. And Mary Catherine? She was cut out. What has Mary Catherine ever done that garnered Mama's attention, let alone her respect? Mama belittles Mary Catherine's faith, suggesting Mary

Catherine's beliefs are comparable to the ancient Greeks' faith in thunderbolt-toting, cloud-gathering, godly-offspring-producing Zeus. But it's not just that. It's everything—everything Mary Catherine wants, everything she is.

"I want to be an artist," Mary Catherine told Mama four years ago, when she was twelve. "A sculptor, like Camille Claudel." Mary Catherine and her classmates were studying Camille Claudel and Rodin at school. Mary Catherine had always loved building things with her hands: sand castles and gingerbread houses. She'd even abscond with Yllis's Play-Doh and fiddle with it for hours. She'd see a large rock or the fallen trunk of a tree, and her mind would carve it up, make it into what she was sure it longed to be. She never made the connection, never realized it was something she could do with her life. Until Camille Claudel. And then a whole new world was born for Catie. Until Mama flattened the world, like a ball of clay.

"A sculptor? Why?" Mama had said (just like she'd say when she'd find Mary Catherine steeped in Play-Doh and ask her why she was playing with Play-Doh and didn't she have something to read?). "So you can end up waiting tables for a living? Because you're going to have a heck of a time supporting yourself as an artist, Catie. You don't want to wind up being financially dependent on a man. (Like you? Mary Catherine thought.) Did you know Camille Claudel was Rodin's mistress? Do you know what that means, to be a mistress? She and Rodin were in a romantic relationship that lasted years, but Rodin was married to someone else, if you can believe that. Camille Claudel must have had very little self-respect. It's no wonder she eventually went crazy. Financial independence is far more likely to land you sane, with self-respect. Just between us, Catie, you could do anything you want. That's not true about everyone—it's not true about Grace. Please don't tell her I said that, I'm just trying to make a point. You're lucky. You have a great brain. Don't spit in the face of luck. Don't waste your brain. Being a sculptor is something you can do on the side, as a hobby."

But it isn't something Mary Catherine does on the side, as a hobby. It isn't something she does at all anymore.

Mary Catherine sticks her fingers in her mouth now, gnaws her nails. Papa hates it when she does this—yells at her for it—but Papa can't see her, and Mama won't say a word, because Mama's transgression is far worse: she and Mary Catherine both know that.

"I'm not eating anymore." Mary Catherine removes her nails just long enough to spit out the words. "I'm fasting, for Jesus. Saint Catherine ate only the sacrament. And I'm doing the same. 'Cause Jesus loves me. More than you love me. More than Papa."

"You have to eat," Mama says. "Why would Jesus not want you to eat?"

Mama and Mary Catherine have this conversation yearly, during Lent, when Mary Catherine gives up TV in Midland and ice cream and chocolate to show Jesus her love. That she loves Him more. Most. "Why would Jesus care if you eat chocolate?" Mama says yearly. "Seems Jesus has more important concerns."

"That's not the point, Mama," Mary Catherine always says. "That has nothing to do with the point."

Mama tries to put her arms around Mary Catherine now, but Mary Catherine pushes her, too hard. Mary Catherine hadn't really meant to push Mama at all. She just meant to nudge her a bit. Let Mama know she has no intention of pretending she doesn't know what she knows. But Mama's body slams against the wall, and it stays there, splayed.

"I know . . . ," Mary Catherine says, even though what she wants to say is, "I'm sorry—I didn't mean it." But other words come out. "I know what you don't think I know, and I'm not going to not know it, no matter what you say or do."

"I don't know what you're talking about," Mama says. "You're not making sense."

But Mary Catherine sees the splotches of cranberry red pop up—one, two, three, four—between Mama's chest and collarbone. Mama knows full well what Mary Catherine is talking about. Mary Catherine may not yet know the *why* of the truth—*why* Mama loves Yllis more. But, as Papa would say, you don't need to know how God made the universe to know that He did. The truth is the truth is the truth, whether it makes sense to you or not.

Mary Grace

Danish Landing, Michigan

Summer 1976

Old Lady Clara calls the gazebo "the bandstand"—as if Dick Clark himself were there dancing to the bandstand boogie. Mary Grace stares up at the bandstand's cherry red ceiling, its boards carved with names from a hundred years. *TILLY + OLAF, ELLIE MAE + WALTER.* Even Old Clara has her name carved there. *CLARA LOVES EMIL*, it reads, hugged by a misshapen heart. Old Clara claims bands used to play in the gazebo when she was a teenager like Grace—a hundred years ago? She and Emil would shake it up, Clara said, doing the grizzly bear and the turkey trot, the bunny hop and the camel walk. It's a bit hard to imagine Old Clara with her bowed legs shaking it up any which way, but the bunny hop? Rocky and Grace had a good laugh about that one, lying with their backs on the cement, shining the flashlight from lover to lover. And they laughed even harder when Rocky stood up to imitate Clara doing the bump. "Do the bump, Clara baby," he said, gyrating his hips in a way Grace would like to forget. "Do the bump."

In all honesty, Grace doesn't like making fun of Clara, although she'd never admit this to Rocky, and she certainly wouldn't admit it to her sisters—although Yllis probably already knows. Grace initially started making weekly visits to Clara two summers ago as a means of fulfilling her school's community-service requirement. She and her classmates were obliged to perform ten hours of "good works" over the summer, and "visiting with an elderly person outside one's own family" qualified. Grace's sisters (possibly excepting Yllis, of course) think this community-service obligation is why Grace still visits Clara. But Grace doesn't have any obligation this summer—she's graduated, remember, Einsteins? Grace suspects neither Tess nor Mary Catherine can fathom any teenager visiting Clara—unless forced—and Grace is perfectly happy to let them fool themselves.

Truth is, over the years Grace has come to feel more comfortable with Old Clara than she does with her own mother, not that that's saying much. Apparently there was a time, when Grace was much younger, when she actually was close to Mama—Grace knows this from looking at old photos. Seems Mama used to read to Grace and play dolls with her. There are even pictures of Mama baking with Grace—who knew Mama could bake?—and laughing with Grace and snuggling Grace. If it weren't for the photos, Grace might not believe she and Mama ever had such a warm relationship. They snuggled? When Grace is around Mama now, she feels like a footnote. Less than a footnote: Mama pays heed to footnotes.

But Grace is no footnote when she talks to Clara. Clara listens, and Grace is a *person*, a person who's both younger and older. It's like Clara remembers the girl Grace was before she became "that girl," the one men and boys—and women, too—can't take their eyes off. Like she remembers the girl who couldn't stop doing math calculations in her head, no matter how hard she tried. Like she remembers the girl who dissected every mechanical toy she owned, until Papa punished her for being wasteful. Like she remembers the eleven-year-old girl in 1969 who was obsessed with Neil Armstrong, but who was more obsessed by the idea of being the future: the first woman to walk on the moon. When Grace speaks with Clara, Grace senses the math-calculating, toy-dissecting, moon-walking girl might still be in there, somewhere.

Yet Grace feels more like a woman, too, in Clara's presence. Because even though Clara sees the girl, seems Clara knows the girl inside Grace has grown—like there's a woman in there, too, who has nothing to do with Grace's woman's body. Neither Mama nor Papa seems to remember the girl, and they certainly don't see a woman in Grace—although they sure as heck see Grace's woman's body. Papa's determined to hide it. And Mama's determined to belittle it: apparently the development of Grace's body hollowed out her insides; she's now only surface deep.

Grace studies the freshly carved ROCKY + M.G. FOREVER, and she wonders how many of the carved lovers remained lovers. Clara didn't marry Emil, after all. She married his brother, Egan. Grace certainly has no intention of marrying Rocky, despite that word "forever," and despite what they'd just done, prior to carving their names.

It wasn't what Grace had expected. Not after she'd sneaked *The Flame and the Flower.* And not after all the hoopla: this act was a mortal sin, able to drive sanctifying grace from her soul?

Adam and Eve's original sin had already driven away sanctifying grace once, thank you very much, but Grace's baptism had restored it. DOING IT apparently was sufficient to expel that restored grace. Not that Grace really takes these Catholic teachings all that seriously, but given the supposed stakes, she thought IT would feel good at the very least. She hadn't anticipated uncomfortable and messy and bewildering. And quick. It was over before she was fully aware she and Rocky were doing IT, scraping themselves against the gritty concrete, sanding their skin. You'd think one of them would have thought to bring a blanket, given how long they'd been planning IT. But no, they'd sneaked out at two A.M., Rocky's primary concern being that Grace's lunatic father was a hundred miles away, and Grace's primary concern being that all-seeing, all-hearing, all-knowing Yllis, having been shaken up by Mary Catherine's horror show, was sleeping not in the girls' room but with Mama.

Grace had lifted and now wore one of Mama's nighties—a teddy—which proved idiotic given it was glacial outside. Hot days do not correspond to hot nights on the Danish Landing. Neither literally nor figuratively, Grace found out. Because days with Rocky were hot, literally and figuratively. Grace would sit on the screened porch, waiting for Rocky to strut out from Cozy Cabin. She'd watch as he'd pass Tall Oaks and Sunset View on his way to check his minnow trap. On most days he wore no shirt, and Grace couldn't help but think of those scenes in *The Flame and the Flower* while she looked at his smooth skin. When she was sure she'd have his attention, she'd bang open the screen door and head on down to the dock, wearing the skimpiest bikini she could find when Papa wasn't around, and the skimpiest bikini she could get away with when Papa was around. She'd lay out her reflective blanket, and then she'd sprawl, knowing she was driving Rocky crazy. Eventually Rocky would join her on the dock, pretending he'd just happened to notice Grace lying there. Grace would feel his eyes creep across her body as the moisture crept into her bikini.

But that was day, when light could obscure the truth. Grace had never realized before this (fated?) night with Rocky that light does just that. You'd think it would be the opposite, that darkness would obfuscate. But as Grace lies on the concrete, her backbone raw, she sees herself and Rocky, and even Old Clara and all those other lovers who had carved their names into the ceiling before her, with a clarity she'd not experienced in the day, in the light. Rocky is a doofus, bless him. Grace is just another in the long (carved) line of hormones, missing a brain. And Old Clara might just have had her head screwed on straight—her hairdo notwithstanding—when she'd intimated to Grace that rocking with Rocky was best left to the imagination.

Profound conversations with Rocky revolve around fish bait and pectoral size. Honestly. Why had Grace not noticed this during the day? Apparently she was too distracted by the spectacle of those pectorals to realize she didn't give a shit. She'd convinced herself her sisters were jealous of her relationship with Rocky, not incredulous, as they appeared. But as Grace freezes and perspires at the same time, not only does she see they truly were incredulous, she realizes she's incredulous herself. She's just given herself to a seventeen-year-old boy who uses a pet name for his private. And she expected a love scene worthy of *The Flame and the Flower*? Christ. Grace is willing to play the role assigned to her, to be the airhead she's expected to be. But to a point. To a point.

And this? It passes the point.

Grace disentangles herself from the concrete, now, leaving a good slice of her back behind. She stands, then hops. Girls can't get pregnant if they shake it all out—that's what her girlfriend Suzette said. And Suzette seems the type to know.

The only satisfaction Grace musters as she hops is the realization neither Mama nor Papa was able to stop her from doing what she'd just done, even if there was no satisfaction in the act itself. Papa may be able to stop her from showing her cleavage. Mama may be able to stop her from feeling good about her cleavage. But neither could stop her from letting Rocky touch her cleavage, and much more. Because it's her cleavage. It's hers. This is Grace's life.

Good luck getting me to go to Africa, Grace thinks. I'll go to Africa when snakes fly.

Clara

Clara knows those Slepy girls call her the Old Biddy. Knows they make fun of her hair, and her legs, re-formed by rickets—not that they have any idea what rickets are. They probably think she came into the world an old hag with enough wrinkles to map out the globe. Probably think her legs were as fickle as a toddler's forever and a day.

Clara can't deny she gets some pleasure from scaring them. She puts on her stern don't-cross-me look she learned from watching her own mama when she was a wobbly toddler, sans rickets. She twists and twists her gray braid up to a Boyne Mountain peak on the crown of her head—if left down, it would pass her rear—and it gives her a bit of height, makes her more imposing. And she makes certain to use her cane whenever she passes the lot of them as she heads down to the dock for some vitamin D.

For whatever reason, the cane engenders a sense of awe in those girls—each and every one. The young one, Yllis, asked Clara if she's a witch. "You take that thing for a ride?" she said as she eyed the cane. At least Yllis sees Clara still has spunk. Mary Tessa, on the other hand, seems prepared for Clara to swat her with the cane. In all honesty, Clara wouldn't mind. She's a spitfire, that Tessa. Could use being knocked down a notch. And Mary Catherine? That child. She'd like to think Clara is some sort of saint. Clearly wants to admire Clara. Based on the look in Mary Catherine's eyes, Clara wouldn't be surprised if Mary Catherine expects her to throw down her staff, like Moses, turn it into a snake, then grab the tail and transform it back into a staff. Bible learning aside, Clara knows from experience if you're fool enough to grab a snake by the tail, expect a bite, not a staff.

Lord knows Clara would disappoint that Mary Catherine if Catie got to know her. If there is anything Clara can do, it's spin a yarn, and she's not referring to her knitting—although Clara does work her knitting needles in a way she can't fathom she ever worked her legs. Clara grew up despising Catholics, to boot, not for any good reason other than that's what Danish Lutherans did. She can't say she feels that way now, but even so. Even so. If Mary Catherine had any notion of the lies on which Clara has based her life, she'd think Clara was the devil. Well, maybe Clara is.

Clara turns from her knitting to find Grace's nose pressed against Clara's screen door. This isn't the first time Grace has come poking, seeking some mothering. To Grace, Clara's cane may as well be a magic wand: someone as ancient as Clara just might be able to fix anything. All summer Clara has watched Grace do the mating dance with that testosterone-oozing boy. She even tried to warn Grace off him on Grace's last visit, saying he reminded Clara of Emil, the brother she didn't marry. Clara told Grace she and Emil had had their fun, but Emil was far more trouble than he was worth, in retrospect. At the time Clara sensed her comment lacked the force to make it in one of Grace's ears, let alone out the other.

"Miss Clara," Grace says now, which Clara finds both annoying and endearing. "You mind if I come in?" Grace pushes open the door and steps onto the porch. Then she spies Egan asleep in the green rocker, which sets her on edge for what Clara senses is a reason other than the unappetizing sight.

Clara puts down her knitting needles. "Come on." She jostles herself to standing, leads Grace off the screened porch and into the bowels of the cottage. "We'll leave Egan out there to snore himself awake."

"He's gonna wake up?" Grace halts, clearly ready to turn around, make a beeline.

Looking at Grace, at that self-conscious way she straightens her back, adjusts her bikini top, draws in her belly, passes her tongue across her front teeth, Clara sees herself and all the mistakes she's made. "He's not going to wake up. But even on the off chance he does, he won't move from that chair until I light a firecracker under him."

Grace's eyes intimate she isn't sure whether Clara is joking, but it's all the same: Egan won't be privy to their conversing.

"My parents are going to Africa." Grace waggles over to the dining table, pulls free a chair. "They're taking my sisters, leaving in a month. But I'm not going."

"Africa?" Clara says. "Why on earth?"

"You know that boy we talked about?" Grace lowers her bikini-lined rear into the chair. Back straight, chest out, ankles crossed. "The one you said reminded you of Emil?"

What's the boy got to do with Africa? Clara thinks. "You drink coffee?" she says, knowing full well Grace is unlikely to have ever touched the stuff.

"Sure." Grace scrutinizes the bowl of cubed sugar.

Clara hands Grace the cup and Grace selects two cubes. Plops them in. Three more. Plops them in. She stirs, watching the sweetness get absorbed by the bitter.

And then out it comes: Grace's confession. Just like that. As Clara stands by the counter, without her magic wand of a cane, her bowed legs have the workout of their rickety lives.

Seena

They wash the green beans, snap them, bag them, and before Seena and Mary Catherine pile them deep in the chest freezer, Seena wishes Mary Catherine would eat even one. It's been nearly two months since the day Mary Catherine stopped eating. She eats nothing but crackers now, which she refers to as "the sacrament," even though they're saltines. She drinks nothing but grape juice (also "the sacrament"). Mary Catherine herself has become a narrow bean—which she doesn't eat. Not even one.

Seena and Mary Catherine had gathered the beans together as they buried themselves with the moist dirt of their Midland garden, still sodden from that morning's rain. And while they gathered, they listened, not to the chatter of each other, but each to the chatter in her own brain. Seena's chatter moved from Dick's seeming impulsiveness, to Mary Catherine's starvation and self-mutilation, to Grace's recent one-eighty—her refusal to attend college, her inexplicable desire to go with them to Africa. And to Father Amadi. Had he really suggested they go?

Then her thoughts moved on to Yllis, because Seena's thoughts always move on to Yllis, her daughter who sees what can't be seen and smells what can't be smelled and knows what can't be known—who has never seemed quite right, even as she seems the sanest of them all. Everyone in the family knows it's impossible to discount Yllis, no matter how hard they try. Because Yllis does, at times, know what she shouldn't be able to know. Still, as Seena collected bean after bean, she prayed to the God in whom she doesn't believe that Dick and the girls had managed to discount Yllis this time. "Enough about the Indian," Dick had said several weeks ago, when Yllis again mentioned the native man she and Tessa had met. "I don't want to hear that rubbish spoken of ever again." And Yllis hasn't spoken of it since—at least not with words.

But what of Mary Catherine's chatter? What had she been thinking while her hands searched each plant for the long, narrow and solid green amid the soft and loose green? Seena asks herself this now as she stands shoulder to skinny shoulder with Mary Catherine. But Seena can't even guess. Mary Catherine has become Seena's Hestia, the virgin goddess of no personality, the goddess of the hearth, the progenitor of life, not the alive.

Ever since they learned they'd be going to Africa—since that day two months ago when Mary Catherine butchered her hair—Mary Catherine has seemed emptied out. She barely leaves the house. She seems the great void before the big bang. Although she still wears her rosary as a (benign?) snake circling her wrist, she rarely fingers it, as if she's forgotten even the Mary for whom she's named. And Seena has seen the tiny razor blade slices on Mary Catherine's inner, upper arm—deftly situated to suggest she's hiding the cuts, even as Seena suspects she wants others to see them. Are they a cry for help? Or for attention? Seena assumes the latter. Just as she assumes this not eating is a stunt. Mary Catherine was the toddler who screamed bloody murder with every scrape. She was the kindergartner with weekly stomachaches—that inevitably vanished the moment Seena offered her an ice cream. She was the elementary school student with perfect vision—tested innumerable times—who was certain she needed glasses. ("I can't see the blackboard, Mama. I can't!")

At some point Seena's patience waned with regard to Mary Catherine's antics. Seena hadn't had a mother AT ALL—not one she can remember. It was difficult for Seena to tolerate this child who did have a mother—an imperfect one, but nevertheless—yet who wanted more of Seena, and more of everyone. More and more. Of Dick, Mary Catherine received more. *Receives* more. More than Tessa does, for sure. More than Grace. Certainly more than Yllis.

Yllis: was her birth the turning point? Was that when Seena could no longer tolerate Mary Catherine's constant demands for attention? Was that when Seena saw Tessa less as lively and endearingly clever, more as annoyingly defiant? Was that when Seena began to fear Grace's charms rather than be charmed by them? Seena had such a longing to shower baby Yllis with love—a motherly longing more poignant than she'd ever before known. But she felt such guilt about this longing. And such conflict inside, because she herself had never been loved—not by a parent, never with depth. Did she pull back from all of her children then, because the love she felt for Yllis felt so right and so deep, yet so wrong?

Whatever the reason, Seena's river of patience—shallow as it is—has dried to a trickle with regard to Mary Catherine. But that trickle was sufficient for Seena to have discarded every razor blade in the house, and she has tried to interest Mary Catherine in something, *anything*. Even God. She's encouraged Mary Catherine to attend mass. She's encouraged her to again go to confession, even though Seena hates the idea of it. But even Mary Catherine's obsession with holiness is a withered, overripe bean.

Seena's daughter cares for nothing, about nothing. Seena believes this because she can. She tells herself this because she can't bear to tell herself what she really thinks, what she really suspects: that Yllis's comment about Dick not being her father made Mary Catherine doubt everything—Seena, Dick, God, herself.

Mary Catherine went to confession two days after Yllis first referenced the Indian, the morning Catie cut her hair—before she cut her hair—and the very same morning Seena discovered Dick had left for Midland in the middle of the night. And yet Dick had managed somehow to meet with Father Amadi and decide to send them to Africa before leaving Grayling? It didn't make sense. Seena had dropped Mary Catherine off at the rectory at eight, and by then Dick was long gone. Dick had lied about meeting with Father Amadi, lied about Africa being Father Amadi's idea. Of course he'd lied. But Mary Catherine? She did meet with Father Amadi. What did she tell him that morning? What did Father Amadi tell Mary Catherine? Seena can't let herself ask these questions, even though the questions are gnats. They are horseflies. They are that subtle stench of mold that hovers in the cottage each spring.

"Do you miss the Danish Landing?" Seena says to Mary Catherine now. They left the Danish Landing two weeks ago. They are back in Midland preparing to leave for Africa. Seena capitulated to going to Africa—but what choice did she have? The girls have not started school, they will not start school. Seena will homeschool the girls once they get settled in Africa, a perfect opportunity for her to bore the girls even more than she already does.

"No," Mary Catherine says.

That's it? Seena thinks. Just no?

"How do you feel about going to Africa? Can you believe we'll be there the day after tomorrow?"

"I don't," Mary Catherine says. "I don't feel anything about going to Africa."

"You'll miss mass, I bet. But Papa says our contact person in Africa—the man who runs the aid organization there—is Catholic. Seems we may have an opportunity to go to mass in Africa."

"As if you care."

"I care for you," Seena says. "I care because it's important to you."

"Well, it's not important."

"But it *was* important," Seena wants to say. "It *was*. What's happened to you?" But Seena doesn't say this. Seena can't approach that place inside her own self where she first buried what's important. She can't even remember the girl she was when her mother was alive, before her father gave her away, when her siblings were her siblings and not just some people she was forbidden to mention. Seena was the baby of the family, the youngest of four and the only girl. And although she wasn't a baby when her mother died, she was far younger than her brothers. Caring for her in addition to caring for her three brothers would have pushed her single father "over the edge." At least that's what Seena was told, when she was old enough to ask her grandmother—her mother's mother—before her grandmother told Seena to never ask again, and long before Seena understood what it meant to reach the edge, take the plunge. Seena never saw her father and brothers again; they were erased from her life. But why did her father allow himself to be erased? Why did her brothers allow it? Seena's grandmother had forbidden Seena from asking her about them, from seeking them out. But why hadn't they asked about Seena? Why hadn't Seena's father or her brothers sought Seena out? No one could have forbidden their seeking, certainly not once Seena was eighteen. When Seena started college, she was sure they would find her, particularly because her grandmother had died that July. Seena arrived at college alone—mourning her grandmother—and watched the other girls be unpacked, settled in, hugged, kissed, missed. As Seena unpacked herself—as she settled herself in— she told herself, One day my father will arrive, or one of my brothers, and he'll explain their absence, confirm their love, fill this void in me, make me feel whole. And I will be hugged and kissed and missed. But the only person to find Seena was Dick.

"Clara wanted to know where we're going in Africa," Mary Catherine says now. "Why would she care?"

"Who?"

"Old Clara, at the Danish Landing. When we were leaving the cottage for the summer to come back here, to Midland, when we were driving away. We stopped because I forgot my rosary. Remember? I ran back to get it and you all waited on the side of the road, in the station wagon. She ran out of her cottage and met me."

"She ran? Clara ran?"

"No. I guess, no. But, she seemed sort of . . . I don't know. Hurried. Kind of desperate like. She asked where we would be in Africa. How she could get in touch with us."

"Old Clara asked that? Why would she want to know that?"

"I asked you that."

"Well, I don't know," Seena says.

"I didn't tell her," Mary Catherine says.

"You could have."

Mary Catherine shrugs. "She likes Grace. Why didn't she ask Grace?"

"I don't know if Old Clara likes anyone," Seena says.

"Everyone likes Grace."

Everyone likes to *look at* Grace, Seena thinks. "Everyone likes you, too."

"Liar."

"Grace is just more outgoing," Seena says, knowing Mary Catherine is right: Seena is a liar. "Grace makes it easy on people."

"Grace is easy, all right."

"What's that supposed to mean, Catie?" Seena feels unusually protective of Grace. Why?

If Seena honestly were to consider this question, she'd discover Yllis's comment yet again. Did Grace change her mind about attending college because of Yllis's comment? Did she decide to join the family in traveling to Africa because she couldn't allow herself to separate from them for fear they would unravel in her absence?

And was Dick's seeming impulsive decision to remove his family from everything they knew—send them and himself to a place where they have no business going—spurred, somehow, by Yllis's comment as well?

These are more gnats, more horseflies, more mold. And Seena shoos them away. She plugs her nose.

"Don't ask me," Mary Catherine says. "I'm just the crazy girl who thinks she's Saint Catherine. I heard you on the phone before we left Grayling. Isn't that what you told Father Amadi? That I'm crazy? What do I know?"

"I never called you crazy," Seena says, but she can't stop herself from glancing toward the razor blade cuts, the thin scars, the arms the width of pogo sticks. Seena told Father Amadi about those cuts, about Mary Catherine starving herself. He's the one who used the word "crazy." "I just was asking Father Amadi to call you, talk to you, since you wouldn't go see him." But Father Amadi had refused to talk to Mary Catherine. He said she needed professional help. He said her problems went beyond what he could handle.

"Well?" Mary Catherine says. "He hasn't called."

BOOK TWO

West Africa

"Christina Slepy?" the witch doctor says again.

Seena had gone silent, claimed she'd nothing to say. But this wise man isn't satisfied. And Seena thinks, If only he were wise. Yet she knows the indignation she continues to feel is just another sign that she who was not a racist is a racist. She knows her arrogance is the rose-colored lenses shattered, making her see the world in disconnected pieces. She's been choosing which rose-colored shard to look through, forgetting the shard was part of a whole, forgetting it was rose colored at all. She and her children and their choices are not the product of this wise man who is not wise. He may have opened Pandora's jar, but Seena stuffed it.

Still, she hates the man—she loathes him. Perhaps more than he loathes her. She tries to acknowledge him now, to acknowledge that she is this: Christina Slepy. But she can't. Slepy, she thinks. Slepy. She'd always hated the name. Hated that she took it. Hated that she'd lost part of herself when she married. She'd suggested she keep her own name, Michels, but Dick had insisted. "Why would you do that?" he'd said. "Keep your own name? I'm not even sure that's legal." And she'd thought,

He thinks he owns me. For years he'd even insisted on calling Seena by her given name, Christina, because he preferred it, even though Seena's mother had referred to her as Seena from the time she was born. Other than her mother's pearl necklace, which Seena never removes, the name Seena is the only gift from Seena's mother that Seena still owns.

Even so, Seena mostly complied, let Dick own her on the surface, let him touch nothing beneath. He'd possess her body at times, but that was the surface—another incarnation of taking his name. It was form. Not content. Ritual, not meaning.

So she could cling to the meaningless.

Why didn't she see this? she wonders. Why was she so determined to hollow herself out, let nothing in? So that when lust rained down on her—this torrent—there was nothing at all to keep it out. It trickled into every crack, through every seam. Every cranny and crater and concave void in her being was transformed from parched to pulsing. And she mistook this pulsing for meaning.

Now? Now the name Slepy has meaning, and she can't touch it—attach it to herself—because she doesn't deserve it. This part of her that she denied is now denying her. This part of her children that she discounted is now leaving them, too: the father, the name. And she yearns for them to hold it—to not let it pass away.

Yllis

I've come to learn there is a name for what I am, and I don't mean "half blood," although I'm that, too, more or less. But the name I'm referring to is "synesthete," meaning I have synesthesia, from the Greek *syn,* which means "with," and *aesthesis,* which means "sensation." Being "with sensation" is a diagnosis—not a neurosis or psychosis. That's what I'm told.

With sensation. Not "of sensation." Not "from sensation." But *with.* Sensation is not my essence. I do not grow from it, change from it, become something more, or less, because of it. I am *with* it: its mirror, its filter, its constant companion. Sensation is not in me, but with me. When I'm stripped of sensation, what am I? Mama often told me I'm one in a million. We synesthetes actually are ten in a million. But we're ten in a million what? Is every synesthete like me: a reflection, an absorption, a sponge?

As the plane slid across the heavens toward a place Papa intimated might be heaven on earth, I didn't know the name synesthesia, and neither did my family. Yet I knew her all the same. She was Mama's guilt and Papa's fury, Catie's hungry envy and Gracie's blooming fear. She was Tessa's joy and selfish greed, her cruelty and the rare but real swell of her heart.

I now know some synesthetes taste shapes, and some see letters and numbers as having intrinsic color. If I were a grapheme synesthete, the plane's neon orange EXIT sign may have been neither neon nor orange. The *e* may have been blue, the *x* purple, the *i* pale yellow and the *t* green. The blinking numbers on Papa's new digital watch may have been blinking pink. If I were a synesthete with ordinal-linguistic personification, the month of September, which it was, may have been irritable or gregarious or stingy, while Thursday, which it was, may have been easygoing or laconic or generous. Or vice versa. September could have been generous and Thursday stingy.

But as we passed from America to Africa, I, Yllis Slepy, synesthete that I am, saw orange neon and digital black during a personality-free Thursday in the personality-free month of September, even as I tasted and smelled and otherwise sensed what seemed an ocean of feeling in that plane. Because I am an emotional synesthete. For synesthetes like me, the world is a layer cake of emotion, and we are its consumers. We don't make the cake—stirring and whipping and baking are for those without a diagnosis. With so much to consume, how could one possibly have the energy or an appetite for one's own creation?

For eleven years I'd been a consumer, slogging down others' pain, inhaling others' rage, drinking their love, jittering with their joy. Yet I'd never considered who I was. Until the Day of the Snake.

And then, for the first time, I tried to see myself like I saw that snake, outside the context of others' emotions. But I couldn't. I couldn't at all. And I wondered why.

Was it because I'd been formed without a father's love? I'd

seen my father, and he'd turned away, as if I wasn't worth a second glance. Was I just half a person—a semblance of a human—formed by my mother's will, defined solely by her love? Because Mama did love me—that I knew. I tasted her love with every breath of my life.

Mama squeezed my hand, squeezed it like she sensed the weight in me, sensed I might drop from the plane before it dropped to the earth. "Papa wants this," she'd told me shortly after the plane took flight, when the air around us was still Michigan air, after I'd asked her, "Why Africa?" "Papa wants Africa," she'd said. "This has nothing to do with anyone but Papa." But everywhere I looked, I saw and felt and smelled, not so much Mama, but what she was avoiding.

The book, *A Wreath for Udomo,* lay open on her lap. "It takes place in Africa," she told me, when she noticed my examining it.

"Damp earth and no grass," I read over her shoulder. "Dank heat and no air. Giant trees and dark waters. Rustle and whisper, hiss and silence. Stealth and menace . . ."

I looked away, out the window. The land below was a puzzle of squares and rectangles and squiggly lines. Patches of green were aligned with patches of differently hued green that were aligned with patches hued like straw. Swimming pools were blue pancakes. Cars and trucks were army ants.

I'd never before been on a plane. I knew about gravity—I had a vague sense of what it was. But I didn't understand how it worked, only that it did work. Objects like people and vehicles didn't float, they were sucked to the earth and held there. Trusting the plane could defy gravity seemed yet another version of what I had been doing my whole life: believing in something I didn't understand at all. Is this plane going to crash down? I wondered. Is it going to realize like I did that it can't defy gravity after all?

Some say it's a gift, what we synesthetes have. Some say we're given a richer planet, one that lies somewhere between heaven and earth. Some say it's like experiencing the world straight on, while everyone else stands behind glass. Some say it's like entering God's mind, seeing the dimensions intended for God alone. Some say every person on earth is a synesthete, but that the remaining 999,990 people out of a million experience synesthesia only on a subconscious level.

Well, maybe so. But maybe God knew what He was doing when He hid these sensations in the great subconscious of the masses. Maybe the mistake He made was handing this so-called gift to me. While I was defying gravity on that plane, I would have handed the gift back had I known then what I had. I would have told God, "Thank you just the same." Because even then I longed for what I would never have again: a father who was mine, a family to which I belonged.

———

The plane landed in a swell. I felt the wheels slam the earth as Africa rose up around me. She was in the air, she was the air, I breathed her in—this scent that said, "The earth and air are not so separate here." Like an enormous woman with folds of warm flesh, I felt her enfold me. As I looked out the window at the African earth and the African people on that earth, I sensed Africa summon me, and I let go of Mama's hand. Seemed Africa had butted in: she wanted this dance.

So I wasn't completely surprised when we passed through immigration that I didn't pass through, not right away. Africa was making her point. The immigration officer waved Papa through, then he waved each Mary by. When it was my turn, he held the wave, studied my passport, studied me. He spoke something unintelligible to his cohort, the only part of which I understood was, "A-mar-e-can." He stamped Mama's passport and returned it to her; he tried to wave Mama through before me, but Mama resisted.

"She is your daughter?" the officer said. I felt Mama pulling one way, Africa pulling the other: I was the rope in this tug-of-war.

Papa had moved on, having assumed, I suppose, that Mama and I had moved on. I could see him following the Marys in the distance, making his way along a narrow hall—and I'd become Alice in Wonderland, unable to follow this White Rabbit. Were the locks too large or the key too small?

"Of course," Mama said. "Of course she's my daughter."

"Is this your mother?" the officer said to me.

"Yes," I said, but what would I have said if he'd asked me about Papa, whether Papa was my father?

"What is your name?"

"Yllis."

"Amaryllis," Mama said. "Yllis is her nickname."

"Is it true?" he said to me. "Are you A-mary-lis Slee-py?"

For a moment I felt I had the power to be the shed light, or not. I was no more a Slepy than I was Papa's mother, Mary Ann. "Yet are you Amaryllis?" I felt Africa asking me. "Are you truly the shed light? Or are you just the shadow, cast by those around you?"

But Mama took the power. "Of course it's true."

Once again the officer spoke to his companion, with what I knew were words with meaning, but to me they were meaningless. "What is he saying, Mama?"

"Shhh, Yllis."

I knew then, when I looked into Mama's golden eyes, that she, too, sensed Africa wanted me, and she was scared.

"My friend thinks perhaps you could prove this to me." The officer rubbed his palms together. "A little something from A-mar-e-ca might prove this to me."

Mama shifted from scared to skilled. She rifled through her purse, through her wallet. She dislodged a bill, tucked it into her passport and handed her passport back to the officer. He opened the passport, as if checking it afresh, then he folded the note into his fist.

"Go," the officer said. He stamped my passport, gave me the wave, but it was a different wave than he'd given my sisters and Papa. This wave had meaning I could understand, unlike his words. "You don't belong with them," it said, "but I'm leasing you out." And I thought, Mama's fit the key into the lock, but have I shrunk, or has the door grown? Is this stamped passport the little bottle with the label DRINK ME? Am I shutting up like Alice's telescope? And what of the key? Is it again lying on the table but now out of reach? Is there no going back?

"It was your name," Mama said when we were free of the officers' hearing. "That's all it was, you know? It's why he stopped you. The other girls are all named Mary. You're not. He was trying to make sense of that."

I was trying to make sense of that.

"Sometimes people kidnap children," Mama said. "These people who work in immigration, they're trained to look for things like that, things that could indicate something fishy's going on."

As if I hadn't seen Mama give him the money, as if I didn't know something fishy was going on.

And the word "kidnap," it hit me. I wasn't adopted so much as I was kidnapped. Nobody had ever asked me what I wanted.

My silent tears started then as Mama and I journeyed through the paint-peeling hall. Soon enough I'd be swimming in the Pool of Tears. And soon enough we'd meet the King and Queen of Hearts and the whole pack of cards.

"There are no damn signs," Papa said after Mama and I had caught up and we'd collected our bags and Lint. "Where the hell are we supposed to go? And what did I do with those damn disembarkation cards, or whatever the hell they're called?"

Papa looked from Mary to Mary to Mary to me, as if one of us had absconded with the cards. None of us was accustomed to Papa swearing. Usually his words didn't match his rage.

"You're holding the cards, Dick," Mama said. "Aren't those the cards you have?"

Papa looked at his hand. "Why would they make these cards so ridiculous, so confusing?" he said, as if the cards' content had something to do with his not being able to find them in his own hand.

"We go over there, I think." Mama pointed toward several men dressed like soldiers, each of whom rummaged through bystanders' bags. "That must be customs."

"What are they looking for?" Grace said as we approached

the rummaging. "Are they gonna look through our stuff like that?"

But no one answered her—not even Tessa, who under most circumstances had something to say. Not one of us spoke again until a third officer looked through Papa's bag, and then Papa asked Grace's question himself. "What on earth are you looking for?"

"Welcome!" the officer said in response. Or not in response. I've heard that phrase, "smiling from ear to ear," but I'd never until that moment seen someone do it. And perhaps the officer wasn't doing it—perhaps it was an illusion caused by the bright white of his teeth against the darkness of his skin. Or perhaps it was his humming I heard, his joy, a joy that seemed misplaced in the moment.

"Go in *that* direction." The officer pointed, then he zipped up Papa's bag.

"We're supposed to meet a driver." Papa's eyes darted from his bag to "*that* direction" to his bag. "Somewhere here there's supposed to be a driver."

"Go in *that* direction," the officer said again.

———————

I'd never seen so many people. The number of people waiting outside the airport far outweighed the number within, at least twenty to one. "You need security?" one man said as we pressed through the throng. "I give you security for small fee."

Mary Catherine squeezed her barely there self between Mama and me. "What are all those people waiting for? What do they want?"

What do they want? Again I was Alice: all relativity seemed out of whack. My eyes saw squalor, my eyes expected to see *want*: envy's dust, melancholy's shimmer. If people are poor, doesn't that mean their life is hard? Doesn't that mean they *want*? In the world I knew, poverty and envy went hand in hand. The kids in the "free lunch" line at school were embarrassed and envious, and sad, too—I'd seen their shimmery dust. I'd wanted to switch places in line just to give them some reprieve from those feelings. Compared to most of those surrounding us at the airport, the free lunch kids seemed rich. So where was envy's dust? Where was melancholy's shimmer?

Bathing us Slepys, that's where. We were all dust and shimmer and fear's cotton candy smell, and those eyeing us seemed interested and amused and happy to see us. "Welcome!" person after person after person said. And they meant it. They did. I heard their hum.

"Stay close," Papa said, as if we had a choice. We were surrounded by people on all sides. Lint, released from his crate just moments before, had nearly urinated on my feet, as there was nowhere else to go. We weren't sardines so much as we were popcorn kernels sizzling in hot oil, pressed kernel to kernel to kernel. We could only sizzle this way for so long before one of us cracked.

Mary Tessa

West Africa

Fall 1976

"There!" Tessa says. "Over there!"

Over there a man holds a sign that reads, SLEPY. He leans against some sort of truck. Inscribed on the side of the truck are the words, GOD IS MY SHEPHERD—AND I DON'T KNOW WHY.

At least someone here has a sense of humor, Tessa thinks. Even she feels some relief when she sees this sign and the truck and the words—same as she felt at Disney World when the Space Mountain car would glide to a stop. Not that she wouldn't get back in line, ride the coaster again. And again. And again. But those moments of reprieve while waiting in line gave her the gumption to ride again. And at the moment, she's ready for the line, ready for the restoration of gumption.

But there's no restoration to be had.

They board the truck, which clearly is not what Pa had had in mind. Just an oversize pickup truck—like the one Pa borrowed from their Midland neighbor to make a dump run—with benches in the rear. They and their luggage are the equivalent of trash. White trash, Tessa thinks, noting they are the sole white thing within eyeshot—the only exception being people's very white teeth and the not-so-white whites of their eyes.

The truck rattles and coughs and sputters and starts, and they're off to Oz, following the red clay road. They definitely need the scarecrow here directing traffic, Tessa thinks as they approach an intersection. There's no traffic light, no stop sign, just a lot of clay dust and honking. They fall in and out of a pothole, and then another. As Tessa feels her stomach hit her heart, she knows without a doubt they're not standing in line waiting for Space Mountain.

Nor is it a small world after all. Tessa hated that ride, It's a Small World. They'd made the trip down to Disney World the year before last. Drove all the way from Michigan to Florida on spring break, staying along the way in KOA campgrounds. For *this*? Tessa had thought when their very first ride was It's a Small World. She'd spent days on the road crammed in a camper, being forced to play Twenty Questions and I Spy and the License Plate Game, for *this*? Tessa sensed even then, as she watched the children of the world frolic, their different faces not really different, their singing voices all the same, that the ride was all wrong. But oh how wrong it was. The world is far bigger than Tessa imagined, and she's seeing just a corner of it at the moment. Probably not even a corner. Probably just a couple inches of a corner. But even in these few inches, the faces are truly different and the voices are not the same and, like Space Mountain, which Tessa eventually had the pleasure of experiencing, she gets the sense this ride may well be worth the journey, even if she doesn't get a stand-in-line break.

Life is a feast, true. But little did Tessa know she's been eating all s'mores and frankfurters and missing the smorgasbord. She'd always thought Grace's interest in clothes was an utter waste, but the women here wrap themselves up in layers of glee, patterned and bright, each woman an original Matisse. Tessa's art teacher at school had described Matisse's work as "expressive," saying his use of color was not intended to mimic reality but to express meaning. Tessa can't help but wonder if Matisse himself journeyed to Africa, if he saw these same blues and reds and oranges, these geometric shapes and organic shapes, all layered and wound. Just looking at these women makes Tessa feel not so much happy as brimming, alive. There's meaning here—Tessa senses this. Just like with Matisse. And as with Matisse, the meaning's out of reach—but Tessa feels like reaching for it anyway. Seems Tessa's been sleeping her life away and the noise in Africa woke her up. Engines roar and girls hiss and buses honk, and Tessa digs it all.

The truck bounces past roadside stalls that seem miniature garages, and every garage is having a sale. Some sell food in boxes and cans, some sell furniture, some sell clothes. Interspersed with the garages are stands selling husked corn and tomatoes, mangoes and dwarf-size watermelons. The truck pauses at an intersection, sits in a red cloud, while buses and trucks and taxis blow past and around. One passing truck is emblazoned with the motto, NEVER TRUST A PRETTY WOMAN. Another reads, FEAR WOMEN AND GROW OLD. A third: SEE BEFORE YOU SAY.

The driver seems to be calculating when to make his move, reenter the fray. Children selling newspapers and what looks like candy swarm the halted truck like flies to meat. Passing vehicles blare as they swerve around the swarm, but the children seem oblivious to the danger.

Tessa surprises herself: she's not oblivious to the danger. "Get out of there!" she wants to yell. "Are you trying to get yourselves killed?" Tessa is used to being the one who takes the risk. She's not used to seeing others do so with no seeming regard, like it's no big deal. "Life isn't cheap," Ma has said to Tessa countless times when Tessa has taken a risk with no seeming regard, like it's no big deal. Like the time she jumped from the top of the pear tree and broke her arm. Like the time she tried to swim across the lake and nearly drowned. Tessa wanted to say in response to Ma, "I know life isn't cheap, why do you think I jumped? Why do you think I swam? Why? Because unlike you I want to experience life—I want to know what's possible. I don't just want to read about it in some book." But watching those children dodge traffic just to make a dime—or a cedi, as the money here is called—makes Tessa wonder whether she's been missing another point. Seems this point may be a different Matisse, out of reach.

The truck jolts forward and the children scramble, having made not a cedi. At least they have their lives, Tessa thinks—and she feels like Ma. This time the truck doesn't move far before it halts again, and there's not even a faux stoplight to justify this halting. What's going on?

What's going on is increased honking, as the vehicles behind make their point. And this point Tessa understands. What does the driver think he's doing, stopping square in the stomach of a busy road?

The driver exits the truck, and for a moment Tessa thinks he is going to leave them here to be more of a spectacle than they already are with their white skin. But then Pa points out they have a flat. And now there is another risk taken with no apparent regard as the driver proceeds to patch the tire while standing inches from his death.

Tessa can't watch. She scoots from one side of the trash bin to the other, nudges away Lint and takes his spot. From this new vantage point the honking is somewhat diminished—the vehicles pass by opposite her now—freeing her to hear something other than horns. Still, she feels the beat before she hears it. Then she hears it and sees it. Four men sit in a half circle yards from the road, their hands flapping like wings as they beat their drums. Passersby pause. Some dance, their movements fast and jerky.

Before now, dancing to Tessa meant tutus and frill. For how many years did Ma force ballet on her, telling her she needed discipline? "My body doesn't move like that," Tessa had said. "And even if it does, I don't want it to move like that." But she wants to move like this. No pliés. No relevés. Just energy and power and rhythm. Tessa has the itch to stand up in the truck, give it a go, but she knows better: she's due a whole lot of payback—from Mary Catherine and Grace and particularly Yllis—and she has no intention of making it easy for them.

Behind the drumming, near the rear of a small tin structure that just might be a house but looks more like a cage, three women squat around a fire. A fire? It must be ninety degrees. It takes a moment before Tessa realizes they're cooking. One of the women props a metal pot over the fire. The others chatter as they slice and stir. A fourth arrives and pounds a long, wide stick into a thick clay pot, mashing up something.

Ma's cooking at home is horrendous, no doubt about it, but maybe it wouldn't be quite as horrendous if she had some company while she cooked. But what company would she have? Books can't cook. And Tessa and her sisters couldn't keep her company, not that they'd want to. Not one Slepy girl could make burnt toast: Ma's never taught them to cook anything. The message Ma's sent about domestic endeavors has always been more than clear. There's no joy in any of it—she wants more for them. So what's the point in teaching them?

Yet watching these African women now, Tessa is not so sure Ma got it right. Meals at home were a chore just to get through. While cooking here seems even more of a chore, based on the fire and stick mashing, the just-getting-through part doesn't seem to apply. Tessa can't be sure, of course, but those women don't so much seem to mind the chore. Tessa would venture to say they're having a good time. When is the last time she saw Ma laugh or smile while preparing a meal?

That would be never.

The driver reboards the truck. He doesn't apologize or explain because patching a flat while risking one's life is just no big deal, okay?

They're back skipping along the red clay road, and Tessa thinks again of Oz, of its wizard. Pa thinks he's the wizard of the Slepy family, but that man behind the curtain isn't a man at all: it's Ma. Tessa doesn't need Yllis's "perspicacity," as Ma calls it, to discern this. Ma can say all she wants that Pa brought her to Africa kicking and screaming, but Tessa doesn't buy it. Ma is a person who gets what she wants.

Didn't Yllis say Ma was lying about Africa being Pa's choice?

Tessa looks over at Ma, who doesn't have her nose pressed in a book for a change: seems Ma's reading Africa. And Tessa is even more convinced some part of Ma wanted Africa. *Wants* Africa.

Seena

The women's clothing is as the ground itself, as if the ground were picked up and wound and wrapped and tied. Red-orange and orange-red, the African earth shows like a magic carpet, bubbled beneath by a lifting wind. And the women's clothing is this magic carpet worn. Dust rises about the Slepys as their truck bounds across the clay, as they gawk at the shining black skin, the blueberry sky, the many bare feet, the plodding of feet. Walking. Walking. It seems at first everyone is walking. And they seem a spectacle because they are not. And then they seem a spectacle just because.

What are the girls thinking? Seena wonders. They've rarely left Michigan. What do they make of these palm trees, these expansive green fans? The trees look, to Seena, artificial. Like oversize plastic toys.

And what of these women wound in earth who seem miracle workers, who balance laundry-size baskets on their heads while sleeping babies swing from their backs? The women move up and down and around, and the baskets stay put and the babies still slumber, while the women's hands buy and sell and sew and slice. Hermes had nothing on these women, Seena thinks, even with his winged sandals and magic wand.

Many of the children wear school uniforms. But they're not in school? And the girls hiss—to get the Slepys' attention, it seems. And they sell, sell, sell. Mostly gum, reminiscent of Chiclets, and water in clear plastic bags. But also newspapers, and laundry detergent—all the same brand, Omo. And cigarettes, too—also only one brand, Embassy. What have Seena's girls ever sold? Girl Scout cookies. In many flavors.

The farther they pass from the airport, the more traffic they see. Taxis. Nearly every car they pass is a taxi. Every truck is some sort of bus—*trotro?*—as is the one in which they ride, but most of the other *trotros* are jammed with both people and chickens. Seena sees Dick thinking: at least we're not riding with chickens.

Or goats for that matter.

Who owns all these goats? Seena wonders. They wander, yard to yard, across roads, munching whatever. It seems their owners would want to contain them, be sure they could claim them, as poor as everyone seems. And yet the goats are a world unto themselves. Seena grabs Lint's leash to make sure he doesn't leap from the *trotro*. She hears in his frantic panting that he longs to enter their private world.

The Slepys' *trotro* pauses for what seems the millionth time and honks at an intersection. A woman approaches the *trotro*, a pyramid of peanuts on her head. Each peanut has its place—like the Slepys' house of cards. Seena is tempted to buy some, just to see the house of peanuts fall.

By the time they reach their destination, the clay dust has

wrapped itself around them and their white skin is as orange as the magic carpet, as if they, too, were made of this earth. Seena yanks a wipe from her fanny pack and swipes the girls clean. Even her eldest, Grace, allows the washing, stunned as she is.

Just days ago Mary Catherine and Seena were steeped in Michigan dirt as they gathered beans after the rain. That Michigan dirt seemed chocolate earth. Moist. Heavy. This African earth is fairy dirt—bright, light, airy. And magical: it colors the air, too. So Seena's swiping proves fruitless within minutes.

The office before them appears war torn, stripped bare. Plain concrete walls, windowless windows. The shape is simple, spartan. But the roof is orange. A mixing, Seena thinks, of heaven and earth. A stalk of a man emerged from the building while Seena swiped, and he stands watching them now with eyes that seem seeing eyes, like Seena's baby's eyes. Except his are Michigan earth, Yllis's African sky—and Yllis is not a baby. The man studies each of them, but his gaze lingers on Yllis. And Seena feels his eyes asking her, How do *you* belong with *them*?

"*Akwaaba,*" the man says. He is a beautiful man, a man of angles: sharp cheekbones to sharp shoulders to narrow waist. "*Willkommen?*" He smiles wide, and the orange light strikes a gold tooth, front and center. The man looks only slightly older than Grace—although the tooth adds age. He wears Western slacks and a white button-up shirt that seems immune to the orange. His skin is dark, but not so dark. Just the right shade, Seena thinks, to remind me.

"He thinks we're German," Dick says, as if the man is deaf.

"Ah, the Americans," the man says. "You are welcome, my friends. I should have known. The melting pot. You seemed

German minus one. I am Kwadzo Mawuli Atoklo. Born on Monday. Please, you will call me Mawuli?" He gestures toward Yllis with his right hand. "This one here was born on Saturday, no?"

Seena feels her cheeks fire beneath the coating of orange, and she is glad, now, for the orange.

"Medical missionaries," Dick says, ignoring the question. "We go Avone." He speaks as if the man would understand a toddler's English best.

"Yes," the man says. "You will go to Avone in time. For now, you are here in our lovely city. No? And Ama," again the man signals to show he is referring to Yllis, "wants to look around."

"Who?" Dick says.

"It's wonderful to meet you," Seena says. But what she wants to say is, *Why are we here? I have no faith in the pope's God. Dick is a pathologist, for God's sake. What does he know about treating dysentery and malaria and guinea worm? We have nothing to offer you.* "Forgive our rudeness. We've had a long trip."

"You are Richard?" He takes Dick's hand.

"Call me Dick. And this is my wife, Christina."

Seena thinks of clarifying, then she thinks again. "Please meet our daughters. Mary Grace, Mary Catherine, Mary Tessa—"

"And Ama," Mawuli says. "The Saturday child."

Ama is not the youngest's name, and yet it is her name: Amaryllis, Seena's Yllis. Seena's child of shed light. "Yes, her name is Amaryllis," Seena says, "but we call her Yllis."

"In Twi her name would be Ama. And in the village of Avone, where the people speak Ewe, those born on Saturday are called Ame."

Seena parses, calculates. Over eleven years have passed since Yllis's birth, yet the birth colors all Seena sees, like this African earth. Yllis was born on Saturday—Seena remembers this. Of course she remembers this. But how could this man, Mawuli, know this? Is he implying he knows even more? In coming to Africa, Seena hoped to escape their house of cards. Now she's met a man halfway around the globe who can see into her soul?

In ancient Greece, Khaos was thought to be the primeval state of being, the great void of emptiness that gave birth to all life. The term "chaos" evolved from this concept. From where did Yllis come? Seena wonders. Is she the daughter of Khaos, or chaos? Was she birthed from Seena's very essence, or from the chaos that was Seena's life?

Seena watches Dick adjust the strap of his camera for the seven hundredth time. Until this very moment, Seena believed Dick alone was on the line in coming here. Grasping, as he is. As if he who knows microscopes and mitosis and meiosis—and dead people—would know anything about healing living people.

Suddenly other children appear, as if in a flock. "*Obroni! Obroni!*" they call. The children look at the girls, at their lanky limbs that protrude from shorts that only now seem too short. And at their hair. "*Akyere!*" Seena thinks of the small gifts she's brought to give the children: packs of bubble gum, small picture books, playing cards, postcards of the Statue of Liberty and Mount Rushmore (places they've never even been, Tessa has repeatedly pointed out).

Mawuli of the gold tooth laughs. "Yes," he says. "Yes."

"What?" Dick says.

"The children say the white girls are ugly," Mawuli says. "But what they mean is they are skinny."

Now it is Dick's skin that fires beneath the orange. "Our girls are beautiful," he says, forgetting to speak as a toddler, and forgetting he doesn't think their youngest beautiful.

Has Dick forgotten why they've come? Seena wonders. Does he notice what she notices? These children are skinny and fat at once, but in all the wrong places: limbs like twigs, stomachs protruded. They smile—laugh even—despite the unhealed sores on legs and feet and arms and cheeks. What does it matter whether the children think the Slepy girls are ugly? Mary Catherine chooses to not eat—she chooses to starve—while these children can't choose to eat, at least not enough, not what their bodies need. Mary Catherine's self-inflicted starvation is far uglier than these sores, these swollen bellies, even though Dick characterizes Catie's fasting as "pious." Apparently these children don't have the luxury of being "pious."

The children circle Mary Catherine, Grace and Tessa while they chant, "*Obroni!* Hi! *Obroni! Obroni!* Hi!" And they pet the girls, as Lint wags and rolls and Yllis uncharacteristically nestles into Seena's skirt. The children finger Mary Tessa's waist-length hair, with delicacy, as if those blond strands that have been singed by Mary Grace and yanked by Mary Catherine and torn by Yllis have become fragile in Africa. As if Tessa herself has become fragile. Seena looks down at Yllis. Yllis looks up at Seena, and Seena realizes what Yllis already has realized. Like the immigration officer, the children made an exception for Yllis. They referred to the "white girls," didn't they? It isn't Tessa who's become fragile: it's Yllis. The seed was planted in Yllis two months prior, on the day she saw the rattler. And the seed grows gangbusters now: it is disposed to this African light.

"Yes, of course," Mawuli says. "Of course. All God's children are beautiful. But the children are not accustomed . . ." He says something to the children in what Seena assumes is Twi and the children peel away and run near the building's rear. They call out as they run, "*Obroni!* How are you! How are you!" Each word jerks out and stops. Clearly separate from the next. How. Are. You.

"And the others?" Mawuli says. "When were they born?"

Seena hears the children in the distance playing a hand-clapping game. Their rhythmic voices accelerate. The clapping accelerates. Seena feels herself accelerate further and further away. "The girls?" she says, as she tries to find the West African ground again. "Mary Grace is eighteen—"

"No," Mawuli says. "What day? What day of the week? You have one Saturday child, born on God's Day. When were the others born?"

Born on God's Day? Seena thinks. *God's* Day? Are you referring to the God who was supposed to lead me not into temptation but deliver me from evil?

"I was born on Sunday." Grace speaks as she swats a fly from Mary Catherine's shoulder. Grace is a grown woman, taller now than Seena. Yet she's come along to Africa. Why? When Grace first learned of their going, she was apoplectic, thinking she'd have to join them—until Dick, with uncharacteristic calmness, reassured her that she didn't have to go, that they'd wait to leave for Africa until after she'd started college. And now? She's deferred her acceptance, followed them into Africa, not wanting to be a world away.

"Ah," Mawuli says. "You are Akosiwa. That is your Ewe name. Ame means Saturday born. Akosiwa is Sunday born. You have the gift of patience, no? A caretaker?"

Seena hears her own breathing then. It seems she's only just remembered to breathe. Grace couldn't care for a hamster. And patience? This naming is superstition, nothing more than the African version of the horoscope.

Mary Catherine moves her left hand toward her mouth to chew her nails and Mawuli watches her, waiting for her to state her day of birth, Seena presumes. But when Mary Catherine's fingers meet her mouth, Mawuli says, "You must not do that."

Mary Catherine freezes, her nails held inches from her lips. She's chewed almost nonstop since they entered the sea of hands at the airport. "Who are they all waiting for?" she asked, as they pressed through the crowd, and Seena saw her longing to disappear. Catie's hair is still so short—Seena sees through it to her sunburnt scalp—it makes even her relatively small eyes appear too large for her face.

"A habit," Dick says. "The nail biting." Dick has hounded Mary Catherine for years about this. Yet Seena sees Dick is enraged now, and not by Catie.

"Nail biting?" Mawuli says.

"It's unsanitary, of course. As a physician I've told Mary Catherine—"

"The left hand," Mawuli says. "She may use her right hand."

"What?" Dick says.

"You may bite the nails of your right hand," Mawuli says to Mary Catherine.

"She was born on Tuesday, I think," Seena interjects, although she doesn't remember when Mary Catherine was born. But it's time to move beyond discussing hands in the mouth, for Mary Catherine's sake. And because Seena sees Dick's simmering fury, usually kept warm by Seena, usually contained by Dick. But not always contained. "Yes, I think Mary Catherine was born on Tuesday."

"Hmm," Mawuli says. "Tuesday is the day God created the sea. A child of the sea is neutral. Steady. She never takes sides."

"She can't swim," Tessa says. "Unless you call the dog paddle swimming."

"You seem more a Wednesday child," Mawuli says to Mary Catherine. "I don't think you like to be told what to do."

"So what's my name?" Mary Catherine says, ignoring Tessa, same as she ignores most things.

And Seena is astounded, astounded Mary Catherine would question Mawuli, astounded she cares about what he has to say. Yet in this moment those eyes that seem too large for her face don't look at the ground or the sky or to escape. They look at Mawuli's seeing eyes. And for the first time in months, Mary Catherine's expression shows neither boredom nor fear. Nor boredom masking fear.

"Or perhaps Thursday," Mawuli says. "Perhaps you're a Thursday child. God created the earth on Thursday. You are observant, I think—connected to the earth. Tell, which name do you like? Abla, Aku or Ayawa?"

"I don't like Abla," Mary Catherine says. And Seena wonders if this coming to Africa was for Mary Catherine rather than Dick. When was the last time Mary Catherine had an opinion about anything? Anything to do with this life? "Aku and Ayawa are okay."

"Yes," Mawuli says. "Perhaps Aku Ayawa for you? You are still deciding inside, I think. Perhaps you were born at midnight." And he laughs.

"I like your jewelry," Seena's baby who is not a baby says then. Yllis emerges from Seena's skirt, thank God. Buoyed by distraction. "We don't have jewelry for teeth in America."

"My gold tooth." Mawuli smiles to show her.

"But when you smile I can't see you. My eyes like the gold."

"You are not alone in that, Ame," Mawuli says. "Americans have a tradition of seeing gold when looking at West Africans."

"Excuse me?" Dick says.

"I'm sorry," Seena says to Mawuli. Then to Yllis: "It's for a cavity, Yllis. It's a filling."

"Oh." Yllis then burrows again, plants herself between Seena's legs. And Seena wishes she'd let Yllis's comment slide.

"We're here to help, for God's sake," Dick says. "We're not interested in your gold."

"Dick . . . ," Seena says.

Mawuli raises his right hand and waves it from side to side. "Of course. A joke. The Gold Coast . . ." Yet Seena wonders. Because she knows they are in Africa searching for gold, in a sense. For that gold at the end of the proverbial rainbow. And she can't help but think, Hades is the god of gold, and Hades rarely leaves the underworld. Are they leaving hell only to find hell?

"What about me?" Tessa asks now, which doesn't surprise Seena. Tessa is Seena's Artemis, her lady of wild things. "What day was I born? What's my African name?"

"Friday," Seena says. Seena remembers this. Somehow. Or does she? "Tessa was born on Friday."

"Yes," Mawuli says. "Afi. This I see. You are an explorer, no? And tenacious."

"She's tenacious all right," Dick says.

"What if I said I didn't like that name?" Tessa says.

"You don't like it?" Mawuli says.

"And what if I was born on Friday, but I wasn't tenacious?"

"But you wouldn't have been born on Friday if you weren't tenacious."

"That's malarkey," Tessa says.

Seena is relieved to see that Mawuli seems amused.

Dick's definitely not amused.

"What's your name mean?" Yllis says, venturing out for a second time. "Mawuli means 'born on Monday'?"

"My first name, Kwadzo, means Monday born, but I see you are listening, Ame. Mawuli means, 'There is a God.' It is the name my parents gave me in thanks to God for my birth."

"So you are a God's child, too," Yllis says. "Kind of. What does it mean to be born on God's Day? To be named Ame?"

Seena thinks again: God's Day. She feels that longing for Yllis to be quiet. It's just superstition, she reminds herself.

"Here, in West Africa, we say, '*Otwedeampong Kwame.*' 'The Great God Whose Day Is Saturday.'"

"So you think God was born on Saturday?" Yllis says.

"That's not biblical," Dick says.

"God was not born," Mawuli says. "In the great nothingness, Nyame just was."

"Who?" Dick says.

"In Twi we also say, '*Kwasi Buroni*,'" Mawuli says, but to Dick now. "That means, 'White Man Whose Day Is Sunday.' The white man got it wrong, you see. He worshipped God on Sunday, not Saturday, so we call him *Kwasi Buroni*. Because Saturday is God's Day. Not Sunday. That is the white man's day."

"You were born on the white man's day, Grace," Tessa says. "I guess you were supposed to be a boy. Good thing Yllis wasn't born on the white man's day. Then we'd know for sure all this day naming is nonsense. Because Yllis is half Indian, aren't you, Yllis? You couldn't be born on the *white* man's day."

"Shut up, Tess," Grace says.

Dick wants to say something, too. He wants to scream something—Seena sees this in the stiffening of the tendons that rail his neck. Instead he circles his tongue through his mouth. Seena imagines the fire in there, in his mouth, and she wonders if this tongue stirring is stoking it. Over the course of the past months, it's taken less and less to stoke Dick's flames. And it's taken less for Dick to unleash the flames.

"Yllis knows I'm joking," Tessa says. "Don't you, Yllis?"

"I still don't get it, though," Yllis says. "I don't get what I am."

Yet Seena knows she understands far too much.

"There is a Ewe saying, Ame. '*Vi-bia-nya-ta-se medzoa— lao.*' 'The child that goes about inquiring is never an animal.'"

"But I wouldn't mind being an animal," Yllis says. "I wouldn't mind being Lint."

"What's that supposed to mean?" Dick says to Mawuli.

"Lint?" Mawuli says.

"This," Yllis points, "is Lint."

"The dog should not have come," Mawuli says, which is true, of course. What was Seena thinking? She thought it would help the girls with the transition. A bit of home in West Africa. But Lint doesn't belong here. That's obvious, isn't it? It's enough for them to figure out why they've come, to negotiate their way, to figure out how—and if—Dick can do any good. Lint is just another tenuous card in this new house they're building.

Lint's fur, normally an amalgam of tan, gray and blond, is now dusted a goldish, pinkish orange. He oscillates between wiggling and wagging, and hiding like Yllis, as if he's embarrassed by his presence here, too.

Dick agrees with Mawuli that Lint should not have come. It was a point of contention, their bringing Lint. Another point of contention. But Seena also knows Dick won't say he agrees with Mawuli. The battle of egos between Dick and Mawuli has overtaken Dick's battle with Seena—at least for now.

"There is another Ewe saying," Mawuli says, but to Yllis alone. " '*Nya nusi wom viwo le da.*' 'Look at what your child is doing.' I have looked at you, Ame. I see you are not foolish. Our tradition says a child born on God's Day possesses the medicine for snakebites. Perhaps you will assist your father with his work here? Yes? But remember this: once you get hold of a snake's head, what is left is just a piece of rope."

Mary Catherine

West Africa

Fall 1976

Cholera, guinea worm, malaria, meningitis, hepatitis, typhoid, river blindness, yellow fever. Did they get immunized against all of these? Mary Catherine wonders as she listens to Mawuli describe what Papa will encounter at the clinic he's to set up in a village named Avone. The diseases seemed foreign, distant, unreal, just notions, when she was in the health clinic being immunized against them. Even taking her antimalaria pills seemed, until now, all form, no content.

But the diseases don't seem unreal now. And the malaria pills: did she remember to take hers today? What about that DEET she was supposed to use, to keep the mosquitoes away? Where is it?

"You may leave for Avone after you've registered with the police and immigration," Mawuli says. "Once immigration returns your passports, you are free to go, if your visas are extended. It will take just a week. No more than two."

Mama and the other girls have gone to unpack, to settle the family into the adjacent dorm where the Slepys will stay until leaving for Avone. But Mary Catherine needed to rest, sit, wash her hands. Wash her whole body. Wash her mind. After riding that *trotro* through the city—seeing the omnipresent filth—she feels exhausted and dirty, inside and out.

"Come," Mawuli had said, when he'd heard Mary Catherine beseeching her mama, explaining to Mama why she'd no energy to unpack. "Sit with me, while I talk with your father." Then he'd taken Mary Catherine's elbow, guided her to swelter in this office, cupping her elbow like she was his cool drink of water. But he was the cool drink of water: his touch was arctic compared with her hot skin. How can he stay so cool? she'd wondered, as she followed him. It must be 120 in this room.

"Immigration will take our passports away? For more than a week?" Papa says to Mawuli now. "And the visa extensions might not be approved? Why didn't anyone tell me this before, before we came? Why didn't anyone tell me this was a possibility?"

They sit in a triangle, the three—Papa, Mary Catherine and Mawuli—so Mary Catherine can see in her papa's eyes the fear she feels in her own. Fear of the diseases that lurk, now both in and out of their minds. Fear they'll be caught, without passports, like trapped flies in this country of flies. The steamy office where they sit is alive with them, the flies. And Mary Catherine assumes they carry at least some of the diseases Mawuli mentioned.

What was Saint Catherine thinking when she ventured out into the world? What good can anyone do when she's diseased? Trapped? Or dead?

"Do not be afraid," Mawuli says, but he looks at Mary Catherine now, not Papa.

And Mary Catherine wonders what she sees in Mawuli's eyes. Because she sees something there, too. Something other than fear.

Mawuli turns back to face Papa. "You will get your passports back. And the visas will be approved in time. We will go there this afternoon. Yes? The offices are closed now for lunch. But perhaps they will open this afternoon."

"Perhaps?"

"Or on the Monday, if not today. Immigration may open on the Monday. You must not worry."

That's what Mary Catherine sees: the lack of worry in Mawuli's eyes. She sees a desire for living. She sees desire. Mawuli is scared of nothing: not disease or Papa, not even God. He's like Father Amadi, she thinks. He even looks like Father Amadi, but with dark eyes. He has the same high cheekbones, the same wide jaw, the same cleft in his chin.

"Unbelievable," Papa says. He strokes his mustache, spreads it. "What are we supposed to do here for a week? Or two? Just wait?" But he doesn't wait, not for an answer. He's out of the office before Mary Catherine realized he was leaving, before she realizes he's left her behind. Apparently he'd forgotten her presence beside him.

But Mawuli has not forgotten her presence. "I want to show you our city," he says to her. "You have energy, now. No? To walk with me?" Again he cups her elbow, again he is her cool drink. They exit the tiny office and enter the large world. As they walk, she longs for him to guide her nearer to him—to shield her from this world. She wishes she could climb inside him, hide. She wishes the children with eyes like walnut shells would find something more interesting to gawk at than her white, white skin and her bald, bald head. She wishes the passing men with lips and tongues and palms of neon pink would stop calling out, asking her if she's a boy. If she's not a boy, if she's married. If she's not married, why not? And, if she does plan to marry, then why is she so skinny?

"Leave her be," Mawuli says to the men and gaping children, while he shoos them and encircles her. "Stop staring," he says to them. "Move on."

But they don't stop staring. Seems being skinny should make Mary Catherine less visible, not more. But Mawuli explains, "If you're white you're thought rich, and if you're rich you should be fat, which is beautiful." Being a skinny, hairless white girl who looks like a boy is akin to *aaaiiiswutuh!*, the piercing wail of the girls who prey on them now, trying to sell them bags of water.

Bags of water: Mary Catherine is terrified of them. Mama's worried Mary Catherine will starve to death, but she'll die of dehydration long before she starves. Fasting no longer feels like a sacrifice. Mary Catherine has no appetite: it's eating that's the sacrifice. But drinking? She longs to drink. She wants to nab a passerby's Pee Cola, but she'd have to smash it to the ground. She wants to tackle those water-toting girls, tie them up in her rosary beads, not to take their water, but to stop their taunting. Because Mary Catherine can't drink, even though she's drying up from the inside out. Her lips are cracked, her spit's run dry, her eyes can't tear to clear out the dust. Mama assumes Mary Catherine is not drinking as a sacrifice for Jesus, but Jesus has as much to do with her not drinking as He has to do with West Africa. Jesus may be here in name—hanging from signs and buildings in logos. But He seems to have forgotten to show up in spirit.

Everything here is dirty: the streets, the sidewalks, the buildings, the air. Even the water is dirty, coming, as it does, from the river. Mary Catherine watches a woman walk to the river, dip in a pot, then carry away the pot of filthy water balanced on her head. How can you wash a bottle clean, if you're cleaning it with unclean water? In the off chance the so-called "pure water" in those bags actually is pure, what about the bags themselves? Where did they come from? Were the bags washed dirty, as it seems most things here are? Was the bottle for the Pee Cola scrubbed in water from the river—that toilet water? That's what the river is: a toilet. People do their business right out in the open. Boys spray into the river, or into the open sewers that line the streets. Women squat over the river, also spraying (dysentery), then they gather the river water to wash their clothes, their dishes, their babies and themselves.

Mary Catherine looks at all of this as she scrapes her sandpaper tongue across her sandpaper lips, and she thinks, Where is God? Did He get so caught up in all the beauty and perfection on the other side of the globe, He forgot spheres don't end— that you have to turn a sphere to see the whole? Is He hanging in a hammock on the Danish Landing admiring His artwork— the glass-top lake and the setting sun—while sipping truly pure water out of a truly clean cup? Or is He like Mary Catherine when she marveled at her hair? Is He marveling at all the people on earth praising Him while He forgets the people themselves? Mary Catherine used to think God created beauty and humans destroyed it. But now it seems God is the selfish one. Maybe humans are just trying to tie up all the loose ends God couldn't be bothered with tying.

Suddenly Mary Catherine can't believe she ever thought Jesus would care if she sacrificed herself for Him. He can't even concern Himself with providing clean water, and she thinks He cares about her hair?

Her rosary beads hang from her wrist, wrapped there like a bracelet, like multiple bracelets, as the African women wear. Only Mary Catherine's bracelet was different: the bracelet of no vanity.

Wrong.

She unwraps the beads, pockets them. Mawuli watches her erase the beads as he leads her into the Art Centre, into buckets of beads and reams of cloth and masks and drums and carved figurines. Mary Catherine feels herself relax in this world within the world. Then she feels her heart speed up again, but not from fear. She reaches out, touches one of the wood carvings—Mawuli describes it as a fertility doll. The figure is stylized but beautiful. Tall and flat, yet rounded at the head, rounded at the torso. A piece of wood that's given birth to life. A man sits nearby carving, working magic. "I want to do that," Mary Catherine says. "I want to learn to do that."

Mawuli watches Mary Catherine, not the man. "You are a powerful woman. You are different from your sisters. Your beauty is that of a woman. They are girls, your sisters. But, you. You are a woman."

"I look like my mother, I know. I've heard it a million times."

"Your mother?" Mawuli says. "No. You are not your mother."

"I'm not beautiful, anyway, remember? You yourself explained. I'd have to be fat to be beautiful."

"There is a greater beauty I see in you. If you were an African woman, you would be a queen mother."

"A queen mother?"

"She is the most powerful woman of each village—the woman who is closest to both the earth and the sky. If you were to marry me, for example, then you would become Queen Mother of Avone. Eventually. Perhaps you should marry me?"

"Perhaps," Mary Catherine says, and she laughs for the first time since the day she lost her hair.

Dick

◈ Death. Dick has known him for so long. Body after body after body he's known, in a way that was intimate. Almost sensual. Alone with Death: Death and Dick, together in an austere room. Sometimes Dick would wait for Death to be wheeled in, and for a moment they would be three: the pathologist, the wheeler and Death. But usually Death waited for Dick. He'd get the call, and he would excuse himself from Life—from Seena and the girls—and he'd drive to Death. He would park, climb from his car, walk through the lot and wonder, How will I meet Death today? Will Death be a she or a he? Old or young? Riddled with disease? Snatched by chance? Donned by grief? Or relief?

Autopsy. According to Seena, the word is Greek in origin and means "to see for oneself." Dick has seen for himself so many many times—far more than anyone should ever see. He has seen mothers who have hemorrhaged and fathers who have blown out their brains and children flattened by speeding cars that never stopped. He has seen hearts imploded and veins corroded and livers that are little but mush. Cancer that ravages and brains ravaged and lungs like tissue, torn. With each of these, he questioned Life, then turned again to God. How else can one make sense? God is the author of Life. It seemed only God could explain the horror of Death.

Dick was drawn to pathology by the wonders of the human body—by the ingenuity of God. Every cell of the human body seemed a miracle in itself, far more original and capable and remarkable than anything of human design. Yet seeing those cells turn on themselves was—and is—like seeing the death of God. It's seeing his father turn on himself and his family again and again and again. It's seeing his mother turn on life and him, until her body developed cancer and turned on itself. His father had used gas, in his very own car in his very own garage, and Dick had found him there, blue, his cells oxygen parched.

Dick never told Seena of these sights—of Death's horrific artwork. He never told the girls what can lie beneath the surface or be around the corner or appear as if from nowhere. Dick told them only that his father had died when he was a child, and that his mother had died of cancer when Dick was just nineteen—and that Dick had persevered, as he always persevered.

Now he has brought his family to Africa, and he knows in a way he wishes he didn't know what lies beneath the surface and around the corner. He knows what can appear as if from nowhere. Death is here. He is in the bloating of bellies and yellowing of sclera, in the perpetually loose stools and fever-induced stares. Dick recognized Death the moment he stepped from the plane. Death was waiting as he and his family disembarked, and Death swarmed them. The airport was an ocean of Death. As Dick pushed through the crowd—as he tried to make way for Seena and the girls—he met Death over and over again. Each time he pushed past the face of Death, he met Him another time, in another face, another body. The face of Death, the body of Death, the smell of Death. Even the sound of Death: this, Dick hadn't heard before. He'd never before encountered the frenetic sound of Death lurking, speaking in words Dick couldn't understand, and yet he did understand. Not the words, but the desperation: Death's yearning. And he was terrified. Is terrified. He came here not chasing Death, but running from Death—from causing it.

Because he knew he could kill, that he'd become capable of it. The more he'd tried to believe Seena would never betray him, the more convinced of her betrayal he'd become. Already Dick had offended God: he'd committed murder in his heart. He knew he had to turn his back on the temptation to kill— otherwise he'd commit the mortal sin and it would drive God's grace from his heart forever. "Lead us not into temptation, but deliver us from evil." God had delivered Dick, through Amadi: He'd enlightened Dick's mind and strengthened Dick's will.

And Dick ran from temptation, he ran from Death—he tried. But he didn't realize Death would be circling in Africa like the children peddling water. And he didn't realize how incompetent he would feel here—how incompetent he would *be* here. Seena warned him—tried to warn him. "How can you help?" she'd said. "You're a pathologist." But Dick thought it was a ploy, her cautioning. Another of her ploys. An intimation he was headed to repeat the blunders of his father, who had lost his license after performing a surgery he never should have performed.

But Seena was right. Dick is the Doctor of Death, not the Doctor of Life.

Dick has brought medical instruments with him to Africa. Stethoscopes and syringes, scissors, scopes and scalpels. And blood pressure cuffs and needles. And every bandage and gauze imaginable. He's brought penicillin, amoxicillin, doxycycline, iodine and quinine. And vaccines. But to him these instruments and medicines are toys. He played with them in medical school, hardly since. He's a fraud—a child playing doctor. He has the right clothes, the right play tools. And about as much know-how as Yllis, whom lecherous Mawuli suggested should be his assistant.

Well, she may as well be. Yllis has nearly the same chance of curing those diseases Mawuli mentioned as Dick does. And Mawuli knows it—he knows Dick's a fraud.

Dick and his family had gone with Mawuli to the police station and immigration office the prior day, hours after they'd arrived. And as Dick fumbled through, seeming more and more helpless at every turn, Dick saw Mawuli grow in the eyes of the girls and Seena. But nothing made sense. How was Dick supposed to make sense of the senseless? No signs directing. No apparent process to follow. Which line to stand in? Which fee to pay? If Mawuli had not been there guiding Dick, Dick would have accomplished nothing.

In fact, Dick did accomplish nothing. When all was said and done, nothing was done, as far as Dick could tell. Their passports had been taken. Temporarily? They were told to return when—if?—their visas were extended. "But how will we know?" Dick had asked. "You will come back," the administrator had answered. "But when do we come back?" Dick had asked. "When the visas are extended," the administrator had said.

Dick stands outside the latrine, now, waiting to enter that den of disease before trying to sleep on a cot that is a full foot too short and nearly as much too narrow. Dick smells Death in the dysentery of the person inside the latrine. He hears dysentery's groaning and splattering and gas passing, and he smells Death's sick embrace. I can help this person, Dick tells himself. I can be the doctor, I *am* the doctor. I can help him, or her. I have doxycycline—it will stop the dysentery.

The latrine door opens, Mawuli steps out. Dick sees the fleeting humiliation in Mawuli's face when Mawuli sees Dick. (What did Dick hear? Did he hear the groaning? The splattering? The gas passing?) But almost immediately Mawuli is again the Mawuli who cares little about what this white man thinks.

Dick doesn't mention the doxycycline.

Dick came to Africa to save his own soul—he realizes this now. He hadn't really intended to save anyone else's.

But maybe I can save others, Dick thinks as he traps the stench, shuts the latrine's door. He pinches shut his nose.

Maybe. But, if so, the soul saving will begin with someone other than Mawuli.

Clara

Clara sits on the porch listening to Egan snore as she watches the Danish Landing fall off to sleep. Her knitting needles and yarn lie in a confused heap on her lap. The light outside is different. Already the gray haze of winter is trying to sneak itself in, reminding Clara that summer in Michigan quickly turns to fall, and fall quickly falls away. Cozy Cabin is boarded up. Tall Oaks is boarded up. Sunset View is boarded up.

And Deezeezdaplas is no longer the place: the girls are gone. Left shortly after Grace and Clara's last tête-à-tête. They must be in Africa by now. Hard to imagine. Particularly hard to imagine Grace there. Like Clara herself, Grace isn't the type who likes getting her hands dirty. But if it weren't for Clara's dirty hand, Grace wouldn't be in Africa, now would she?

As Clara watched the Slepys' station wagon drive off the Danish Landing, she lied to herself, told herself she was looking forward to some peace. No more dodging Yllis's questions, Tessa's acorns, Mary Catherine's worshipping eyes. No more shooing that mutt Lint from her geraniums. No more feeling annoyed by that hoity-toity Seena Slepy, who can't be bothered with the

mundane, even when the mundane may well mean grandchil-
dren. No more wanting to slap some sense into that Dick Slepy,
who thinks he can will himself a Dane and will his wife affection-
ate and will his children respectful, who thinks demanding a perfect family, while snapping a photo of what looks like one, is the
equivalent of having one.

Well, lying or not, peace is not what Clara got. Grace seems
more here than when she was here. Shows how old Clara's get-
ting—she keeps confusing the two of them. She keeps thinking
Grace's predicament is her predicament. Grace told Clara the
Slepys were headed off to Africa intending to save lost souls.
Seems to Clara they should have started with themselves.

"Clara?" she hears Egan say, but she pretends to not hear
him. She's not quite ready to disentangle herself, remember
she's an old thing, not a young thing carrying her fiancé's
brother's baby. "Clara?" Egan says again, and this time she hears
it, not her name, but the lack of it, the hollowness: Egan needs
his inhaler.

"I'm getting it," she says. She turns toward Egan, but that
hazy, morphing light makes him hard to see. Where's that damn
cane? Clara thinks, as she tries to unwrap herself from the chair.
Aging is the most irrational thing. Your brain fools you into
thinking you're eighteen, the same time as your body can't
fathom you ever were eighteen.

The cane lies on the floor. Seems Clara dozed off and let the
damn thing slide. She performs a bit of geriatric gymnastics as
she tries to get hold of the cane, but finally gives up and leaves
it on the floor. She wobbles around the cottage looking for the
inhaler, to no avail.

When Clara finds Egan dead, she has no broomstick, no miraculous staff, no magic wand. But Egan has the inhaler. He grips it like he was trying with all his life to hold on to something. And Clara remembers that grip on her a lifetime ago. She remembers it crushing her fingers when she was in labor trying to push out that baby she didn't think she wanted, until it was born dead. Then she wanted it more than she'd ever wanted anything. She begged God to give her baby back, to resurrect her. But God ignored Clara. And Clara has spent every day of her life since then angry with God. Angry that He gave her insight only when it was far too late.

Now, as she sees Egan before her—as she sees him dead— she has that same feeling of seeing something she didn't think she wanted pass away, only to realize how much she wanted it.

Clara rips Egan's inhaler from his cool grip. It crashes to the floor. She collects her cane, this time with surprising ease, only to return to the inhaler and beat it with the cane until the inhaler is pulp. The inhaler and God are one and the same, she thinks: useless. Worse than useless. They make you think you're safe. They make you depend on them. Then when you need them most, they fail you.

But just as Clara is about to give the inhaler one last blow, she's given the gift she's been waiting for her whole adult life: God did resurrect her baby. He did.

Clara's baby was resurrected.

As Grace.

Grace came to Clara. Grace needed a mother.

Clara is the one who failed. Not God.

Mary Grace

West Africa
Fall 1976

Grace feels inside out, like she's been living in a shell, but now her innards are exposed for all to see. It's at once claustrophobic and sprawling, as if she's oozing while unable to breathe. And the droplets of her, they follow her like a trail. A little of her here. A little of her there. A smear of her on the wall. A stain of her on the concrete, climbing the stairs. Amazingly, she never runs dry: she just keeps oozing away, even as the shell where she lives feels more and more cramped.

Grace and her family are in West Africa: they're here to save the world. It's four in the morning and the damn roosters are crowing. They'll crow until the sun rises, when at last they'll slumber. Grace longs to snap the roosters' necks, chop off their heads, watch them dart around headless, their blood spewing. At least then they'd be quiet.

Yesterday, as they toured the city, Grace saw a man beat a woman with a switch. And when Tessa with her big mouth asked that handsome Mawuli what's-his-name what the hell was going on, he matter-of-factly said perhaps the woman was insane—perhaps the beating was to rid the woman of evil spirits. Grace felt like telling Mawuli to bring it on, because Grace feels insane. Even during the few hours when she did sleep it was noisy, even before the roosters began their screeching. The vendors shouted, "*Obroni! Obroni!*" in Grace's dreaming, mad mind, begging her to buy *kelewele,* the spicy fried plantain "almost like banana" that's nothing like banana, or red red, a mixture of plantain and beans that's not even red.

They've been in Africa for forty-four hours; the building where they're staying has been without water for sixteen. No one seems particularly concerned about the lack of water. Apparently even the water company, appropriately named African Water Company *Limited,* is on AMT, African Maybe Time. Maybe the *trotro* will pass this way. Maybe the electricity will come back on. Maybe immigration will return their passports.

Maybe they'll have water.

How does anyone survive in this godforsaken place? Don't they realize: people die without water. According to Papa, God sent them here. Well, yeah, one of Mama's gods, Hades.

How did Grace get herself into this? She could be at college now, living in South Quad, surrounded by football players and edible food and *running water.* And no roosters. Instead she's in a schizophrenic country where the official language is English, but hardly anyone speaks it—certainly no girls. Instead they speak Twi or Ewe or Ga or Grusi or Gurma or Dagbane or God knows what else. You'd think they could make up their minds.

You'd think Grace could make up her mind. Is it her mind that's keeping her awake, or the roosters? Is it the heat that's making her sweat like Papa, or her nerves? Is it the hideous *kelewele* that's making her ill?

She thinks of Rocky. He's in college now. And he's in her. And she's in hell. Apparently performance satisfaction has little to do with target accuracy. What feels like a complete miss can turn out to be a bull's-eye. Grace wishes she'd had the sense to discuss the specifics with Old Clara BEFORE. AFTER Clara explained how experience has nothing to do with aim. How first comers can get knocked up just like anybody else. How hopping is best left to those doing the bunny hop.

"Gracie?" Grace hears Yllis whisper, but she ignores her. Grace's entire family has to sleep in the same room—the West African version of the dorm. And Grace thought U of M's dorms looked bad. Their cots aren't much wider than puny Yllis. The rest of them have to lie on their sides just to keep from toppling off. Apparently Grace should be grateful for the cot. When they head out to the village where Papa will run his clinic—where they'll have no electricity EVER and no running water EVER—they may well be sleeping on mud, just to add some icing to that cake. When Papa questioned Mawuli about the cleanliness of sleeping on mud, Mawuli said: "Oh, but the floor is clean. We sweep the floor often in the day." Sweeping a mud floor? What is Grace missing here?

"Gracie?" Yllis says again, and Grace knows Yllis is well aware Grace is awake. How Yllis knows is another matter, but Grace has learned to stop questioning when it comes to Yllis. "Mary Grace?"

As Grace hears Yllis whisper her name, she thinks of Papa's explanation as to why he named her Grace. "Grace is God's mercy," he'd said. "It's the love God shows us of his own initia-tive—not on account of our merits."

Not on account of our merits: seems for once Papa knew what he was doing.

Grace turns her head toward Yllis, although it's so dark, she couldn't see Yllis to save her life—which would be pointless anyway, given Papa is going to kill her soon enough. "What, pinhead?" Grace says.

"Do you love me?"

"Go to sleep, Yllis," Grace says. But she imagines Yllis's little face lying there on no pillow (none of them has a pillow), those pale eyes of hers staring at the darkness, those teeth that are far too big for her mouth biting at her lip. Grace remembers her-self when she was Yllis's age, when her teeth were too big for her own mouth. That was about the time she realized she was pretty, despite her teeth. Pretty, and a girl. "You don't have to worry about being good at math," her teacher Mr. Kane had told her when she'd asked him for the more challenging math the boy seated behind her had been given. "You're a girl," he'd said. "A pretty girl. Pretty girls don't need to be good at math." "But I like math," Grace had said. "And I'm good at it. It's not a question of whether I want to be good at it." "But it is a question," Mr. Kane had said. "And you're asking it—you're asking for harder math. I'm telling you, you don't need to ask. It's unnatural, unattractive, girls liking math. And you're not unattractive, Mary Grace. You're just not."

"I love you," Grace says to Yllis now. "'Course I do."

Grace does love Yllis, same as she loves Tess and Mary Cath-erine. Only that love isn't simple like it once was. When Grace and her sisters were much younger, they would have stuck up for each other no matter what. That's not to say they didn't fight. That's not to say Grace didn't hate her sisters at times. But back then they were swimming in clear water. While Grace and her sisters would deck each other, they'd defend each other, too, particularly when one of them was threatened by someone outside their circle: that someone would be decked with far greater force. But now Grace and her sisters are swimming with the Loch Ness Monster in water that's been so muddied by Grace's own lies and deception—while Yllis points out every speck of floating dirt—there's no way Grace could even find her sisters, let alone save them.

Yllis lies quiet for a minute—maybe two—and Grace thinks she's dozed off. But as is usual with Yllis, she's out to prove Grace wrong. "Gracie?"

"Hmm."

"I love you, too."

"You need to get to sleep, Yllis," Grace says. "We have to go to mass in the morning, remember? Papa is going to wake us early."

"Where do babies come from? I mean, I understand, sort of. But, do you have to love someone to have a baby with him?"

Yllis knows, Grace thinks, and Grace is pissed. Grace feels like she's living with the CIA. How a midget like Yllis figures things out is beyond Grace. "What are you talking about, Yllis?" Grace says, although she knows all too well what Yllis is talking about.

"I just want to know if every baby comes from love. Or whether some babies just come."

"Sometimes love has nothing to do with it." Grace figures she may as well tell Yllis the truth. "Sometimes people just screw up."

———————

Grace wakes the next morning, surprised she's slept. Apparently there was something soothing about Yllis's knowing: Grace isn't entirely alone here in African hell.

Yet all of a sudden Grace needs to puke. She feels anything but soothed now. She battles to get out from under the mosquito net so she can escape outside and avoid others seeing her upchuck. But the more she battles, the more she's tangled.

I'm going to wake Papa, she thinks. Please don't let Papa wake.

Her prayers are answered: Dick is dead to the world. Even Yllis still sleeps, miracle of miracles. Grace finally finds her way out of the mosquito net, out of the dorm. But she doesn't make it inside the latrine. When Mawuli literally stumbles upon her, she is hunched outside the latrine's door.

"Akosiwa," he says, but he says it in a different way, like he understands for the first time why Grace was given this African name. He lifts her hair into a ponytail, holds it away from her face, touches her cheek. "You are pregnant," he says, after he apologizes for running her down. It's sort of a question, sort of not. Grace doesn't feel the need to answer. It never occurs to her to lie, even though she would have lied to anyone else who'd asked, including Yllis—although a lot of good that would have done. "You are not married." Again: sort of a question, sort of not. "Your parents are not aware."

In more ways than one.

Mawuli figured it out, Grace thinks: he figured it out. When Grace wipes her mouth and turns his way and looks into his dark dark eyes—eyes so beautiful but so different from Rocky's—she knows without a doubt that he knows without a doubt.

Clara said to never tell a soul, and Grace didn't. But Mawuli knows anyway. That Grace's own family, excepting Yllis, didn't put two and two together when a perfect stranger did says something—something about Grace's family or something about Mawuli. Grace isn't sure.

Strange thing is, Grace isn't troubled by Mawuli's knowing. She actually feels that weight people talk about, that weight people say gets lifted. She sensed a bit of the same kind of lifting last night with Yllis. But Mawuli's knowing? There's something about him that makes Grace feel at once lighter and stronger, as if he's wrapped his powerful arms around the baby inside her and lifted some of her burden. Even before he speaks again, Grace senses they have a deal of sorts—that he won't tell. She trusts him. And she's found some respite knowing she'll have someone to confide in who's older than Yllis and younger than ancient.

Seena

Seena wakes, claustrophobic in her mosquito net, to the sound of a rat invading her fanny pack, tearing through the foiled snacks she'd stored there. She shoos the rat, observed by an audience of children who stand outside the open window, watching her.

Apparently Seena slept—she has witnesses to the fact.

Still, she feels she's not slept for years; she feels a thousand years old. She props herself up, looks around. Dick lies snoring, but even he can't compete with the roosters and rats. Tessa and Mary Catherine lie in matching fetal positions, clearly seeking some comfort. Grace is absent. Attempting to escape the throng of eyes? Or the rats?

And Yllis watches Seena.

"What?" Seena whispers to Yllis—although what's the point of whispering? "Is something wrong?" But Seena knows something is wrong, and it has nothing to do with rats.

Yllis looks away from Seena, at the children, and Seena ducks beneath her mosquito net, wanting as much as Yllis to avoid what is wrong. She locates the trinkets she brought to give the children, then tugs free one of the picture books and hands it to Yllis. "Take it to them, Yllis," she says. "One of them might like to read it to the others while we get ready for mass."

Yllis complies. She unravels herself from her mosquito net, collects the book from Seena and delivers it out the window to the eldest child, a girl who looks Tessa's age, maybe older. "You can read it out loud to the little children," Yllis says.

The girl takes the book and flips through the pages, looks at the pictures. The remaining children jockey to see. Yllis lingers, apparently wanting to listen herself. The book is *Make Way for Ducklings,* a story Yllis used to love when she read picture books, but that was years ago now.

The girl tries to hand the book back.

"But you can have it," Yllis says. "You can read it."

The girl gazes at the book.

"You can have it," Yllis says again.

"She doesn't understand," one of the boys says. The girl looks at her feet as the boy pushes to the front of the crowd. He is younger than the girl. Perhaps he's ten—or eleven, like Yllis. "She doesn't speak English."

"But you learn English in school?" Seena speaks from across the room.

"Yes," the boy says, but he doesn't explain. "I will read the book." He opens it. "Meester . . . and . . . Meesus . . . Mall . . . aired . . . wear . . . loooo-king . . . for . . ."

My God, Seena thinks: he can barely read. Does that mean the girl can't read at all?

In this question Seena finds yet another distraction from that which is wrong.

Yet she also finds a seed of feeling. Seems the African sun has seeped through, drenched that light-starved, parched seed.

Yllis

People have a cloudy blanket that hovers over them when they sleep, as if the blanket holds in their souls, keeps their souls from flying away and forgetting to come back. Nyx, the Greek goddess of night, was born of Khaos, Mama said. Nyx gave birth to a slew of children, including Thanatos, "death." I figure that's why the blanket forms, to keep death at bay.

But I could see from the starlight and Gracie's own light that her blanket was missing, so her soul could have floated off if she hadn't been paying attention. But she was paying attention—that was obvious. She was thinking hard on something, and nothing was going to pass her by. She was super bright in the relative dark. And the lines and angles of her body were sharp. I couldn't taste her love. Whatever she was thinking seemed to be standing in love's way. Or perhaps it was her sweet-scented fear that obscured love's taste. Because something was eating at Grace, too. "Mary Grace?" I knew she'd pretend to be asleep, yet I knew she'd pretend for only so long. "Gracie?"

I wanted to comfort her—I knew she needed me. But how could I soothe her when I couldn't find me? "Does every baby come from love?"

"No," Grace told me. "Sometimes love has absolutely nothing to do with it. Sometimes people just screw up."

"Well, it's sort of easier to think of people making babies with*out* that *lov*ing part anyway," I said, even as my mind replayed her words. "Particularly Mama and Papa."

Grace busted up.

She fell asleep then. Her fear waned and her blanket formed—as if in answering my question, she'd answered her own—and the blanket that hung over her was thick and still, not jittery and see-through, like some blankets are. Yet I knew that, unlike me, Grace belonged, that my question couldn't have been her own. Grace was a Slepy inside and out. She had Papa's coloring. She had his eyes. And he had his eyes on her much of the time.

I, too, have my papa's coloring, I thought, thinking back on that day: I have these blueberry eyes.

But his eyes are never on me, to protect me.

Does that confirm Grace's words, that love had nothing to do with it?

When he saw me there in the woods that day, he studied Tessa as much as he studied me. And then he let me walk away, just like that.

As I watched the absence of Grace's blanket transform to the heaviest blanket in the room, I thought about her answer: screw up. Is that what I was? What I am? I tried to remind myself: the words a person speaks sometimes are less like the pictures Papa takes, more like their negatives. When I'd hold up those negatives in the light, look at the Marys' black skin and my less-black skin, at the Marys' black hair and my white hair, I knew I was seeing some version of truth. But there was no taking that particular version at face value. In order to parse out truth, I'd have to hold what I'd heard to the African light, do some adjusting.

Because Africa had something to tell me about myself—I was sure of this.

Yet Africa wasn't making it easy. The next day at mass, love made no sense. And I found I couldn't find envy or melancholy in the congregation at all, like the blackness of the people's skin drank those colors up. Or maybe it was the other colors that got in the way. The women looked as beautiful and poisonous as monarchs in their shocks of red and orange.

Thinking back on that scene now, I can't help but wonder whether it was a sort of foreshadowing of later, of Mama being judged while looking bloodless, like pasty Jesus, as the elders of Avone eyed her without envy or melancholy.

But unlike at Mama's trial, love was at mass. Those handsome black people sat worshipping and loving a pale and very white Jesus. And on Sunday, no less. The white man's day. I'd learned of colonialism at school. And I'd learned of slavery. I knew the coast of West Africa had been a gateway where whites herded Africans onto boats as if they were cattle, where Africans passed from being free to being slaves. And I'd seen that back and forth between Papa and Mawuli when we'd first arrived—I'd seen Mawuli's distrust of this White Man, and I figured his distrust made some sense. Africans had many reasons to hate whites and few reasons to love them.

Yet there the Africans were at mass loving white Jesus anyway. And I felt Africa telling me, "Love is not what you thought."

Seena

Seena remembers the feel of him when she closes her eyes, when she imagines she is the other person living the other life. She recalls the first time her fingers traced his hand, his wrist, his forearm. She can almost feel his arm now: the warm caress of skin beneath the shelter of coarse hair, the curved beauty of his muscle, his veins pulsing. She recalls the taste of him, too, and the moist blanket of his lips. She longs to taste him now, to smell him. To touch him. She allows her mind to trace the triangle of his upper body: this stretch of straight shoulders, dipping inward, falling low, to a waist that was narrow and firm, a back that was smooth stone come to life. And when his fingers found her, they were a quiver of air. Her lips, circled. Her neck, molded. Her collarbone and rib bones discovered for her. And then, her tears shared, because he knew as she knew the cost of commission, the cost of omission: that nothing is free.

Africa may be another world altogether, so far away from the familiar. Yet Heimdall has found his way here. He is every-where. Again and again Seena's eyes fool her. She sees him driving a taxi, carving a tool, praying, drumming. He'd told her stories of Africa. He'd described the drumming, the praying, the carving. She'd smelled Africa through his stories: dry earth, fish soup, open fires, roasting corn. She'd worn African colors in her mind: these exotic-bird hues. And she'd imagined the sensation of the kente cloth, when Heimdall described it draping across the body like a warm, securing weight. Heimdall had been her window into this world long before she arrived in this world. And now, as she wanders down this one-lane road that's barely a road while the girls and Dick attend mass, her imagination sees Heimdall reflected in the dusty window of every passing *trotro,* his smile lines creasing, his mouth a powdery pink, and she stumbles again into the world within the world within the world of his eyes—that are her baby's eyes. And she wonders whether Mary Catherine was right—does she love Yllis more? And then she thinks, What kind of mother would love one child more?

What kind of woman would do what I've done?

Seena couldn't attend mass. Not here. Not today. If he is in the passing *trotros,* he most certainly would be in mass. "I want to walk the streets," she told Dick, the girls. Then she turned to Mawuli. "Tell me, Mawuli. Where should I walk for the hour while you're in mass?" But as Mawuli described the location of the Art Centre and government headquarters and the fishing port, what Seena wanted to say was, "Tell me, Mawuli, where can I go where I won't find him?" Because she longs to avoid Heimdall—thoughts of him—as much as she longs for him. Isn't that the very reason she prodded Dick those many years ago to buy the cottage at the Danish Landing? Because she couldn't bear being away from Heimdall any more than she could bear being near him? Living with never seeing Heimdall had proved more difficult than seeing him, even with the knowledge she would never touch him again. And so: the purchase of the cottage, the regular visits to Grayling, and the facade of attending mass.

But here, in Africa, she has no chance of seeing Heimdall, even while she is reminded of him at every turn. And these reminders of him are reminders in the exponential, because they serve to ensure she remembers she is an addict and she can't get her fix here, leaving her able to think of little but how to get more, of him—even as she tells herself she can't have more, she won't have more. She made that decision when Yllis was born.

Seena is Psyche and Heimdall is Eros. He visits her, yet he is invisible to her, and she is in love with him even though she can't see him. Yet isn't it Seena who lit the lamp? Isn't it she who made him run from her? And now she roams the earth, trying in vain both to find him and to lose him.

Seena thinks these thoughts as she stumbles over a woman who washes clothes in a pan. The woman squats near the side of the road; the soap bubbles in the pan like spit. And now the soap spit splatters, speckling the woman's dark skin and transforming the orange clay to blood.

"I'm sorry," Seena says. She has no idea whether the woman understands.

The woman resumes scrubbing with barely a pause.

How did I not notice her? Seena thinks. She was right in front of me.

Then Seena sees: washing women squat all along the street,

splashing the roadside like fountains. Each one of the women looks at Seena, sees Seena—this spectacle of obtuse paleness.

Seena turns off the street, onto a small alley, wanting to disappear. She's not eaten since yesterday. As Seena prodded the girls to eat this morning before they attended mass, she emptied her fanny pack of its corpses: rat-nibbled Pop-Tarts and rat-picked-through Chex Mix. And she felt she could follow Mary Catherine's lead and never eat again.

But now her stomach quietly rumbles, responding to the smell of eggs and sweet tea and doughy bread. Seena proceeds down the alley, follows the smell. And she finds the soft eggs and tea, and the pillows of bread, being sold at a stall by a woman with no teeth.

"I want some of each." Seena gestures toward the items on the table, assuming the woman may not understand her words. "How much?" She shows the woman her cedi, this Monopoly money.

"This cedi." The woman points to two coins.

Upon their arrival in West Africa, Dick had warned Seena and the girls, "You must barter when you buy things. Otherwise you'll be taken advantage of. Your white skin is a neon sign saying, 'Take advantage of me!' Even if the item you are buying is worth just a few cents, it sends the wrong message to pay more for it than it's worth. Bartering is part of the culture here. It's expected."

"No." Seena holds up one hand, as she would if she were warning Tessa to hold her tongue. "This amount?" She tries to hand the woman one of the two coins.

The woman disregards the money. She pours steaming tea

into a plastic cup and hands it to Seena. Seena sips the tea, against her better judgment. "Was it boiled?" she hears Dick ask in her head. "It must be boiled to ensure you've killed the parasites."

The tea tastes both bitter and sweet, and Seena thinks, How appropriate. Seena feels she's living inside Heimdall here. She feels closer to him than she has for years—for *years*. Yet she's farther from him now than she has been since she first met him. Has it really been twelve years? More than twelve years. A bitter, sweet, more-than-twelve years.

The woman with no teeth mounds a square of paper with the eggs and bread.

Seena offers the coin again. "Okay?"

"This cedi." The woman gestures toward the same two coins.

Seena shakes her head. "Too much."

A man who stands behind Seena in line speaks to the woman in Twi or Ewe—rather than in gestures and grunts—and the woman pushes the heaping paper into Seena's hands. Then the woman reaches toward the ground and into a basket of tiny bananas, bananas that look to Seena like runts of the litter. Each bunch is a bunch of runts. The woman with no teeth grabs a bunch and thrusts them toward Seena.

"No," Seena says. "I want to buy just the eggs and bread. And the tea. I don't want bananas."

"For you," the woman says. And Seena finds herself holding the bananas she didn't want.

"I don't want them." Seena tries to hand the bananas back.

"For you," the woman says again, then she nudges Seena aside, begins helping the waiting man.

"I have to pay you," Seena says. "I didn't pay you."

The woman ignores Seena. She now focuses solely on the man: Seena no longer exists. The man orders, then pays, as Seena stands motionless, unsure what to do, no longer certain she does exist. Everything she's experienced in Africa could as well be a dream, and she could be a mere actor in someone's sleep—an actor who has become irrelevant and faded from the dream.

But after the man pays, he turns to Seena. "Eat," he says in English. "I have paid."

"But . . . ," Seena says. "You don't have to do that. Let me pay you."

"Some things are unimportant," he says. "Such a small amount. Not worth arguing about. You were asking her to give you the food, you see. Her cost for the food was higher than your offer. Prices of such items are set. A certain profit. A certain cost."

"I didn't know . . . ," Seena says. And then: "Please. Let me pay you."

"It is unimportant."

"The bananas. I didn't want to buy them. I didn't mean to . . ."

"The bananas?" The man laughs, and Seena feels herself grow more ridiculous in his eyes. "The bananas were her gift to you."

"My gift?" After I tried to rob her? Seena thinks. "I have so much more than she does," Seena wants to say. "I can't take these from her." But she stops herself. Perhaps Seena doesn't have more, at least not of what matters.

"Thank you," Seena says to the woman, who now acknowledges her, albeit briefly. The woman smiles at Seena with her smile of no teeth.

"Thank you," Seena then says, turning to the man.

But the man has gone.

I'm an embarrassment, Seena thinks. I'll never understand this place.

But when she returns to her family—when she finds them in pieces outside the church—she realizes her daughter Grace is more foreign to her than Africa.

Mary Tessa

West Africa
Fall 1976

✳ The girls sit in mass, having been dragged there by Pa on their third day in Africa. Flanked by him on one side and Mawuli on the other, they recite the Our Father.

"'Our Father, who art in heaven, hallowed be Thy name. Thy kingdom come. Thy will be done, on earth, as it is in heaven. Give us this day our daily bread. And forgive us our trespasses, as we forgive those who trespass against us. Lead us not into temptation, but deliver us from evil.'"

Tessa is surprised, and disappointed, she can recite the Our Father, that it's the same as at home. The Hail Mary is the same, too. And the white Jesus hanging from the cross is as white as the Marys themselves, just like at home. They've come all the way to Africa, and Tessa still has to attend mass. And the mass is the mass is the mass. Even in Africa.

Why is it Ma gets to escape this "cultural experience" (as Pa called it) to walk the streets and have a true cultural experience? Watching black Africans worship a pasty Jesus who is wearing what Tessa can best describe as a diaper is a cultural experience Tessa could live without.

"Tess," Grace says. She slips Tessa a note written on the back of a "Jesus Is Lord" pamphlet. "Maybe we shouldn't be praying for God to lead us not into temptation," the note reads. "After passing that market, I'm having difficulty finding anything here tempting."

Walking to mass, they'd passed their African daily bread: a market of groundnuts, tomatoes, onions, yams, a root called cassava for making *fufu,* snails, crabs, whole fish, plucked chickens hanging from their feet and feathered chickens hanging from their feet.

Other than the vegetables from Ma's garden, and the occasional pet chicken that became dinner, Tessa was accustomed to the A & P, to cans and cartons, and to meat that bore little resemblance to any particular kind of animal. But the food in West Africa is food in motion, crawling and swinging and smelling. All of it's smelling. And the cooked-up food, even that is frenetic, given how it's eaten. *Fufu* and *kenkey* and *banku,* all pastes of bland sorts finger-dipped into communal bowls of soup. And although Pa told the girls and Seena to be careful, to eat only food they knew was well cooked ("to kill the parasites"), Tessa wants to eat it all—to feel that goop on her fingers, to slide it into her mouth while in a circle of others doing the same.

She imagines sitting white shoulder to black shoulder to black shoulder. She imagines her gooey fingers brushing against the gooey fingers of those who actually want to hear her speak. Because people here *talk* while they eat. And listen and laugh. The only people who talk at home in Midland during dinner are John Chancellor and David Brinkley—and Pa, who speaks only to hush anyone not employed by NBC News.

And dinner in Grayling where there is no TV? Most of the time no one even bothers to sit at the table. What's the point when there's no news to watch? Instead, Ma stacks the plates on the counter next to the tuna surprise or its equivalent, and the girls, Pa and Ma each pile a plate whenever they please—or more likely when they're starving and willing to eat even Ma's cooking.

Up until now, Tessa regarded the Slepy eating ritual—or lack thereof—as a blessing. She wasn't particularly interested in hearing Ma talk to herself about the most recent myth she'd ingested. She wasn't particularly interested in hearing Pa nag her. She certainly wasn't interested in the unique nonsense espoused by any one of her sisters—the only exception occasionally being Yllis, whose unique nonsense at least sometimes is entertaining.

But now? Now Tessa wonders whether it might be sort of nice to have someone give a hoot about what she has to say. It might even be nice to give a hoot about what others have to say. Seems she and her family might have a thing or two or three to learn from their African "brothers and sisters," as Mawuli calls them. Tessa expected to feel annoyed by Mawuli's "brothers and sisters" business, but she finds herself feeling less annoyed, more of something else, something resembling the hunger she experiences when she sees those same "brothers and sisters" sharing a meal.

Apparently Tessa is alone among her Slepy sisters in feeling anything that resembles hunger. Generally speaking, eating is more of an afterthought with Yllis, even on the rare occasion when she isn't acting faloupoo. (Being in Africa isn't one of those occasions, just FYI.) Mary Catherine isn't eating, period. And Grace's note pretty much says it all.

On their walk to church, they'd also passed Blood of Jesus Hair Care, Jesus Is Able Stationery Shop, Innocent Blood of Jesus Restaurant and Immaculate Conception Rewinding Service, et cetera. As Tessa folds and unfolds Grace's note, she wonders whether all those other incarnations of Jesus are white, too. Is the Jesus of that hair salon white? The Jesus of that restaurant? If so, she figures there are about as many white people as black people in the country—the white people mostly being Jesus.

The sermon is an exploration of the Gospel of Matthew and, specifically, of the Aramaic sentence, *Eli, Eli, lama sabachthani?* meaning, "My God, my God, why hast Thou forsaken me?"

"Jesus asked God this very question when hanging on the cross, waiting to die," the priest says. "Even Jesus questioned God. Even He temporarily lost faith. We all at times have moments when we doubt. But doubt is rational. Faith in God is not dependent on rationality. Faith is having belief despite our rational minds."

Despite our rational minds, Tessa thinks. *Despite our rational minds.* But it's hopeless. Tessa can't turn off her rational mind. She can't stop herself from thinking, If Jesus and God are one and the same, wasn't Jesus sacrificing himself as much as He was being sacrificed? And if that's the case, what right did He have to complain?

Tessa didn't want to be bothered with the members of her own family any more than they wanted to be bothered with her. What right does she have to complain?

They leave mass and Ma shows up, just in time to hear Mawuli announce that Pa's a soul stealer. Heck, Tessa could have told him that. Not that she would have named it as such. Tessa prefers to call Pa a grueler. "Soul stealer" sounds more like something Yllis of God's Day might conjure up—she with her rambling on about colors and blankets and souls vanishing in the night. But Tessa has seen the effect Pa has on Ma, and on Yllis at times, and even on Grace. Something seems to dry right up inside them when he's around, like he's stuck in a straw and sucked.

Which he's just done, in Pee Cola no less. *Pee Cola*. Now that's something Tessa wishes she'd thought to make up. She watches Pa's lips hug the straw, his mustache making the sight particularly unappealing. "How's your pee, Pa?" she'd love to ask, but Pa's already teed off at Mawuli. Tessa would hate to have that soul stealing unleashed on her.

"Put that thing away. Now," Mawuli says again to Pa. He points to the camera Pa had used minutes before to snap a photo of a round-bellied girl trailing a kindling-carrying woman. The girl saw the flash and yelped, and the woman turned to face Pa head-on, the kindling like a teeter-totter on her head. There was an explosion of spit as the woman told Pa off in Ga or Twi or some other lashing tongue—at least Tessa thinks the woman was telling him off based on the spit and the violent teetering of the kindling. Next thing Tessa knew every passerby had joined in the fun. They all were spitting and flailing at Pa—clearly in need of a chill pill—until Mawuli saved him, ordering him to pack up the camera IMMEDIATELY and stop stealing people's souls IMMEDIATELY.

"Steal their souls?" Pa says now, after the great multitude has parted and departed. "You're an educated man, Mawuli. And a Christian. And we've just come from mass. How can you believe in that superstition? It's a camera, for goodness sake. I told you already, it can't steal people's souls. Only the devil can do that."

"You're setting yourself up here, Pa. Talking jive. You may as well just call yourself the devil," Tessa nearly says—although she manages to hold fast to her lashing tongue.

"Superstition?" Mawuli says. "Can you explain this to me, this word, 'superstition'? You Americans like this word when referring to African beliefs, but I see little difference between your beliefs and this so-called superstition. You won't eat meat on Friday. Is this superstition? You trickle water on the heads of babies to save their souls, while you talk about being washed in the blood of the lamb. Superstition? You believe a wafer and wine become the body and blood of Christ, and you eat it. Superstition?"

Tessa recalls the words the priest spoke just minutes ago, during mass, before the Eucharist. He quoted Jesus, saying, " 'Unless you eat the flesh of the Son of Man and drink his blood, you shall not have life in you. For my flesh is food, indeed, and my blood is drink indeed, and he who eats my flesh and drinks my blood abides in me.'" Does seem a bit whacked, now that Tessa thinks of it.

"Are you not a Christian, Mawuli?" Pa says, which Tessa senses he's been longing to ask ever since the Slepys arrived in

West Africa and Mawuli started in with his birth days and corresponding name calling—which Tessa has to agree is idiotic, and oh how she hates agreeing with Pa.

"I am a Christian," Mawuli says. "And I am an African."

"So that gives you the right to believe in nonsense?"

Ma watches the whole exchange like she used to watch Grace's tennis matches. Her eyes swing back and forth, from whack to whack, but her pallor suggests she'd just as well disappear, all things being equal. The photographed girl and woman have parked themselves a half block away, selling their kindling, and Yllis picks apart the robbed pair with her eyes, no doubt trying to figure out whether their souls are intact—Tessa would bet David Cassidy on that. Mary Catherine consumes her righthand fingernails (at least she's eating something) while hiding the offense from Pa by standing in Mawuli's shadow. Grace vomits—having eaten something other than fingernails—but only Tessa notices.

Tessa feels like she's hovering above it all, just taking in the sights—like a soul, Yllis would say, escaped from her body, just waiting to be snatched. But Tessa would rather think of herself as Wonder Woman, soaring above the mere ordinary humans. If only Tessa weren't feeling so ordinary at the moment. So unlike herself. So needy.

"Nonsense, you say?" Mawuli says to Pa. "Like the virgin birth?"

"How dare you!" Pa says.

"How old is this daughter?" Mawuli says, seemingly changing the topic. He gestures toward Grace. And now everyone sees what Tessa had already seen: Grace's puking.

"Grace," Ma says. "Sweetheart." But she doesn't embrace Grace. Neither does Mary Catherine, who finally does cease and desist (the gnawing). Even Yllis hangs back, and that means something given Yllis usually is a sap. Tessa thinks she may have an inkling of what Yllis might be seeing, some aura around Mary Grace warning them all to keep their distance, which Tessa does.

Only Pa seems clueless. He and Mawuli. "Seena?" Pa says. "She's ill," as if Ma were the clueless one. Pa reaches and touches Grace and bursts the aura, and Grace gets a dose of those screaming meemies. Her whimper turns to a wail and her heaving seems a mix of some frenetic tribal dance and an upchuck.

"The girl is marrying age, yes?" Mawuli says. "Even in America she is marrying age. But she is not married, yes?"

"What?" Pa says.

"Mary Grace is eighteen," Ma says, "I told you before . . ." But she looks on the verge of having the screaming meemies herself. She glares from Mawuli to Pa like she can't decide who to murder first.

"I will marry her," Mawuli says. "She will be my wife."

"What in the world?" Ma says.

"I'll be damned if she will," Pa says. "I'll be damned if you will."

We're definitely not in Kansas anymore, Tessa thinks. We're far far away from the *Little House on the Prairie*. Mawuli is no John Boy.

Grace stops shrieking. And puking. "Yes," she says. "Yes. It's what I want."

Mary Catherine

Ad nauseam. It's Latin, meaning "to the point of nausea," according to Mama.

Seems everyone here has reached the point of nausea, with Grace being the example du jour. Even Lint's got the runs. Mama defined the term, ad nauseam, after she'd asked Papa to stop describing ad nauseam the parasites likely to be in the uncooked food and water. "You're scaring the girls, Dick. We want them to *eat*," she'd said, but Mary Catherine knew "the girls" meant her. Ever since Mary Catherine accused Mama of loving Yllis more, Mama has loved Mary Catherine more, but only on the surface and mostly in the form of trying to get her to eat—which has only highlighted the guilt Mama feels for preferring Yllis, which makes Mary Catherine hate Mama more.

Mama. She's just realized Mary Grace is puking, only Grace isn't puking now, she's screeching. Mary Catherine moves toward Mawuli, since he hasn't moved toward her. She wishes Mawuli would take her elbow again, pull her near him again, try to protect her from the world as he opens new worlds—like he did before. But Mawuli glowers at Papa, apparently thinking about how to outwit Papa, not thinking about Mary Catherine.

Passing people stare, but not at Mary Catherine for a change. They stare at screaming Grace, and at Papa and Mawuli, who still volley too many words and looks Mary Catherine can't decode.

But then Mawuli says something Mary Catherine does hear, does understand. He speaks of marriage, and Mary Catherine feels a rush, like from water that's so cold, it feels hot. "I want to marry her," he says.

Mary Catherine is surprised—before she's not surprised. He told her before, didn't he? Mawuli told her he wanted to marry her. She'd believed it was a joke, but it wasn't a joke. Maybe Mary Catherine will marry him. Maybe she will become the queen mother: Mary Catherine, Queen Mother of Avone. She feels drawn to Mawuli, like she's felt drawn to only one other person before. And she actually can imagine living in Africa—despite how scary much of it is—if it means being with Mawuli. So, why not?

Why not?

Because it's Grace he wants, that's why not. "She'll be my wife," Mawuli says, after Mama responds to his question about Grace, telling him Grace's age. "I'll marry her."

"But that's Grace," Mary Catherine nearly says. She thinks for a moment Mawuli's confused them—he thinks Grace is Mary Catherine and Mary Catherine is Grace. But then Mary Catherine remembers she has no hair. And she knows Mawuli hasn't confused them. He knows perfectly well who she is, who Grace is. And she thinks: Mawuli held my earth in his pink palm, and he's dropped it like a bomb. First Father Amadi, then Mama, then Jesus.

Now Mawuli.

"Yes," Grace says. "Yes. That's what I want."

Mary Catherine slips her hand inside her pocket, grips her rosary beads. She feels one bead crack. Then another. Bitch, Mary Catherine thinks. Bitch. How could she? Grace only wants Mawuli to prove she can have him. She doesn't care about Mawuli. She just wants to hurt me.

Mary Catherine longs for the razor. The blade. She wants to hold a different pain. But she has no blades here—not even to shave. Mama forgot them. Even long-legged Grace has to suffer furry legs.

"I want to marry Mawuli," Grace says. "And I will."

"I'll be damned if you will," Papa says.

I'll be damned if you will, Mary Catherine thinks.

Clara

He's coloring the earth now, death is. Or sucking out its color, as the case may be. As Clara stands looking at Egan's face drained by death then blushed pink by some mortician, she can see death out the window of the funeral parlor, absconding with the foliage, leaving the trees looking as naked as she feels. Clara has been stripped clean by the vulture of life. It's not death that's drained her: it's life. Death is just that stranger who's come by again to point out Clara's a stranger to herself, mourning all the things she never wanted.

Clara met Egan in 1920, but she can't remember it. What she remembers is Egan's brother, Emil. Emil had come to the lake directly from university, wearing a pair of plus-four knickerbockers with boots and a belted, one-button coat with large patch pockets. Clara had never seen anyone so beautiful. Having been too young to serve in the war, Emil had a light about him that had dimmed in Egan—and maybe that's why meeting Egan evades Clara's memory, being in the shadow, as he was, while his younger brother blazed. That blazing light sure did fade a year later when Emil blew out his brains, apparently deciding not getting into law school mattered more than the baby he'd planted in Clara.

Egan had served in the war. He'd seen death, he told Clara after they married, while she carried the baby he thought was his. Egan claimed death had a face, that when a person would die, death would climb in, and death's face would mold with the face of the dead, changing the person's features. Clara never got to see death's face on Emil, as he didn't have a face left when he died. She didn't see death's face on her baby, either, because the nurse carried the baby's blue body away before Clara had a chance to know her baby's face. And Egan had insisted they have a closed casket, not wanting to encounter death again himself.

Clara wonders now whether she's looking at death's face—whether Egan's features have been contoured by death's. Truth is, she'll never know. She hasn't seen Egan for years—she can't picture his living face—even though she's looked at him every single solitary day for the past fifty-plus years. Seeing and looking are not the same thing. And now, as usual, it's too damn late.

This is what Clara is thinking when Mary Grace's face merges into Egan's. Grace's long lashes sprout through, draping Egan's closed eyes. Grace's sunburnt nose turns his nose pink. Her cheekbones thrust his sagging skin. Her high forehead stretches his wrinkled one.

Next thing Clara knows, she's supine. How she arrived this way, she couldn't say. She looks up and sees fat-baby angels. It takes a minute before she appreciates it's the painted ceiling of the funeral parlor she sees, not heaven, although she's still quite certain she's dead. She figures she's lying in a coffin now—as stiff and shiny and blushed as embalmed Egan—until she hears the funeral director, Mr. Hayes, speak to her in his funeral-director voice. "Mrs. Eihlerson?" he says, far too slowly given the situation. "Mrs. Eihlerson? You okay?" Clara figures she's either alive or in hell.

"Do I look like I'm okay?" she feels like asking, even as she realizes she's a bit disappointed she is relatively okay, not dead or dying. What on earth does she have to live for?

Then Clara remembers Grace melding with Egan, and she springs up, which she can't say she's done in recent—and not so recent—memory.

"I have to go," she says.

"But the wake . . . ," Mr. Hayes says.

Clara hobbles out the door. It's too late for Egan: he's gone, wake or no wake. Grace is the one Clara's waking for.

When Grace came to Clara's cottage, seeking Clara's guidance, asking Clara to help her with her "situation," Clara told Grace to hold fast to her child, that losing a baby is akin to losing your life—thinking that's how she'd lost her own life, because she'd lost that baby and Emil.

But that's not right, is it? Clara thinks now. That's not right. Clara still had her life: she had Egan—Egan would have loved her till the end of the earth. And she had Grace. Clara is the one who stole her own life and tossed it in the trash.

"But what about Papa?" Grace had said. "He'll kill me, Clara. He will, if he finds out I'm pregnant. And he'll kill Rocky. Or worse. He'll make me marry Rocky, and I can't marry Rocky . . . I can't."

"Do what I did, then," Clara told her. "Find yourself a man quickly you can marry, and marry him. Let him think the baby is his child. And never tell a soul."

Please, Clara thinks now, let me find Grace. Let me tell her I was wrong. *Please*. Just this once let it not be too damn late.

Mary Grace

Mawuli asked Grace to marry him, right then, right there, while she crouched by the latrine. And for the first time Grace could remember, she believed in God. Not that she hadn't believed before, she just hadn't given God much thought. Attending mass, reciting the Our Fathers and the Hail Marys was just something the Slepy girls did: believing wasn't a choice. And because of that, Grace never really considered whether she herself believed.

But now? Grace has proof of God—proof He exists. Proof He actually is paying attention to Grace in particular. Because God answered Grace's prayers: he granted her the impossible.

When Clara told Grace to find a man she wanted to marry, and marry him, what Clara said seemed right even as it seemed ridiculous. And impossible. But it wasn't impossible. It wasn't.

Mawuli is a man Grace respects. Mawuli stands up to Papa—while Rocky stands behind Papa's back, flipping him the bird. Mawuli talks about saving the lives of people in Avone, and throughout West Africa, and throughout the world—he's dedicated himself to this aid organization—while Rocky thinks he's done his good deed for the year if he felt sorry for some trout and exercised catch and release. *And* Mawuli understood Grace when no one but Clara—and Yllis—did. He wants to marry her even knowing what she is, what she's done.

Truth be told, there's something thrilling to Grace about marrying a black man. There is a part of Grace, hidden beneath thick layers of tanning lotion and mascara, that wants to live on the edge. She'd wanted to be the first woman to venture into new worlds at one point, hadn't she? Before she knew about tanning lotion and mascara. And this? This marrying a black man certainly is a new world. Sure, interracial marriages happen, but they hadn't happened to anyone Grace knows. When she thinks back on giving herself to Rocky, she feels like a teenager cliché bordering on white trash. How many times have people intimated Grace has no brain? How many times have people suggested a girl who looks like Grace is sure to wind up getting knocked up? "Better keep your eye on *that* one," people would say to Mama in front of Grace, as if Grace were not only brain dead but deaf and mute. "You might want to think about sending *that* one to a nunnery."

Grace can't say she didn't take some pleasure in their comments—it would be a lie to say she didn't. The comments were intended as a sort of compliment, even if they implied Grace was little but a pretty shell. Truth was, Grace herself no longer was sure she was anything but a pretty shell. It had been so long since she'd made any notable attempt to use her brain. Still, Grace didn't like the intimation she'd end up knocked up. She told herself people were just envious, that their comments stemmed from envy. It didn't follow she would end up knocked up just because some envious people suggested she would.

And then what did Grace do? She got knocked up, and by a boy named Rocky. Rocky. Talk about stereotypes. Marrying Rocky would have confirmed Grace as nothing but a bubble-head blonde who couldn't see beyond pectorals. But when Grace imagines herself being with Mawuli, she feels special, courageous, like the kind of woman others couldn't help but respect. The kind of woman Grace herself could respect. Marrying Mawuli means entering the future. *Being* the future: this is Grace's second chance. Grace doesn't love Mawuli any more than she loves Rocky. But if she marries Mawuli, she won't hate herself.

Grace doesn't expect Mawuli loves her any more than she loves him—although part of her wants to believe he does. Part of her wants to believe they were meant to be: Grace and Mawuli. But Grace is too old to believe in fairy tales. She's too old to believe Mawuli is Prince Charming who's come to save the damsel in distress. Grace knows Mawuli may be using her, too, at some level. Maybe he sees her as his ticket to America. But Grace doesn't care. She needs a short-term fix. The long term is the long term. Grace will deal with that when it comes.

Besides, Mawuli makes Grace feel comfortable. He even likes her ears—which shouldn't matter, but it does. Rocky teased Grace about them, playfully, but still. When Grace asked Mawuli what he thinks—whether her ears are too large—he said long, soft ears like Grace's are a sign of great beauty.

Mawuli and Grace spent the hour planning—the hour after Mawuli discovered Grace puking by the latrine—while Grace's family overslept. Her family was supposed to be getting ready for mass, Grace knew.

But she let them sleep.

While she learned.

About Dipo.

Dipo is a puberty rite for girls. It's a means of preventing promiscuity and unwanted pregnancy. A bit late for that. Nevertheless, the people of Mawuli's home village regard Dipo as essential. Mawuli's family will not allow his marrying Grace if she doesn't undergo it. "You will learn personal hygiene as part of Dipo," Mawuli said to Grace as he inhaled her vomit breath while eyeing her dirty fingernails, greasy hair and wrinkled, reeking clothes.

"You try staying clean and pressed without running water," Grace nearly said. But then she realized somehow he'd managed to do just that.

Maybe Grace does have something to learn.

"What else will I learn through this Dipo?" Grace asked him, still incredulous she'd agreed to marry this man she didn't even know. It feels like a game—the pregnancy, and the idea of marrying anyone—and yet it feels nothing like a game when she's heaving out the lining of her stomach, sure she's on the verge of death.

"You will learn to manage a home and care for children," he'd said.

Grace thought he was joking. Not that she knows anything about caring for a home or children, but it's 1976 not 1956. Still, Mawuli wasn't joking. And Grace couldn't help but think, What will Mama say? Ever since Grace realized she was pregnant, Grace thought about Papa: what he'd think, whom he'd kill. But what would Mama think if she knew Grace would be participating in a ritual where she'd dedicate herself to personal hygiene, home economics and child care? Mama, who clearly regards such endeavors as a waste of time—even though she's dedicated her own life to them.

———

Grace sees the coast now. The fishing boats scattered along the beach look like oversize bicycle seats—banana seats—discarded, each donning a flag not unlike the tassel that flails from Yllis's banana-seat bike at home. According to the driver, they're nearing the first stop on their tour along the coast, a so-called slave castle. Papa insisted they leave Mawuli the morning after Mawuli's public proposal. But Papa believes leaving the city means leaving Mawuli. He's in for a surprise.

Grace sees what may well be the building of torture. She can't say she understands the point of seeing the site of slaves' suffering. Confined as she is in her own personal torture chamber (this *trotro* and her body), she'd rather not have an audience. Isn't it a bit sadistic—voyeuristic—visiting such a place, imagining such a scene? And that they call the buildings where the slaves were housed *castles*. Grace doesn't get it. Seems such places should be bulldozed, not revered. But what does she know?

What does Grace know? She knows she feels she's about to vomit again, but she also knows there's no possible way there's anything left inside her to vomit. She knows her legs are glued with sweat to the plastic seat, and that every time she tries to move—when she takes a crack at the impossible feat of getting comfortable—she skins the backs of her thighs. She knows being with Rocky was the most asinine thing she's ever done, and that's saying a lot given she's done her share of asinine things.

And she knows she's grateful to Mawuli for agreeing to marry her, even with the Dipo.

Avone, the village where Papa is to set up his clinic, is the village of Mawuli's birth. Avone is on the border between the country's Ewe and Krobo regions. Mawuli chose Avone as the location for Papa's clinic because Mawuli's family is there. Although Mawuli's family is Ewe, and his father is the local priest, his family has adopted the local Krobo practice of Dipo. Grace will participate in Dipo there, in Avone. The ceremony will take a week. Then she and Mawuli will marry, and they will be the only ones to know—at least in the short term—that the baby inside Grace is not his. And then? When Papa finishes his African penance, Mawuli will return with the Slepys to the States. They'll leave before the baby is born—Papa himself will insist on this, for sure. The baby will be "premature." No one from Mawuli's family ever will see Rocky's pale Danish skin and pale Danish hair mixed with Grace's pale Polish skin and pale Polish hair. And Papa? Grace expects he'll be so relieved by that pale Polish skin and pale Danish hair, he won't say a word.

Seena

Mawuli is behind them now, still in the city. After his comment yesterday about Mary Grace, it seemed long past time to go. Dick hired a *trotro* to carry them and their supplies along the coast, where they will visit the slave castles before heading to the village of Avone.

Dick managed to arrange within minutes what until this morning he'd deemed impossible: immigration had returned their passports and extended their visas. After Seena's experience with Yllis at the airport, she was well aware that a little bribery goes a long way in West Africa. But this from Dick, a man who called it a sin when Seena convinced the librarian in Grayling to waive an exorbitant fine for an overdue book. "You have to teach the girls responsibility, Seena. You can't go around skirting the rules for your own benefit. If you turned the book in late, pay the fine. It's as simple as that."

Well, apparently it's not as simple as that. At least not when one's eighteen-year-old daughter is involved.

Seena expects Dick was right when he moved quickly to separate Mawuli from Grace, even as she tries to make sense of what still seems senseless: Mawuli's proposal, Mary Grace's response. It's difficult to parse out which was more bizarre. Yet seeing Yllis's and Mary Catherine's expressions as they watched Mawuli and Grace, Seena sensed there was more to the situation than met her eyes—that there just might be some sense to it after all. Is it possible Grace fell in love with Mawuli? And he with her? Like the young priestess Hero and her lover Leander? Or like Pyramus and Thisbe? In just days? Before, Seena would have thought these myths just that: myths. And she would still think such love impossible, if it hadn't happened to her.

But Grace? With an African man? Tennis-playing, cheerleading, sunbathing Grace? The same girl who fell for Rocky Rasmusson?

Then Seena thinks again, It happened to me.

Who would have thought it would happen to Seena? She was as white bread as anyone when she fell in love with Heimdall. She'd interacted with a handful of black men in her life, at most. Yet the color of Heimdall's skin barely entered the equation: the love they shared was color blind.

Maybe Mawuli stirred up something deep and real in Grace.

Mawuli certainly managed to stir up something in Seena.

As the Slepys left the city, Seena hoped by escaping Mawuli's seeing and naming and stirring, she could settle back into her world of make-believe. Because looking back as she is, remembering Heimdall as she is, she feels like Orpheus peering back at Eurydice—like she'll send Heimdall to Hades forever. Even as Seena hoped, however, she knew Mawuli alone hadn't conjured up Heimdall. This country conjures him, even while he's half a world away.

But hasn't he always been half a world away, or more? A world, even. Although he seems, like Yllis, Seena's soul. He seems her body. As Seena jostles in this *trotro,* as Lint cowers beneath her sweating legs, as the bones in her rear feel bruised, as she tumbles to the side toward Yllis and away, forward toward Dick and Mary Catherine and away, backward toward Tessa and Grace and away, her body leaves her. She can't remember which body is hers, which is Heimdall's. She can't remember whose soul is whose. And she thinks, Why does it matter? Both our souls are damned.

"Mama?" Yllis says. She points out the window toward a splattering of children who circle an abandoned building: no doors on its entryway, no glass or screens on the windows. Seena nods to acknowledge she sees the building, she sees the children, that she can imagine the malaria-laden mosquitoes zipping in and out of the building's absent windows and doors. It's too noisy to talk with the *trotro* rattling, the luggage clasps clanging against the *trotro's* metal frame, the wind an orange screamer, spitting through the *trotro's* three open windows (still open, despite Dick's efforts). But Yllis tugs at Seena's blouse; her eyes insist Seena look again. Seena does, and she sees the children are in uniform, this abandoned building is their school.

Seena brought bubble gum to give to these children: bubble gum.

The *trotro* stutters to a stop, and the children fan about it, their uniforms the color of Lake Margrethe sand. "Hi, *Obroni!*" they shout. "How. Are. You. *Obroni?*" Their toothy smiles are bright moon white. Their feet are sandaled; their stomachs are either very thin or very round.

Too round.

"That's from protein deficiency," Dick yells back at Seena, as if he's read her mind—as if he's Yllis. "That widening around the middle." He speaks like he's discussing the dimensions of the surrounding mud houses, not the dimensions of children. Seena feels a surge of rage when she hears this, when she sees Dick's face. He has that look, now, similar to his feigned expression when he asked her, "Is it because you won't be able to ice-skate in Africa, is that why you don't want to go?" He knew when he asked the question that skating on the creek behind their house early on winter mornings—or on Lake Margrethe in early spring—comes as close to religion as anything for Seena. But he also knew skating had nothing to do with Africa, nothing to do with her not wanting to go. There was every other reason in the world not to go: the girls' schooling, the threat of disease, his career.

And the reason Seena would never acknowledge.

Seena reaches into her bag, now, finds the bubble gum. She passes a pack to each of the girls. "Hand it out," she says. She feels ashamed of the gum, but she feels more of something else. "Now. Quickly. Before we pull away. Through the windows."

The girls clamber from their seats, toward the open windows, as Seena tries unsuccessfully to open the window nearest her. When she turns back to face the girls, she sees Mary Catherine already has distributed her pack, apparently fearing the sugar might enter her through osmosis. Seena longs to shake her. "Can't you see these children?" she wants to scream. "Can't you *see*?"

Unaware Seena is watching, Tessa tucks the pack into her shorts' pocket, just as Yllis's pack slips from her hand, out the

window, into the orange dirt. The *trotro's* engine fires as three
of the smallest children leap upon the pack and each other, and
Seena feels sure the pile of them will be crushed beneath the
trotro. "Stop," she shouts. "Stop!" The driver ignores Seena,
but the children jerk back, leaving the gum in the dirt, clearly
thinking Seena was speaking to them. One child lifts the now
pink-orange package from the ground. He holds it between his
thumb and forefinger—as if the gum were fragile—and reaches
toward Seena, trying to hand it to her as the *trotro* pulls away.

When Seena finally turns from the boy, she realizes the girls
are looking at her, as is Dick. She feels the wetness they see—the
tears that grip her chin. Seena is as surprised as they are by these
tears: she is not someone who cries.

Again she thinks of Heimdall. For him, she cried. Yet she's
also crying for this. Why is she crying for this?

And then she knows: she can give these children something
other than bubble gum. She can teach here, in Africa. She
taught her girls to read when they were small. She can teach the
children of Avone to read, and to love reading the way she does.
It will open up a whole new universe for the children, like it did
for her—before she shut the door on that new world.

"It's okay," Seena says now to the girls. And she thinks, It
is okay. Now, it truly is okay. "Sit down, girls. Before you fall."

Grace and Mary Catherine listen, and sit, which is remarkable. Neither is really speaking to Seena, one because she won't
eat, the other because she can't eat. Yllis moves along the aisle
like a caterpillar and crawls in beside Seena. Tessa stands in defi-
ance just to show she can.

How ironic. Seena has two children who won't speak to her

and one to whom she'd rather not speak. Once again she hears Mary Catherine in her head: "You love Yllis more."

Seena wishes she were certain she loved all her girls the same. She wishes she could bridge the distance between herself and Grace, Tess and Catie. But no one taught her how to bridge the distance; no one mothered her. Her grandmother took her in, owned her. But she had raised her children. She was done raising children. She felt affection for Seena—that was clear— but underlying the affection was resentment, bitterness. Not a mother's love. Seena has no memory of feeling a mother's love. How is she supposed to know motherly love? She's been playing the role of mother, like Dick plans to play doctor. But neither of them knows what they're doing.

Yet Seena didn't always feel this way. When Grace, Catie and Tessa were small, she'd felt swarmed by her love for them, hadn't she? It ran rampant, this love, and Seena had found herself petrified of herself—of her feelings. Love was unpredictable, love didn't last: it died or vanished or changed its mind. And because of this, Seena yanked in the love, harnessed it. She tucked it away and forgot it. But then Yllis was born, and she couldn't forget the love. It was a torrent. A terrifying torrent.

The *trotro* hits a bump—a bigger bump—and Tessa hits the roof, literally. Her head slams hard. The sound is audible despite the clanking and blowing. Part of Seena can't help but think Tessa deserves it, after she swiped that gum, after her disobedience now. But the other part of Seena is horrified by her own coolness. "Tessa, sweetie," she says. And she tries to rise, to ease her way around Yllis, reach Tessa. But Seena gets bounced back down as the *trotro* hits a pothole and sinks a good foot. By the

time Seena recovers enough to try again, Dick has reached Tessa
and is comforting her, and Tessa lets him, proof she's not fak-
ing it—as she's been known to do, seemingly for the pleasure of
watching others jump.

The *trotro* takes a blind curve, and the driver speeds up, toot-
ing the horn as if he derives joy from noise—as Tessa used to as
a toddler, whenever she could steal her way into the front seat,
lay on the horn. But, when Seena hears another horn respond,
she realizes this honking has a purpose on this one-lane road:
the preservation of life. The *trotro's* brakes screech and the
trotro runs off the road, into what may as well be the road (it's
all relatively the same), as an oncoming taxi barrels by, blowing
the orange dust into an orange cloud. Seena longs to float away
with the dust; she longs for each of them to float safely away.

Instead, she sinks into the seat, as best she can, as the *trotro*
returns to the one-lane road and they again play what Seena
now understands is the West African version of Russian roulette.
What if they hadn't heard the taxi's horn?

Bang. You're dead.

Seena closes her eyes again, in part to shut out the sight of
Lint's vomit, which she only just saw and which lies inches from
her flip-flops. Apparently Lint feels the same way about West
African roulette as Seena. She can't clean up the vomit, best to
not see it. Seena strokes Lint now, with eyes closed. The feel of
his fur reminds her of home, of the living room in Midland, the
last place she recalls petting him before now. If she believed in
God, she'd pray to be back there now.

She wishes there were a God to whom she could pray.
Let us get back home alive. Let us survive this trotro. *Let Mary*

Catherine eat. *Let* Grace *eat. Let Tessa stop acting spoiled and selfish and reckless. Let Yllis stop looking for answers she doesn't want. Let Dick forgive me, even if he doesn't know what he's forgiving.*

But Seena wasn't raised to believe in God. Her grandmother considered herself an intellectual, and she scoffed at faith. And Dick's faith? Early on in their relationship Seena had been moved by his beliefs, even if she herself couldn't fathom believing as he did. But then she found his girly magazines: this was the man who worshipped the Virgin Mary?

Dick was a hypocrite. His faith was a sham.

Heimdall's faith wasn't a sham.

Isn't a sham.

The mere thought of praying returns Heimdall to her, now behind her closed eyes. And she thinks, Can you really seek forgiveness when you still want the thing for which you need forgiveness?

Heimdall now looks in her imagination as he did when she first met him, his hair only beginning to gray. Dick was supposed to have the meeting, not Seena. Dick had arranged an appointment with the local Grayling priest, Father Amadi. Although they didn't own the cottage yet, they spent a month each summer in Grayling, and Dick had insisted the family attend mass while there. He'd been taking the girls to mass—Seena had refused to go. But Dick was on call that weekend, and he was called away, so he arranged for Old Clara to watch the girls, and he arranged for Seena to take his place, forcing her to introduce herself to Father Amadi.

As it turned out, it was Father Amadi who took Dick's place.

The day before Seena met with Father Amadi, she had discovered Dick's stash. She'd been cleaning when she came upon the magazines. At first she thought they had been left there by the previous renter. They couldn't be Dick's—Dick was a religious man. And Dick loved her. He told her when they made love: she was the only woman in the world to him.

She'd left the magazines where they were—not knowing what to do with them—only to find, the next morning, the pile rearranged. The magazine with the cover of the bulbous-breasted brunette no longer topped the stack. It had been replaced by the rear-facing blonde, long legs spread-eagle.

The magazines were Dick's. They were.

And this reality: what did it make Seena?

An object, that's what she was. Another object. A piece of meat. Not a thinking, feeling human being. Why hadn't she realized this before? To Dick, she may as well have been paper. Just like she'd become to her father and her brothers: nothing but a person on paper. But, for Dick, paper couldn't have sex. Dick was obsessed with Seena before he even knew her. Meaning he wasn't obsessed with *her*. Seena knew this—and yet she didn't, did she? The first time Seena and Dick made love, Seena fell in love with the idea of love: the idea of being in love, the idea of being *loved*. *At least someone loved her*. If not her father, if not her brothers, than *someone*. And over time, she'd come to care about Dick. To love him?

No. How foolish could she be? She and Dick weren't in love. Dick adored her eyes, she knew. He adored her neck, she knew. Dick told her these things when they had sex. But she was not her eyes, she was not her neck. Or was she? Is this what she'd become? Yes. What else was she? She, who'd been given up by her father. She, who'd been forgotten by her brothers. She, who'd given up the schooling she so loved to marry someone who didn't love her. She, Seena Michels, had become Christina Slepy: eyes and neck.

These are the thoughts and feelings that tortured this paper woman whom Seena had become. And these are the thoughts and feelings she carried to Father Amadi.

Heimdall Amadi. The name still ripples through her. Half Scandinavian, half African, his face seemed to embody the world. He was wearing his clerical garb, his Roman collar, garb which until that time seemed the equivalent of a costume to Seena, nothing more. But in that hour while he spoke with Seena, as she looked for answers in his pale blue eyes, the black clothing and white collar became far more: a wall between them, his wedding ring, a podium on which he stood far above her. And she was overwhelmed with the yearning to knock down the wall, remove the ring, lead him down.

She was not yet thirty, then. He was not yet forty. She had three children, all named Mary. He had a flock of children, none his own. She had a husband she didn't love because she was a person who had no faith in love. He had no wife, but he was married nonetheless, because he was a man for whom living and loving were indelibly intertwined. He was a man, but to Seena he was a freak. Because Seena believed love lived in literature, mythology: between Alcyone and Ceyx, Hero and Leander, Orpheus and Eurydice. Not in real life. Real life was messy. Even lovemaking was a messy business. Something to be tolerated, not exalted. She could intellectualize romantic love, but not feel it. She could parse it, explain it, rationalize it, but she couldn't experience it. And she wondered, Does anyone? Or is sexual love a human fabrication, some glorification of our animal instinct? Because instinct, she had. Has. The first time she made love to Dick, instinct won out, no question. As did biology: Mary Grace. But love?

These are the things Seena told Heimdall Amadi—these are the things she confessed. She, who had maligned the idea of confession, found herself confessing away.

And his answer to her: "Yes, Seena. Love."

He told her his experience of love became the foundation of his belief in God. He explained how his rational mind could make a compelling argument against the existence of God, but his experience of love was more powerful than his brain could hold. "Love opened me to the mysteries that lie everywhere," he said. "My faith doesn't rest in any doctrine—not really. It grows out of a respect for—an awe of—those mysteries. So much of life we can't explain, not with our rational minds. Science abounds with what we don't know, what we can't explain. Gravity, for instance. You understand gravity, right? The apple falls from the tree, et cetera. But the fact is, you don't understand gravity. No one really does. Scientists can describe how gravity works—not why it works the way it does. Science often explains the how, not the why. And sometimes science can't even explain the how. The speed of light. Nothing can go faster, right? But there are particles—quantum particles. They respond to one another, immediately, even when millions of miles separate them. How can this be, when nothing is faster than the speed of light? Mysteries lie everywhere, Seena. For me, faith is being open to those mysteries—being open to what we can't understand, what we can't explain. And love. Love is one of those mysteries. Love between a man and a woman is, perhaps, the most powerful mystery of all."

"But you're a priest . . . ," Seena said.

"Yes," Father Amadi said, and he laughed. "That I am."

Seena thinks back on this conversation as the slave castle appears in the distance, and she knows: she and Heimdall are those quantum particles. They are connected—and always will be—even though a universe lies between them. Because in Heimdall's spoken words, Seena found herself baptized, born anew. This man who made her feel safe—so safe she'd opened up to him, allowed herself to be vulnerable in front of him— believed in love. Maybe true love was possible.

Maybe she could love and be loved and be safe. Maybe love was, in fact, a powerful, beautiful mystery. Perhaps the most powerful mystery of all. Maybe love did not equal abandonment. Or betrayal. Maybe love wasn't a myth. Until this moment, when Seena had permitted herself to feel tenderness toward her daughters, so often the fear that love was fragile and fleeting would grip her by the throat, steal her breath, steal the love. Then she'd found Dick's girly magazines, and she knew the love she'd thought she felt for Dick wasn't love at all, and the love she'd thought Dick felt for her was nothing but a cruel joke.

Love was a cruel joke.

But it wasn't. Sitting across from Heimdall Amadi, Seena realized love could happen. It was *happening*. Seena longed to know this man, his mind, his body. She longed to understand his past, fears and dreams. She wanted to know what made him laugh, what made him weep. She yearned to be familiar with even the most mundane aspects of his life. And the passion she felt toward him did not feel like animal instinct. She wanted to explore his body, every inch of it. She wanted to love his body, not procreate. Seena *wanted* to love. For the first time in her life, she wanted to love, not just be loved. Before when she'd felt love sneak into her heart and mind, fear had risen up, tried to stamp the love out. Then Dick's girly magazines had landed the final kick, and love became the last thing Seena wanted.

Until this moment.

Then, for a time, love became the only thing Seena wanted.

Yllis

Love is not what I thought.

Love is impatient. It's not always kind. It does envy, it does boast. At times it is proud and rude and self-seeking. And easily angered. It does, now and then, keep a record of wrongs. And it doesn't always avoid evil or rejoice in truth. It can't always protect. It doesn't always trust or persevere: sometimes love fails.

Until Africa, I'd believed love had one taste. The taste could be stronger or fainter, hotter or colder, but its essence remained the same. And while I knew hate and love sometimes mixed—that love could be peppered with hate yet still be love—I hadn't realized hate is integral to love, that it's within the reach of love's expanse. I hadn't realized what makes love Love is not its consistency, but its malleability, its magnanimity. Its abundance: love holds it all. Love is ugly and full of hate even as it's tender and kind. There's nothing pure about love. It's the impurity that is love. I know that now.

Love *hopes* to be patient. It *hopes* to be kind. It *hopes* to not envy or boast or be proud. It *hopes* to persevere.

But love is not perfect.

I tell myself this now. Every day.

Yet as I moved through the colors and smells and tastes of Africa—as the colors and smells and tastes moved through me—I didn't know this about love. I longed to hold fast to the only taste of love I recognized. I wanted to bottle up the love I had, keep it safe, never let it change. I was willing to open the bottle, let more love in. But I wasn't willing to let any seep out.

If you love something set it free?

No.

Love's not yours to set free.

Love's not mine.

It didn't matter whether I was willing to let love seep.

Love seeps. And it grows. And it dries up even as it blooms.

I should have realized this. Just knowing Tessa's heart, I should have realized this. Just watching love starve Mary Catherine as Grace starved love, I should have seen the signs. Even looking at Mama and Papa, I should have recognized the chameleon of love. I'm the one who should have accepted the chameleon. I'm the one who should have stood up for it, protected it. I should have told Mama and Papa—and my sisters, too—that love can withstand a lot. I should have told myself this: that love is hardy because it's impure.

Dick

Dick sees the slave castle lording over the dark sand, ominous and white and architecturally out of sync with its surroundings. Usually Seena, or Yllis, makes these poetic connections, but this one is too obvious for Dick to miss: the ominous, white castle built by the ominous whites to subjugate the dark land and its dark people. Why Dick thought visiting the slave castles was a good idea is lost on him now. Already Dick sees Death everywhere. Already he hears Death taunting, "What can you do to prevent me?" And now he will pass inside a building built by people who did nothing to prevent Death and everything to cause it. And Dick will feel more responsibility to do something and less capable of doing it.

"The castle!" Tessa says, and she points.

Dick turns backward to look at Tessa, but Seena sits in front of her and instead he sees Seena. The yellow of Seena's irises has softened as she's aged, become more golden. Her eyes are less shocking, now—or perhaps Dick has become accustomed to them in a way he expects he'll never become accustomed to Seena herself. He still feels a surge of something primal when he sees her, when he touches her. There are times when he wishes he were a simple primate, an animal driven by instinct, without a conscience, incapable of heartache. Because he longs to mate with her like an animal and to not care that she feels nothing for him. Then he wants to slap her or shake her to make her feel *something*. Just as he'd love to slap around that pugnacious Mawuli who has the audacity to call himself a Christian while performing African voodoo and lusting after his child, his Mary Grace.

Seena is a cold person. She watched Tessa smash her head, and she did nothing but sit and stare. She watched Mary Grace empty her insides, and she appeared more disgusted than anything. When Mary Catherine cut her hair in devotion to God, Seena's primary concern was the loss of hair, not the love of God. And Mary Catherine's fasting? Seena can't imagine such love. She can't imagine anyone would suffer for love. She thinks Mary Catherine is self-centered, that the fasting has little to do with God and much to do with Mary Catherine's need for attention.

And Dick thinks Seena is projecting.

But he loves her anyway—he longs for her. He can't imagine life without her.

In rare moments of lucidity, Dick sees Seena's heart aches, too: for the boy with the pack of gum who turned her yellow eyes red, for the teenage girls who hiss to live, for those with sores and bloated bellies. And in these rare moments he remembers her heart: there was tenderness in their early relationship, wasn't there? There was passion. They barely left their hotel room on their honeymoon. They'd gone to Niagara Falls, but they heard the falls far more than they had opportunity to see them. When Seena was in her last trimester, pregnant with Grace, Dick would lie with his head on her roundness, and she would pet his hair, outline his ear with her pinky. Even when Grace was a toddler and Mary Catherine was a baby—and when Mary Catherine was a toddler and Tessa was a baby—there was a sweetness in Seena. She would make mud pies with Grace and Catie. "Delicious!" she'd say, "Yum, yum!" And she'd pretend to gobble their pies up, smearing mud across her face. The girls would squeal and giggle. "Do it again!" Grace would say. "Eat more!" Catie would say. Seena would blow raspberries onto Tessa's bare tummy, and Tessa would flail her plump baby thighs and wail in delight. When Tessa came down with croup when she was two, Seena stayed awake for three full nights, listening to that seal's bark, watching Tessa breathe, assuring herself the croup hadn't sealed Tessa's tiny throat—that Tessa could breathe. But knowing Seena's heart can feel—that it can ache—is almost more intolerable than believing she is incapable of feeling, because it raises the ultimate question: does her heart ache for him?

Dick has no idea when she was with the damn Indian last. Has it been days or years? He did try to question the girls when they were in Grayling—had they seen anyone unusual around?— but asking the girls questions without being questioned is a rare occurrence. And getting any reliable information from them is rarer still. Yllis and Tessa saw Seena's lover that day in the woods—the day before Dick made the decision to go to Africa. This Dick knows. Did Seena see him around that time, too? And where would she and he meet when they did meet? Where did they meet when they made Yllis? In the cottage Seena later asked Dick to work to the bone to buy and keep?

Damnit. God damnit: the redskin has no right to Seena. He has no right to Yllis. Regardless of blood. It was Dick who took care of Yllis night after night when she was a newborn, warming her bottles, changing her diapers, rocking her as she mourned the absence of her mother—of Seena—who lay delirious with fever, her breast rock hard with mastitis. Dick was there when Yllis said her first word, when she took her first step, when she celebrated her first birthday, mashing her cake into her fist and her fist into her face. Dick was there on her first day of kindergarten. It was Dick who cried at her first communion.

Where's that damn redskin been? The bastard.

Not in Yllis's life.

And now he won't be in Seena's life either, will he?

Death may be in Africa, but at least that son of a bitch is not.

BOOK THREE

West Africa

Victims of murder usually arrive at night.

Dick rarely worked on such victims. Their bodies normally were sent to medical examiners—forensic pathologists—which Dick was not. But occasionally he would be called to do an autopsy on a person believed to have died a natural death, only to discover the death was anything but natural. Dick would be summoned to the lab: an elderly person had stopped breathing in his sleep, or a newborn had died, presumably from SIDS; a long-term sufferer of disease had finally succumbed to disease, or some genetic abnormality had stolen another life.

Seena remembers these calls, there were hundreds of them. The phone's ringing would barrel through her sleep like a siren—a portent of death. Dick would rise from bed, and Seena would watch him move about the dark room. He was an outline, lacking substance: he was a ghost. He would vanish from the room, and Seena would tumble back into luscious sleep where her lover was not a ghost, not a memory, not a longing. And there, with him, Seena would find life while Dick found death.

In the morning, when her lover was again a ghost and Dick was again a man, Seena would hear the story of the lost life.

Normally, Dick would be vague. He wouldn't describe the routine slicing and unfolding and peeling away. He wouldn't speak of the smell, or of the feel of cooled blood wetting rubber gloves. He wouldn't refer to the scalpel or forceps, the blunt-nose scissors or hand saw, or the brain knife, the coronary artery scissors, the electric saw or probes. Instead, while Seena under-cooked the oatmeal or overcooked the eggs, Dick would speak in categories: age, gender, cause of death. He provided further details only on those rare occasions when he himself had been surprised—when he'd expected to find the handiwork of nature and God and instead found the handiwork of man: murder.

Dick would ramble then, fueled by the adrenaline of murder, and Seena would learn of murder victims' activities and pro-pensities—of how they tend to disembark life in the dark, how they must be weighed and measured, how their temperature is taken once and again and again, how samples are plucked at the root, cut from the nails, swiped from the eyes, how orifices are examined, modesty disregarded.

When finally they are sliced, they are sliced in a Y, from the ears to the neck to the pelvis, and the skin is peeled across the larynx, from the face, over the skull. The skull is sawed through, the brain momentarily freed, before it is sliced into sections, like a fruitcake. Then the remaining organs are removed in blocks—the heart with the lungs, the liver with the kidney—as if the pathol-ogist were unpacking a suitcase, unloading the shirts with the shorts, the slacks with the socks. The exposed blood is analyzed and tested, as is the urine and the contents of the stomach: the hallowed last meal is no longer hallowed.

Seena thinks this as she paces the cell of a room—as she

awaits her (last?) meal—before she returns to the schoolhouse to face the questions, the accusations, the misinterpretations. Dick's last meal was sticky *kenkey,* she remembers. It would hardly look different when removed from his stomach than it did before it entered: a whitish-brown glob. Did they find the *kenkey* there in his stomach? Do they slice and peel and swab in Africa as they do at home? It is a horrid thought: Dick in a Y, his brain a fruitcake. Yet it is a dogged thought—it won't leave her. She imagines Dick on the morgue slab even as she endeavors to shut this door, seal out this image.

There was a time—a time before Seena became just another paper girl—when Seena was awed by Dick: by his understanding of the human body, by his composure when faced with the gory details of death, by his devotion to God and to his family. By his devotion to her. When Dick fell, he fell far. His obsession with the intricacies of the body became his obsession with the intricacies of each centerfold. His choice of profession— to work daily with the dead—became evidence to Seena of an unhealthy mind. His seeming devotion to God and his family—his devotion to Seena—were all building blocks of the Dick Slepy charade. Snap a picture, Dick, Seena used to think. Set up the tripod and the timer and snap a picture of your happy family, being protected by you, this God-fearing father and husband who worships the Virgin Mary. Then hang it up alongside your centerfolds.

But just days ago, Seena had again felt awed. By Dick. She'd forgotten she'd ever felt it. Until she felt it again. And then she remembered.

Now she wishes she could forget.

Yllis

They float like jellyfish, the souls. But in air. And they look like jellyfish, hued by their surroundings and see-through, as if they're part there, part not there. Stepping into that slave castle, the souls hung everywhere. The air was thick with them, undulating with them.

I wasn't sure they were souls—not at first. I'd only seen souls in the dark, when I could feel them more than see them: their warm-wet breeze. Souls were a vague outline to me, a moist brush against my nightgown, when I'd pass Papa in the hallway in the middle of the night, in need of a drink of water; when Papa had returned from a midnight call, trailed by a soul that seemed unsure where to go in this life after life. Before entering that slave castle, souls to me were a window into mystery—a window into my realizing that even my eyes only scratched the surface of what there is to know about life and death. Yet seeing those souls packed into the light of the slave castle, I realized this about souls: they can feel.

Because the jelly beings in the slave castle were sad: I saw their shimmer. And they were angry, too. The smell in the castle—that fish-guts stench—was pungent, and it wasn't coming from the nearby ocean. And it wasn't coming just from Papa. It also hovered high and low, depending on the hovering height of the souls. Some of the souls were tiny, the smallest jellies imaginable. But others filled a good amount of space with their see-through presence.

As I think back on those jelly souls now, I wonder whether the size of the souls corresponded to the size of the bodies they'd left behind. Were the largest jelly souls from the brawniest slaves? Were the tiniest souls those of babies trapped—babies who passed on with their mamas before they ever touched the earth? Or did the size of the souls have more to do with the size of the hurt left behind? Could the largest soul have come from the smallest life, depending on the size of the lingering pain? Or was the size normative in a different way, related to the quality of the life lived? Had the largest souls led particularly good lives, or particularly bad? And vice versa, the smallest?

By the time Papa's soul moved on, I knew the jellies were souls, and I knew what to look for when I looked for Papa's. But I didn't know whether to look for a big jelly soul or a small one, or something in between. Because Papa himself was large, as was the hurt left behind, and Papa led a relatively good life, all things considered. But Papa did some very bad things, particularly as the end neared. And maybe those bad things served to shrink his soul, or inflate it.

I wonder now about Gracie's baby's soul. Will it forever be trapped in Africa? Or can souls travel the globe? And if they can travel, then why did the slave souls stay put, clinging to their slave castle as if clinging to life? Why did they not ride out the door like a hitchhiking butterfly on the shirtsleeve of a visitor like me? Why did they not slip through the bars that covered the windows, blow out with a gusting breeze? Or is there some comfort in the familiarity of one's earthly home, even when that home becomes hell on earth? Did the slave souls remain in the slave castle because they didn't want to leave the souls of those they loved?

If that's the case, maybe Gracie's baby's soul will come looking for Grace—looking for the mama she never had the opportunity to love. Maybe she'll come and peek through the windows, like Clara used to do.

Sometimes I imagine Clara's soul and Egan's passing by Deezeezdaplas. Clara's is peering through the windows, of course. Egan is finally able to breathe without his inhaler. It's nice to think of Old Clara floating, given how hard it was for her to walk. I imagine her as a jelly soul with silver tentacles flowing—the tentacles being her hair. You hear stories, you know. And I've heard some about Clara, about how she died. But I'd rather think of her floating and flowing and spying in on me.

I envision being back at Deezeezdaplas, looking out the window and seeing Clara's soul. I imagine it's evening and the lake is a sheet, so still it looks dry, as if Mama could tie on her ice skates, skate on water. The lake seems a mirror of heaven— so peaceful, so vast—as if you could run and jump in and be transported there, to heaven. But what looks like heaven and what is heaven are very different things. And what looks like hell and what is hell are different, too. I remember thinking this when we passed by that school on our way to the slave castle— the school that looked like it had been bombed. The children around it hummed with joy, even as their school appeared a version of hell. I pointed this out to Mama—I tried to point out this amalgam of heaven and hell. But Mama had begun to leave me by then; I couldn't reach her.

Seems to me now if I actually were back at the Danish Landing—if I were to jump into the heaven mirror of Lake Margrethe—I'd fall through the earth and land right back in Africa, because Africa changed me: I'll never escape her. And I'd be in a heaven of sorts, in Africa, being there again with Papa and Gracie's baby; being back in the place that opened my synesthete's eyes. But I'd be in hell, too, being back there with my eyes open.

Before Africa, I knew feeling: joy's humming, melancholy's shimmer, the flavor of love. Because I *was* joy's humming, melancholy's shimmer and the flavor of love. But did I *feel* these feelings? Or was I merely the bearer of others' sins, others' joys, brought into the world like a sacrificial lamb, without a father's love?

In Africa, joy and melancholy and love weren't always where they belonged. When I couldn't get hold of these feelings—when I saw myself without feelings swirling, like I did that snake—I was no longer sure I had a soul.

Mary Tessa

West Africa

Fall 1976

✳ Okay, Tessa's not that much of an icicle. Even if she were, they're in Africa, so a lot of good it would do her. But, she gets it: slavery is appalling to say the least. But what did she have to do with it? She wasn't even alive. Old Clara wasn't even alive. We're talking ages ago.

Humans can be a cruel bunch—there's no question about that. And Tessa can't say she doesn't see a little cruelty in herself, being honest. But slavery? It's the past. Let bygones be bygones. Seriously, people could spend their entire lives regretting all the atrocities committed by their forebears, but what good would come of it? Even in the highly unlikely event there is a God out there racking his Holy Brain in an attempt to understand the barbaric behavior of those made in His image and likeness, seems to Tessa He would rather humans start appreciating what they've got rather than worry about whether and why and how and when their ancestor's ancestor's ancestor was enslaving someone. Americans, in particular, should start counting their lucky stars. Comparing their standard of living to that of people in West Africa? Let's just say Tessa had never squatted over a latrine before coming here, let alone a latrine where the waste on which she's doing the duty appears to be alive—and she's not making that up. She'd never given a second's thought to the water she used when she brushed her teeth before she set foot in Africa. Brushing seemed enough of a nuisance as it was. But here? Here they have to boil the water before they brush, heavily prolonging the nuisance. In Michigan, it seemed they were roughing it at the cottage, where the water is so laden with minerals it can tint Tessa's blond hair orange. But those minerals seem wimpy compared to what's swimming in the water here (Tessa's not referring to people). And let's talk about electricity. Here, it means a lightbulb—one per dwelling—and that's if you're lucky and the power happens to be on, which it isn't a good portion of the time, based on their four days in Africa. And this is *city life*, which apparently is downright luxurious compared to the village where the Slepys are headed.

Anyway, humans have learned their lessons, haven't they? Nobody's enslaving anybody anymore, so Tessa doesn't understand why Pa thinks they need a tour of torture to understand torture so they'll never torture again—unless he's talking about the daily torture he inflicts on his own family: he, the High Priest of Irritability. Besides, Pa's not exactly the most sensitive when it comes to such issues. Consider the way he refers to the Indians at home. You'd think they all were mass murderers given the way Pa warns the girls to stay away from them. They can't even explore the Old Trail anymore without his questioning them about whether they've "spotted" one, as if he's referring to one of the wild beasts he insists they'll see in Africa (lions and tigers and hippos, oh my!), not a human.

Why Pa's suddenly become Mr. Compassionate—transporting them first to Africa and then to the slave castle to witness (further) torture—has gotten Tessa wondering what he's been up to, for what sin he's atoning. Tessa expects Yllis would have some theory about the matter, if Tessa were to ask Yllis, which she won't. Yllis no doubt would start in on her Indian-daddy business, and that while describing the wafting of colors and the seeping of smells and the sounds accompanying the colors and smells, and Tessa would be more convinced than she already is that she's living with Regan MacNeil herself and should seek out a local fetish priest to perform *The Exorcist*.

Speaking of fetish priests, Tessa looks forward to seeing one. She imagines they look something like Gene Simmons, tongue and all. According to Mawuli (whom Tessa liked well enough until he crashed off his rocker, thinking Grace is some catch), the fetish priests are far more entertaining than the purely Catholic variety. Here, in Africa, magic is not relegated to the realm of *Bewitched* and *I Dream of Jeannie*. *Au contraire*. Mawuli's father is a fetish priest. He's called Okomfo and he eats razor blades and hangs out rags each night to appease the flying spirits, while Catholics eat stale wafers they call "flesh" and hang Jesus—their so-called bread of life—from a cross in a rag. Mawuli's father damns those who commit evil by sprinkling them with magic black powder, which causes them to suffer a fatal accident or become deathly ill, while Catholics just send the damned to burn in hell and no one gets to view the burning. Tessa doesn't expect she'll get out of going to mass by communing with a fetish priest, even if the fetish priest in question claims to be a Catholic, which Mawuli's father apparently—and perplexingly—does. But it certainly is worth a try.

At the moment, however, there are no fetish priests flavored Catholic or non-Catholic in the vicinity, as far as Tessa can tell. All she sees from the *trotro* are a beach and boats and a building that looks half prison half palace and which she expects is the castle of slaves. She can't say she's unhappy about getting out of the *trotro,* even if it means a tour of torture. The *trotro* trip has stirred up every organ in her body. She feels like soup inside, despite having swiped that gum in hopes it would settle her stomach (it didn't). Fortunately, her soup stayed inside, unlike the soup of Grace, whose entrails must resemble the Sahara Desert at this point. And Tessa had to sit next to her the whole way (the choice being Grace or Pa, so she took Grace).

Tessa feels a bit bad about having swiped that gum, especially given that it turned out to be for naught. And especially after seeing those children dog-pile. Easing her conscience is the reality that it wouldn't have done the children any good and may have done them harm. Why Ma chose to give malnourished children bubble gum so they can rot out their teeth is just another of the many mysteries involving Ma.

Tessa looks ahead at Ma's neck and the top of Yllis's head, then farther on to Pa's thinning hair and Mary Catherine's absent hair and absent flesh. She wonders if they're all seeing what she's seeing: their next stage of torture is imminent.

"We are to this place," the driver says, which Tessa assumes is confirmation they've arrived.

Mary Catherine shifts in her seat, sits sideways, which makes her next to invisible. She's up to something: making jewelry?

Yet it's her rosary beads she fondles. Most puddle in her skirt. A few she holds in her hands while she restrings them, but the string is short. Bracelet short. Mary Catherine–size bracelet short, meaning it's little larger than ring size. Funny thing, Mary Catherine is older than Tessa. Tessa's growing while Catie's shrinking. Another facet of the Slepy family that functions backward—if that can be called functioning.

Mary Catherine finishes her stringing within seconds. "Tie it on me," she says to Pa. "On my wrist."

"Huh?" Pa says. Apparently not noticing Mary Catherine has just reassembled her rosary into a bracelet, he ties it on her, no questions asked.

Typical. Mary Catherine starves herself to death, apparently while doing a one-eighty on God, and Pa thinks she's just doing some beautifying. Grace pukes herself to death, apparently while doing a one-eighty on love (Mawuli?), and Ma blabbers on about Orpheus and Eurydice. Hello? Yllis is Yllis, which is enough to scare anyone to death—anyone but the members of this head-in-the-fog family. Does any Slepy but Tessa ever pay attention to what's going on? Anyone but Yllis, who doesn't count. The Slepys are all islands unto themselves, and while each island may have clean water and electricity and toilets that flush, being isolated on an island is lonely indeed.

A string of women pass by the *trotro*. Each has a baby tied snug to her back. How many babies has Tessa seen since they've been in Africa? Seems nearly every female over the age of seven has a baby in tow. But Tessa has not heard one baby cry. Not one. The West African people may be wanting in material comforts, yet they sure seem to know something about comforting.

The *trotro* shudders and dies, and Pa directs the girls out of the bus. They climb down, the four of them: Marsha, Jan and Cindy Brady. And Yllis. A crowd appears from out of nowhere, which is ordinary here in Africa. Whenever the Bradys show up, people sprout up out of the dirt. The eyes of these particular sprouts crawl first across Mary Catherine's white stick legs and her white stick arms and her peach-fuzz head. Then they move on to Grace. The men, in particular, study Grace. Their eyes linger mostly on her legs, which have turned more golden in the African sun and even Tessa has to admit are something to see. Then the onlookers check out Tessa. No one pays any heed to Yllis, which also is usual.

Ma exits the bus looking like she's journeyed to hell and back. Then Pa exits looking like he's not so sure this slave endeavor was a particularly astute idea after all. Various of the admirers approach and offer to guide a tour of the slave castle, but the driver hollers something in what Tessa thinks is Ewe and the guides disperse, leaving the Slepys looking as lost as Tessa expects they feel. "What are we doing here?" Pa's body seems to say. He swings his arms to and fro, like he can't figure out where to put them, and his feet stir up a small cloud. Mary Catherine fingers her rosary, which is what Mary Catherine typically does when she's not consuming dead nails. Only this time her rosary is a bracelet, and rather than finger-count the beads as would be the norm, she sort of spins them around the twig that's her forearm. Grace looks on the verge of puking, of course. And Ma gazes at Mary Catherine's dry lips while licking her own dry lips.

Only Yllis appears to know how they got here.

"So?" Tessa says. "Shall we?" But what she feels like saying is, "Chickens!" Tessa figures she'll lead the train. This wasn't her idea, but she's not chickenshit.

But Yllis beats her to the punch. Yllis is halfway to the castle when Tessa catches up with her. "What are you doing, midget?"

"This place hurts," Yllis says.

Here we go, Tessa thinks. "Places can't hurt, Yllis. They can't feel. They're not *alive*."

"I know that," Yllis says, and Tessa thinks, You do? "It hurts me," Yllis says. "This place hurts *me*."

She's telling the truth, Tessa knows, and Tessa feels a little jealous. Not that she's a masochist or anything, but sometimes she wishes she could experience things the way Yllis does—sometimes Tessa feels she's missing out.

Pa gets his rear in gear and pays. They enter the building through two massive dark doors over which hangs a sign reading, DOOR OF RETURN, and Tessa wants to ask, "Do we have to?" The building looks a bit like the fort on Mackinac Island back at home, the fort through which Pa dragged the girls, lecturing all the while about the American Revolution and the War of 1812. And all the while the girls wished they were peddling around the island or splashing in icy Lake Huron or eating Murdick's fudge.

The slave castle's interior is anticlimactic: an uneven stone floor, peeling white walls, arched doorways, shuttered windows above a courtyard, potted plants that pepper the courtyard. They paid for a horror movie and got Walt Disney. This is what they drove here to witness? This experience is supposed to be life altering? Other than annoyance, all Tessa feels is achy and itchy and a bit nauseous, and how much she'd like to exit through that DOOR OF RETURN.

But then she notices Yllis. "What do you see?" Tessa asks Yllis. She's surprised to hear herself ask this, yet she wants to know. Because Yllis definitely is looking at something Tessa can't see and feeling something Tessa can't feel. Most of the time Tessa thinks Yllis is the looniest of them all. In this rare moment, Tessa wonders whether she and the other Bradys are the loonier ones. Yllis is dealing with being here in her Yllis sort of way. The rest of them? They're not dealing. Tessa's trying to make a joke out of something that's just not funny, and the others still appear to be doing what they were doing when they first exited the *trotro*: wondering where they are and how they got here. And this includes Pa, who's the one who actually decided where they are and how they got here.

"I'm not sure," Yllis says. "I'm not sure what they are."

Tessa tries to follow the path of Yllis's eyes, to see the "they" she refers to. But Tessa sees only floating dust particles in a stream of sun. Why, then, does she feel different all of a sudden? Why does she feel she's being watched? She looks around, expecting to find the eyes she feels, but all she sees are tourists and Ma, and not one of them looks at Tessa. Still, something grips Tessa inside, like a sticky fist.

Tessa hadn't heard Ma approach. Ma clasps Yllis's hand. Tessa clasps Ma's. Ma looks as amazed as Tessa feels that Tessa just took her hand. Still, Ma gives Tessa's hand a squeeze. Together the three pass through what soon becomes the horror movie Tessa longed for, and Tessa wonders why she longed for it.

They walk under one placard, around another placard, over a

third placard, and as they step into the cold confines of the MALE SLAVE DUNGEON and the WOMEN'S DUNGEON, Tessa's imagination becomes the movie reel. And by the time they reach the door that leads directly to the ocean—the door from which the slaves embarked on their journey across the sea—Tessa squeezes Ma's hand so tight, she knows she's hurting Ma, but she just wants to make sure Ma doesn't let her go.

Because the placard above the door, describing the door? It's clear: THE DOOR OF NO RETURN.

You get one life, Tessa thinks. You may as well live it up?

Those slaves, they had one life, too. And what happened to that life? It got snatched, as if it meant nothing at all. Snatched by people like Tessa's family—people who believe living alone in comfort on a desert island is living.

Mary Catherine

Transubstantiation. The term describes the bread and wine transforming, becoming Christ's body and His blood. But transubstantiation is different from transforming. It's the opposite in a lot of ways, because the bread and wine don't change in appearance, they don't come to look like flesh and blood. But their substance changes. It's like that term Yllis uses, prestidigitation. "Your eyes tell you one thing," Yllis says, "but your brain tells you another, and it's hard to make your brain and eyes agree." During the Eucharist, your brain tells you the wafer is Jesus' flesh and the wine is His blood, but your eyes are convinced they see just another stale wafer and glass of germy wine. And it's hard to make your brain and eyes agree.

It's hard for Mary Catherine to make her brain and eyes agree, and this has nothing to do with her not eating, not drinking. Nothing to do with the fact that her brain has become a slow-moving *trotro,* low on fuel. Nothing to do with her eyes seeing things she imagines no one but Yllis normally sees, hallucinating as she's doing here and there, from dehydration, she expects. No, every time Mary Catherine thinks of that scene with Mawuli and Grace—every time she pictures it in her mind's eye—it's sharp in her dry eye and sharp in her starved brain. And, still, she can't make her brain agree with her eye. Why would he want to marry her? Why?

Saint Catherine had visions. She'd see into heaven, and into purgatory and hell. Mary Catherine is like Saint Catherine after all: she saw directly into heaven and purgatory, and now she's seeing into hell. Her heaven was Mawuli, her purgatory was waiting to be near him again, and her hell is the realization that Mawuli wants Grace.

Mary Catherine longs to cut herself, to hold the blade between her thumb and forefinger and slice. She wants to see her white flesh pop free, she wants to see the bursting blood. She wants to feel that pain only she can cause—the pain she can control.

From the moment they arrived in Africa, Mary Catherine noticed Mawuli looking at her. She wouldn't have admitted it before—she wouldn't have admitted to liking his looking. But he was looking, and not like the others here who look at Mary Catherine like she's some freak, and who offer to marry her anyway. Mawuli looked at Mary Catherine and saw a woman, and for the first time in her whole life, she felt like a woman: not a little girl trying to be a woman, not a child mistaking priestly love for human love, not a younger sister needing to be Holier Than Thou, not a middle daughter needing to stand out, be loved. Not a teenager wasting her brain on Play-Doh. And although she felt scared inside—of all the scary things in this country—she felt alive, too. She felt she had something to live for—something to be scared of losing. It seemed she'd undergone her own transubstantiation. She looked the same, but her substance had changed.

Only it hadn't.

That something she thought she had to live for? She lost it, just like that.

Mawuli wants Grace.

And Mary Catherine knows she's a fool. She's the magical Rudolph the Red-nosed Lizard with Porcupine Quills whose tricks have fooled only herself.

She needs to sit down. Mary Catherine stands on the path between the castle and the *trotro*, but she needs to sit down. It feels like someone's stuck in a needle, drained her of all blood. Even if she had a blade—if she were to cut—she'd be dry inside. Dry.

The distance from where she sits to the *trotro* seems like the distance from Africa to Michigan—and not just the physical distance. It's a gap that feels more and more impassable each day they're here, even though they are here—like the more time they spend in Africa, the harder it is for them to find it. Does that make any sense? Mary Catherine's brain is oatmeal. Or *fufu*.

Mary Catherine sits. As her rear sinks into the clay, she wonders whether transubstantiation is just some fantasy. Is the bread and wine like her? Just bread and wine mixed with hocus-pocus? And what of the rosary—that string of holy beads with which she'd journeyed through the Seven Sorrows and Fifteen Mysteries, prayed the Hail Mary and the Our Father, meditated on the Holy Face of Jesus and the Sacred Heart?

Mary Catherine looks ahead at the odd threesome of Mama, Yllis and Tessa, who'd left the castle before she did and now have nearly reached the *trotro*. They've yet to look back at the puddle that is Mary Catherine. Mary Catherine's fingers tally her rosary beads and find far too few. Then she remembers the remaining beads await her in the *trotro*. She'll make earrings with those. Maybe a choker, like Mama's pearls. Because the rosary does seem hocus-pocus. What did it get Mary Catherine? She has fingered those beads countless times, counting her countless prayers of devotion, only to have her prayers denied.

Grace had exited the slave castle before the rest, claiming she needed fresh air, and she circles the *trotro* now, her bare legs like neon signs reading, LOOK AT ME! LOOK AT ME! As Mary Catherine watches her, she thinks of a few other things Grace needs, namely a brain and that mirror mirror on the wall to tell her she's not the fairest of them all—despite her trying to be a Nair girl even here, daring to wear short shorts in a country where it's rare to see a woman's ankle, let alone her knee. Idiot.

Mary Catherine forces herself to try to stand up, urged on by the desire to board the *trotro* before Grace, determined to not get stuck sitting next to Grace. No one has noticed Mary Catherine in the dirt, anyway. They probably would have been halfway to the next slave castle before they realized she was missing. That wouldn't have happened if Mawuli were with them. He'd have noticed she was missing when she first sat down. He wouldn't have left her sitting here, wasting away. He would have come to her, helped her up. He would have found something for her to drink that appealed to her more than it repulsed her. He would have urged her to eat a banana, like he did before. "It has a tough skin," he'd said to her. "But when the peel is removed, inside it is sweet and pure, like you."

Mary Catherine thinks this, then she thinks again of Grace, and she feels more than ever she'd rather dry up like sun-baked dung than sit next to Grace on that *trotro*. But whenever Mary Catherine tries to stand she's caught in some wave—or some whirlpool, like she's being flushed.

Flushed. Mary Catherine sits back down. She never thought she'd have fond memories of flushing.

Or of toilet paper, for that matter. Fortunately Mama's taken to carrying tissue with her everywhere. As it doesn't seem to be anywhere.

The last time Mary Catherine used a toilet, which had nothing to do with flushing, Mama gave her tissue, and she saw her urine on it. The urine was thick and brown, as if infused with Africa.

Mary Catherine finally manages to overpower the flush. She stands, stumbles forward. But soon she's hit with another wave. She hangs her head, like she's Grace, like she's puking. And she waits for the wave to wash away. It does. Mary Catherine then pieces together every single solitary particle of energy she can muster, and somehow she manages to cross the impassable divide. She boards the *trotro* before Grace does, determined to seal her fate: keep Grace far far away.

But Tessa thinks along the same lines and trumps her. "I'm not sitting next to Grace again," Tessa says, just after Mary Catherine boards the *trotro*. "I risked life and limb once—risked having my limbs puked on. It's someone else's turn to be the target. I'm sitting by Ma."

"But I'm sitting with Mama," Yllis says. "I was sitting with Mama."

"Actually, girls," Seena says, "I need to sit next to your papa. I need to talk with him before we get to Avone."

Outside the *trotro*, Papa stands urging Lint to empty his insides, assumingly so Lint won't have anything more to empty on Mama.

"But?" Yllis says.

"I'll sit with you this time," Mary Catherine says to Yllis. Mary Catherine will not be the duck sitting. She will not allow Mary Grace to set her sights on her. It's not the vomiting Mary Catherine is concerned with. It's just Grace: her stuck-up, self-absorbed self. Mary Catherine can't bear the thought of listening to Grace drone on about HORRIBLE Africa or her GOD-AWFUL stomachache or her LONGING for home— and all this while Mary Catherine starves to death and thirsts to death and is moments from death.

And Mary Catherine certainly does not want to hear any nauseating account of Grace FALLING IN LOVE.

Mary Catherine scoots in next to Yllis.

"That's not fair," Tessa says to no one in particular.

Yllis looks somewhat ambivalent about sitting next to Mary Catherine, probably because this not eating and not drinking has made Mary Catherine irritable. "You don't want to get stuck sitting with Gracie either," Mary Catherine says to Yllis. "Trust me."

Trust me, Mary Catherine thinks: trust *me*. From now on Mary Catherine will not rely on God or Jesus or any facet of the Holy Trinity to take care of her. The Holy Trinity has served Mary Catherine about as well as the Unholy Trinity (that is, Mama, Yllis and Tessa) that boarded the bus before Mary Catherine did. Both trinities probably would have Mary Catherine sacrifice herself—offer up her earthly body as a receptacle for Grace's literal and figurative run at the mouth. No thank you.

Mary Catherine looks at Yllis's scrunched-up face. She expects Yllis wants to say something nice about Grace. "I feel sorry for her," she can imagine Yllis saying. "I don't mind sitting next to her." But Yllis is astute enough to keep the sugar to herself. Mary Catherine is starving and thirsty and feeling homicidal. She imagines her eyes, which Yllis eyes now, look wild, given she can't stop their shifting.

"Catie, what's purgatory?" Yllis says, still looking pouty, but clearly doing her own shifting. Yllis's question would seem out of the blue if it weren't coming from Yllis.

Mary Catherine doesn't answer.

Papa and Grace climb onto the *trotro*.

"Dick," Mama says. "Sit with me."

Grace deposits herself next to Tessa, who's clearly doing her own pouting.

"What's purgatory?" Yllis says again.

The driver fires the engine and barrels forward and Papa drops partly into his seat, partly on Mama.

"It's having to visit slave castles," Tessa calls back. "More. Even when visiting one is more than enough."

"It'll be okay," Mama says—to Tessa, Mary Catherine assumes—although she's not sure why Mama says this, what she means. What will be okay?

"Purgatory is an essential element in the Cycle of Redemption," Mary Catherine says, quoting word for word from catechism, amazed she can remember anything given how worn down she feels. And amazed she can sound so convincing given she's no longer sure she believes a word she says. "We're all sinners, you know, Yllis. Each of us. We came into the world tainted by Original Sin. And we all sin. Some of us more than others." Mary Catherine looks at Grace, trying to think of a way to use Grace as an example. "And some of us commit mortal sins. You know, like adultery. And murder." Mary Catherine is confident Yllis knows what these things are: adultery, murder. Tessa loves teaching Yllis anything and everything R-rated. "And for those mortal sins," Mary Catherine says, "people go to hell."

"Just like that?" Yllis says. "You get one chance?"

"Pretty much."

"But aren't there exceptions? There must be exceptions. What about that capital punishment Papa talks about? And what if . . ."

"What?"

"I don't know," Yllis says.

"Well, I don't know either . . ." Mary Catherine needs to sleep. "You can ask Father Amadi when we go back home. He'd know." But Mary Catherine wishes she hadn't mentioned Father Amadi. She doesn't want him in her brain. She puts her head on Yllis's shoulder. Yllis is so short, Mary Catherine may as well put her head on Yllis's lap, which she does.

Yllis strokes Mary Catherine's hair—what's left of it. "But what about purgatory?" she says. "What does that have to do with purgatory?"

Mary Catherine would like to tell Yllis to leave her alone, let her sleep. Shouldn't Yllis herself have learned about purgatory in catechism? But Yllis is being so sweet, petting her. Besides, until just seconds ago, Mama was talking nonstop to Papa, something about Avone and teaching. Actually, she was more or less yelling, apparently so Papa would be able to hear despite what Mama calls "the shake, rattle and roll" of the *trotro*. It would be hard to sleep now, anyway, given all the noise. "Well, there are other sins besides mortal sins," Mary Catherine says into Yllis's skirt, which she sees is way dirtier than anything Yllis wears at home, and Yllis is not the cleanest. "Like when Mama serves us meat on Friday, or you tell a white lie. Sins you commit even though your heart is in the right place." Mary Catherine turns her head to face upward, away from Yllis's skirt, which stinks. And she notices the sweat beads that hang on Mama's neck. The curls around Mama's hairline are dark—must be wet—and her back is board straight, her shoulders high. If Mary Catherine were to touch those shoulders, she knows from experience they'd be rock hard. Something about Mama's conversation with Papa has made Mama tense.

"Those sins are called venial sins," Mary Catherine continues. "If you die with some of those lesser sins not atoned for—like if you haven't done penance for them—then you go to purgatory. And the souls in purgatory, well, they still suffer a lot. But it's not like being in hell." Hell actually sounds kind of nice at the moment: Mary Catherine is freezing. *Freezing.* Even though Yllis is a furnace. Even though Mama is just inches away and she's melting. Even though Mary Catherine could see the heat outdoors, and that wasn't due to the flushing. "And, eventually, the souls get out of purgatory. So it all works out in the end."

Mama turns. "Stop!" she says. "Just stop it. Stop scaring Yllis."

"I'm not scaring her," Mary Catherine says. She would like to sit up, say it to Mama's face. But she can't. Mary Catherine's body has an agenda that has nothing to do with what Mary Catherine thinks she wants.

"Tell me, Catie," Mama says. "Is it murder if you kill yourself? Or is killing yourself just a venial sin? Do you just go to purgatory?"

Mary Catherine sees fire shoot out of Mama's eyes. Real fire. But she knows she's hallucinating. If Mama's eyes were burning, her whole face would be burning. And it's not. But the brightness: it's too bright. It hurts Mary Catherine's eyes. She lifts one hand with what seems ridiculous effort, and she covers her eyes. But the burning light doesn't go away.

"Is it a real place?" Yllis whispers, and Mary Catherine knows Mama must have looked away, despite the light. Otherwise Yllis wouldn't be asking. "Or are the souls just stuck here for a while? Like a bird with a broken wing? You know, like the bird knows its nest is up there waiting? Like the nest is heaven. But the souls just can't seem to get off the earth?"

She is asking all of this for a reason, Mary Catherine thinks in a blur. What is it?

"Are you planning to do something you shouldn't, Yllis?" Mary Catherine says, but barely.

Just barely.

And the light goes out.

Clara

Danish Landing, Michigan
Fall 1976

Amadi. He's the man.

Clara doesn't even know where the Slepys make their home when they're not at Deezeezdaplas. When they're in Grayling, Deezeezdaplas seems the only place on earth. She never thought to ask them—not even Mary Grace. The Danish Landing has a way of making you forget, and Clara doesn't think it's just her. You forget there's a world out there that doesn't involve acorns and moss and sunsets and teenagers in bikinis. You forget there's something more important than whether the blueberries are ripe, and if they're not yet ripe—or they're past ripe—then what in heaven's name are you going to put in your pancakes? You forget the country may well elect a peanut farmer as president—unless Dick Slepy insists on reminding you. You forget Comaneci's seven perfect tens. You forget Patty Hearst. You forget the Vietnam War has ended. You don't give a hoot Vietnam is now ruled by communists.

And you forget people live anywhere else, until they're gone. And then you tell yourself you'll ask them next summer. You'll ask them where they go when they leave the Danish Landing, when they leave Deezeezdaplas. But, of course, when the next summer rolls in, you forget to ask. And you tell yourself it doesn't really matter if you know. It doesn't matter that you forget.

Until it does matter.

Now Clara has to track those Slepys down, not knowing a lump about them, other than they are in Africa. Africa. It's a continent, not a city. Not a state. Not even a country. A continent.

And the only person on this planet she can imagine who might have any idea where they've gone is Father Amadi, excepting that Rasmusson child, who also is long gone—and who seems far too young to be making children. But then, who doesn't seem young to Clara?

Father Amadi. The only Catholic priest in town. The only person off the Landing whom Clara knows has had any contact with the Slepys. Having heard a snippet of a conversation on the party line between Seena Slepy and Amadi, Clara is a bit underwhelmed with the man, in all honestly. Mrs. Slepy had been pleading with him to see Mary Catherine—something about Mary Catherine chopping her hair and chopping herself—and Amadi had refused. Said the girl needed professional help. Well, ain't he a professional? Call that the love of Jesus?

But where else is Clara to turn? Amadi might even know something more than Clara's nothing about Africa, given he's one of the few dark-skinned people in the near and not so near environs, the local Indians aside. Clara would venture to guess every single parishioner at that church is the color of Wonder bread. She has to feel for that priest—even if she doesn't like him. He, no doubt, wouldn't choose to reside year-round in Wonder bread Grayling if he had a choice. Then again, who would, excepting the poor, old and decrepit, given winter here is cold and gray and damn long? And imminent. Shit.

Hence, Clara, who was raised a Catholic hater, is off to plead with a Catholic priest to take mercy on an old woman, tell her how to find the Slepys. She figures she's got her work cut out for her. Why should he tell her? She'd like to play the Egan card—that she's recently a widow, that she needs to inform the Slepys of Egan's death (as if they'd care). But skipping out on Egan's wake is one thing. Using his death is quite another. There's not one Slepy who'd give a happy rat's ass Egan's passed. No, she'll have to play it straight with the priest. Tell it like it is, that she can't tell him a damn thing, but she'd like him to tell her where the Slepys are all the same, as she needs to get in touch with them. She doesn't particularly want to get in touch with "them," of course. The only one of "them" she's touching is Grace.

Clara calls up the Dial-a-Ride. "Clara Eihlerson, here. At the Danish Landing. Number 1888. I need a lift to the Catholic church in town." Clara can drive. Managed to fool the DMV yet another time. Her eyes still work. Her legs: that's the problem. Fortunately, she'd had a good day her last go-round with the DMV. But she's not having a good day today.

"Mrs. Eihlerson?" the dispatch person says. "It's Alfred. I used to take Egan . . ." But he stops, starts inhaling as if he were Egan.

And Clara thinks, I'm definitely not having a good day. Chances are this Alfred fellow was at the wake and he's going to want to know about my ditching it.

"I need to see the priest," Clara says, hoping Alfred might think she's seeking solace because of Egan. Maybe that will stop his prying.

No such luck. "You're not Catholic, now are you?" Alfred says. "Aren't all you . . . Danes Lutheran?"

"'OLD Danes' is what you mean, isn't it?" Clara feels like saying. "Aren't all we OLD Danes Lutheran?" But instead Clara lies. "That Mary Grace Slepy—one of the youngsters who summers out at the Landing? Well, she's a Catholic, and she showed me the light." Lit up the sewer, Clara thinks. "You Catholic, Alfred?"

That shuts him up. And the Dial-a-Ride is on its way.

When Clara hears its honking, she realizes she's dozed. She yawns, and a bit of dried spittle cracks in the corner of her mouth. She wipes at the spittle as she hobbles out the door toward the red-and-white Dial-a-Ride parked in the foreground, framed by the red-and-white Deezeezdaplas. It's a bit much to take in when one's just woken up. She feels like she's looking at an inkblot, trying to determine which part of the blot is the Dial-a-Ride, which part is the cottage. Her wrinkled lips themselves feel a bit like dried spittle. She's not sure whether she's still got white crust lining her lips, or whether the crust is just her lips.

She's glad to see the driver is one she doesn't recognize— not Alfred. The driver's name tag reads, BOB—apropos given the way he bounces down the Dial-a-Ride steps. Reminds Clara of one of those Weebles Wobbles. And he's bald to boot.

"You need the lift?" BOB says, referring to the elevator used to raise invalids from the ground to the bus.

"I need *a* lift, not *the* lift." Clara's not riding that elevator, most certainly not with a man who resembles a Weeble. Seems people start riding the elevator up the Dial-a-Ride and next thing they're riding is a hearse. All things being equal, she wouldn't mind the hearse, actually. But all things are not equal, she made damn sure of that. "Do I look like I can't walk?"

BOB's expression indicates that's the very reason he asked if Clara needed the lift.

Clara tries to climb the stairs onto the bus, but her foot refuses to lift more than an inch off the ground. She tries the other foot. Same result. Apparently BOB the Weeble was right: Clara can't walk. Clara feels wobbly herself, like she might fall down. Being a Weeble suddenly doesn't sound all that bad, given Weebles can't fall down.

Clara jams her magic cane into the dirt to steady herself, stop the shaking. Then she uses the cane to try to hoist herself onto the steps. But it seems she's sinking directly into hell, passing right through the earth, not waiting on the hearse. Christ.

She hears the groaning of the lift, hears it rattle to a stop.

"You have a chair?" BOB hops from the ground to the lift, lickety-split.

"Dump that salt right into the wound, BOB," Clara feels like saying.

"Is there a wheelchair inside the cottage?"

Just rub it in, Clara thinks. Rub the salt right in there, make sure I've not a drop of dignity left. "No-I-don't-have-a-wheel-chair." She knows better than to ask whether it looks like she needs one. She shuffles onto the lift. BOB holds her steady as they rise.

At least Clara's not sinking into hell anymore.

But when she sees inside the Dial-a-Ride, she realizes she's wrong. Sinking is a relative term: Clara's sunk. The Dial-a-Ride is full of broken people who drool and shake and ramble and are altogether lopsided.

And Clara knows she belongs right here.

Seena

West Africa

Fall 1976

Mary Catherine is dying.

While the rest of the Slepys visited the second slave castle, Mary Catherine remained in the *trotro*—sleeping, Seena thought. But upon their return, they could not wake her. And now? Now she's the color of mold, like her insides rotted days ago, but the rotting has just reached her surface. Her body has wilted as this new form has spread—this fungus of death. Why did Seena not see this coming?

Even as Seena asks herself this question, she knows she did see this coming. She watched Mary Catherine's cheeks become little but bone as the flesh and skin concealing the bone grew transparent. She watched Mary Catherine's once-small eyes grow huge and her once-full lips wrinkle and parch and become Old Clara's. She watched Mary Catherine's wrists and ankles and knees grow as the rest of her shrank. She watched Catie's body hunch under the burden of her weight that was barely any weight at all. And she watched Yllis hunch, too, weighted with insight: "That quiver around Mary Catherine, Mama. It's different, Mama. As if it's part of her skin. Like a scar." A scar.

Scars. The cutting. Seena saw those, too, the scars that line Cat-ie's inner arm—and she sees the scars now, these steps that lead to hell.

Seena saw this, she heard this. And she dreamed of Heim-dall.

Heimdall was her refuge from worry. Heimdall was her place of peace. Even as he was anything but. Her affair with Heimdall was reckless, dangerous. Yet when she was with him, she felt safer than she'd ever felt, more peace than she'd known. And when she dreams of him now, it feels reckless and dangerous, safe and peaceful. Had she ever felt safe before Heimdall? No. Had she ever felt peace or wonder or passion? Doesn't it make sense, then, that her troubled mind would turn to Heimdall, seek refuge in thoughts of him? Doesn't it?

No, Seena thinks: I watched my daughter starve herself and fantasized about my lover.

"Where's the driver taking us?" Seena says now to Dick, who seems almost more scared than Seena—and Seena is terrified.

Dick doesn't answer. He talks to the driver—tries to talk. The driver either can't understand Dick or doesn't want to. He shakes his head, nods his head, wobbles his head, but not in any discernible pattern that corresponds to Dick's questions.

"Is there a hospital nearby?" Seena says. "Or some sort of clinic? Ask him that, Dick. Tell him we need to go there now."

"Stop it, Seena," Dick says. "Shut up! I can't think."

Dick can't help Mary Catherine: Seena knows this, Dick knows this. Dick examined her and as he did, he turned grayer and grayer, as if the mold had spread to him, too. "She needs to be hydrated, nourished," he'd said, as if Seena didn't know. As if

Grace, Tessa and Yllis didn't know. "She needs an IV. Her heart rate is slow. Way too slow. And her blood pressure. It shouldn't be low like that. I think she needs potassium." It seemed Dick was trying to remember something he'd learned in another life. Seena felt a softening toward him as she saw his longing to be more than he is and to remember more than he can.

"The driver says we have to get out," Dick says now. "He says a taxi will come along."

"Come along? What? You must be kidding. Get *out*? Our daughter needs a doctor." Dick is a doctor. "A hospital. We can't wait for a taxi."

"We don't have a choice. He won't take us."

"Bribe him. You did it to get the visas." Why isn't Dick fighting? Why isn't he yelling? Why didn't he think to bribe? Seena begins to sob. She who doesn't cry, cries and cries. She doesn't mean to cry. She tries to stop herself from crying. What good comes of it? Yet hot tears rush down her face as she heaves and gasps: her daughter is going to die.

"Mama?" Yllis says. She nudges Seena with her shoulder.

Seena ignores her.

"He has a sick child," Dick says, "the driver."

And Seena thinks, Welcome to our world.

"He drove to the capital to get medicine," Dick says, "but he lives here. He was just driving back here. He brought us since he was coming this way. When I hired him, I didn't real- ize . . ."

"Our child is *dying*," Seena says. "And he can't be bothered? She's *dying*. Did you tell him that?"

"Catie's dying?" Yllis says.

"Ma's just saying that," Tessa says to Yllis. "She's just trying to get Pa to do something." Tessa speaks as if Seena can't hear her, as if Dick can't hear her.

But they both hear her. And they both know she's being classic Tessa: the know-it-all who knows-it-not. But then Tessa grips Yllis's grimy hand with her grimy hand and holds on. This gesture is anything but classic Tessa.

"She's not gonna die," Yllis says. It's a statement, not a question. Seena tries to find some solace in this: Yllis the seer doesn't see death. But Seena can't.

Dick looks at his hands. "Two of the driver's children recently died. They were twins. Babies. He has just one child now."

"So we're lucky?" Seena says. "We're lucky since we'll still have three?"

"That's what he said."

"I'm not getting off this *trotro*. He's taking us to a clinic whether he wants to or not. He can go to his damn child afterward." As Seena speaks, Grace climbs from the *trotro* and resumes her dry heaving. "Looks like we may end up with just two children left." Seena gestures toward heaving Grace. "But I guess we'll still be lucky."

As soon as Seena says this, she wishes she could take it back. For the first time, Grace's nausea scares Seena—really scares her. Maybe Grace won't get better. Maybe the death mold will reach Grace, too. Maybe Grace also will be on her deathbed, slipping further and further away from Seena even while Seena remains inches from her.

Maybe Seena will lose two daughters to Africa.

The horseflies and gnats Seena shooed for months swarm

her now. The stench of mold she sealed out now emanates, but from inside her. Seena is the reason Mary Catherine is starving herself. Seena is the reason Grace is here in Africa, not in college. Seena is the reason Grace might die here, too. Seena is the reason Dick brought them to Africa, because Yllis saw what she saw, spoke what she spoke. And although Yllis was wrong, she was right, too. Right enough to start this avalanche.

"There's no clinic nearby," Dick says. "I'm the clinic. Remember? I'm supposed to be the clinic for this region. We need to go to a larger town, or a city. It's too far. He won't take us."

"I'm not getting off," Seena says again.

Mary Catherine seems to be barely breathing—her breaths are so shallow, her chest hardly moves. Seena holds a bag of water and dribbles the water across Mary Catherine's cracked lips. "Catie?" she says, for the hundredth time. She dribbles more water. It runs out of Mary Catherine's mouth and cleans a path to her jaw. "Mary Catherine?"

"She could have a heart attack," Dick says. "It happens. These girls who won't eat."

"'These girls'?" Seena says. "We're talking about Mary Catherine, Dick. Not 'some girl.' You're saying Mary Catherine could have a heart attack?"

"It's her heart," Yllis says.

Yllis is getting on Seena's nerves. In this rare moment, the irritation Tessa and Dick regularly display toward Yllis feels justified. It seems Tessa and Seena have swapped skins: Tessa coddles Yllis while Seena feels like throttling her.

Seena looks past Yllis and Tessa to Mary Grace. Grace sits

in the dirt. Her head hangs between her splayed knees. Her pink panties are visible, extending just beyond the crotch of her shorts. Why did Dick allow her to wear those shorts? Why did Seena? A group of boys watch Grace. They're just old enough to be thrilled by the sight of panties. But maybe not, maybe this, too, is different in Africa.

"I thought it was different, Mary Catherine's not eating," Dick says, as if he himself were striving to make sense of his senseless behavior. "She was doing it for God. I didn't think it would go this far. I didn't know it had gone this far. I thought God would take care of her."

"You were proud of her for starving herself," Seena says. "I can't believe that." But Seena can believe it. Then she thinks, Who's worse? Dick may have been thinking on God, trying to pump up his family and himself. But I was thinking on Heimdall Amadi. It's not Dick I'm angry with. It's not Yllis who's getting on my nerves.

"I didn't know . . . ," Dick says.

Seena realizes they're talking as if Mary Catherine is not with them, as if she's dead. A shiver runs through Seena—an icy, jagged knife that slices her from the base of her back up her spine. "Is she going to die, Dick?" Seena says now. "Is she? Don't let her die."

"No. No, she won't die."

But Seena doesn't trust Dick. In this moment, she feels she's never trusted him. He knew she didn't love him—she never told him she loved him—and he let her marry him anyway. He knew what she was giving up, even if she didn't. And now she's left a loveless, self-hating woman whose daughter is about to die.

Mary Catherine opens her eyes. "I'm thirsty," she says, as if she's just woken from a nap, not a coma. "Where's Mawuli?"

Seena lifts the bag of water toward Mary Catherine's mouth. "He's not with us . . . Remember?" Mary Catherine's not all here, Seena thinks: her mind's not right. But she's here enough. Seena wants to fall into Mary Catherine's body, hold her, not let her get away again. She wants to apologize—to acknowledge directly the horseflies, the gnats. "I was selfish," she wants to say. "I did something that was very selfish, very wrong. But I made the right choice in the end, Catie. I walked away. I came back to you—to all of you. All I want, now, is to be your mother. To be a good mother. All I want is to take care of you." But Seena can't say this—she knows it's not completely true. She never fully returned to them. She couldn't walk away, even though she wanted to, even though she tried. Her relationship with Heimdall is not over, not in her heart.

"But I heard him . . . ," Mary Catherine says. She pushes away the water, lifts her head, looks around, and Seena finds herself looking around, too.

Maybe Seena's the one who's not all here.

"Sweetheart, drink this," Seena says.

But Mary Catherine looks at the bag of water like she's looked at every bag of water since they arrived. Seena would get more water into Mary Catherine if Catie were still unconscious.

"No," Mary Catherine says. She looks at Seena as if Seena were the wretched bag of water, then she again looks beyond Seena.

Seena is on the verge of screaming, "I'm your mother, god

damnit. You don't just get to refuse to drink. I'll pour it down your throat if I have to."

"Mawuli is here," Yllis says. "I saw him."

Seena expects Tessa to correct Yllis, as would be usual, to clarify that Yllis's seeing and normal people's seeing do not correspond. When Yllis says she sees something, that something is the equivalent of nothing to anyone with a normal brain. But Tessa is remarkably quiet.

Seena has to step in. "Yllis didn't really *see* Mawuli."

"Yes I did," Yllis says, with far more insistence than Seena knows she feels, because Yllis has shrunk under Seena's words. The words seem a palpable presence hanging in the air, and Yllis appears afraid of their weight, as if they could crash down and crush her.

Seena has never before expressed doubt like this about Yllis, about the things Yllis claims to see and know. But you can't see someone who's not here. Mawuli can't be here and not here at once.

Mawuli is *not* not here and here at once.

Mawuli is here.

He steps onto the *trotro,* following green Mary Grace who climbs aboard first. Mawuli clutches a bunch of banana runts. Seena notices Yllis study her face, as if Yllis is trying to determine whether Seena is able to see Mawuli.

"I had a feeling," Mawuli says, avoiding Dick's gaze, "that you might catch trouble. I will take you to Avone. Yes?"

"I'd say trouble caught us," Dick says, but Seena hears in his voice the relief she feels. Mawuli may be here to prey on Grace, but predator or not, he's their savior.

Mawuli waits for Grace to sit, then he approaches Mary Catherine. He takes the bag of water from Seena's useless hands and lifts it to Mary Catherine's lips. "Akosiwa tells me you are unwell," he says to Catie. "You must drink, Aku Ayawa. And you will eat a banana." Seena watches as Mawuli performs this miracle: Mary Catherine drinks, she eats.

And now it is Seena who falls in love with Mawuli.

"We should take her to a hospital," Seena says as they collect their things in preparation to transfer to another *trotro*. "Before we go to Avone, Mawuli. Dick says Mary Catherine should go to a hospital."

"But you are the hospital," Mawuli says to Dick. "You are bringing the hospital."

"Mary Catherine should be hydrated and fed. Intravenously," Dick says. "I don't have the means . . ." Dick decided not to be "that kind of doctor" in Africa. He'd told Seena, after attending a bush-doctor seminar at home—before coming to Africa—that he was no bush doctor. He could administer medicine and shots, he said, but he'd no intention of doing anything "invasive."

Mawuli looks from Dick to Seena. Seena thinks she sees in his expression the question, This is modern medicine? "She does not need to be fed with a tube," he says. "She can eat, no? She can drink."

"But she won't . . . ," Dick says—although she just did. "And she was unconscious."

"She is awake. Fully awake," Mawuli says. He turns again to Mary Catherine. "My father also is a doctor," but Seena senses some hesitation before he uses the word "also." "He will help to care for you when we arrive in Avone."

"Your father is a doctor in Avone?" Seena says. And she thinks, Why are we going there, then? How many doctors does one village need?

"Your father lives in Avone?" Dick says.

"You told me your father is a priest," Mary Grace says. "I thought he was a priest."

BOOK FOUR

West Africa

In the days after Seena first spoke with Heimdall Amadi, her world split open wide. Everything she'd known—everything she'd thought she'd known—became new to her. She'd been drawn to mythology because she'd no faith in life. In myth, true love existed. In myth, honor existed, and beauty and passion. In real life, love was a charade, an empty promise. Passion, too, was an artifice: airbrushed photos, plastic parts. Beauty? Beauty was surface deep. Scratch off the top layer, find the hollow beneath.

But in this rebirth, everywhere Seena looked, she saw promise. Her world, which until then had seemed known, knowable, mundane—even ugly—became a treasure chest. Seena could feel loved and feel safe. Seena could love. And because of this, her world brimmed with mystery. For the first time, Seena experienced the sunrise as a miracle: the light and warmth played across her body as she imagined her body lying across his. For the first time, she experienced the miracle of water—its giving of life, its sustaining of life—while she became one with the lake and imagined herself becoming one with him. And sleep: this melting away. Sleep, too, seemed a miracle, because there, in sleep, Seena disappeared into the dream of his arms.

It took more than a month before her imagination took root, before these fantasies became real. And, during this month, Seena became a stalker, determined to be God's Other Woman.

She went to mass, not for the girls or for Dick, but to watch Heimdall. He would stand with his legs wide, arms crossed, back straight, looking after his sheep, sometimes looking at her. She felt his eyes more than she saw them. He looked when he didn't think she would see him looking, but his eyes caressed her skin, shooting chills up her spine, along her shoulder blades, her neck.

She loved his hands. She imagined touching them, being touched by them. His fingers were graceful, yet masculine. How could that be? It seemed inconsistent, contradictory. So much of what he was—of what he appeared to be—seemed a contradiction: a perfect, beautiful contradiction. The veins that lined the back of his hands and forearms were prominent, reminding her of the blood that pulsed through him. When he would hold the communion wafer—pinching it between his forefinger and thumb—then place it on her tongue, she wanted to forego the wafer, taste him. Did she sense his hand quiver? Did she sense his breathing grow unsteady when he would pass the wafer between her lips?

Did she believe she had pierced his soul the way he had pierced hers?

Yes, she did sense these things, she did believe them. And they fueled her, they justified her. She tried to believe they absolved her. She and Heimdall belonged together, despite his being black and her being white. Despite her being married and his being a priest. Because, in finding him, she found life. It was too late for their love to be unblemished, but perhaps it was not too late.

These are the things Seena told herself before she stalked. These are the thoughts that absorbed her while she sat curled in a helix on the Danish Landing sofa, trying to find succor in Apollo, Athena and Aphrodite, but finding only Heimdall.

Then: she left her purse at mass so she could return to the sanctuary alone, in search of it, in search of him; she parked outside the rectory late at night while the girls and Dick slept, scanning each lit window for him; she concocted reasons to detour by the church each time she drove into town, and more reasons to linger in town should she see Heimdall there. Finally, when she could bear it no longer, she called on him again. She needed his counsel, she said. She was struggling, she said.

And it was true. She was a wreck: a neglectful mother, a neglectful wife, a lost soul.

Father Amadi welcomed her—perhaps he expected her. He trembled, she remembers—his whole body trembled. But his blueberry eyes were still.

"Why are you shaking?" she said, but she knew why. She touched his hands—these hands she'd touched so many times in her mind. She kissed his hands, then his lips and his neck. She touched his hair, she kissed his eyes.

And Heimdall kissed her and touched her. And as he did, he cried.

Seena did see sunlight embrace her body as it melted into his, then. She did feel reborn in him as the lake became their world. She did fall asleep in his real arms and wake to find she wasn't dreaming.

And she knew life could come from love.

Yet she knew, too, the pain of betrayal—of being the betrayer. And she knew the malignant disease of deceit. She knew anger she'd never before known—anger because she could not love the man who seemed her destiny without enduring this disease. Anger that she could not rejoice in the baby she carried, the baby she feared was Heimdall's even as she feared it was not. She knew guilt, because she thought about Heimdall more than she did her girls, because she believed if it weren't for her, Heimdall's soul would be clean. Because she felt Dick's love, still—even though she was determined to believe he didn't love her, he'd never loved her.

And she knew jealousy of the God she'd never believed in.

Now? As Seena follows Queen Mother, who leads Seena from this makeshift cell back to her makeshift trial, Seena wonders about this woman: Seena the Stalker. Until months ago—even days ago—she seemed a friend, a confidante. Seena would remember this version of herself with tenderness, understanding. On the turn of a dime, would she have become this woman again? Yes, Seena thinks. Yes.

But now this former Seena seems a distant dream, a silly child, a selfish bitch. If Seena and her girls live past this—if they survive Africa—will Seena look back on herself as she is now and again see someone else altogether? Will she again see a distant dream, a silly child, a selfish bitch, scheming her way through and around and about?

The queen leads Seena to the front of the schoolhouse room where Seena again will face her accusers. But it is not Seena's accusers she sees this time when she turns toward the crowd, it is her Marys, her Yllis. They huddle in the rear of the room; the three older girls encircle Yllis as if to protect her. They appear like petals encircling the eye of a black-eyed Susan. Except she's blue eyed, this Amaryllis. And no one can protect her.

Yllis

When we arrived in Avone, we arrived first to death, then to VIPs and to superstition—to spirits in the bush and spirits in the river, to sacred fish and enemy rings. And we arrived to Mawuli's cousin, a boy named Addae, who tried to explain what couldn't be explained.

Mawuli introduced us to Addae moments after we'd arrived. "*Woezor*," Addae said. "You are welcome. You must come."

Tessa, Grace and I followed him, not realizing what we were doing or why we were doing it, while Mama and Papa escaped with Mawuli to battle death, to keep it from claiming Mary Catherine.

The whole village was gathered; the whole village was red, or so it seemed. Because in the village of Avone, red is the color of death. "They're having a party," Tessa said. And it was true. The villagers of Avone were having a party: a three-day party for death. Dressed in their most beautiful garb—garb of red upon red upon red—the villagers were dancing for death and drumming for death and feasting for death.

Tessa, Grace and I were taken into the red fold. "*Woezor!*" people said again and again. They took our hands. They smiled. "*Woezor*. You are welcome." We drank palm wine. We danced.

Tessa, in particular, danced. Grace did not. We laughed. Grace left.

"Was this party for us?" Tessa said to Addae when the drumming and dancing stopped and Addae offered to show Tessa and me around the village. "To welcome us?"

"You are welcome, yes. This was the third day of a girl's funeral. She was two."

"What?" Tessa said. "A funeral? You don't mean 'funeral.' A funeral is when someone dies. You mean the girl's birthday? She turned two?"

"She died, yes. She was the favorite daughter of our priest, Okomfo. So we celebrate her birth day, yes. Her life."

"She died?" Tessa said.

"She had the diarrhea," Addae said.

"I don't understand," Tessa said. But she did understand. "I thought it was a party. It seemed like a party."

"Yes," Addae said.

"She died of diarrhea?"

"Yes," Addae said.

And I knew Africa again was stirring this pot, even before Addae explained about the spirits. Two-year-olds died from diarrhea. Where melancholy should have gathered, drumming and dancing and feasting had. Sadness and joy were holding hands, and something else altogether was hugging everyone. I'd seen the shimmer of sadness at the funeral, but I'd heard the hum of joy, too. And overriding all of it was something I didn't recognize. It wasn't so much peacefulness as it was acceptance. Life is a gift, it seemed to say. When it ends, you don't ask, "Why me?" You ask, "Why not me?"

Why not me? I thought. Why shouldn't I, who has a life, be grateful for that life, no matter whether my life was formed with love?

Yet life was a gift I didn't understand. I thought of those slave souls in that slave castle, how they seemed to be forever trapped. They once had a life, too. But it was the life of a slave.

Addae pointed to the forest that aligned the village. "On the Sunday, the woods belong to the spirits," he said. "You must not go to the bush on this day. You must not hunt on this day."

"What about the other days? It's Monday. Can we go to the woods on Monday?" Tessa said.

"On the Friday, the river belongs to the spirits. You must not go to the river." He gestured toward the river in which several funeralgoers squatted. "But you may go to the bush. And on the Monday, yes. You may go to the bush. But you may never fish. Not on any day. Not in this river. The fish of the Avone River are sacred fish. Not edible."

"Not edible is right," Tessa said, but quietly, only to me. "Do you see what those people are doing in that river? That's one way to save people from killing themselves by eating contaminated fish. They're sacred, those fish. Of course they are. Tainted with human waste, they're as sacred as can be."

Addae noticed Tessa's murmuring. "What's this you say?"

I braced myself. It was unlike Tessa to not challenge anyone and everyone who said something she considered nonsense. But she didn't challenge Addae. "Speaking of the sacred, what about that priest you mentioned. He's a fetish priest, right? One who heals people?"

"Oh, you would like to meet Okomfo." Addae said. "Perhaps you would like an enemy ring? But you've had a long journey, and I've forgotten to take you to our VIP. First you visit the VIP, then I take you to Okomfo for an enemy ring."

"What's an enemy ring?" Tessa said. "And who's the VIP if it's not that Okomfo?"

Papa often referred to himself as the VIP of the Slepy family, causing Tessa to sputter and Grace to roll her eyes.

Now it was Addae who sputtered, smiling. "Okomfo will sell you a ring to protect you from your enemies. But do not call him the VIP."

"I should get one for my sister," Tessa said. "One of those enemy rings. She's an enemy to herself. She can wear it with her mood ring."

"This little sister?" Addae said, pointing to me. "Mood ring?"

"Not Yllis," Tessa said. "Mary Catherine, the one who's ill. The one who's with my parents. Although come to think of it, Yllis . . ."

"Who's the VIP, then?" I said to Addae, interrupting Tessa. I needed no mood ring to tell me I was not in the mood to be teased by Tessa. I was in the mood to be comforted. By Mama. But Mama and Papa had disappeared with Catie the moment we'd arrived in Avone—that is, with Catie and Mawuli. The four of them had holed up in a hut, after Mama had shooed me away.

"The Ventilated Improved Pit," Addae said.

"The what?" Tessa said.

"The toilet. Our new toilet in Avone is the VIP."

"A toilet is the VIP?" Now Tessa did sputter. "You have just one?"

"Of course, no," Addae said. "The VIP has ten toilets."

"That flush?" Tessa said. We hadn't seen ten toilets that flush since we'd arrived in West Africa.

"Flush? No," Addae said. "The pit is cleaned out every five years."

"Cleaned every five years?" Tessa said. "I guess that's why people use the river."

"What about the river?" Addae said.

"Nothing," Tessa said, apparently realizing making jokes about the river—the home of the sacred fish—might be taboo. "The river has nothing to do with anything."

Only it did. In the coming days, the river of Friday spirits and sacred fish had something to do with many things. But that night there was no river; there was no fetish priest selling enemy rings. There was only Addae hunting bats in the spiritless bush, and Tessa teaching him to play Truth or Dare.

I ran from Addae and Tessa that first night—before the bats, before the Truth—because I couldn't hunt. I say I ran, but I only tried to run. Like the slaves in the slave castle, like the spirits on this Monday and on the three days that followed, I found I'd nowhere to go.

Mary Tessa

Night had settled, bats had died. Some truth had passed from Addae to Tessa. Some courage had passed from Tessa to Addae, although not with ease. Addae had then invited Tessa to his home, to the communal bowl, to the hand-dipping ritual of *fufu*.

"Can I help cook?" Tessa had asked Addae as she and he journeyed to his hut. She was thinking of the scene she'd viewed from the *trotro* when she and her family first arrived in West Africa—of the women cooking, talking and laughing.

"Yes," Addae said. "It is not normal for a guest. But I will ask my mother, Abla."

When Addae and Tessa arrived at Addae's hut—a bare concrete structure surrounding a courtyard—Tessa found herself in the courtyard, without Addae, encircled by women and girls and cooking, and language she couldn't decipher. And instructions, conveyed with gestures and this indecipherable language: chop this like *this*, not like *that*, grind this, seed that. They were preparing soup for *fufu*, she knew—Addae had told her this before he'd vanished. Apparently boys are excluded from this *fufu* preparation. Or perhaps girls are excluded from whatever Addae is doing now. What is he doing now? Probably pouring libations of palm wine to the spirits, which seems to be one of the few things men around here actually do—witch doctoring excluded. According to Addae, the females cook and farm and clean and care for children and sell goods at market. "What do the men do?" Tessa had asked. "Do?" Addae had said. "The men are in charge."

Thinking about that now, Tessa is glad she's where she is. She'd rather be here than pouring libations. She feels sort of useful here, where she's doing something more than the nothing she's done since they arrived in West Africa, hunting bats aside. She's learning something to boot, even if that something involves tomato seeds. And although she can't understand anything anyone around her says, she can understand these women seem to like one another. They seem happy. And they seem happy to have her with them.

In addition to Addae's mother, Abla, and his three sisters, Addae's two aunts are here, along with their children. Altogether, fourteen people prepare this meal—the youngest looks to be about four—while three babies swing from three backs. The four-year-old climbs on Tessa's lap now. She touches Tessa's hair. Then the other young girls crowd around Tessa. They stroke her hair, they hold her hands, they brush their pink fingertips against her cheeks. One of them reaches her tiny hand into Tessa's pocket, locates Papa's old Casiotron watch that Tessa lifted back in Michigan after Papa bought a better one. (Tessa figured he didn't need two.) She'd kept the watch lodged in the pocket of her shorts since, afraid of getting caught with it.

The remaining children scramble off Tessa, scramble around the watch. Tessa takes the watch back and arbitrarily presses buttons. With each press, the numbers change, the children squeal.

"Afi. Afi!"

It takes a moment before Tessa realizes Addae's mother—this large-voiced, petite woman named Abla—has spoken to her. Tessa made the mistake of sharing her African day name with Addae at the funeral, not realizing he'd take it seriously, use it. But he'd introduced Tessa to the group of women and girls as Afi, not as Tessa. And now Abla looks at Tessa—this girl who doesn't even know how to seed a tomato—as if she's not only dumb but deaf. Abla pushes a bucket between the children, into Tessa's hands. "Water," she says in English. "You get." You are disrupting the children's work, her eyes say: enough is enough.

"From the river?" Tessa says, as if there were options.

"You get," Abla says again.

In the short time she's been in Avone, Tessa has seen woman after woman after girl after girl scoop water from the river, carry it back on her head, not spilling a drop. As Tessa approaches the river now, hardly able to see in the dark, she thinks of the human waste in this toilet of a river, and she wishes it were Friday—the day the river belongs to the spirits. She wishes the river always belonged to the spirits. That way, she'd not have to go near the river now. That way, the villagers would be forced to use the Very Important Potty rather than the river, even if the VIP is cleaned out only once every five years.

But it is not Friday.

Tessa reaches the river, dips her bucket, fills it. Then she heads back up the bank dragging the bucket, spilling as much water as she keeps. Children circle her, bathe her in the light of a torch. They giggle and point.

Okay, Tessa thinks, I'm an embarrassment. I get it.

"*Obroni!*" the children say. "*Obroni!* How. Are. You. Where. Are. You. Go-ing. How. Are. You. *Obroni?* Where. Are. You. Go-ing." One of the smallest girls takes the bucket from Tessa, plops it on her head, not spilling a drop. She literally runs up the bank with the bucket on her head. Still, she doesn't spill a single drop, the show-off.

When they reach Addae's hut, the girl hands back the bucket, and she and the remaining children evaporate into the night. "Bye. *Obroni!* Bye!"

Tessa's again alone. She considers leaving the water and making her own exit. But why does she consider this? She wanted escape from the desert island, didn't she? She pushes her hip against the door, enters the hut, enters the courtyard, looks around for Addae, who's still nowhere to be found.

"Afi!" Abla says. She takes the water, pours it into a pot, sits the pot atop a burning fire.

And Tessa feels the tension she barely knew she felt release. Abla is going to boil the water—she is going to boil away the human waste. No one here is going to die from diarrhea.

Except Abla doesn't boil it.

The water is barely warm when Abla instructs Tessa to remove the pot from the fire.

"It hasn't boiled yet," Tessa says, knowing Abla is unlikely to understand her words. "Shouldn't it boil?" Tessa well knows, as every one of the Slepy girls well knows, the water must boil to be certain it's safe to use. How many times did Pa explain this? Ad nauseam, as Ma would say.

Abla waves her hand, waves away Tessa's words, whether she understood them or not. She picks up a large bowl, demonstrates to Tessa how to wash the bowl in the water. Then she hands Tessa a bowl. "You," Abla says. She then says something to a girl who looks to be about Tessa's age.

The girl takes Tessa's hand, squeezes it. "Friend?" she says.

"Yes," Tessa says. "Yes."

The girl smiles, releases Tessa's hand, picks up another large bowl, washes it.

And Tessa mimics her. She dips her bowl into the unclean water, she scrubs it dirty.

The bowls are still wet when Abla fills one with *fufu* paste, one with soup, one with chopped vegetables.

Addae returns. The women now disappear, the girls disappear. The men and other boys arrive. They loop themselves around the *fufu* paste, the soup, the vegetables.

"Where are the others?" Tessa says, confused. "Where's your mom?"

"You are our guest," Addae says. He motions for her to sit next to him in the circle. "You want to learn to cook. You learn to cook. Now you eat."

"But what about everyone else? Aren't they eating?"

"The men and boys eat. The rest will eat later, when we are done."

"But I'm not a man," Tessa says. "I'm not a boy."

"You are white," Addae says, as if that explains anything.

Addae's father then says, "You are welcome in our village, Afi. You are our honored guest." He lifts a cup of palm wine, says something in Ewe, then pours a small amount of the wine on the ground. He repeats this several times.

"He is thanking the spirits for your coming here," Addae says to Tessa.

"If you die here, Afi, in our village, your life has been blessed," Addae's father says.

Die? Tessa thinks. What do you mean, die? Yet at some level she knows what he means. Death is part of life here. According to Addae, funerals are common even in this small village. Many children die before age five. And Tessa has not seen anyone who looks particularly old. Even the so-called elders aren't much older than Tessa's Ma and Pa. Does that mean there are no older people—that people don't live to be much older than Ma and Pa?

Tessa wishes she believed in God, in heaven. She wishes she believed in an afterlife. She wants to imagine that two-year-old who died from diarrhea dancing along the golden streets of heaven. She wants to imagine the African elders actually growing old, in heaven if not on earth.

Addae's father demonstrates how to roll the *fufu* into a ball, how to hand-dip it into the soup, how to slide it into one's mouth. He nods at Tessa.

Tessa barely hesitates before she rolls the paste, dips and eats. The *fufu* is delicious.

Dick

West Africa
Fall 1976

Dick remembers Mary Catherine's birth. He hadn't seen Mary Grace's—it just wasn't done, the delivery room was no place for fathers. But by the time Mary Catherine was born, Dick was a medical student, and he insisted he had a right to be there. He was a doctor, after all. Or soon to be one. And a well-known physician named Robert Bradley had made his public case that, in fact, the delivery room was absolutely a place for fathers. Hence, Seena's ob/gyn grudgingly let Dick in, after he pulled Dick aside to warn him, "You might never again find your wife attractive after seeing what you're about to see."

Dick almost hoped this was true, that his attraction to Seena might wane. The less he felt her love, the more he wanted it, just like with his father and mother. Dick had taken their love for granted, until it was gone. And, then, his want was great. Could there really be something capable of altering that want?

The answer to that question? Yes, absolutely. The problem? With Seena, the altering happened in the wrong direction. Watching Seena give birth was like watching the sun become an egg, and when it burst, it birthed more light. The birth was gory—there's no question about that—but Dick had become accustomed to gore. What he wasn't accustomed to was seeing Seena made raw and vulnerable. By necessity, she left her mind and occupied solely her body, where she panted and pushed. Sweat streaked her face like tears. She, who seemed the ultimate in selfishness—who seemed annoyed by having to cook Dick's meals and do Dick's laundry—became ultimately unselfish. She endured what Dick could see was excruciating pain, and she did so with no apparent annoyance or regret. She was strong and capable. And beautiful. More beautiful than Dick knew she could be. And when Mary Catherine slipped into the world and Seena held her, Dick loved Seena more than he realized anyone could love. He thought, as he watched Seena cradle Mary Catherine, as he watched plump, pink Catie learn to nurse: I will never do as my father did and leave them. I will never do as my mother did and leave them in spirit. I will never let them down.

And now, what has Dick done but let them down? Mary Catherine lies on a dirty cot in West Africa, in a room that seems a shell stripped of fruit. Bare mud walls and a bare mud floor. No paint. No carpet. No bed, couch or comfortable chair. Catie's teenage body lies exposed on the cot—not covered by a blanket or sheet—and Dick is forced to see her torso is no wider than that of a small child: her limbs are all elbow, wrist and knee. She is gray and scaly and trusting some lecher more than she trusts Dick. For good reason. Mawuli convinced Mary Catherine to eat and drink while Dick insisted she be fed intravenously, with what might well have turned out to be contaminated needles, given where they are. And before that? Dick had been proud of Mary Catherine's not eating and drinking—her fasting for God.

Dick had told himself Mary Catherine's fasting showed character. Truth was, Dick was pleased Mary Catherine had thumbed her nose at Seena.

Mawuli sits holding Mary Catherine's hand now, while Seena sits across from Dick, the heel of Mary Catherine's cot a bridge between them. Or a barrier. Another barrier. There were already so many barriers, including that Dick loved Mary Catherine's flouting of Seena's wishes, Catie's proving to Seena that the God Dick worshipped and Seena scoffed at was worth some sacrifice. Even a lot of sacrifice. Even so much sacrifice it might make one deathly ill.

God, I'm a fool, Dick thinks.

Because Mary Catherine was deathly ill, until Mawuli stepped in. And Seena will always hate Dick's guts; he's given her plenty of fodder. And Grace thinks she wants to marry a man she met days ago, who not only is black and lives thousands of miles from home, but who also apparently is the progeny of a witch doctor. Tessa is out cavorting with the village boys—none of the girls here speaks English—doing God knows what. And Yllis is living proof it's nothing new, Dick's being a fool.

Speaking of the witch doctor, he's arrived, having appeared in the hut as if from nowhere. He probably conjured himself up out of thin air, given he has magic powers. Except this dusty air is anything but thin.

"Father," Mawuli says. And then to Seena and Dick, "This is my father, Okomfo, elder and priest of Avone. A great healer."

Okomfo looks to be about Dick's age. He wears a free-flowing white tunic and a thimble-shaped hat. The sclera of his eyes is pee water, his sweaty face a sticky pool.

"Not now, my son," Okomfo says. His eyes shift from Dick to Seena then back to Dick. "You must come, Doctor. My girl needs you."

"*My* girl needs me," Dick wants to respond. "I can't leave her." But he knows he can leave Mary Catherine—that she doesn't need him. Mawuli's the one who saved Mary Catherine, not Dick.

"Come quickly, Doctor," Okomfo says.

Dick complies. He feels grateful someone thinks he has worth—even if that someone is a witch doctor. He follows Okomfo out of the hut, then out of the village. "Where are we going?" Dick asks when he realizes the village is behind them.

"My hospital," Okomfo says, but Dick doesn't understand: there is no hospital near Avone.

The two men pass through a small jungle of trees, into a sprawling compound of huts. As they pass hut after hut, Dick sees shriveled women and shriveled men, open sores, missing limbs, tumors the size of limbs, children as thin as limbs, scorched scabbed skin, pussy eyes.

This is a hospital?

"So many evil spirits," Okomfo says. He gestures toward the broken people. "I mix medicines from our local plants for them. I say prayers. Most I cure. But my two-year-old daughter . . . She, I did not cure."

"You're able to help them?" Dick says.

"Yes, yes. I know the medicines to frighten most evil spirits.

I know the prayers. I learn these things from my grandfather, the greatest medicine man."

"I think I can help you," Dick says, and he believes it. He could treat some of those people they passed, for sure, just using disinfectant, some antibiotic ointment. "I have medicines, too."

"We will share medicines. I will teach you, you will teach me. But first you will help my girl. My medicines cannot help her."

"Your two-year-old?"

"No. No."

They reach the largest of the huts. It is far larger than the others, more a house than a hut, made of concrete but with shingles and a garage.

"Please come," Okomfo says, and Dick follows Okomfo into the garage where he finds a Mercedes.

A Mercedes? Swindler, Dick thinks, but then he stops himself. Doctors at home are well compensated, they have Mercedeses and Cadillacs. *I have a Cadillac.* Why should Okomfo not have a nice car? It's a racist thought, this notion that he shouldn't. He's caring for these people with his local medicines. He's curing disease, even if he thinks he's scaring away spirits.

"She is here," Okomfo says, as he passes from the garage into one dark room and then another.

But Dick has heard the girl; he knows where she is.

She is fifteen, Dick later learns. Younger than Dick's Mary Catherine. And like Mary Catherine, the girl is a twig, but swollen in the middle, like a knotted branch—or a contorted limb of a baobab tree. She is surrounded by other twigs and limbs and contorted branches: a hut full of girls and women who kneel, bend, pray, wail—all wanting to help, all unable to help.

Dick steps inside this baobab tree of fear and pain. He stands above the writhing, panting, perspiring girl whom Dick assumes is Okomfo's daughter, not his wife.

She is neither his daughter nor his wife.

"She's in labor?" Dick says. He barely believes it could be true. The girl's hips are narrower than one of Dick's thighs. Her fisted hands are so tiny, Dick feels the urge to slide his finger into her grip, let her hold him, the way each of his daughters did when newly born, with that infant grip. Her face is full, perhaps plumped by hormones or the retention of water, not by baby fat. Yet it appears to Dick—even as he wonders if he truly is helpless again or if he only feels helpless—that a baby is having a baby.

"She can't have this baby," Dick says. "Not naturally. She's too small, her pelvis too narrow." As he speaks, he realizes he stands in the girl's blood. She lies on a bed that isn't a bed at all. Just a mat of straw—a mat of bloody straw. The blood has seeped past the mat onto the concrete floor, which now appears more fertile than the clay earth outside.

Dick looks toward Okomfo, intending to pull him aside, explain the girl will die. Dysentery, Dick has decided he can handle. And inoculations. And malaria, provided the medicine works. And sores. But surgery? A C-section in the bush? No. Never. It is beyond Dick's skills, his mental strength. He'd taken a "bush doctor" seminar before arriving in Africa, but as he'd listened to the instructor explain how to perform primitive surgery, he could no more imagine himself performing such surgery than he could imagine himself walking on water. I'll draw the line, he'd told himself. I'm not going to become my father, butcher some person in surgery the way he did. I'm not a surgeon. I know my limitations. I'll just say no.

But an image of Yllis as a newborn fills his mind's eye and other words flow forth. Grace's birth he was not permitted to see, but Mary Catherine's and Tessa's he saw. Yllis's birth was stolen from him. This birth will not be. "I need water," he says. "A lot of it. In a large pot. And a fire, to boil the water, to sterilize the instruments. I'll need sheets, too. Or rags. Some sort of cloth. Rip the cloth into strips. We'll boil that, too."

Okomfo translates Dick's words. The wailing women and girls stop wailing and scatter. Large swatches of cloth appear as Okomfo did, as if from the air. The women tear the cloth. Dick hears the river water splash. He smells smoke drift in from the courtyard.

He opens his black bag. He actually has a black bag—he'd purchased it along with the medical instruments he'd bought when he decided to play doctor.

But he's no longer playing doctor.

He checks the girl's vitals: her low temperature, her low blood pressure, her slow pulse. It feels as if something or someone other than Dick is acting—as if God has infused Dick's mind, his body, and given him a surgeon's decisiveness and confidence, a surgeon's skilled hand. For the first time in so long—since meeting Seena?—he feels God's presence deep within his body, he feels the Virgin Mary's nurturing love. "My grace is sufficient for thee: for power is made perfect in infirmity." God has granted Dick an actual grace. And now Dick himself can care for, nurture.

When he pours the scotch onto the girl's tongue and orders her to swallow, he doesn't question performing surgery with no anesthesia other than scotch. And when Okomfo offers his magic herbs—one for sedation and one as a coagulant—Dick somehow knows the herbs aren't magic but medicine, and he gives his blessing.

Dick removes the scalpel from the pot of boiling water and holds it in his scrubbed, gloved hand. He doesn't pause in doubt before he slices open the girl's abdomen. He's not surprised when the girl screams as he feels her stretched uterus beneath the blade. He doesn't long to stop what he's begun, to sprint away and never look back. He looks instead at the steely determination in the girl's eyes just before he pierces her uterus— just before he watches it spread. Only when his hands plunge into her body—only when he touches the new life—does he feel overwhelmed. Yet he is not overwhelmed. He lifts the breathing baby boy, hands him to the helpless horde that's no longer helpless: the women pat, suck and wipe, as if they've done this a thousand times. And Dick? He removes the placenta, cuts the cord then stitches the girl, as if he's done this a thousand times.

Seena

Like the school they'd passed while in the *trotro,* Avone's school resembles an abandoned building. At least there is a school, Seena thinks as she walks toward the building, a construction of concrete blocks with a corrugated iron roof. Seena passes child after child—mostly girls—on her way. Why are these children not there, not in school?

The school-skipping children walk barefoot, balancing buckets of water and stacks of kindling. Some carry babies. Some carry teetering baskets of pineapples and bananas. "Where. Are. You. Going?" each child Seena passes asks her. "Where. Are. You. Going?"

Where is Seena going? Where? She's still trying to understand where she is, who she is, who her children are, who her husband is. How can she possibly know where she is going? But she says, "I am going to school. Why aren't you in school?"

"Where. Are. You. Going?" the children respond.

Seena left Mary Catherine with Mawuli. Perhaps it is more accurate to say Mary Catherine left Seena. After Dick raced off with Okomfo, Seena sat feeling superfluous. "Is there a school here?" she finally said to Mawuli, who seemed more than happy to give Seena directions, send her on her way.

Seena climbs the steps of the school now. She enters and discovers seventy-five or more students who range in age from six to twelve and who sit along benchlike tables and mimic one teacher's words. The school has no electricity, as far as Seena can see. The "blackboard" is a smoothed square of plaster, painted black. Seena sees only a handful of textbooks, a splattering of paper, a few pencils and pens.

The teacher stops speaking, looks at Seena. Then every one of the seventy-five plus students turns toward Seena.

"I'm sorry for interrupting," Seena says. "I'm Seena Slepy. We're new here, my family and I. We've just arrived. My husband is a doctor. He'll be opening the clinic. Is it okay if I watch?"

As Seena says this, the rain begins, falling in a torrent of water and noise. Standing beneath the iron roof, Seena feels trapped beneath a stampede. The teacher appears to be speaking to Seena, but Seena hears only the stampede.

The rain pounds through the open windows and bathes those children who sit closest to the windows. How can the students learn with this noise, while getting wet? Seena knows they have a rainy season. Do they endure this daily then?

The children disperse, run out the doors, get more drenched.

The teacher approaches Seena. "I am Kofi."

"The school day is over?" The Slepys arrived in Avone around noon—it must be no more than one or one thirty.

"It is over now," Kofi says. He gestures toward the rain.

———

Seena spends the next hour with Kofi, learning all she can about the school. Only the children whose parents can afford the fees attend. Usually a family will pick one or two of their many children to send to school, particularly in the older grades. Girls rarely get sent. Instead, they help their families with farming, housework and child care.

Sounds familiar, Seena thinks.

"Can I see some of their work?" she says. "I'd like to see the kind of work the students do."

"They worked on these today." Kofi hands Seena a stack of essays.

The first essay is entitled, "Cassava Root," as is the second, third and fourth. Seena reads through the first, then she skims the second, the third. "But these are about the baobab tree? Not the cassava root. And the essays are almost exactly the same."

"Yes," Kofi says. "The assignment was to write about the cassava root."

"I don't understand."

"I gave the children a sample essay about the baobab tree. Then I asked them to write a comparable essay about the cassava root. Most titled the essay, 'Cassava Root,' then copied my essay about the baobab tree."

"So you fail them," Seena says. "They should fail."

"No. I have seventy-eight students. Their parents pay me to give them a pass. I fail no one. If I fail anyone, parents stop sending the students. It is not worth it to the parents to pay the fee if the student fails."

"School is for learning. They need to learn. If they don't

learn the material, they should fail. What's the point if they don't learn?"

"The point is to give them a pass."

"I want to open another school here." As Seena says this, she realizes this.

"But we have a school. Some children walk miles from other villages to come to our school. There are many villages without schools."

Seena thinks of the girls she passed on her way to the school. "I want to start a school here for all those girls in Avone who don't come here."

"It is not so important about the girls," the teacher says. "Most of them will marry."

Seena stands to leave. "Thank you for your time."

"And their families need them for the chores."

Seena barely hears. She is out the door, into the rain.

"You are an American, though," Kofi says to no one. "You, of course, know better."

But Seena doesn't hear this. She is in the torrent, wishing she could talk with Heimdall. This is his homeland; she longs to tell him about her school.

———

The last time Seena was alone with Heimdall was the day Yllis was born. She knew Yllis was coming—after birthing Grace, Mary Catherine and Tessa, how could she not know? She recognized the bloody show in her panties. She knew well the deep aching in her lower back as the baby dropped and her hip bones spread. She felt intimate with the squeezing, rhythmic waves of pain as Yllis worked toward her release. She'd phoned Heimdall, she'd told him the baby was coming. And he'd met Seena in the woods, along the Old Trail.

Dick thought Seena had gone to pick blueberries while he and the girls prepared to celebrate the Fourth. But the only blue thing on Seena's mind was the eyes of her lover: would the baby have her lover's eyes?

Heimdall begged Seena to go to the hospital, but she refused. She needed to know in private who fathered this child. She needed to see the baby's skin, her hair, her eyes, without some doctor's or nurse's prying. And she wanted Heimdall to be with her the first time she saw the baby's skin and hair and eyes.

And he was. When Yllis entered the world, she fell into Heimdall's hands. And before Seena knew, Heimdall knew: he and Seena were forever bound.

Heimdall folded himself over Yllis's small, bloody body, and he sobbed, so loudly Seena feared someone might hear and come. What if Dick were to find them?

"I need to cut the cord, Heimdall," Seena said, and Heimdall stifled his sob, looked up. "Let me cut it." Seena had come prepared. She snipped the cord then wiped Yllis clean. As she did these things, Heimdall held their baby daughter for the first and last time.

"I'll leave the priesthood," he said. "I can do something else, Seena—be something else. A professor, maybe. We can be married. We'll be a family."

"But you love being a priest." Seena took Yllis from him. "It's who you are." And it's who I love, Seena thought. After losing her father and her brothers—after her grandmother died—school had been the only thing that mattered to Seena. But then Seena married, and she lost that, too. She couldn't let Heimdall lose himself. She couldn't do to Heimdall what Dick had done to her. Besides, love was fragile, wasn't it? Love was unpredictable. Look at the kind of mother Seena had become. At one time, she'd been unable to squelch the love she felt for her daughters—no matter how frightened she was of these feelings, no matter how hard she tried—but with all the deception, the sneaking around, even that stubbornly persistent love had begun to fade. What if Heimdall lost himself and Seena lost her love for him?

He would be left with nothing.

At that very moment Seena knew: she wouldn't leave Dick. She loved Heimdall, and because of that love, she and Heimdall and their baby would never be a family.

Seena left life, then. She returned to mythology, not because mythology was richer than life—it wasn't anymore. But because real life was too beautiful, too painful.

Now, Seena moves through the rain, which has become a blinding sheet. Where is Dick? Seena needs to tell him about her school.

Mary Grace

West Africa
Fall 1976

Grace didn't know Mawuli meant a fetish priest, a witch doctor, but that's what Mawuli's father Okomfo is. According to Mawuli, Okomfo tends to the body and soul "in one fell swoop."

One fell swoop. Mawuli's using that phrase brings to mind Mama's explaining its meaning to Yllis. "The word 'fell' in that context used to refer to something evil," she told Yllis. "It didn't have anything to do with falling. 'Fell' referred to something particularly ferocious. Something deadly."

Let's hope it's no omen that Mawuli used that phrase. That Grace is going to have a witch doctor for an in-law is omen enough.

Grace waits for Mawuli in a mud room in a mud hut belonging to Mawuli's aunt. Mawuli fetched Grace this morning, only to have her sit here alone—which Grace figures is just as well, given the options.

"Akosiwa?" Grace hears Mawuli's voice now through the mud hut's door, but she pretends to not hear. She's fathoming that people live this way, that Mawuli lived this way while growing up, that in the short term she'll be living this way. They arrived in Avone yesterday and found sparse huts of mud or concrete that make the cottage on the Danish Landing seem palatial, and narrow ditches that snake the ground—between huts, around the open school, to the dirt road, parallel to the dirt road—then descend to the river. Grace thought the ditches a curiosity of natural topography, until Tessa pointed out the sewage that passes between the huts, around the school, along the road and into the river. And to think Grace came here bringing her own nausea.

"Akosiwa?" Mawuli says again. And now he knocks. Grace wishes she could find some way to distract him, to get him to focus on something other than her.

Mama and Papa were distracted most of yesterday—and not just with Mary Catherine's shenanigans—while Grace suffered her way through a funeral where Tessa made a dancing fool of herself. Tessa may utterly lack judgment, but Mary Catherine pushed it too far this time, smack into the danger zone. Even so, Grace can't help but find comfort in Mary Catherine's and Tessa's determination to snag the attention, given Grace would prefer at the moment to have no attention at all. Truth is, even Mary Catherine being on her deathbed apparently isn't sufficient to hold Mama's or Papa's attention for long. So what does Grace have to worry about? Once Mawuli stepped in, began caring for Mary Catherine, Mama and Papa stepped way back. Papa found his calling as a bush doctor, and Mama transformed into Mother Teresa before their very eyes, deciding from out of nowhere to form a school for girls.

Grace feels like reminding Mama that Mother Teresa doesn't

have any girls of her own, let alone a stew like Grace and her sisters, each of whom could use some mothering. Where was Mama when Grace gave up math for makeup? Where was Mama while Grace wilted beneath some stranger's comment about chastity belts? Where was Mama when Grace sought out Old Clara for sex education? Where is Mama NOW? Even Grace can see neither Tessa nor Yllis is acting like herself—Tessa's dancing being an exception. And Mary Catherine is a mess, even if she is eating and drinking again, no thanks to Mama. Grace should be with Catie now, being the mother to Catie that Mama can't be—not here preparing for Dipo, preparing to be a real mother that Grace can't be. But Catie doesn't need Grace any more than she needs Mama, thanks to Mawuli.

Seems Mawuli could get Mary Catherine to do just about anything. For the past two months, Mama had utilized every carrot and stick imaginable trying to get Mary Catherine to consume a calorie. Mawuli shows up and says, "Eat the banana," and Catie does, just like that. "Eat the *kenkey*," he says, and down it slides.

Mawuli's seeming magic power has gotten Grace wondering whether there is something to this witch doctor business. The influence Mawuli has over Mary Catherine sure seems like the product of sorcery. Does he have that kind of power over Grace? Is that why Grace agreed to marry him? Is Mawuli's father, Okomfo, performing some hocus-pocus that's making the Slepys into modeling clay and making Mawuli the sculptor? Grace does feel shocked by her own decision, at times, as if someone's made her think she wants what she doesn't want at all.

Grace thinks this, then she thinks of Rocky. She certainly is appalled by that decision, and there's no blaming that one on voodoo.

"We must begin, Akosiwa," Mawuli says, and now he eases open the hut's door. Grace looks up at him. Mawuli has eyes you could fall into: moist, dark and soothing. When Grace looks into his eyes, that voodoo takes hold. She's making the right decision; she knows she is.

"Your parents are occupied now."

"Yes," Grace says. What's new? she thinks.

"This is a good time to start Dipo."

Mawuli is conniving, Grace sees this. He knows as Grace knows that Mama and Papa are far less likely to make a stink about Grace being part of this ritual that's supposed to teach her how to be a caretaker, when they themselves reek with neglect for having failed to care for Catie.

"They're not going to stop me," Grace says. "Mama and Papa aren't going to stop me from doing Dipo. You don't have to worry."

Grace knows her parents will allow her participation in Dipo, based on the exchange she and Mama had earlier in the day when the two were sharing some unsweet "sweet bread." "You want to take part in that tradition. Fine by me," Mama said, after Grace explained Dipo. "Frankly, Grace, I don't have time for this nonsense. And neither does your father. You want to make a fool of yourself, fine. As long as you're breathing, I don't really care. But don't think that means you're marrying anybody, because you're not."

"This isn't the Danish Landing, Mama," Grace felt like saying. "You're not the village queen here." There actually is a village queen of Avone, Queen Mother. According to Mawuli, the elders of Avone, namely Queen Mother and Mawuli's father, Okomfo, will decide whether Grace and Mawuli marry. Mama has nothing to do with the decision.

Mawuli leads Grace out of the hut and to the palace of the queen. "Queen Mother will explain to you Dipo," he says. "Prepare you."

It's concrete, the queen's palace-hut. Not mud. Grace steps inside and sees even the floor of the hut is concrete. Apparently a "clean" mud floor is good enough for the gander but not for the goose—at least not when the goose is the queen.

She looks like a man: the queen looks like a man. Most of the women in the village wear head scarves and traditional clothing, these brightly hued wraps. But Queen Mother wears no head scarf. Her head is shaved, her garb drab. She certainly doesn't look like she'd mind sleeping on a pea.

As the queen leads Grace farther into the hut, the queen rambles nonstop, but she doesn't speak in English. If this is her explanation of Dipo, it's sure not doing much good. Mawuli will need to translate. But where is Mawuli?

The queen pulls aside the curtain that separates the entryway from the hut's interior, and she and Grace pass from lightness to darkness. Grace's eyes need to adjust. When they do, she sees she's standing in the center of a ring of girls.

Naked girls.

Each of the girls wears nothing but a swatch of patterned cloth between her thighs. Some of the girls look nearly Grace's age. Some are younger than Yllis, as young as five. Some are prepubescent, with breasts like flower buds.

What is going on?

Grace feels the girls and the queen disrobe her with their eyes. And then Grace herself imagines her white skin next to their black skin, her small white breasts next to their full black breasts and medium-size black breasts and nearly absent black breasts.

Grace looks again for Mawuli. She has to tell him she's made a mistake, she can't do this.

But Mawuli is nowhere to be found.

Only his voodoo remains.

Dick

West Africa
Fall 1976

◆ Dick and Seena sit inside the hut, head to head, discussing their plans for Avone—Dick's clinic and Seena's school for girls—when Tessa bursts into the mud pod. "Gracie is naked!" she says. She's either sunburnt or flushed. Her hair flounces in golden wings as she bounces up and down.

"You're waking Mary Catherine . . . ," Seena says, and then, "What?"

"Naked?" Dick says. "What do you mean 'naked'?"

Mary Catherine opens her eyes.

"Grace," Tessa says. "And the whole village is watching."

Dick wants to believe Tessa is just being Tessa, trying to stir the soup, make things interesting. He hopes she's the boy crying wolf, that she just longs for some excitement, bored as she must be. But the flush on Tessa's face—it is a flush, he sees this now—is Tessa embarrassed. This is a Tessa Dick rarely sees.

The shell of Dick's world may have cracked long ago, but he senses the shell may be in shards now: no one is climbing back in that egg.

Seena sees what Dick sees; maybe she senses what he senses. She's on her feet before Dick is, then she's gone.

Mary Tessa squeezes her left hand with her right hand, then she squeezes her right hand with her left. Dick expects Tessa to chase Seena down—it's not like Tessa to miss the action. But Tessa wants to hide, Dick realizes, she wants to hide away from what's happening outside. And Dick knows he'd better get the hell out there.

"Where are you going?" Mary Catherine says as Dick barrels out. "Why are you leaving me? Where's Mawuli?"

But Dick doesn't stop—not this time. He's been stopping his whole life, thinking somehow it would all work out. Thinking somehow if he just waited, prayed, believed, endured, it all would work out in the end. His father would recover after losing his license, his mother's depression would wane, Seena would love him, his children would love him, he would do good in the world just by not doing bad. He may have looked at girly magazines, visited the Rent-a-Girl, but those were victimless acts.

After he delivered that baby yesterday, though, Dick knows what it feels like to do something. Had he done nothing then, the girl and baby would have died. This time, Dick is going to do something.

But when Dick exits, he again finds nothing. That's what Mary Grace wears: nothing. Nothing but a rag tied like a fancy diaper. She parades in a parade of girls who all wear these diapers. Okomfo stands off to the side with his many girls, all of whom are dressed.

Dear God, Dick thinks when he sees Grace: my daughter is

a woman. When did it happen? She has breasts, real ones. And a body that reminds him of the girls in the girly magazines. Every boy and man in this village—including Okomfo—knew Grace was a woman before Dick knew. Each and every one of them was eyeing her when Dick stepped on the scene.

Dick feels paralyzed, even as rage thunders through him. The rage is a breaking wave in his body, he hears it pound inside his ears. How dare they look at his daughter this way? How dare they parade these girls like they're merchandise? Okomfo is not allowing his own girls to be treated like merchandise.

"What the hell are you doing?" Seena pushes herself into the parade, grabs at Grace. "What the *hell* do you think you're doing?"

"Mama," Grace says. "Please don't. Please."

Seena pauses, her arms fall to her sides. She steps back.

Grace turns away.

Is Seena crushed or humiliated or furious or scared? Dick doesn't know. He doesn't know what she'll do; he doesn't know what he'll do. He doesn't want to stop, but his body won't move. He doesn't want to wait, endure. But his body won't do anything else.

Dick hears music. Maybe it was playing all along, but he hears it only now as the girls begin to dance. They arch their arms and legs, their shoulders rise and fall, as do their breasts. Then Grace starts to dance—the girls teach her. Dick sees pleasure in Grace's face. She laughs.

She looks beautiful and primal and peaceful.

These strangers understood something about Grace Dick didn't understand himself. It never occurred to Dick something like this would have meaning for Grace. These people are celebrating Grace becoming a woman, when Dick's only concern was keeping Grace away from Rocky Rasmusson.

And Mawuli.

How is Dick any better than his father, who left Dick to figure out for himself how to become a man? How is Dick any better than his mother, who watched Dick struggle to become a man and saw only her own needs?

Dick realizes he's crying as Seena backs farther away from Grace. Seena scans the crowd, her eyes meet Dick's. And Dick knows Seena was scanning the crowd for him. Seena runs toward Dick and, when she reaches him, Dick pulls her close. He envelops her body inside his. He presses his face into her hair that smells nothing like her hair—and yet it does. Beneath the layers of clay dust and the lingering scent of their onion-rich lunch, Dick detects Seena's perfume: Primitif, the same scent she's worn for how many years? As long as he's known her. In his mind's eye, her eighteen-year-old self stands before the mirror, spritzing her neck, wrists and hair. But this woman in his arms is not eighteen: she's twice that age. Yet the way she's melting into him reminds him of another time—a time his mind had forgotten but his body remembers. There was a time when Grace was a preschooler, Mary Catherine a toddler and Tessa a baby, when Seena did melt into Dick, when he had felt her love. But that time had come to a screeching halt. When? How? Dick doesn't know. Somehow he'd moved ahead, not noticing he'd left Seena behind. Until he did notice. But by then she'd been picked up by someone else—someone who realized she was standing alone at the edge of the road.

Seena may have allowed herself to be picked up, but Dick had responsibility, too. Didn't he? He should have realized he was driving alone. He should have turned around, looked for her.

"Okomfo's daughters aren't doing this," Seena says. "Why aren't they doing this?"

Dick closes his eyes, allows his body to fully remember his wife. Then he opens his eyes, tilts Seena's face upward, toward his. He looks through his own well of tears into her well of tears—then beyond the well into her golden eyes. From now on, Dick won't steer alone.

"We'll leave here, if that's what you want. We'll go home, Seena—we'll go back to what we had. It will be like we never came—like none of this ever happened." Dick says this, even though he doesn't want to go home, not after yesterday—not after saving that girl and her baby.

"But I don't want to leave," Seena says.

Yllis

Mary Grace was grinding corn while her breasts swayed. I knew everyone was watching her and the other grinding girls, and I was watching them, too. Mama had sent me away again. "Go play with Tessa. Find something to do. Your father and I are busy, Yllis," she said as she melded into Papa. "Mary Catherine is sick, remember? And you yourself can see what is happening with Grace. Go play."

Go play.

Mama had never spoken to me this way. Go play?

I didn't go play. I hid in the crowd.

Grace and the other girls knelt on the ground, knees splayed, their bodies shifting forward and backward as the corn transformed from kernel to dust. The queen mother had shown each girl, one by one, how to grind—including Grace. The queen then weaved between the girls, half singing, half shouting.

Okomfo stood near me, strung as I was in this ring of voyeurs. But, unlike me, Okomfo didn't stand widemouthed. He was an active voyeur, translating the sing-shout words of the queen—for the enrichment of Grace, I assumed then. Although I'm quite certain now Okomfo was most concerned that Mama and Papa understood the meaning of the ritual—understood what was at stake.

"You are becoming women," Queen Mother said. And Okomfo translated.

Okomfo then stepped forward, trailed the weaving queen. As he examined the girls and powdered corn, he purred. Or maybe the purring I heard was joy's, because joy was there. I'd heard it before while the girls danced. But everything had become jumbled: the light had shifted color and the smell had shifted scent. I had difficulty deciphering the sound of the shout-song from the sound of the fetish priest from the sound of joy. I sensed the nude dancing and nude grinding was a precursor for something far bigger, though, in part because the light around Mama and Papa was changing fast. They were wrapped around each other and Papa seemed to be soothing Mama. But he shouldn't be soothing her, I thought. He shouldn't be telling her it will all be okay, because it won't be.

It wasn't.

I broke from the ring and sprinted past the circle of eyes. I ran to Mama. "I think something bad is going to happen, Mama."

Mama rotated her face from Papa's chin to me. But Mama's face didn't look like Mama's face. "Something bad has already happened, Yllis."

"Something really bad, Mama."

Mama turned back toward Papa, nestled her head in the hollow of his neck. "You don't call this really bad?" she said, but was she speaking to me?

Mama was only a foot away, maybe inches—I knew this, yet I didn't, because she seemed so far away. I couldn't taste her love for me. I couldn't taste my love for her. "Mama?" I said. She didn't answer this time.

She can't hear me, I thought. She's so far away, she can't hear me.

I'd always believed in my love for Mama; I'd always believed in her love for me. While all the world could be hued and stinking and noisy, Mama's love was the constant for me—that unchanging core. It didn't matter that Mama was imperfect. It didn't even matter that she was a liar. Her love for me was perfect. Her love was the perfection.

Only it wasn't.

Maybe I was incapable of love—only the reflection of love. Maybe that's why I no longer tasted any love. Maybe Mama's love for me had faded away, and my love for her had been nothing but its mirror. It seemed to me in that moment that the screen of love had been ripped wide, and I saw through the hole, saw straight outside for the first time. I realized then: I'd been looking through the security of what I thought was love, seeing the world that way my entire life. Without that love screen, the world was a different place. A scary place. The quivering was still there, and the scents and colors, but there was an edge to all of it that the screen of love had softened. I tried to remind myself there is beauty in seeing truth—in seeing things for what they really are. But I couldn't focus on anything I saw or heard or felt, other than the sharp edges.

"Today you crush corn," Queen Mother said, then Okomfo said. "This symbolizes your initiation into the world of womanly duties—the most important duty being maintaining virtue. Truth is the essence of being a woman. You must hold it. Keep it."

But truth isn't like that, I thought. Truth can't be captured and trained like an animal. You might think you've got hold of truth, just like I did. You might think you're seeing it straight on. But all the while you're touching it and seeing it through a screen.

"Tomorrow is day two of Dipo," said the queen and Okomfo. "The day of Ke Pam Yami. You will be washed in the river, cleansed of your childish life. You will eat the meal of Ho Fufui Yemi, as a reminder that you will leave your family one day to join the family of your husband. For the next five days, you must not eat corn or rice. You may not look in a mirror. You may not giggle. You may not show childish behavior."

"Brilliant," I heard Mama whisper, her mouth pressed against Papa's ear. "Some of those girls are younger than Yllis."

She'd referred to me like I was too childish to understand the import of her words. Who was this woman? Where was my mama? "Those girls who are younger than Yllis?" this mama said. "They're not supposed to be silly, act like children?"

I'm a child, I thought. Just a child. A silly childish child with a wild imagination. She's been patronizing me all along. Making me think she trusted in me, had faith in me, when all she really had faith in was not having to take me seriously, because I'm a silly child.

———

I couldn't sleep that night. My blanket wasn't going to form—I knew it. But I also knew it didn't matter: I had no soul to lose.

Mary Tessa

✳ Day two.

Grace is a streaker.

Again.

But in the river this time, and Mama is saying nothing—she's not even here to watch. She and Papa are off doing God knows what, while Mawuli and Mary Catherine are in their hovel. Those two are probably eating corn and rice and giggling. Mary Catherine sure is eating now, and giggling, particularly when Mawuli is present.

Mawuli spends more time with Mary Catherine than he does with his betrothed, which is no surprise, Tessa figures, given Mary Grace is forbidden to speak to anyone but Queen Mother and the local witch doctor, Mawuli's father, Okomfo. Grace won't even speak to Tessa in private, which isn't all that unusual. But when Mama and Papa try to speak to Grace, she behaves as if they're a figment of her imagination, not worth a second glance.

The other name for this Dipo is "outdooring," which Tessa would venture to guess is some bizarre contortion of "coming out," a term that, frankly, better describes what's going on here in Africa than what goes on in the southern states at home. These African girls—and Grace—truly are coming out, and of their clothes no less. They certainly aren't leaving much to the imagination, trumping even Yllis's imagination based on the way Yllis is acting. Yllis has started nagging Tessa to tag along— as she's doing now—as if suddenly she's frightened to be alone with herself.

Tessa thought the "coming out" ceremony in the U.S. was the oddest thing—not something midwesterners could much relate to—until she saw this. Mary Grace wouldn't have considered having a "coming out" ceremony at home, but here she is, coming out in a nude, full-body dunk. Reminds Tessa of the baptism ceremony she witnessed when she accompanied her girlfriend Margot to the Assembly of God at home. But at least the holy rollers at the Assembly of God kept their clothes on.

Tessa wishes she could find all this funny: Grace and the nude dancing, cornmeal making and river baptizing. It is funny—her head knows that. It keeps placing the scene on *The Gong Show*, it keeps giving Grace the gong. But that slave castle stalks Tessa like a burning fire. As does that dead two-year-old with diarrhea. As does Tessa's rear end. She's spent far more time in the VIP over the course of the past twenty-four hours than she's spent anywhere else, and she understands now why people die from diarrhea. "If you die here," Addae's father had said, "your life has been blessed." Well, at least Tessa has that to hold on to. A blessed life, one that includes making and eating that *fufu*, despite where it's left her: the VIP. Every time Tessa starts to make fun now, the fire reaches her head or her rear, and the fun is fried. Each and every one of these naked girls is a naked slave in Tessa's fried brain, and she imagines each crammed into the women's dungeon, dying from diarrhea. The fact that white-skinned Grace has stolen this Dipo show—because she has—somehow seems an incarnation of that slavery. Tessa feels a great need to slap Grace, but only after she dresses her.

"Afi? Psst."

Tessa turns and sees Addae. He motions for Tessa to join him at the peak of the riverbank—and Tessa is more than happy to comply, make her exit. Addae's name is an Akan name meaning "morning sun." His Ewe family gave him the name because Addae had refused to be born, forcing his mother to labor from dawn till dawn. Addae told Tessa this story when she'd first met him the day before last—the day she ate the *fufu* that has been leaving her ever since, the day she taught Addae how to play Truth or Dare, and he showed her how to shoot a slingshot, hunt bats.

"Tess?" Yllis says as Tessa runs up the bank trying to hold her insides in. "Where you going?"

Addae motions toward Yllis. "She comes, too," he says. The softy.

"Oh, c'mon, then," Tessa calls back, and the scaredy-cat trails her.

Addae holds the slingshot. Apparently the dripping breasts have lost their allure: Addae's off to hunt. The slingshot looks more like a two-headed voodoo doll than a weapon. Addae said his father made the slingshot as a gift for Addae when he became a man. Tessa felt like pointing out Addae is no man—he's probably twelve. Fourteen at most. But now that Tessa sees five-year-olds being initiated into womanhood, Addae may as well be an elder.

The slingshot is a talisman, Addae said. It's in the form of a masked woodland spirit, and it protects him while he hunts. One of the masks is oriented upward, one downward, so no matter the source of the danger faced, whether from the sky or the ground, "I'm protected," Addae said.

Good luck when you encounter a lion, Tessa thought.

Tessa—with Yllis attached—meets Addae at the top of the bank. The early sun lights him, makes his black skin shine. He is the morning sun standing in the morning sun. Tessa thinks this and then she thinks, There are no flying bats to shoot now—it's day. What's he have in mind?

"I'm going to shoot the dog," Addae says.

"Shoot Lint?" Yllis says.

Lint paces the riverbank, barking and whimpering and barking. Lint's considering wading in to save Mary Grace, Tessa knows. But Lint is scared of everything, particularly water.

"You can't shoot my dog," Tessa says. "Why would you do that?"

"Rabies," he says. "The dog has rabies. Look at him."

"Rabies?" Yllis says.

"Lint doesn't have rabies," Tessa says.

"The dog has rabies," Addae says. "See him. The dog is crazy."

"That's crazy," Tessa says. "You're crazy."

Addae lifts one shoulder. Tessa assumes it's some version of a shrug.

"We could shoot my sister," Tessa says. "We could shoot Grace."

Addae arches his eyebrows and tilts his head, like he's considering it.

"No . . . ," Yllis says.

"I'm joking," Tessa says.

Addae performs his second one-shoulder shrug, just as Tessa notices the sharp tip of the slingshot rock is violet colored. Something smells like egg yolk. "Why's it painted?" she says. "Why's the rock painted?"

"Poison," he says. "Flint-bark sap."

"Sap?" Tessa says. "Sap's not poisonous."

"The girl is stupid," he says.

"Oh yeah," Tessa says. "Well, you can stuff that slingshot where even the morning sun doesn't shine."

"What is this you say?" he says. He's not the sharpest rock in the slingshot. He seems downright surprised Tessa's pissed. "I was not talking of you," he says in his singsong-far-too-articulated way, once he gets it. "You are not the girl."

"And you're calling girls stupid? I am a girl, Addae. What? Because I can speak English, you think I'm a boy?"

"No . . ."

"Are you talking about my sister, then?" Tessa's ready to take him on. "About Yllis?"

"No," he says. He pats Yllis like she's Lint. "I like this little one. I will take care of her, teach her. She is good." He gestures toward Grace and her harem. "That sister."

"Well, you have a point there," Tessa says. "That whole thing seems idiotic."

"But it is not 'idiotic.'"

"You're the one who started this," Tessa says. "You're the one who said she's stupid. I'm just agreeing."

"It is different. For us, it is different."

"Well, that Okomfo apparently doesn't think so. He's not letting his own daughters dance naked and splash around naked." Tessa gestures toward Okomfo. He stands in a circle of clothed girls.

"Daughters?" Addae says. "Those girls are not Okomfo's daughters. They are *trokosi*. They are his slaves."

"Slaves? What are you talking about, slaves? People can't be slaves. Not anymore."

"You don't know everything, Afi," Addae says. "This sap is poison." He holds up the purple-painted rock. "And those girls are slaves. They are Okomfo's slaves. When a person in our village commits a crime, his family must give a virgin to calm the angered spirits. The girl becomes Okomfo's slave. His *trokosi*. It is our system of justice."

Justice?

Tessa needs the VIP. She feels like she's about to lose it again, but from both ends. Her knees shake, then the shaking moves up her middle, through her arms. Her head feels light, like it's floating off. "Well, I wouldn't be doing that Dipo even if I lived in this freakin' place," she says. "Seems to me the girls who are doing it are the slaves."

Addae looks at Tessa like he's considering taking her down with his slingshot.

"Truth or dare?" Tessa says, trying to get his mind off shooting her—trying to get her own spacey mind off the slaves and the shaking and the soup that's determined to fly.

"Truth," he says.

"If you had to pick one of those girls who is not a slave and not stupid after all, who would you pick?"

"I have chosen," he says. "It is no matter."

"Chosen what?" Yllis says.

"The wife for me," he says. "If she fails, I will choose again."

"Fails what?" Tessa says. He's not joking. "You chose one of those girls? You're getting married?"

"When I'm ready." He points toward a girl who has just emerged from the river. Her breasts are the size of strawberries. She's younger than Tessa. She might be younger than Yllis. "That one."

"How old is she?" Tessa says. "Eight?"

"Eleven," Addae says, as if that's plenty old. "But I will marry her only if she's a virgin."

"That's disgusting," Tessa says. "And you shouldn't be talking like that in front of Yllis," who just so happens to be eleven. Addae apparently assumes Yllis is more like six, given he referred to her as the "little one." Tessa is tempted to tell him the "little one" is the same age as his betrothed, just to make a point. But she doesn't want Addae getting any ideas about Yllis. "What? Are you gonna check?"

"She will tell Queen Mother. If she lies, the spirits will know of her lie."

"Yeah," Tessa says. "And Santa Claus is coming."

"Santa Claus," he says. Tessa can't tell if he knows who Santa is. "You will see tomorrow."

"I can hear the sleigh bells ringing." Now it's Tessa's turn to shrug. This conversation is making Tessa's head throb—as if she needed more throbbing.

"Come," Addae says then, and he takes off, sprinting bare-foot along the upper bank of the river.

Where did he learn to run like that? It's like having to keep up with the Six Million Dollar Man. Better than he was before. Better. Stronger. Faster.

Tessa considers staying put given the idiot is about to marry a child "if she is a virgin," and given if Tessa is going to run at all, she ought to be running toward the VIP. But Tessa is at once horrified and bored with this Dipo. And she'd like to take another whack at that slingshot. Addae showed her up big-time with the bat shooting. He's up five to her one. Tessa doesn't like being beat.

"Wait here," she says to Yllis, then she runs through the brush down to the river, squats where she can't be seen in a tangle of overhanging trees. She empties her insides, as if her body were filled with water. Then she heads back up the bank.

Tessa's gasping when she and Yllis finally reach Addae. Addae gives them both a look, like he's been waiting around for days. Then he hisses, "Ssh." He turns back to look at whatever he was eyeing when they arrived, while Tessa doubles over, kicks off her Dr. Scholl's.

"You have bionic eyes, too?" Tessa says.

"Ssh," Addae says again.

"What are you looking at?" Tessa whispers, as she still sees only her feet.

"Truth or dare?" Addae says.

"Dare," Tessa says, because she always says "dare."

Addae shoves the slingshot beneath her gasping. "You shoot it," he says.

Tessa looks up: the bird is the most beautiful thing she's ever seen.

"The purple heron," Addae says.

The bird reminds Tessa of Mama, with its long legs and golden neck. It wades in the river. It even moves a bit like Mama does, jerky, but graceful even so, as if its seeming frailty is just the calm before the storm. Seems its power is in abeyance, just awaiting the surge. The heron flaps its wings twice, as if to confirm Tessa's thinking, show a tad of its might. But even the flapping is beautiful. The wings stretch as long as Tessa's arms, and they ripple like Lake Margrethe waves, like the waves when the sun has just set and the lake has calmed, and the waves move in what seems slow motion.

"Shoot it," Addae says.

"No, Tess," Yllis says.

Tessa realizes she's standing upright, holding the slingshot. When did she stand up? She looks at Addae and he sees what she can't say: she can't shoot this bird. Herons are protected birds; Tessa learned this in school.

Addae grabs the slingshot from her and aims. "For my mother," he says.

But Tessa pushes him to the ground. Addae sprawls in a

cloud of orange dust. The slingshot thumps onto the ground, but the rock remains in Addae's fisted hand.

The heron looks straight at Tessa, but it doesn't take flight.

Tessa picks up the slingshot. Its downward mask faces her, its upward mask faces the heron. Herons are protected, but humans aren't? Tessa thinks of the slave mothers, the slave daughters, the slave sons. She thinks of the girl who died from diarrhea. "Give me the rock," she says.

Addae does, because he knows before Tessa knows what she's about to do.

Tessa inserts the rock, makes certain the sharp painted edge faces outward, toward the heron.

Then she sends the purple poison flying.

The heron falls, Addae hoots, and a part of Yllis dies.

Mary Catherine

Purgatory. If Mary Catherine is not there now, it's where she's headed, if she doesn't land in hell.

It's the third day of this Dipo, and Mawuli fed Mary Catherine *fufu*. He dipped his pink fingers into the gluelike cassava paste, then he plunged the paste into the soup. His hand dripped with palm oil and chicken fat and stringy, stewed chicken bathed in tomatoes and onions as he slipped his fingers between her lips. Mary Catherine isn't sure what day of the week it is—it may well be Friday. But the last thing on her mind is fish.

And that's the least of it.

Mary Catherine definitely covets what belongs to her neighbor, who happens to be her sister. And she's thinking of committing murder. All that hatred she felt toward Mama has ricocheted to Grace, and it's stuck on Grace, like flung cassava paste.

When Mawuli left Mary Catherine to watch the third day of Dipo, he told her, "We are like the Holy Trinity. I am the Father, made in His image. Your sister Grace is the Son. And you, Aku Ayawa, are the Holy Ghost, always present in spirit."

Mary Catherine didn't understand what Mawuli meant, but she knew it was blasphemous. Humans can't be compared to God or Jesus or the Holy Ghost. Yet she found his words soothing, anyway, his telling her she would be present in spirit. Because she's still too weak to get up—to watch Grace make a fool of herself. It's probably just as well: prevents her from committing murder.

But it doesn't prevent her imagining the murder, imagining how she'd kill Grace. As she lies listening to the chanting and drumming, Mary Catherine hates herself for what she sees in her mind's eye. Yet even as she hates herself, she feels exhilaration because of what her mind conjures up: poison. She'd do it with poison. Tessa killed a bird, using poison sap from flint bark. Mary Catherine would mix a little of that sap into *fufu*, let Mawuli feed it to Grace, hand to mouth.

Who knew Mary Catherine's soul was so dark?

For the first time ever, Mary Catherine hopes there is no God. She hopes Saint Catherine was a Froot Loop.

The chanting and drumming stop, and Mary Catherine wonders what's happening now. According to Mawuli, this day of Dipo is called Bua Sia Mi. Grace will be painted with clay, then she must tell the queen mother of her virginity.

Mary Catherine felt herself heat up when Mawuli said that word, "virginity." Virgin. She tried to think of the Virgin Mother, not her own virginity. But Mary Catherine felt Mawuli's eyes, like she's felt his eyes so many times. If he weren't about to marry Mary Catherine's sister, she'd feel certain he was thinking of her virginity, too.

"And then what?" Mary Catherine asked Mawuli, as if it

weren't eating what's left of her—this idea of Grace painted in clay, discussing her virginity so she could lose it.

But Mawuli told Mary Catherine nothing more. Instead, he pressed those same fingers that had nourished her body against his lips, then he touched Mary Catherine's lips. "You are no longer deciding inside," he said. "You will have a new name soon, I think." And he left.

———————

Mary Catherine hears the commotion now. It's not the rhythmic commotion of the past two days. This is real commotion— not orchestrated, not planned. Mary Catherine realizes this even before Yllis bursts into the hut. Yllis's blue eyes fidget, like she's watching something only Yllis can see. Even so, Mary Catherine knows Yllis truly has seen something, not just imagined it. And now Yllis is trying to escape what she saw.

Yllis's gaze finds Mary Catherine's. Yllis stares before she screams, "Run! Catie. Get up! Run! They're coming for you."

"What?" Mary Catherine says. She feels panic overtake her body, as if a volcano inside her has given birth to an earthquake. Could Mawuli see inside Mary Catherine's soul? Did he see the darkness inside her? Did he see her mind killing Grace? Did he tell the others what he saw? Are they coming for Mary Catherine, now, because Catie's a murderer in her heart?

"I didn't mean it," Mary Catherine says. "I never would have done it. I know it's still a sin, my thinking it. But I wouldn't have . . . I was just upset, mad."

Yllis shakes her head; her hair and face become indistinguishable. "C'mon, Catie!" she says. "C'mon!"

But it's too late: Mawuli's father has come for Mary Catherine. He stands in the doorway of the hut. "He is a powerful juju man," Mawuli had told Mary Catherine, explaining that a juju man is a type of traditional healer, "but one who has the gift to avenge as well as heal."

Mama and Papa seem to fall into the hut. They stand, now, flanking Mawuli's father. Mama's face is streaked with mud or clay, and Papa's looks swollen. "That's my daughter, Okomfo," Papa says. "I don't know what you're thinking."

Tessa scoots in beside Mama and grabs her hand.

"Tessa, go," Seena says. "Take Yllis—take her away from here. She shouldn't see this. Go find that boy—the boy you like. Take Yllis with you."

Tessa minds, no questions asked. She sprints to Yllis, takes Yllis's hand, drags her from the hut, just before the juju man speaks.

"Yes," Okomfo says. "She is your daughter. And Mawuli is my son, Doctor. It is only right, based on the crime. And this is the one I want." Okomfo points at Mary Catherine. "You must give this one to me."

Clara

The Catholic church is nothing to look at. A rectangular, one-story brick building with relatively small windows, it looks as much like a prison as it does anything. Not that Clara has ever seen a prison. But she can imagine. At least the Danish Lutheran church looks like a church—although at this point in Clara's life, given the choices she's made, she's not sure whether entering a church is any less terrifying than entering a prison. Fortunately (or unfortunately) for Clara, she doesn't have to decide, as the Catholic church combines the two. Apparently the Lucky Day continues.

BOB parks the Dial-a-Ride in front of the church, then bobs on up to lower Clara on the lift. The only clear upside of Clara's current situation is that over half of the passengers are now sleeping, not able to take in the sights—that is, Clara's humiliating herself. Again. She's not even going to bother trying to negotiate those stairs this time. She's already in hell. May as well ramp up the temperature.

"You have an appointment, Mrs. Eihlerson?" BOB says as

he and Clara descend. "You here to see the interim priest? You supposed to meet him in his office? In the rectory?"

"I'm not meeting any interim priest." Clara shakes off BOB's grip on her arm as the lift meets the ground. "I want to see Amadi. Father Amadi. Where do I find him?"

"Father Amadi? He's not here, Mrs. Eihlerson."

"What do you mean, 'not here'?"

"He left," BOB says.

Would be Clara's luck, now wouldn't it? "Well, when's he coming back? I'll wait."

"He's not coming back, Mrs. Eihlerson. It's been in the paper. Haven't you read . . . ?"

"What are you talking about, BOB?" Clara says.

"He's left the ministry, ma'am. He was having a relation-ship. You know. An affair . . ."

"A love affair?" Clara say.

BOB shrugs.

Lordy be. Something tightens inside Clara, like her will to live has gripped hard—like it's trying to hold on. She not only has to find Grace, she has to find Amadi to find Grace. Feels like she's on one of those scavenger hunts, looking for a paper clip, a yo-yo and a dill pickle. But to what end? There's nothing to win in this hunt. Only something to not lose.

What has Clara done to that poor Grace, trying to sentence her to a loveless life? A life where she's responding, not acting. Constantly trying to mask her past wrongs. Clara may not be dead, but she's been burying herself her whole damn life. And now, Grace? Clara has sent Grace off to follow in Clara's own foolhardy footsteps. Clara's not only old, she's old and asinine, clearly not having learned her own lessons: it's Clara's baby she wanted Grace to save.

Oh, God, Clara thinks. Let there be a God and let that God hear this prayer: guide Grace to know I'm just an old fool, not worth my salt. Let her know not to heed a damn word I've said.

"You can see Father Quinn," BOB says, apparently seeing Clara is on the verge of a breakdown that has nothing to do with her broken-down limbs. "He came up from downstate. Gave mass last Sunday."

"Will he be able to tell me where I can find Father Amadi?" Clara says.

Clara is making BOB nervous—she can see this. He bobs, still, but the bobbing isn't the oh-how-fabulous-I'm-not-as-wretched-as-you-are bob, but a sort of jumpy, twitchy bob, like he's worried whatever Clara has that's making her wretched might turn out to be contagious.

"Can't say, ma'am," BOB says, but he's leaving her just the same. "Father Quinn's office is over there." He gestures toward the rectory as he backs onto the bus, then he flips the switch. The lift lifts.

Clara is left.

"You call now, when you need a pickup," BOB hollers out the door, just before the door flaps close.

But Clara knows with a clarity that catches her unaware there's a good chance she won't need a pickup, that she'll find her own way home. Because she understands, even before she discovers Quinn snoring, there's almost no chance he'll be able to lead her to the Slepys. And Clara has no interest in living to see her life relived through that girl.

"Father Quinn?" Clara says, after she's managed to hobble into the rectory, find the office and knock. When no one responds, she pokes her head through the partially opened door. She feels like a Peeping Tom—peeping on God—especially after hearing that juice about Amadi. Certainly seems possible some other Peeping Tom got an eyeful while standing in the very spot Clara stands in now. It's more than Clara would like to imagine.

The view Clara does take in is more than she'd like to imagine, as well. The man is ancient, and that's saying something coming from a woman who just rode the lift on the Dial-a-Ride. The room has that old-person smell of rancid grease mixed with Ben-Gay. Clara will be damned if she ever allows herself to reek like that.

Come to think of it, maybe she does reek like that.

GODDAMN.

Quinn's head lolls on the desk, his mouth hangs wide. He snores and drools. A little puddle has accumulated on his ink blotter. Clara figures the parishioners won't have to worry about this one having wandering eyes and hands, et cetera. Then again, this interim priest—as BOB called him—might drop dead while preaching, which wouldn't exactly be a clean transition. Anyway.

"FATHER QUINN," Clara hollers, like he's deaf. She abhors when others do that to her, when they holler after seeing her cane, like somehow she's using the cane because her ears are crippled. But what else is she to do? She's afraid if she approaches Father Quinn, she might startle him into a heart attack, and she already has enough deaths on her plate.

Father Quinn stirs—thank God—then clears his throat and swipes his mouth with the heel of his hand. It's even less of a pretty sight seeing him straight on. He has little tumbleweed tufts of hair above his ears, but otherwise he's as bald as a newborn's bum. His nostrils are bigger than any Clara has ever seen. They face more forward than down, giving a full-on view of their hairy interior.

Well, Clara's certainly no Liz Taylor herself.

"Father?" she says, and she feels like the fool she is. Clara's father has been dead for forty years. This old geezer is no more a father to Clara than Clara is a mother to that Grace.

Or to Grace's baby.

Or to my baby, Clara thinks.

Suddenly, Clara bobs like BOB. She shakes like piss in the breeze. But this shaking, it's from the top down, not the bottom up. It's her torso that started it, and now the quivering has made its way down her limbs.

"You need to sit down, Mrs. . . . ," Father Quinn says.

At some point, apparently, Quinn rose to his feet and made his way to Clara. He now helps Clara across the room, eases her into a chair.

Just a little payback for Clara's thinking he was ancient. She can imagine the old geezer asking, "Who's smiling now?"

"What ails you today, my sister?"

Clara would like to point out she's no more his sister than he is her father, but she hasn't quite mastered the shaking. Feels like her baby's still in there, trying frantically to find a way out.

"Where's Father Amadi?" Clara says. "How can I get in touch with him?"

"That is God's business, Mrs. . . . What is your name, my dear? It's God's place to deal with Father Amadi. His transgressions are between him and God."

"I don't give a hoot about his transgressions. I just need to find the man. It's about the Slepys."

"Yes. I know," Father Quinn says.

"You know?"

"About the Slepy girl."

"What?" Clara says.

"The girl . . ." But Quinn knows he's said more than he should have said. His words trail off.

Clara needs to get her wits. And fast. "Yes, the Slepy girl. I know all about it," she says, even though she knows squat.

"You do know," he says then, like he's trying to convince himself. "Father Amadi says it was her, you know—that she came on to him. That she'd been coming on to him all summer. But, given his secretary—that Mrs. Mahoney—given what she saw . . . I imagine that's what you heard."

Clara wants to kill him. She wants to kill both of them: Amadi and Quinn. Goddamn bastards.

"I've heard stories," Clara lies, "but not directly from Mrs. Mahoney. It's hard to parse out the truth, Father. I'd like to know exactly what Mrs. Mahoney did see."

"Says the girl came running out of the office only partially dressed and crying . . ."

"She's pregnant," Clara says then. "The Slepy girl is pregnant." It comes out before Clara's old brain catches up with exactly what she's saying. But it doesn't take even her brain that long. Rocky Rasmusson had nothing whatsoever to do with Grace being pregnant: it was Amadi. Clara knew Amadi didn't give a damn about the welfare of those girls, after hearing that conversation between Seena Slepy and Amadi, when Amadi refused to help Mary Catherine. But who would have thought he was capable of this?

Mary Grace didn't trust Clara after all.

And Clara loses a child for the second time.

Seena

Mary Grace was speckled with gray, as if she'd spun clay on a pottery wheel and lost control. The clumps clung to her pale shoulders, her pale breasts, her pale stomach. Its flecks peppered her hair. Strand upon strand of colorful beads circled her neck and plummeted between her clay-splattered breasts, as did strands of golden twine.

Seena had actually felt some relief on this third day of Dipo—before the pot cracked, before Okomfo staked his claim on Mary Catherine—because Grace hadn't seemed as exposed—as naked—because of the clay and the beads and the twine.

Seena had forced herself away from her plans for the school to watch Dipo. The day before she'd scouted a location, a clearing on the outskirts of the village, land that apparently no one owned. "Could I build a structure here?" she'd asked. "Who owns this property?" She'd been received with shrugs, blank stares, half nods, as if her questions were senseless. So she'd changed course: "I want to construct a building here. I want it made of concrete, like those buildings over there. It needs a solid foundation, and windows that open and close. And a roof that's made of a material other than iron." Within minutes she had an entourage of village men and boys, all with suggestions, ideas, connections. They assumed she was building a home for her family, and she didn't avow or disavow this. Soon enough Kofi would make her real intentions clear to them, she knew, but by then she'd have the information she needed: she'd be on her way. And when Seena was on her way—when she wanted something—there was little that could stop her.

Nevertheless, she'd stopped today to watch Grace. She'd conceded to Grace's participation in this Dipo—or realized she had little choice but to concede. Her only hope was that some-day she would be able to look back on Dipo and laugh. She had images of teasing Grace. She imagined them back at the Danish Landing, with Grace home from college, a boyfriend in tow. She imagined telling this imaginary boyfriend about Grace's parading in Africa, naked but for beads and clay. She envisioned Grace's embarrassment, the boyfriend's laughter, and Seena thinking even Dipo was somehow worthwhile in retrospect.

And now? Like the make-believe pottery spinning on the make-believe wheel, Seena's fantasy of the happy family looking back with nostalgia on their African adventure has burst wide: the shit has hit the fan. And it's not only Grace who's speckled. They're all dripping with shit.

Because Grace is pregnant. When the queen mother placed the clay pot on Grace's chest, the clay pot cracked. Or so the queen mother said. "She is not a virgin," the queen declared. "She is a liar, this girl."

Mawuli had explained before the ritual that on this day, Bua Sia Mi, each girl must swear to the queen mother that she is a virgin, after which the queen mother places a clay pot on the girl's chest. "If the girl lies," Mawuli had said, "the pot will crack." Listening to Mawuli, Seena couldn't help but wonder if this was the origin of the term "crackpot."

And when the queen mother made her announcement—claiming Grace was neither a virgin nor truthful—Seena called the queen just that, a crackpot. "C'mon, Grace," she'd said as she pushed her way through the crowd, through the uproar in the crowd. "She's a crackpot, that woman. That so-called queen. This has gone far enough."

Dick had traced Seena's path through the horde and stood beside Seena, stroking her hair.

"No, Mama," Grace had said, her eyes brimming with tears and fear. "No, Mama. She's right. I'm pregnant. Papa, I'm so sorry."

"You're not pregnant," Seena had said. "A cracked pot doesn't make you pregnant."

"I know that," Grace had said. And she'd looked at Seena like what Seena was, what she is: a crackpot. "It was Rocky," Grace said. But she spoke to Dick, then, like she'd given up on Seena. "Forgive me, Papa. Forgive me, please."

For the briefest moment of blissful ignorance, Seena actually thought, What was rocky? Then she realized: Rocky. Rocky Rasmusson. And right there, in a sea of eyes and ears, Seena learned her daughter is neither a virgin nor truthful.

"But Mawuli knew," Grace had said. "I mean, he knows. And he wants to marry me . . ."

"This is the outrage!" Seena heard these words, but her memory of this moment is a blur of color, flesh, fabric and beads. And noise: unintelligible murmurs and grunts. Mawuli's father, the priest called Okomfo, burst through the throng like a freed pomegranate seed. He wore a red flowing garment and a woven cap that resembled an oversize thimble. "A disgrace. Of my family. My honor."

And now Seena knows something she never would have imagined: slavery is not a thing of the past. The slave souls Yllis claims she saw, Seena sees them, too. Only they are not dead in body, only in spirit. They are the girls who'd been circling Okomfo—they are "his girls," that handful of girls who did not participate in Dipo, whom Seena had regarded as the lucky ones. But that was before she learned the word *trokosi*, meaning "slaves of the gods." That was before she looked at the girls closely—before she saw she couldn't look at them closely, because they won't look at her. Their eyes are still. Their expressions are still. Their will? If it lives, it lives beyond where Seena's eyes can reach. They are slaves, these girls. They are Okomfo's slaves.

And Seena's daughter—her Mary Catherine—wants to be enslaved.

After Grace announced to the throng that she was spoiled goods, Mawuli's father Okomfo demanded unspoiled goods: a virgin, Mary Catherine. "It is the law," he said. "You have shamed my family. Your daughter has offended my honor and the honor of my son. You must give me a virgin to pay for this offense. She will be my *trokosi*. Otherwise, I will curse your family. Death will fall upon you."

Seena laughed in Okomfo's face, threw out a few curses of her own. She had followed Okomfo into the hut—in to find

Mary Catherine. Catie sat in her makeshift bed, wrapped in kente cloth, looking far too much like the queen mother—with her short hair—than Seena could stomach at the moment. "This is the one I want," Okomfo said. "You must give this one to me. As payment."

"People aren't commodities," Seena said. "They can't be owned."

"Tell your Indians that," Okomfo said. "Tell the descendants of those you Americans enslaved."

Only later did Seena have a chance to contemplate the irony of the situation, and of her words. He was right, in a sense, of course. They'd just visited slave castles, hadn't they? But that was the past, she'd thought: the past.

But it is not the past.

Slavery is alive.

According to local law, if a person commits a crime, the person's family must give a virgin daughter to the village priest in order to appease the gods for the crime. The girl becomes the property of the priest—his *trokosi*. The *trokosi* farm and fetch water, wash clothes and cook. And after the onset of menstruation, the *trokosi's* bondage involves sexual servitude as well.

Apparently the Slepys are "lucky" in this regard, because Mawuli's father has agreed to "give" Mary Catherine to Mawuli instead of keeping her for himself. "And she will be my wife," Mawuli said, "not my slave."

What luck.

Mawuli planned this. Seena knows in her gut: he planned this. Mawuli wanted Mary Catherine all along—it's as clear to Seena as any of this could be. Grace told him she was pregnant and he set her up, just so he could get his hands on Mary Catherine.

Seena had seen the way Mawuli looked at Catie from the moment he met her. But she'd discounted it. How could any man be attracted to this boyish girl? A girl with no breasts, no hair. Catie looks more like a young man than many men. But that was just it, wasn't it? Queen Mother looks masculine, too, with her barely there hair and her men's clothes. Catie's lack of breasts and hair represented something to Mawuli: she was, to him, like Queen Mother. Still female, but strong, powerful, independent. Exotic, yet familiar, too. And sexy because of this. Seena should have realized. When she met Queen Mother, she should have put the pieces together.

But did Mary Catherine realize? Did she know Grace was being set up?

Maybe she did.

Pandora's jar has cracked open wide. The spirits of deception and suffering, doom and blame, strife and hatred and death have escaped, no question. But where is hope? Where in this dusty Hades is hope?

Seena has plans to build a school where she'll teach African girls, when she can't even teach her own?

Because Mary Catherine wants this. She *thinks* she wants this. "I'll stop eating again if you refuse," she'd said when she learned she could end up with Mawuli while Mary Grace ended up shamed.

"Stop eating, then," Seena told her. "I'd rather you starve yourself to death than enslave yourself."

But that image of Mary Catherine near death—of her lying

cool and still and white like a solidified smear of glue—haunts Seena more than Okomfo's curses. What's caused Mary Catherine to become so selfish? So reckless? So willing to trade in her life—and her sister's dignity?

Seena can't stop the echo in her own brain: What caused you to become so selfish? So reckless? So willing to trade in your family's welfare and your dignity for a man? Isn't she just mimicking you?

———————

It is Friday, four days after they arrived in Avone, a week since they arrived in West Africa. But Seena has relived much of her life here.

She stands alone near the river now, the river where Grace supposedly bathed nude—at least Seena spared herself that scene. Seena looks into the water, at her reflection. She tries to find some semblance of a human, but all she sees is a quiver of color.

"Seena?"

Seena turns and sees Dick, who descends the bank in two strides. Seena expects Dick to embrace her—she wants him to. But Dick doesn't. He lays his camera on the ground. He strips off his shirt. He's sweating, Seena sees. He dips his shirt into the river, then he dabs at Seena's face with his shirt. "You're a mess," he says. "You should see yourself."

And Seena thinks, I was trying to.

"We received a telegram," Dick says, "from the city. I mean, from the States. But it arrived just now, in a taxi that was passing through from the capital."

Something is wrong, Seena thinks. Something *else* is wrong. She knows from Dick's pallor, from the ice in his eyes, that something else is very very wrong. "Is someone hurt?" she says. Dick doesn't answer, and Seena adds, "Did someone die?" But who could have died? Dick's parents are dead, and he's an only child. If Seena's father is still alive, he may as well be dead. Seena may as well be an only child.

Dick twists his wet shirt with fisted hands. "One person is dead," he says. The tendons in his neck protrude. The muscles in his shoulders and forearms grow large and hard before Seena's eyes—as the ice in his eyes becomes steel. "And if it's up to me, another person will be dead soon."

BOOK FIVE

West Africa

"You killed your husband," Okomfo says. "The curse had befallen you, and you were possessed. Death was stalking you and your family. You had chosen the curse of death. You could have calmed the spirits. You could have given your daughter . . ."

For five days now Seena has returned to this school-turned-courthouse. For five days she's been tried here, overtly by Okomfo and Queen Mother, covertly by every other member of the village, including the teacher Kofi, who permitted his schoolhouse to become Seena's courtroom. Now, on this last day of Seena's trial, Kofi sits in the front row, awaiting Seena's reply.

Seena must be careful; she knows this. For her children, she must be careful, hold her tongue. But she'd like to respond to this juju man by spitting in his face. She'd like to tell him he is a fraud, as bad as the white slave traders, a child molester.

Another child molester.

Seena wants to die.

If it weren't for her children, she'd go to death freely. Death is what she deserves. She's a neglectful mother, an unfaithful wife.

This juju man is not a fraud. A curse had fallen upon Seena: she was possessed. With Heimdall. And because of this, death did stalk her family. It nabbed life from Dick and from Grace's womb. It tainted Tessa's soul. It smothered Catie's goodness. It stained Yllis's life. And death stalks Seena still, making her long for it—for its numbness.

But does death still seek her children? Seena doesn't know. She hasn't been permitted to speak with them since the trial began. She doesn't know if Mary Catherine is eating, if Mary Grace is still bleeding. Where is Tessa? She's been away from the trial as much as she's been here. And why won't Yllis look at Seena? Is death tracking Yllis, too? Wanting not only to stain her life but to take her life? Is it tracking Yllis like Tessa tracked animals with that boy—that Addae—searching for any life she could find so she could steal it?

Even as Seena asks herself these questions, part of her doesn't want to know if Mary Catherine is eating, if Mary Grace is bleeding, where Tessa is, whether death still is tracking. Because every time she looks at her daughters, the pain is stark, the loss suffocating. Each has lost her father, and for what? Each is parentless, now, adrift in the dry sea of Africa.

For what?

Today the trial will end. And Seena will be convicted: she has no hope of a different outcome. How could she even hope for a different outcome? Not when she knows what that outcome could be. She is doing what she can in this moment—holding her tongue—to protect her children. But how will she—this murderess—protect her children when the trial ends? She'll be powerless: David against Goliath.

If only she had David's five stones.

If only in these five days she could find a way to take Goliath down.

Dick loved this story: David and Goliath. And he loved the story of the five loaves and two fishes that were somehow enough to feed a hungry multitude.

As Seena thinks this she realizes: for the first time since being with Heimdall, she's not afraid to love. She's afraid to *not* love—to not love enough. For the sake of her children—for the sake of this love—she must sharpen her rock. She must transform these five days into five loaves, powerful enough to turn a miracle, feed the needs of this multitude.

Seena recalls the myth of Amaryllis: so in love was Amaryllis with the shepherd boy Alteo that day after day she stood on his doorstep and pierced her heart in an attempt to win his love. But Alteo had no interest in girls: he loved only flowers. It made no difference how many times Amaryllis pierced her heart; Alteo paid her no heed. Then a miracle happened: on the very spot where Amaryllis's blood had fallen, a beautiful flower bloomed. When Alteo saw the flower, he fell in love with Amaryllis, and he named the blood red flower Amaryllis in her honor.

Seena must do more than pierce her own heart. She must play by Okomfo's rules. She must discover Okomfo's flower: what will get the attention of a man who has spent more time during Seena's trial pouring libations to the spirits than making a case against her?

Seena knows spirits, doesn't she? Hasn't she spent the last

twenty years reading about warring gods and escaping spirits? She knows Apate, the spirit of deceit, and Oizys, the spirit of suffering. She knows Moros, Eris, Geras and Nemesis. And she knows Ker, the spirit of carnage and death.

Hope remains.

Yllis

It's an outline, Death is. It rings people, then squeezes. That man—that witch doctor—was right. The Snake of Death had encircled us, and it circled still.

When Okomfo cursed our family with Death, I watched Death rear its head and flick its tail. Mama had laughed at Okomfo, called him a lecher. "You'll take Mary Catherine over my dead body," she'd said.

But who gave her the right? Who gave her the right to open the gate to Death, to welcome him in?

This and other questions floated around me. They were my jelly souls: these questions that couldn't be answered were lives that couldn't be contained. And I knew then what purgatory is—that it's not a place.

"Is it like dominoes?" I'd asked Papa back in Grayling, after he'd announced there is nothing cruel or unusual about killing a killer. "You have to be a killer to kill a killer. Doesn't it just keep going?"

"Is it murder if you kill yourself?" Mama had asked Mary Catherine, as Catie lay wilting, draining herself of life. "Or is killing yourself just a venial sin?"

"You get just one chance?" I'd asked Mary Catherine after

she'd explained about mortal sins. About murder. About hell. "But aren't there exceptions? There must be exceptions."

Is it an exception if you kill a killer? Or is it like dominoes, no matter? If you kill a killer or kill yourself, do the dominoes fall to the side, does the Snake of Death itself die?

Sometimes I think the significance of each life is defined and miniscule: not even the size of a sparrow in an egg. A child is born, lives, dies of diarrhea. Life goes on. A man is born, lives with an inhaler, dies in a rocker. Life goes on. A woman is born, lives with rickets, dies alone. Life goes on.

Papa was born. He lived a good life. He lived a bad life. He died with a splattered heart.

Life goes on?

I don't know the answer to this question. I don't know if there's room in this world. Because other times each life feels unwieldy to me, all powerful, all consuming, just knowing how much the choices made by one person can affect others' lives. In this respect, each of our lives seems huge: Papa's and Mama's, mine and the Marys', the Indian's, the slave owners' and the slaves' themselves. Each life seems without defined boundaries, as if it could open up and suck the essence from everything around it when the wind changed, or on a whim. Or because of hatred or greed or desire.

Or in a moment of panic colored by Africa and flavored by the impurity that is love.

Mary Grace

Mary Grace hears a woman's scream. It isn't high pitched. It isn't a scream of hysteria or excitement. It isn't a scream of terror. It's almost breathless, this scream—like someone had thought to scream but ran short on air. Grace wants to ignore it. She wants to wallow in her humiliation and fear. Grace is white trash carrying the offspring of white trash, and no black magic is going to change that. She paraded around nude. She degraded her family. And now her sister Mary Catherine is trying to save Grace by degrading herself—by agreeing to let herself be human payment for Grace's transgression.

Grace is in the same impossible situation in which she'd started, but now she's put everyone around her in an impossible situation as well.

Yet Grace isn't the same. That Dipo meant something to her. Standing before all those people, stripped inside and out, she found something inside herself she forgot she had. The world is different from what she'd expected, and she wants to be part of it, this new world. She is *capable* of being part of it: this is the most astonishing thing of all. Grace doesn't have to stay in the jar in which she's been sealed—in which she's sealed herself. She doesn't have to be the cheerleading blonde sunning herself on a reflective blanket—that pretty girl who doesn't need math. She can be that if she chooses, but it's her choice, and she can choose something else. And if she does choose something else, she can handle it. She doesn't need Mawuli to handle it for her. Or Clara. Or Mama or Papa.

Queen Mother helped Grace see this, before Dipo. And Dipo made her feel this. Grace was the one who stood in front of those people, baring her body and soul, while Mawuli stood on the sidelines like a cheerleader himself—a cheerleader who quickly switched sides, joined the winning team. Queen Mother said women here care about their appearance—wrapping their bodies and heads in that beautiful cloth, ringing themselves with those beautiful beads—because they have self-respect, not because they lack it. Part of the purpose of Dipo is to instill this self-respect. Caring about your appearance doesn't mean you care about nothing else—it doesn't mean you're brainless and worthless and as shallow as the Avone River, no matter what Mama thinks. No matter what Grace's former teacher Mr. Kane thinks. No matter what anyone thinks.

And the baby? Grace has options, adoption being a fairly obvious one, as Queen Mother pointed out in private after the pot cracked. Clara sort of failed Grace in the options category. Old Clara's baby was stillborn, she'd told Grace. And Clara couldn't get pregnant again. Maybe there is a younger version of Clara out there—someone who is ready to raise a child, but who can't have one of her own. With the help of Mama and Papa—who, it turns out, love Grace, faults and all—Grace will figure it out. And those people who will look at pregnant Grace and feel justified, who'll decide she became exactly the person they expected her to become? They only seal Grace in a jar if she agrees to be sealed there. And Grace no longer agrees.

But the scream?

In the past, Grace would have heard that scream and stayed put. She would have been scared, and she would have rationalized there was nothing she could do anyway, whatever the situation. But, now? Grace decides to scout out that scream, to try to help, because she actually believes she might have something to offer—something that could help—whatever the situation.

But the pain rushes in moments after the scream—almost simultaneously with it. The pain is menstrual cramps revved. It rides through Grace as if on a roller coaster. Grace doubles over as the waves of pain squeeze and ache their way through her. But the waves never actually pass through—they just keep coming, like they're being recycled, circling back to the beginning every time they reach the end.

———————

Grace wonders now whether her blood started running the same time Papa's did. She wonders whether the life in her passed out of her in a puddle of blood, just as Papa's life passed from this world. It's comforting, in a way, to think they passed on to the next life together: the baby who never was and the papa who left too soon.

Dick

West Africa
Fall 1976

Dick finds Seena by the river. The setting sun illuminates her against the darkness that falls around. Her hair is disheveled, her clothes are filthy. Her pearl necklace looks odd against the backdrop of filth. She hangs over the river as if vomiting. Maybe she is vomiting, made ill by Mary Grace's behavior, or Mary Catherine's behavior, or by Seena's most recent consumption of *kenkey*. Even so, Dick takes out his camera. Just as the sun drops to the other side of the globe, Dick snaps a picture. He wants to preserve this moment. He's not stealing Seena's soul: he's holding it. The love he feels in this instant is driven less by passion, more by Dick's knowing their days in Africa have drawn Seena and him together, not pushed them further apart. Seena is Dick's partner: they will survive this together.

"We received a telegram," he says when Seena notices him. Seena's face is smudged, that beautiful face. Too beautiful to be smudged. Dick pulls off his shirt, dips it in the water, dabs at the orange dirt on her face. The orange smears, but it doesn't disappear.

"What is it?" she says. "What did the telegram say?"

Dick dreads telling her what he's learned. He's less concerned about the news of Clara—he'd never sensed Seena was fond of Clara. It's the report about Mary Catherine he fears relaying. What will happen to Seena when she hears? She's already been pushed to the brink.

But there's no turning back. Seena knows Dick has something to tell her, something important. He feels a rush when he realizes this—when he realizes she can see his thoughts. It's evidence of their closeness, that they've become close—that somehow through their daughters' missteps, their own missteps, Dick's C-section, Seena's school, they've found each other. Again. Nothing will come between them now.

"Did someone die?" she asks, reading even the news about Clara in Dick's face.

"Yes." Dick tells her what the telegram said about Clara first, while he tries to cage the fury he feels when he mentions Amadi: he wants Amadi dead.

Clara had gone to see Amadi, Dick says. But she'd found an interim priest in his office instead. And while with this other priest, she'd had a stroke, died on the spot.

"Clara wasn't Catholic," Seena says, which seems an odd response. "Why had she gone to see Father Amadi? And why was there an interim priest in the office, not Father Amadi? Where had he gone?"

Seena's coldness is rearing up again. This is the Seena who can't be bothered with others' discomfort, others' needs, others' pain. Others' lives. This is the Seena driven by logic, made frantic by the illogical. "You may not have liked the woman,"

Dick feels like saying. "But don't you care at all? You saw the old lady every day of every summer for how many years?"

But instead Dick says, "Clara went to see Father Amadi about our daughter."

"Our daughter?"

Dick explains, then, how that bastard Amadi molested Mary Catherine, how the whole town knows. How Mary Catherine told Clara she's pregnant. How Clara had gone to confront Amadi about the pregnancy but died in the act.

Seena's eyes are quiescent. If she's breathing, Dick sees no sign of it. "Seena?"

"But Mary Catherine's not pregnant. It's Grace who's pregnant. This isn't making sense. Mary Catherine never would have confided in Clara. She was scared of Clara. Besides, Heimdall wouldn't do that. I don't believe it. I won't believe that."

"You're defending Amadi. That devil? I trusted him . . . The bastard. There are witnesses, Seena. How could you defend someone who molested our daughter?" But even as Dick asks this, part of him knows. And then all of him knows: it's obvious, isn't it? It's always been obvious: his daughter with the blueberry eyes was fathered by his father with the blueberry eyes. His priest.

There was never any damn Indian.

His wife not only stole Dick's love, she stole his God.

Dick has been alone his whole goddamned life, and he is still alone. Dick's father abandoned him, his mother abandoned him. He thought the Virgin Mary had loved him—that Mary's love and God's love had carried him and protected him when nothing else could and no one else would. But the Virgin Mary is a slut. God is her pimp.

"You love him," Dick says. It's not a question.

Seena answers anyway, not with words, but the stillness breaks. Seena, who didn't cry at their wedding, or when their first child was born, or their second or third, heaves and sobs. She presses her face into her hands, and when she pulls her hands away, her face is a smear of tears, snot and dirt.

And Dick's soul dies. "I knew Yllis wasn't mine. I knew from the first moment I saw her. But I loved you. I loved you anyway. But I don't love you now."

Dick strangles Seena then. He tries to. His fingers encircle her neck, her pearls. He bends her backward, towers above her. He feels her neck's tensed cords—this grizzle beneath his thumbs—as the pearl choker evolves from snug to lax. Seena's yellow eyes bulge. She tries to scream, but Dick chokes the scream.

He doesn't want to kill Amadi.

He wants to kill Seena.

But something stops him.

Something kills his body.

Too.

————

Ironic that the Doctor of Death doesn't know the cause of his own death.

Dick hovers above his body now, and above Seena, whose body slumps over his. Seeing himself down there, Dick is not sure what he is—what it is that's hovering.

There was a doctor, a man named MacDougall, who performed experiments on the recently dead. MacDougall concluded that a person loses three-fourths of an ounce on average the moment he dies. MacDougall's experiments were faulty, and Dick never gave the notion of "death's weight" much heed. But is that what he is now? Three-fourths of an ounce? Three-fourths of an unfeeling ounce?

Seena

Seena is a balloon, her breath trapped inside. And other air hangs all around. She feels this other air—she feels it touch her skin. Yet she can't draw the outside air into her mouth, her throat, her lungs because the balloon is sealed. By Dick. No air passes in. No air passes out.

But then it does, it passes both in and out. Seena crashes to the ground gasping as the air rushes into her lungs and out of her lungs.

Dick lies partially on top of Seena, partially on the clay earth. Seena realizes she's alive. Dick wanted her dead—she was sure she would die. But she's alive. How is she alive?

She rolls Dick off of her, onto his back. The rolling takes effort, almost more than she has—more than the breath she has found can manage. But she does manage, and then sees: the hole leading to Dick's heart, the rock stuck in the hole. My God, she thinks. Oh, dear God.

Seena looks up—she looks for help. She finds the hazy gray blur of Tessa, Yllis and that boy, that Addae, as they approach her, passing through the river.

Yllis arrives first. Seena looks into Yllis's blueberry eyes as they look down on the face of the father who isn't her father—yet who was her father still. Seena stripped her of one father. And now another? No, she thinks. Please. No.

Tessa arrives then. Seena smells her presence before she sees Tessa's pallor and the feces that snake her leg. But when she does see this—the pallor, the feces—she knows with certainty how Dick died. Tessa her daughter who thinks only of herself thought of someone but herself: Seena. Tessa shot Dick to save Seena's life. But it's not Tessa who really killed Dick; Seena knows this. Seena destroyed Dick's heart.

And because of this, Seena wants to go with him. She belongs in Hades—she belongs in hell. Tessa and Yllis run to get help, and as Seena waits with Dick's body, the river calls her. She imagines Virginia Woolf, weighted down with rocks. She could weight herself down, let the rocks carry her to hell. She feels Dick's pulse—his absence of pulse. She presses her hand against his silent, bleeding heart. Then she stands, walks toward the river.

But Lint stops her. He bounds toward her, coming from where? He barks, circles her. Water is Lint's nemesis: he can't bear it. Nor can he bear to have Seena near it. Even at the Danish Landing, he preferred Seena skate over the lake rather than swim in it. And Seena realizes Lint is her Cerberus, the three-headed dog who guards the entrance to the underworld, who prevents the living from entering. Except this Cerberus has four heads: three Marys and one Yllis. And because of them, Seena will skate over the underworld again.

Yllis

Mama sat at the front of the sparse schoolroom—sparse but for the mass of people. It seemed every person from the village had jammed his way in to watch the last day of Mama's trial.

Okomfo remained Mama's primary tormentor, but the queen—who could speak English after all—took jabs, too, whenever Okomfo lost his stride. Not only was Mama a murderer, the queen said. She was a neglectful mother, having allowed Grace to become a woman with no guidance, no instruction. If Mama had taken care—as the people of Avone take care by giving their daughters Dipo and teaching them to be women—what happened to Grace would never have happened.

"Tell us how you killed him," Okomfo then said to Mama, as if he hadn't said this innumerable times before.

But this time, unlike the prior times, Mama replied. "I'm Apate." She spoke in a near whisper, in a soft wind of words. "Do you know Apate?"

Okomfo stopped what until that moment had been nearly incessant marching and gesturing. His lips pursed.

"I am the spirit of deceit and guile," Mama said. "I was in

love with Dolos, the spirit of trickery. And together we killed Aletheia."

"What's she doing?" Tessa said, having just returned from the VIP.

"She's not making sense," Grace said.

"It's a demon," Mary Catherine said. "Father Amadi told me about demons. About how a demon can take over a person. That's why she's not making sense."

But I knew Mama was making sense.

And I knew, too, that I could feel—that I did have a soul. Because in this moment, Mama carried the burden. Yet I felt the burden all the same. And I realized: souls don't stand alone. What makes a soul a soul is the shared burden and pain, the shared joy: it's the connection between us that carries on.

"Who's this Aletheia?" Okomfo says. "You've killed someone else?"

"I feel Ker, the spirit of carnage, of death," Mama said. "If I stay here, in this village, I fear she'll move through it—that I won't be able to stop her . . ."

"You American Catholics don't know of the evil spirits," Okomfo interrupted, but he didn't flail his arms or stomp his feet or pour yet another libation to appease the African spirits enraged by Mama. "You don't believe in the evil spirits."

"But we do." Mary Catherine spoke from the crowd—seemingly surprised by her own words. "We do believe in evil spirits. In demons. The devil can act like a spirit—a demon. He can take over a person. That's why the church performs exorcisms. Because of the demons."

Mary Tessa

West Africa
Fall 1976

✳ "Okomfo? I have something I must tell you. Okomfo!"

Sitting in Ma's trial, Tessa knows it's Addae who speaks even before she looks up and turns toward him—even before she sees him standing, holding high his protection, his voodoo slingshot. He's lifted the slingshot into the air, above the array of orange and red wraps, the covered heads, the strung and slung beads. The slingshot mask facing him angles upward, toward what Tessa hopes is heaven. The mask angled downward looks on Tessa and her sisters; it looks on Ma.

What's Addae doing? Tessa thinks. What does he think he's doing? She'd like to stand, grab the slingshot, aim it at Addae to shut him up. Ma had made some comment about being an evil spirit or killing a spirit, which had sent a wave through the multitude. Tessa assumed every person in the room was ready to burn Ma and Tessa and her sisters at the stake. And now Addae's gonna stoke the flames? "Protect us," Tessa whispers to the mask. "Please. Protect all of us." Because Tessa couldn't protect anyone if she had to. She's just returned from the VIP where she finished cleaning out her insides. Now she's cleaned of strength.

"Lady Slepy is not the killer, Okomfo," Addae says.

Tessa moves inside herself. Life is a feast, but Tessa wants to fast, like Catie—she doesn't want to take life in. Tessa longs for that divine dullness, that place where she'll want for nothing. Feel nothing.

"I killed him, Okomfo. I killed the man Slepy. Lady Slepy did not."

"What?" Tessa hears Ma say.

And Tessa thinks: Why is Addae doing this, saying this? Tessa should stop him. She needs the energy to stop him.

"With this." Addae rocks the slingshot forward and backward and forward—that damn slingshot—and Okomfo watches. "I killed him. Lady Slepy had no thing to do with it. I was scared to tell before. It was an accident, Okomfo. I was hunting, hiding in bushes. It was dark. Almost dark. There was this bird. In the river. I tried to shoot this bird. But the man Slepy was across the river . . . I did not see him."

The flies and fanning mix with murmurings and shifting bodies. Several in the audience lose interest and push their way out of the room.

Okomfo lifts his hand. The murmuring and shifting stop. "You are innocent, child. You killed no one."

Tessa coughs, then. She gasps and coughs. She hadn't been breathing, but her body arrests air, now—it ignores her mind, which doesn't want to breathe. How does Okomfo know?

Okomfo looks at Ma again, away from Addae. "You unleashed this curse, Christina Slepy—this curse of death. The boy is innocent. You are not." But then Okomfo says something else, something no one expects, least of all Tessa. "You must leave our village now," he says to Ma. "You and your children must leave. And that spirit—that demon. You must take that demon with you."

Okomfo instructs Queen Mother to release Ma, and then he leaves the room.

Ma is free.

But Tessa knows Ma will never be free—none of the Slepys will. Because Okomfo was right: Addae is innocent. He and Tessa and Yllis were together, concealed in the bushes, looking for another bird to take down. But there was no bird—there was only Pa. They watched as Pa took Ma down.

Mary Catherine

West Africa
Fall 1976

Mary Catherine holds Papa's book, his Bible. She's held it since she found it in his suitcase when she'd searched there for a change of clothes.

A change of clothes?

The change of clothes. His last. Mawuli had asked Mary Catherine to pick out the clothes, before Mama's trial began. Now the trial is over. But those clothes won't ever be over.

Mary Catherine waits for Mama in the rear of the school-room. She can barely see Mama through the horde: the room is still jammed with people. And smells.

Grace had insisted on taking Yllis outside to wait because of the smells, while Tessa made another trip to the VIP. But Mary Catherine couldn't move. Will she ever again be able to move?

She pages through the New Testament as she waits, seeking guidance, peace, safety from Matthew, Mark, Luke and John, and from the Acts of the Apostles. But it's hopeless. The trial may be over. They may be free to leave, go home. But Michigan is a stranger. Papa is dead.

Mary Catherine slams the Bible shut. Then she opens it

again. She flips through the beginning, through the section that she learned from catechism also makes up the Jewish Torah: Genesis, Exodus, Leviticus, Numbers, Deuteronomy. But the words seem unreadable, unreachable.

She needs something to hold on to—something to stop her from drowning.

She turns to page one. She forces herself to read. *In the beginning God created the heavens and the earth. The earth was without form and void, and darkness was upon the face of the deep; and the Spirit of God was moving over the face of the waters. And God said, "Let there be light;" and there was light. And God saw that the light was good; and God separated the light from the darkness.*

If only it were so easy to separate the light from the darkness.

Mary Catherine used to think it was easy.

"You're pregnant?"

Mary Catherine hears Mama. She looks up and sees Mama. Then she tries to make sense of Mama's words. But Mama's words make no sense. And Mary Catherine thinks, Mama's crazy behavior during the trial wasn't an act: Mama is crazy. She is demon possessed. "I'm not Grace, Mama," Mary Catherine says. "I'm Catie. You know that, right? It was Grace who was pregnant. Remember? But she lost the baby, remember, Mama?"

"I know who you are," Mama says.

But Mary Catherine doesn't know who Mama is: she's lost her papa and her mama.

"There's no baby, then?" Mama says.

"No, Mama," Mary Catherine says. "No." But Mary Catherine knows Mama was told about the baby—about Grace losing the baby. Mawuli asked Queen Mother to tell her. And Mawuli said the queen did. Mary Catherine knows Mawuli wouldn't lie to her. Mawuli loves her—he told her so. He said, "Now you will be my queen."

But Mary Catherine isn't sure she loves him. Not anymore. Mary Catherine's not sure of anything anymore; she's nowhere near ready to be anybody's queen.

"Were you in love with him?" Mama says.

"I thought I was," Mary Catherine says. "Maybe I am."

"So you wanted it? He didn't force you?"

"He didn't force me, Mama. But I know I caused you and Papa pain. I'm so sorry . . ."

But Mama stops her. "No. I should have protected you, Mary Catherine. You're only sixteen, for God's sake. You've done nothing wrong." She cups Mary Catherine's face, and now Catie is Mama's drink of water. "*I* am sorry. I failed you, Mary Catherine. I failed all of you—each one of you girls. You needed me. You in particular needed me to guide you, to teach you how to become a woman. Because you're becoming a woman, Catie. You're becoming a strong, independent, beautiful young woman. But you're not there yet. I need to help you get there, in a safe way. I will help you get there in a safe way."

Mama frees Mary Catherine's face and wraps her arms around her.

And Mama feels to Mary Catherine like her mama.

Mary Catherine drops the Bible; she holds her mother.

Clara

Clara expects regret. When she realizes she's dying, she expects to feel little but regret for the life she's failed to live.

Instead, she sees her whole life stretched out like a canvas. She sees herself as a child before she had rickets, splashing in the lake, splashing her own mama, then cuddling on the soaked lap of her papa. She sees the joy she gives her parents; she feels the love she feels for them.

She looks further on and she sees herself with rickets. She watches herself persevere. She feels the strength she finds inside to still dance, twirling on Emil's arm as she lets herself fall in love with him.

Then she sees herself digging deeper for more strength when Emil leaves her—when he takes his life. She sees herself wanting to hate Emil but choosing instead to hold on to the love she has for him—and to hold on to their baby because of that love.

When she loses the baby, she thinks she's lost that love. But she hasn't lost it. She turns the love on Emil's brother, on Egan.

Egan is her companion. Her friend. Her lover. And together they live a good life—a worthy life.

A life worthy of Grace—of being her friend, no matter what Grace decided to do. Because Clara is Grace's friend, and Grace is Clara's. On the big canvas of life, friends sometimes lie, and they give bad advice.

Grace will find the strength she needs, whether she's used Clara's bad advice or not.

For the first time in a long time, Clara is not chasing anything.

It's time for her to go home.

Seena

In Greek tragedies, the protagonist always suffers a life-altering loss. The loss is not random or meaningless but a logical consequence of the protagonist's actions. The loss may be more severe than seems deserved, and at times divine intervention aggravates an already bad situation. Yet in every Greek tragedy the catalyst for the protagonist's downfall is *hamartia,* from the Greek *hamartanein,* a term that describes an archer missing the target. In essence, *hamartia* means "mistake," pure and simple—although the mistake is never pure and rarely simple.

History repeats itself.

Seena is a cliché.

She thinks this now, knowing she and her girls will soon leave Africa behind, even as she knows they will never leave Africa behind. Dick's death will forever haunt Seena. The *trokosi* will forever haunt Seena. What Africa taught Seena about herself will never leave her.

Because the upside of being a tragic protagonist is that every such protagonist experiences *anagnorisis,* meaning "recognition." The tragic hero or heroine develops insight, so at the very least he or she understands the situation for what it is.

At least Seena has this: she knows how Dick died—that Addae didn't shoot him. She knows Heimdall never really loved her; he couldn't have. And she knows she didn't really love Heimdall. She didn't even know him. She'd fallen in love with an ideal, not a man. The man himself was no one she ever would have loved.

And she's also certain of this: she will never be forgiven no matter how many times she asks, because the dead can't forgive.

Yet she also knows she is lucky—and her girls are lucky. Because she and the girls have each other, and they have the opportunity—the freedom—to miss the target, to make mistakes, and to experience *anagnorisis, hamartia's* flip side.

Yes: Seena knows they are lucky. Until she knows they are not.

Until she finds another daughter as a smear of glue and realizes she hasn't learned a damn thing.

Seena had not seen Tessa since she'd left the trial. When she'd walked out of the schoolhouse with Mary Catherine, she'd come upon Grace and Yllis, but not Tessa. Tessa had gone to the VIP, or so Tessa had said, according to Yllis. But Seena assumed Tessa was avoiding her, not able to face what she'd done, even if she did what she did to save Seena.

Later, when Tessa was nowhere to be found, did Seena do what a good mother would do? Did she send out a search party, find Tessa, connect with her, soothe her? No, Seena was relieved, at some level, that she didn't have to face Tessa, that she didn't have to face what Tessa had done. As Seena and the other girls packed, prepared to leave, Seena nudged Tessa from her mind.

———————

Seena finds Tessa only when she herself journeys to the VIP. Tessa half sits on the ground, half lies on the ground, her body a smudge against the concrete structure of the VIP. Her eyes are open but . . . do they see? "Tessa?" Seena says. "Tessa?" Seena sees the gray-white skin, the cracked lips. She kneels and feels Tessa's light pulse.

"Mama," Tessa says, but barely. "Mama. You're free, Mama." Her body shifts from the VIP to Seena. She rests her arms around Seena's middle, lays her head on Seena's shoulder. "I'm going to die, Mama. Like the girl, Mama. That little girl. With diarrhea. But it's okay. Because I want to die. I should die. That girl, she didn't deserve what happened to her. And Papa. And those slaves. From the slave castle. And here, too, Mama. There are slaves here, too. None of them deserved what happened to them . . ."

Seena remembers herself saying, "I won't lose any more children to Africa." And now she hears Africa's response: "Life is a gift. You don't demand gifts." Seena feels her last meal stir, feels it climb into her throat, feels it push for release.

But she holds it down; she holds Tessa. She lifts Tessa's body—and as she does she feels how thin Tessa's become. "You're going to be okay, Tessa. I'm going to help you."

Seena carries Tessa through the village. "Where is Okomfo?" she says to every person she encounters. "Where's Okomfo? My daughter's sick." But no one answers her, this demon.

Seena reaches the schoolhouse, bursts inside. The room is transformed, once again just a school, as if what happened to her here just hours ago never was.

Kofi stands talking with Queen Mother. He looks up, sees Seena, sees Tessa.

"Where is Okomfo?" Seena says. "She's sick. Tessa's sick. Will Okomfo help her?"

Kofi nods. "Of course," he says. "Of course. I'll find him. Wait here." Then he leaves the building in a streak.

Queen Mother gestures, indicating Seena should lay Tessa down on one of the long and narrow student tables. But Seena sees a morgue slab, not a table. She imagines Tessa as she imagined Dick: laid out like a slab of meat.

But Tessa is alive, Seena thinks: she's alive.

Queen Mother touches Seena's shoulder; Seena remains ice. Then the queen takes Tessa from Seena, gently. Only now does Seena feel the ache in her arms, her back. "Your daughters are good girls," the queen says as she arranges Tessa on the table, not as if she's a slab of meat but as if she's delicate, a butterfly.

Tessa opens her eyes, studies the queen, closes her eyes.

"You are a strong girl," the queen says to Tessa's closed eyes. "You will see. Okomfo will come. He will help you. You'll get well. You have this spirit like my spirit, like Akosiwa's spirit. It cannot rest long."

The queen then looks at Seena, looks into her eyes. "Your Akosiwa is a special girl."

"You mean Grace." Seena can't look at the queen: she looks down, and now it is Seena who speaks to Tessa's closed eyes.

"Her name is Grace. Mary Grace." Seena brushes a strand of hair from Tessa's forehead. "And this is Mary Tessa."

"Yes," the queen says.

"You humiliated Grace in front of everyone," Seena says. "Everyone. And that was after you marched her around like her body was for sale. How dare you speak of her now as if you care about her."

Seena can no longer see Tessa's eyes: they've become a wet blur. She presses her palms into her own eyes. She doesn't want to cry in front of this woman, this monster.

"You are wrong about Dipo—about the women of Avone. They are powerful women. Not victims. They are capable, strong. Like your Grace. They are not ashamed of their bodies. But they are more than these bodies. They are not limited by these bodies—they are empowered by them."

"What about the *trokosi*?" Seena removes her palms, these plugs, and the tears stream. She knows she should check herself, that she should check her words. But the words spill forth with the tears. "How are they empowered? They are slaves. *Slaves*. And the other girls. Most can't even attend school. Sure, they use their bodies for chores and child care. But do they get to use their brains? Do they get to pursue their dreams? You obviously had the opportunity to be educated. You're the only female I've met here who speaks English. The boys get to learn. Why not the girls? It's easy for you to say, when you were given opportunities the other women and girls haven't been given. You've been empowered. Why you and not them?"

When Seena says these things, she believes she is right. Yet she knows Queen Mother is right, too, in many ways. Grace was a body to Seena. Seena's own daughter was little but a body. Grace was limited in Seena's mind because of her body, her beauty. Seena herself assumed Grace would make her way in life riding on her beauty, her body. She didn't discuss sex with Grace, because she wasn't ready to give Grace over to what seemed a meaningless life. Given this, why would Seena have celebrated Grace's body changing from that of a girl to that of a woman? The changes in Grace's body had only served to confirm in Seena's mind that Grace would never be anything more.

But Grace will be more.

She is more.

———————

"Ah," Okomfo says when he sees Tessa. "She has a bad spirit. No?" Seena expects Okomfo to rub it in—to tell Seena she unleashed this spirit, which Seena already knows. But Okomfo refrains.

Tessa again opens her eyes. "I have diarrhea. I'm going to die, too."

"Too?" Okomfo says. He presses his index finger into Tessa's cheek once, then again. He studies her dry lips and tongue. "This spirit likes best the little ones." He opens and unpacks his basket, then he mixes clear liquid with white powder with white powder. "Big girls like you, this spirit spits back. I make you sweet, then this spirit spits you back."

"What is that?" Seena says. "Are you going to give her that?" Seena assumes Okomfo has concocted some magic potion, but where else is she to turn?

Okomfo says nothing to Seena: Tessa exists, Seena does not.

"Okomfo mixes the boiled water with the sugarcane and the salt," Queen Mother says.

Water, sugar and salt? This is black magic?

"Only this she drinks for two days," Okomfo says, but he looks at Queen Mother, not at Seena. "Then the spirit leaves her."

In two days, the spirit does leave her.

Okomfo's magic works.

Mary Grace

Strange how death makes you see life—how it makes you look at the same people and the same sights you've looked at all along and see something else. It's like the world around got plugged in, turned on. And the people? They've gone from being three-dimensional to having dimensions far beneath the surface. Grace sees these other dimensions now because she's found them in herself. There are spaces in Grace she didn't know were there. Some are vast. Some are barely there. Some come and go, seemingly as they please.

There's a space for Papa in Grace, and it's big—far bigger than she knew. Funny how she feels the space more now that he's gone. And there's a space for Clara and the baby—spaces that make her feel full and empty at once.

Africa will soon be in their past, but there's a space for Africa in Grace, too—a space that brims with colors and smells and music, and betrayal and tragedy and injustice. But there is confidence there also. And there is strength.

Strength. The word brings to mind Rocky and those pectorals he so loved—that Grace so loved. Grace did to Rocky exactly what others did to her, didn't she? She looked at his beauty, his body, and she assumed there was nothing beneath. Isn't that why she never told him about the baby? Because she assumed he was shallow? It never occurred to her that he'd want to know, that he'd care. But *why* didn't it occur to her? Because she'd boxed him up, sealed him in. Shelved him.

As if she had the right.

For the first time Grace wonders about the dimensions in Rocky.

She'll tell him about the baby. After all.

Dick

◆ Seena stands with Dick's girls at his funeral, as Dick watches his body descend into the earth. His body descends, but his three-fourths of an ounce still hovers in this purgatory—this place that is no place. This place of no peace.

The trial has ended, Seena has been freed. The boy Addae claims to have killed Dick. But Seena really killed Dick—she and Dick both know this—because Dick was dead before he died.

Dick watches his girls crumble as his body disappears. Grace doubles over, her hands grip her cheeks, her folded back shudders. Mary Catherine stands as a statue, but tears pelt the ground. Tessa crouches and grips Seena's legs, as if she's a toddler trying to hold herself up. Yllis kneels next to Tessa, strokes her back; and she looks toward the heavens, toward Dick's hovering three-fourths.

Dick senses Yllis's eyes upon him—he senses this gentle touch—as if Yllis is soothing him like she's soothing Tessa. And Dick feels himself feel: he feels soothed. And he realizes this is something Yllis has always done for him: she's helped him to feel. Even when he's done so kicking and screaming.

Even though he usually did so kicking and screaming.

Yllis made Dick's life richer; he knows this. And he knows, too, with surprising certainty, that Yllis is his daughter. Even as he knows she is not.

"Forgive me," Seena says to the sky, to Dick, as she's said many many times since Dick's death.

No, he thinks. No. I won't forgive you. You've taken everything from me: my love, my children, my God, my life.

But then Seena pulls their girls around her, each of them. She eases each to the ground, sits in their circle. And she begins to talk, to tell the story of when she and Dick met—of Loudmouth and Latin. She tells them of their courting and of their wedding—stories she never recounted before, events Dick wondered if she remembered. But she does remember them, in detail. And as she expounds on the width of Loudmouth's mustache and the texture of Dick's raglan-sleeved coat and the intricate design of the lace on her wedding gown, the tears that so rarely fell fall in droves.

And Dick finds the forgiveness he was determined to not find—not just for Seena, but for his own mother, his father. He wanted to possess Seena—to own her—like she was his *trokosi*. But you can't possess someone's spirit, can you? The eyes of the *trokosi* should have taught him that. And his parents? He'd always seen their deficiencies—how their deficiencies took from him. Just as he'd always seen Seena's deficiencies. But had he ever seen *them*? Had he ever considered their lives, separate from his own? No. No. They were his *trokosi*, too, their sole purpose to serve Dick's needs. And when they failed him, they failed, period.

Dick not only finds forgiveness, now; he longs to be forgiven—and he again feels God's love.

Dick no longer hovers, but falls. As he falls, he scatters. He's
not three-fourths of an ounce, he's three-fourths of an ounce
scattered. A drop of him falls into Seena. A drop falls into Tessa
as she tightens her arms around her mother. Both Grace and
Mary Catherine close their eyes as Dick falls into them. And
Yllis touches her heart where Dick settles in.

Mary Catherine

"Father Amadi?" Mary Catherine said, after barely knocking. She peered through the partially opened door, stepped inside, shut the door. He looked at her with the look she'd come to expect. "Do you have a minute?"

"Of course, Mary Catherine," Father Amadi said. "Of course I do."

It was the day Mary Catherine cut her hair—but before she cut her hair. It seems forever ago now—like Mary Catherine has lived not only her own life, but Papa's life since. Still, Mary Catherine remembers noticing Father Amadi looking at her hair, as he always did. She knew he wanted to touch it.

"I saw *The Exorcist*," Mary Catherine said. "Does the church really believe in that? Does it really do that?"

"Well, the church does believe demonic spirits can overtake a person. And priests do occasionally perform exorcisms, to free the person of the demon. But it's nothing like the Hollywood version, Mary Catherine. It's nothing like that."

"What about you?" Mary Catherine said. "Do you believe in demons? Have you performed an exorcism?"

"I believe people sometimes are subject to powers they don't understand. Powers that seem bigger than themselves. And sometimes they need help getting free. Addiction, for instance. That's a demon, in a sense. It makes people act in ways they know are against their self-interest."

"I think you feel that at times," Mary Catherine said. "I think you feel something like addiction."

Father Amadi looked away, and Mary Catherine thought: I'm your addiction.

"What about the term 'consubstantial'? You preached on it at your last sermon, but I don't understand it." But Mary Catherine did understand it. Mama had explained that the term comes from the Latin word *consubtantialem,* meaning "of one essence or substance."

"It describes the relationship between the elements of the Holy Trinity." Father Amadi hadn't moved from his seat. His breathing was shallow. They both knew the real reason Mary Catherine was there. "The Holy Ghost is separate from the Father and Son, yet it has the same divine essence, the same nature. The Holy Ghost is *consubstantial* with the Father and Son."

"I want that." Mary Catherine unbuttoned her blouse. "I want that with you. I know you want it with me."

Mary Catherine believed she did know this, because Father Amadi was overcome when he'd see her. She saw the feeling in his eyes, she heard it in his breath. He'd collect himself quickly, say something like, "You took me by surprise," or "I thought you were someone else." Yet Mary Catherine knew he was lying, because whenever he slid the host between her lips, onto her tongue, his hand quivered, he forgot to breathe. Then he'd grapple for air as the next parishioner stepped up.

"Don't do that, Mary Catherine," Father Amadi said, and he rose, rounded the desk, neared her. "I don't want you to do that. Button up your blouse."

But Mary Catherine knew what he wanted. She unbuttoned further, unlatched her bra.

Father Amadi grabbed her. His hands felt enormous on her shoulders. His eyes looked shiny and hard and too rounded, like blue marbles. His breathing no longer was shallow, but deep. Too deep. Like he was holding something in—and that something was about to implode. Mary Catherine started to scream, but he stifled the scream with the heel of one hand, and with the other hand he yanked her blouse closed. "Get out of here," he said. "Get out. Now."

West Africa

"Truth or dare," Addae says, but to Yllis.

Tessa stands to the side, feeling too sick to play.

"Truth," Yllis says.

"Who do you love most?" Addae says.

But Yllis can't answer this question: she doesn't know anymore.

"Can I change my mind?" Yllis says. "Can I choose dare?"

"You love someone, Yllis?" Tessa says.

"Dare, then," Addae says. "The next one, you shoot it." Addae hands Yllis the slingshot.

Addae had taught Yllis the prior day how to work the slingshot. Yllis holds it now. She feels both the smoothness of the wood and the jagged cut of the masks; she remembers the catharsis of the snap.

She's scanning the riverbank, looking for another heron to take down, when she sees her papa take her mama down.

She never even considers not shooting.

The purple tip of the rock pierces him, it's a perfect bull's-eye. And he drops to the ground like a heron.

Yllis screams. Grace hears the scream. Seena looks toward Yllis's scream and sees Yllis and Tessa splash through the river.

"Mama?" Yllis says. "Mama . . ."

Seena looks up at Yllis, into the face of terror. "I did this," Seena says. "You understand, Yllis?" She looks at Tessa—smells and sees her waste. "You understand Tessa? *I* did this. I'm not going to lose any more children to Africa. Promise me. Promise me you won't tell a soul. Ever."

Yllis nods—she barely nods.

"Yes, Mama," Tessa says.

"Now go," Seena says. "Run. Get help."

Yllis

The day we left Avone, I found Papa's camera. It lay where he died. The very last picture he took was of Mama standing near the Avone River on Friday—the day the river belonged to the spirits alone. Yet I ran through this serpent anyway.

In the photograph, Mama looks as if she'd turned toward Papa just before he snapped. Her hair snakes around her head, her eyebrows ride high, lines etch her forehead.

In the background, across the river, stand Addae and Tessa. And I stand there, too, gazing past the river spirits and sacred fish, gripping the slingshot.

And now I know why snapping a picture of someone is equivalent to stealing the person's soul. Truth can't be held like that. One picture may be worth ten thousand words, but even that many words can't tell the whole story.

Truth doesn't have a color. And it doesn't have a smell. It doesn't quiver or make noise. It doesn't shimmer. Yet it does— it does all these things, depending.

Because truth is capricious. It may be hovering there all the while, but one moment you think you see it—it seems so clear, so well defined, as if you could catch it and hold it steady in your hand. But the next moment it's gone, or at least so fast moving it's a blur, at best. That's the thing Africa taught me about truth. You know it's truth because it's busy. Any seeming truth that's idle? Well, that's just not truth.

————

Now I live day by day without knowing whether killing is like dominoes: will the dying inside me ever end? Are there really no exceptions, does murder mean perpetual hell? Or is this just an idle truth that's not truth at all? Is there something that could save me? Redeem me?

Mary Catherine says I should ask Father Amadi these questions when he returns—after she clears him of the charges against him, which she will. Father Amadi is wise, Mary Catherine says: he'll know how to help me.

Maybe I will.

Maybe he will.

EPILOGUE

Heimdall Amadi

Father Amadi would have given up everything for Seena. Now: he's given up more than everything.

My God, my God, he thinks. Why hast thou forsaken me?

He didn't mean to love her—to fall in love with her. But the love he felt seemed a gift from God. He'd listened to her husband's confessions. He knew Dick had no idea who she was, what she was. She was a prize to him: the hunted deer. The point was to conquer, display the conquered. Love had nothing to do with it.

Dick didn't long to know her. He *didn't* know her: not her questioning mind, not her hungry spirit. He didn't feel closer to God because of her.

But Heimdall did.

Before Seena, God had been a theory—a beautiful, soothing theory. The world was a place of mystery, and God was its author. But being with Seena—knowing her—made Heimdall know God, not just in theory. God filled his body when he touched her. God ballooned his mind when Heimdall climbed inside hers. This woman who had come to Heimdall so lost, so aching and empty, had ignited life in him. And he realized: knowing God means knowing life, living life. Living real life:

its gray areas, its inconsistencies. So he'd given himself over to this love, to its gray areas and inconsistencies. Heimdall was in love with a woman who'd vowed to love another, even though he'd made a vow to love only God. And in his love for Seena, Heimdall loved God more.

When their child was born, the love he felt was a magnificent beast, and Heimdall was in awe. To create life from such love. And then to love that new life. Before knowing Seena, before this baby, Heimdall had barely scratched the surface of love. But now that he'd scratched it, delved deeply within it, nothing— nothing at all—would ever be the same. And he knew: he could be a priest or not. If he remained a priest, he would be a better priest, because he'd delved into love. But if he left the priest- hood, he would do so as a better man—despite appearances. He'd no doubt people would judge him—and judge Seena. He'd no doubt they would see him and Seena as impulsive, careless, selfish. And at some level they'd been impulsive, care- less and selfish. Of course they had: Heimdall accepted this. But he'd had a window into Dick. And because of that window, he could see beyond. He wanted nothing more than to be Seena's husband, to be the child's father, to accept the responsibility for what he'd done.

But Seena pushed him away.

"I can't let you give up who you are," she'd said. "I can't let you gut yourself for me."

Why couldn't she see? He wasn't gutting himself being with her, being with their child. He was gutted when she decided for him—when she took these things away.

She continued to come to mass in the summers. Why? To

torture him? Yet he longed for her to come. He counted the days, the hours, the minutes until she'd step into the sanctuary and back into his life—until he'd see his daughter again.

Seena's girls grew. Yllis grew. Seena's older daughters looked so much like her. Seeing them was seeing Seena multiplied. And Yllis? With every day, Heimdall longed more to be her father. What right did Seena have to take his child away?

And so he shook. Each time Seena neared him, he shook. Each time the girls neared him, he shook.

He suggested Dick take them all to Africa, not because he was afraid of Dick—of what Dick would do to him if Dick learned—but because he was afraid of himself. No longer could he sustain the charade. When Mary Catherine came to him that morning—before he found Dick in the car—and started to disrobe, Father Amadi realized his ability to pretend had forever died.

Mary Catherine had read his longing. Only his longing wasn't for her.

Now? The charade will end—it has to. Heimdall will have to explain his behavior. And Yllis finally will know her father.

Perhaps Heimdall has not given up everything.

Perhaps God has not forsaken him.

In Memory of Jamie

Thank you . . .

Kara Cesare, my Athena, for your wisdom—and for teaching me how to weave a good yarn.

Michael Carlisle, my Apollo, for healing me of Khaos, and for so much more.

Julia Flynn Siler, my female Hermes, my bringer of dreams, for unfailingly guiding this traveler.

Michael Bourne, my Poseidon, for calm through the storm.

Al Duncan, my Zeus, for being the god of my gods.

Amy Laughlin, Tina Laurberg, Melissa Meldrum, Sarah Petrie, and Betsy Bakeman, my Aphrodites, for wisdom in all matters of love and beauty (and life).

Chuck Spencer, my Hephaestus, for passing on the flame, and Liz Epstein, my female (and lovely) Hephaestus, for sculpting and sculpting (and sculpting and sculpting . . .).

Michelle Frey and Laura Rennert, my Akosiwas, for your caretaking and remarkable patience.

Patricia Petrie, my mother and my Ame. You possess the medicine for far more than just snakebites.

Meg Waite Clayton, my Artemis, and Dan Meldrum, my male Artemis, for always lending an arrow in the hunt.

Amy Franklin Willis, Kim Oster, Emilia Pisani, Masie Cochran, and Madhushree Ghosh, my Ayawas, for your keen observations—and for keeping me grounded.

And Doug, Jacob and Owen, my Addaes, my morning suns, for lighting my world.

Finally, thank you to the remarkable people at Gallery Books and InkWell Management.

Because of you, my jar is more than full. And hope always remains.

AMARYLLIS

in

BLUEBERRY

Christina Meldrum

INTRODUCTION

In a West African village, Seena Slepy stands trial for the murder of her husband, Dick, a doctor who brought his family from their home in the United States to do humanitarian work. How Seena got to this crossroads, with her fate hanging in the balance, is told in a series of flashbacks. Richly atmospheric, *Amaryllis in Blueberry* is a stirring, soulful novel about the intricacies of human relationships and the haunting nature of secrecy.

DISCUSSION QUESTIONS

1. *Amaryllis in Blueberry* is told from the viewpoints of Seena, Dick, their four daughters, their neighbor Clara, and finally the priest Heimdall. How do the varied perspectives affect you as a reader? The final chapter is the only one told from Heimdall Amadi's perspective. Why do you suppose the author chose to give him the last word?

2. Consider how truth and reality are portrayed in the novel. What besides individual perspective contributes to each character's view of truth and reality?

3. What are your thoughts on the narrative structure of the novel, which begins with The End—Seena on trial for murder—and intertwines scenes from the past and present? How does knowing about Dick's death at the beginning of the novel affect your perception of him throughout the book? How does it affect your view of the other characters, particularly Seena and Yllis? If the story had been told in a more linear fashion, do you think you would have felt differently about the story and/or the characters?

4. Consider the significance of storytelling and mythmaking in the novel. The author interweaves Greek mythology, African mythology, and Catholic doctrine into the story line of *Amaryllis in Blueberry*. How are these myths/faiths similar? What purpose do they serve? How does religion relate to storytelling and myth making in the novel?

5. The title refers to a Greek myth—the myth of Amaryllis, and Seena summarizes the myth on page 317. What parallels do you see between the myth of Amaryllis and Yllis's story? In chapter two, Seena explains the myth of Pandora (pages 17–18). What parallels do you see between the myth of Pandora and the novel's characters, story and structure?

6. Yllis is the only character who tells her story in past tense. Why do you think the author chose to give Yllis this unique perspective? Although Dick, Seena, the Marys, Clara, and Heimdall all tell their stories in the present tense, each looks back on past events. How do you think their present circumstances impact their memory of those past events? How does their memory of these events impact their sense of the present?

7. Discuss the role of religion in the novel. What drives Dick's strong Catholic faith, including his affinity for the Virgin Mary? Mary Catherine says, "seeing God, believing in Jesus, is like believing in air" (page 53). How does Mary Catherine use religion to construct her identity? How does Dick? How do their experiences in Africa challenge their self-perceptions?

8. Compare the two different settings portrayed in the novel, Michigan

and West Africa. For the various members of the Slepy family, how are their expectations of Africa different from the reality they encounter? How does each setting affect the way each character constructs his/her sense of identity and reality?

9. What role does names and naming play in the novel? Yllis in not a Mary. Tessa, Grace and Catie all share the name Mary. Seena does not use her given name, Christina—except when Dick insists on calling her Christina. Each of the girls receives a West African day name. Mawuli's name has meaning. Addae's name has meaning. Are the characters empowered by their names? Confined? Do any of the characters use naming either to empower or to disempower others?

10. "How can you live with someone for years . . . and see only your imagination reflected?" wonders Seena (page 3). Seena's comment suggests she came to realize her perception of Dick was built on imagination—on myth. Was it? Seena claims she never loved Dick, but do you think she did? Does he love her? To what degree are Heimdall, Seena's daughters and Clara also Seena's "imagination reflected"? What role does imagination play in the formation, nourishment and/or undermining of the other relationships in the novel?

11. Is the "Day of the Snake" (page 90) a turning point in the life of each of the Slepys? Seena seems to think it may be, but is Seena's perception of the announcement's significance fueled by her own needs? Is this another moment when Seena sees only her "imagination reflected"? Do you think a single statement can have the power to irrevocably alter the course of people's lives?

12. Obsession affects several of the characters in *Amaryllis in Blueberry*. Why is Dick obsessed with Seena? Why does Seena become "Seena the Stalker"? Is Mawuli merely a replacement for Mary Catherine's lost obsession, her faith? How important is the theme of secrecy in the novel, and why?

13. What are Seena's strengths and weaknesses as a mother? How does your perception of her as a mother affect your view of her as a person? How does each of her children see her? In what ways is Seena's relationship with Yllis different from her relationship with her other daughters?

14. What are Dick's strengths and weaknesses as a father? As a husband? As a human being?

15. What is the significance of Yllis being a synesthete? In a sense, her gift results in her "carrying the sins of the world," given she is the recipient of

others' unspoken confessions. And in the end, it is she who sacrifices her innocence to save her mother. Do you think the author intended to make a parallel between Yllis and Father Amadi? Yllis and Christ? What other metaphors or symbolism do you detect in the novel?

16. "Grace isn't the same. That Dipo meant something to her. Standing before all those people, stripped inside and out, she found something inside herself she forgot she had" (page 321). What reaction did you have to the Dipo ceremony? Do you think it has redeeming cultural value? Why do you think it is important to Grace? Does the Dipo ceremony make you reflect at all on our own cultural practices related to puberty and youth coming-of-age?

17. Why do you think Mary Catherine is drawn to Father Amadi? Why do you think she cuts herself and starves herself? Is it merely a plea for attention, as Seena suggests at one point? Is it possible Mary Catherine knows more about the relationship between Father Amadi and Seena than she is able to admit?

18. Tessa's family regards her as a "troublemaker," and even Yllis says Tessa is "good at sick. And cruel" (page 15). Yet in many respects, Tessa is more sensitive to and affected by both the joys and sorrows of life in Africa than anyone else in her family. How is this seeming sensitivity consistent with her family's perception of her? How it consistent with her perception of herself?

19. What role does Clara play in the novel? She is not part of the Slepy family, yet she still has a voice in the novel. Why?

20. Now that you know the novel's ending—that Yllis killed Dick—what new insights does it give you into the story and the characters, particularly Yllis? Would your foreknowledge of this and other events—particularly the true circumstances of Yllis's birth and Mary Catherine's meeting with Father Amadi—have altered your perception of the events themselves? How do you think a second reading of this novel would affect you?

ENHANCE YOUR BOOK CLUB

1. Visiting the slave castles along the West African coast has an emotional impact on some of the characters in *Amaryllis in Blueberry*. Further information about the slave castles can be found at http://www.lasentinel .net/African-Slave-Castles.html.

2. Synesthesia is a rare sensory condition that affects Yllis. Find out more about it here: http://en.wikipedia.org/wiki/Synesthesia.

3. Prepare a feast with recipes from *The Africa Cookbook: Tastes of a Con-*

tinent by Jessica B. Harris, or check out the selections at www.epicurious .com/recipesmenus/global/african/recipes.

A CONVERSATION WITH CHRISTINA MELDRUM

Q: *Amaryllis in Blueberry* **takes place in Michigan and West Africa. What personal significance do these landscapes have for you? What appealed to you about using two such dramatically different locations in the novel?**

A: I grew up in Michigan and continue to spend time there every summer. Although I no longer live in Michigan year-round, it will always be home to me at some level. Michigan represents family to me. It represents summers on the lake. It represents holidays. While the characters in *Amaryllis in Blueberry* are purely fictional, the Danish Landing is very real. My family has owned property on the Danish Landing for over a hundred years. Nearly all of my most poignant childhood memories take place on the Danish Landing. I remember my grandmother standing at the stove flipping blueberry pancakes. I remember exploring the Old Trail. The Danish Landing gave me my first campfire, my first sunburn, my first leech! To the degree any place on earth makes me feel grounded, the Danish Landing does. I imagine Yllis would find part of my soul on the Danish Landing.

And I imagine she'd find another part of my soul in West Africa. I worked for a short time in West Africa during my twenties, and I continue to have ties to West Africa through my nonprofit work. To the degree the Danish Landing is my place of peace, West Africa is my place of prodding. West Africa nudges me, with its energy and rituals, its colors and smells. As a twenty-something living in West Africa, I did not feel peaceful, but I sure felt alive. I did not feel grounded; I felt flung from Addae's slingshot. And when I landed, I had a different perspective, one that was far more nuanced.

I was drawn to writing about these two places because on the surface they are so very different, but beneath the surface of each, there's another world. And these beneath-the-surface worlds are surprising—and surprisingly similar in many ways.

Q: Why did you decide to begin the narrative with The End, rather than have the story unfold along a more linear time line?

A: I find perspective fascinating. What if we could begin at The End? Or what if we could take the knowledge of The End and revisit our lives? Would we see ourselves differently? Would we see our lives differently? Would we become different people altogether—are we merely the sum of our choices? Or are we who we are at our core, indelible at some level no matter our choices? Would Seena or Yllis, Tessa or Mary Catherine, Grace or Dick or Clara or Heimdall be the same person to the reader if I had started at the beginning and moved straight to the end? Or did each become a different person to the reader because the reader had foreknowledge of certain outcomes? Did the reader's altered perspective change each character in some fundamental way? I don't know the answer to any of these questions, but I think the questions are worth asking, worth exploring.

Q: Seena is fascinated by mythology, and even the novel's title draws on a Greek myth. Is this a topic in which you had an interest prior to writing *Amaryllis in Blueberry*?

A: I've wondered—and continue to wonder—whether each of our lives is a story at some level: a myth we create. How is our sense of reality and identity influenced by our memory, by our perspective, by our reflection on past events? Seena was a person who struggled with her own life story, because it was a painful life story in many respects. Was she drawn to mythology because others' stories were safer for her, more palatable to her? Perhaps, but how accurate was her perception of her own life? Was the love she shared with Dick a mere myth, as she came to believe? Was the love she shared with Heimdall a myth as well? Or was it her spinning of these experiences the myths-in-making? And what of Yllis? Her entire life's story was built on myth: the myth of the blueberry field; the myth of Amaryllis. Yet Yllis was a person who saw beyond myth, whether she wanted to or not. No matter the myths people created for themselves—and of themselves—Yllis sensed feeling; she could see beyond people's words. Still, truth ultimately evaded even Yllis. Was Yllis right, then, that truth is necessarily elusive, "that it can't be contained in a jar"? Are myths essential to our understanding of ourselves and our world? Personally, I think they may be.

Q: "I am an emotional synesthete. For synesthetes like me, the world is a layer cake of emotion, and we are its consumers" (page 90), says Yllis. What prompted the idea to have a character in the story be a synesthete?

A: I remember being a little girl and wondering whether other people's experience of color matched my own. How do I know, I wondered, whether my blue is someone's else red, someone else's magenta? Perhaps my neighbor sees evergreens as ever-purple, meaning my sense of normal would be utterly abnormal to my purple-tree-seeing neighbor. How would we ever know? As I grew and learned more about the power of our brains to filter information perceived by our senses, I became increasingly interested in the impact of perspective on our understanding of truth, which led to my fascination with synesthesia. That said, Yllis was a character with a mind of her own from the get-go. I personally did not know about emotional synesthesia until meeting Yllis, truly. Emotional synesthesia is a form of synesthesia that does exist. But Yllis led me to it as I came to know her as a character—not the other way around.

Q: The scenes where Mary Grace participates in the ritual of Dipo are intriguing, particularly the reactions of the American characters to something so unfamiliar. What more can you tell us about Dipo?

A: Dipo is a Krobo ceremony, although some form of Dipo exists in many ethnic groups in West Africa. It is a ceremonial rite of passage, ostensibly to prepare girls for the responsibilities of sexual maturity and eventual marriage. As a student of religion in college, I learned that similar rituals—rituals that celebrate young people's passage into adulthood—exist in many cultures. Why? What is gained from such ceremonies? Is there an underbelly to such practices, a dark side? I included Dipo—and Grace's participation in the ceremony—in *Amaryllis in Blueberry*, in part to consider these questions, but also in hopes Grace's experience of Dipo might spur some thinking about our own culture as well. Grace's family was troubled by Grace being "parade[d]…like merchandise." But how do we as a culture express value for girls as they develop into women? How do we guide girls? What traditions and ceremonies celebrate and prepare young women—and young men—in our culture for sexual maturity and adulthood? What are the upsides of our own traditions—or lack thereof? What is our dark side?

I've wondered about these questions, in part because girls—and to a lesser extent boys—in our culture often seem to lose themselves at some level when they reach puberty. I certainly did. Is this because I was unprepared for this stage in my life? Is it because I suddenly felt less like a whole person, more like an object, as a result of the cultural messages I received? When Dick saw Grace in the Dipo ceremony, he noted she had a body that reminded him "of the girls in the girly magazines" and he was enraged his daughter was being displayed like "merchandise." Yet he regarded his looking at the "girly magazines" as a "victimless act." A ceremony like Dipo may seem troubling at first blush—and there are aspects of the ceremony that I continue to find troubling—but I think people tend to be particularly sensitive to and critical of such practices in part because they are foreign. Our own cultural practices may be equally troubling, but because they are familiar, we're more accepting of them. I do believe there may be something for us to learn from rituals such as Dipo. Although certain subsets of our society do provide rites of passage to celebrate, honor and prepare youth for adulthood, on the whole the cultural messages teens in our society receive seem at best confusing.

Q: The slave castles visited by the Slepy family on their journey in West Africa are a haunting aspect of the novel. Why did you choose to include them as a setting in the story?

A: There is a line in *Amaryllis in Blueberry* in which Yllis refers to "the painful, beautiful truths that hover about like gnats . . . so often we just swat them away." To me, slavery is one of those painful truths we often swat away. It is part of West Africa's past. It is part of our past. But slavery is not the past. Like Yllis would say: the slave souls live on; slavery lives on. Be they *trokosi* or victims of the sex trade or the drug trade or the disfigured girl on the cover of Time magazine who tried to escape her Taliban "owner," girls and boys and women all over the world are enslaved everyday. The slave castles are a reminder of that. They're the gnats. They're the decapitated rattler. Like Yllis would say: "[T]here is a painful sort of beauty in seeing things for what they really are."

In that regard, the slave castles are symbolic of a related issue: how was each character in *Amaryllis in Blueberry* enslaved at some level: by others' perceptions, expectations and memories of him/her; by the character's memories and self-perception; by others' choices; or by the confines of his/her culture? How and to what degree is each of us similarly enslaved?

Q: What was the most challenging aspect of writing *Amaryllis in Blueberry*? How was the experience different from that of your young adult novel, *Madapple*?

A: With both *Madapple* and *Amaryllis in Blueberry*, ideas spurred my writing at the outset, more than plot or character did. When I began *Ama-*

ryllis in Blueberry, I was interested in exploring the way myth and perspective help shape humans' sense of reality and identity. I wanted to embed my own story in a myth—the myth of Pandora—and allow that myth to help shape the reality and identities I created. At the same time, I wanted to tell my own story from many perspectives: past and present, first person and third person, eight characters, starting with the end, ending with a voice that until that point had had no voice. I was trying to do a lot with ideas and structure, and at first my characters seemed lost in those ideas and structure. It took my having a terrific editor and agent and some wonderful reader friends who directed me back to my characters. With their help, I really came to know my characters, but it was tough, because there were a lot of them. Unlike with *Madapple*, which I told mainly in first person from the perspective of one character, in *Amaryllis in Blueberry* I had to know all eight characters intimately. In order to do this, I realized I needed to write them all in first person, then shift their voices (all but Yllis) back to third person. This was time-consuming and challenging, but it helped tremendously.

Q: *Amaryllis in Blueberry* and *Madapple* both have a character that is put on trial. Did your background as an attorney come into play in deciding to include these scenes? How is Seena's trial most different from one that would take place in the U.S.?

A: I am interested in justice: What is it? How do we decide? Is justice independent of culture? Or is there some fundamental form of justice that exists irrespective of culture? The trials in both of my books were means by which I hoped to explore these questions. Seena's trial in Africa was dramatically different from the trial in *Madapple*, where Aslaug was said to be "innocent until proven guilty." And yet, was it really that different? Of course, in some fundamental respects the trials were night and day. As Seena said, Okomfo and Queen Mother were her "accusers, judge and jury." But as the trial in *Madapple* suggests, our system of litigation, with its lawyers, judges and juries, does not necessarily arrive at truth in the end—any more than did Okomfo and Queen Mother. Cultural assumptions and prejudices played a role in both trials. Hence, the question: particularly with regard to the rights of any subset of society, be it women or the disabled or a particular ethnic group, should cultural norms be relevant to determinations of what is just and unjust? The more time I spent thinking about these issues, the less obvious the answers became to me. Hence, I stopped practicing law. And started writing.

Q: Did you intend from the start to have religion be a key theme in the novel, or is it an aspect of the story line that developed during the writing process?

A: I see religion less as a theme in *Amaryllis in Blueberry*, more as a vehicle by which I explored other themes, particularly truth and the corresponding power of perspective. Similar to the role of Greek mythology and African mythology—and mythmaking in general—religion was a means by which certain characters in the novel made sense of their world and of themselves. Because of this, religion provided an avenue to explore other themes in the novel, including justice, contrition, and obsession. In these respects, I did intend from the outset to have religion play a key role.

Q: Against Seena's wishes, Dick insists on calling her by her given name, Christina. Is it a coincidence that you share a name with one of the characters in the story? Do you have a nickname?

A: I've often wondered about the power of names and naming: Can we be confined by the names we are given? Or do names have the power to empower? Names are extremely important in West Africa. Every child is named according to the day of his or her birth. And people often have additional names with meaning, as did both Mawuli and Addae. How powerful are these names in shaping each person? Comparatively, how powerful was Yllis's name, and the Marys' names and Seena's name in shaping each of them? Yllis is not a Mary. How did that affect the way she viewed herself? How did being a Mary affect Grace, Catie, and Tessa? Seena talks about her name as a gift given to her by her mother, yet the loss of her mother was a yoke around Seena's neck her entire life—like the pearls. Did Seena's name empower or disempower her? When Dick insists on calling Seena "Christina," what might be his intention, subconsciously or consciously? To control Seena? To own her? To give her "Christ within," make her into a religious person? To the degree names are important in the story, it is for these reasons, not because I share a name with one of the characters. That said, I did grow up with a nickname (not Seena!), as did most everyone in my family. And perhaps that nicknaming spurred my interest in the power of names.